POTSDA

BUDDY GIOVINAZZO

POTSDAMER PLATZ

NO EXIT PRESS

This edition published in September 2004 by No Exit Press
P.O. Box 394, Harpenden, Herts, AL5 1JX
http://www.noexit.co.uk

ISBN 1 84243 115 3

2 4 6 8 10 9 7 5 3 1

Typography by Avocet Typeset, Chilton, Aylesbury, Bucks
Printed and bound in Great Britain by Cox & Wyman, Reading, Berks

For Erich Maas

He who wants the world to remain as it is
Doesn't want it to remain at all.
(anonymous, Berlin Wall)

1

September 1995.

Lufthansa flight 8257. JFK to Frankfurt. Connecting flight 8835 Frankfurt to Berlin. Arriving Tegel Airport at eleven o'seven AM

The flight arrived three minutes early and I waited on line at the customs gate. I fingered my passport firmly between my thumb and index finger, tried to shake the effects of seven Crown Royals out of my throbbing head as everyone around me looked like they were melting. I shouldn't have drank so much and I certainly shouldn't have taken so many pills but there was no way I was making this trip without them; I'd have to find a doctor real soon whom I could trust and rely upon. I checked and rechecked the clear laminate flap on the inside of my passport, still pissed at Hardy for telling me about the time Leo Castillo tried to sneak back into the States with a forged passport until the customs agent noticed his picture had shifted; that's how Leo got nailed on his murder rap – but then, Leo's wife and I had a great eight months because of that.

Hardy bumped me from behind and gave me a torpid, dimwitted grin. He was a clumsy stalk of a lout with a big mouth and a bad attitude. I knew they would barely glance at his face before brushing him through the gate.

His head sat like a cinder block on a stiff green uniform; his ball-bearing eyes were the color of chrome and his lips looked like dried worms stuck together in uncertainty. He looked first at the photo, then he looked at me, then back at the photo, then back at me. He was sizing me up; something didn't feel right to him. He took a small penlight and shined it on the lamination and now I was getting a little spooked. I willed myself with everything inside of me to become the name in that passport.

'Reason for *w*isiting Germany?' he demanded.

'Vacation.'

'*Guten Tag.*' He slammed a large metal stamper down on an inside page, dropped the passport in front of me and reached past me for Hardy's.

We retrieved our bags and walked briskly toward the exit where swinging frosted-glass doors opened automatically into a bustling Terminal 8. I almost wished they hadn't.

Suddenly the signs were in gibberish, the advertisements were unknown to me; nobody here was speaking English! That's when the foreignness of the whole thing slapped me. Slapped me like an angry whore.

'You know where we're goin'?' Hardy asked, with a young boy's hopeful lilt in his voice.

'I'm following the yellow arrow.'

'How do you know where it's leadin'?'

'There's a picture of a car at the end.'

Five black-skinned men in colorful African robes waited on a ticket line. Two flight attendants, a man and a woman, stood directly in our path, both were blond and over six-feet tall and arguing loudly in each other's faces.

'This is fuckin' nuts,' Hardy mumbled under his breath, keeping with me stride for stride.

Ten minutes later the sullen men and women standing like chess pieces at the passenger pick-up stand were beginning to notice us; we may as well have been painted green. Hardy was hopping softly back and forth on the balls of his feet, shivering as if he was cold; never a good sign with Hardy; I can tell you from personal experience.

'Who the fuck we waitin' for?' he mumbled.

'Somebody named Vita.'

'What kind'a name is Vita?'

'I don't know.'

'Where the fuck is he?'

'I don't know.'

'How the fuck long are we supposed to wait?'

'As long as we have to.'

'I still don't see why the fuck we're here. Thousands of miles from home. Any two-bit leg-breaker could do this job.'

'We're two-bit leg-breakers,' I reminded him and he chortled, seemed to relax for a moment. But he was right, it had been eating away at me for a while now, the whole setup felt wrong; it had scapegoat written all over it. But I found you got a lot further in life, and tended to live a bit longer, by doing whatever Riccardo Montefiore asked you do to without question.

A tall brown-skinned guy about thirty years old with well-groomed blue-black hair and wearing a dark brown pinstriped suit and brown alligator shoes came running up urgently waving a crumpled piece of paper.

Hardy mumbled, 'What the fuck is this?'

The guy was anxious and jittery, tugging at his cufflinked sleeves and looking around before stopping abruptly in front of us and throwing a quick look to the paper in his hand.

'Do you have ticket for Giants game?' he said. Words fell out of his mouth like chips of wood, but they were the right chips.

'I'm a season-ticket holder,' I answered and the guy let out a sigh of relief.

'I am sorry,' he said. 'You were waiting long not?'

Hardy grumbled, 'Two fuckin' hours.'

The guy's face dropped as if doused with water, I thought he might cry, then just as instantly he let out a

11

laugh, albeit a nervous laugh. '*Ach so*, ha ha ha. The American humor . . . My car parks near.'

He immediately grabbed our bags, motioned to some older brown-skinned spark plug of a guy with a wild gray beard pointing out in all directions like antennae gone insane, and started for a line of cars at the curb.

'I am Vita,' he said as he walked. 'Your flight okay?'

'Fine,' I answered, not wanting to be rude during my first twenty minutes in the country.

'Long no? From USA?'

'Long enough.'

'My father waits for you at his office.'

'Your father?'

'Yossario.'

That explained a lot. Vita stopped abruptly beside a black four-door BMW sedan. He looked nervously up and down the pick-up stand; once convinced the coast was clear he rushed to the trunk and popped the hood, hoisted our bags in back. With a flourish of his hand he motioned us to get in the car, then hopped in the front passenger seat. Hardy and I shared a glance. The wild-beard guy opened the door for us and we got in. Hardy turned around and watched the airport shrink from view.

'Shit, this place is smaller than Newark.'

I handed a slip of paper over the front passenger seat.

'That's where we want to go,' I said. 'Right now.'

Vita looked at the writing on the paper and I heard him gulp, then he looked over at the wild-beard guy and said something in a language that I knew wasn't German. The wild-beard guy glanced at the slip of paper and turned back to the street in front of him, no expression, no reaction, nothing.

Vita turned around, his face sank as if he was confused. 'We take you to your flat now,' he said.

'No. We don't want to see our flat. We'd like to get started right away. You got the stuff?'

Vita's face sank further. I could tell it would be an expression I'd have to get used to; I hoped for his sake I didn't get used to it too soon.

'*Stoff*?'

'You're supposed to have something for us. We couldn't bring them over on the plane.'

He didn't get it, but a second later he did and said, '*Ach so* . . . I take you to my father now.'

No, maybe he didn't get it after all. 'Are the pieces there?'

'No. We receive them later.'

'Let's receive them now.'

'But . . . *ist* early. Too soon.'

'I have very specific instructions. Trust me on this one, Vita. The sooner we put it into play the sooner we can all go home.'

Vita whipped out a cellphone and started punching numbers on the face of it but Hardy ripped it from his hand and chucked it out the window. Vita gasped and looked back in shock.

'Tony's the chief tonight,' Hardy snapped. 'Now take us where he says.' Then he sat up straight with his head touching the cushioned top of the BMW. Vita whispered something to the wild-beard guy, who grunted without taking his eyes off the road and made a right turn down a side street. That's when I noticed his left hand was missing, gone completely; his wrist ended at a seeping-red, freshly bandaged stump. I nudged Hardy who peered around the seat to get a better look, threw me a glance that told me he was impressed.

We drove along a green park of trees and shrubs and churches with tall spires and cracked turquoise bells inside them. The streets were filled with women strolling in long robes and wearing scarves around their heads; brown-skinned children played soccer in a square where old men with gray beards sold fruit and vegetables out of the backs of their cars. Dogs ran freely in the street and every pub had tables and chairs out front with young people drinking coffee and smoking thin brown cigarettes and it seemed like the whole world just stopped working for a minute and took some time to relax.

Hardy stared out of his window at a group of veiled women pushing baby carriages and quipped, 'Shit, where the fuck are we? Downtown Istanbul!'

Vita turned around and told him, sheepishly, 'We are in *Kreuzberg*. The Turkish *Viertel*.'

Hardy and I waited in the car while Vita and the wild-beard guy went inside.

'I don't like it,' he complained. 'Why the rush? The mystery? The place ain't been staked out. We don't know who the fuck these people are; it could be a setup for all we know.'

He was right, and it was damn foolish of me not to go inside with Vita because if it was a setup Hardy and I would soon be dead.

The back door opened suddenly and a long black duffel bag was dropped at our feet. Vita and the wild-beard guy got in the front and we pulled away. The perfectly cut symmetrical hairline on the back of Vita's neck told me the little prick had called his father the second he got inside. Hardy unzipped the duffel bag and pulled out an oily black piece of steel.

'What the fuck is this? We asked for Mac 10s.'

Vita turned around in the front seat. 'AK 47. *Ganz neue*. Just as good.'

Hardy checked the firing pin and inspected the cartridge bay, pulled the trigger a few times and spat out disgustedly, 'No, not just as good! Just as shit! These are Russian. You know the type of quality they got over there in Russia?'

'We test before you come.'

'Just because you pulled the trigger don't mean it won't jam or misfire. This is bullshit!'

I turned to Hardy; in all matters relating to hardware I deferred to his expertise and judgment, though I'd never known him to squabble over the means of delivery before, having seen him once use a homemade Saturday Night Special that practically blew up in his hand. I whispered, 'Do you want to put this off for a day?'

Hardy slammed the cartridge into the loading bay and waved me off; he was simply negotiating. Hardy's not as dumb as I sometimes play him to be.

We drove through crowded streets of small shops and fruit stands where dirty gray buildings had life-size nude statues on top; there were churches and boarded-up factories and trains rumbling by on elevated tracks and Hardy pointed to a tall cylindrical tower with a big silver ball on top and said it looked like it was going to blast off for Mars.

Vita looked back meekly, and said, as if he were talking about the retarded brother you don't want anyone to know about, 'We drive into the former East Berlin.'

Streetcars scraped along dug-in metal tracks on cobblestone streets and brown brick buildings sat half-crumbling with chips and gouges missing from the facades and construction scaffolds took up entire blocks and scattered on every other corner were cafés and pubs with plastic lawnchairs around small tables.

Hardy mumbled, 'The Lower East Side without the charm and character.' And in that instant, something snapped inside. Because all the buildings and shops and

abandoned lots and crooked narrow alleys made of cobblestone cubes and soft beige dirt – even the names of the
streets which I could barely read or pronounce – somehow
looked familiar to me, as if I'd been here before; as impossible as I knew that to be. Because I'd never been anywhere
before; one time to Washington D.C. when I was fifteen
years old, and even then it was only to go to my sister's
funeral. Simmering in my stomach now was the same
murky soup of dread I'd cooked up then. I was also pretty
damn tired and probably beginning to hallucinate.

We stopped in front of a square yellow building, a newer
building than any other on the block. Hardy and I sat there
for a moment playing the psyche game: I pictured the guys
inside this building doing fucked up things to the people I
loved, like raping my daughter and stabbing her mother
and dragging their naked bleeding bodies through the pot-
holed streets of Newark New Jersey chained to the back of
a Chevrolet. Then for some reason, just for an instant, I saw
Riccardo Montefiore sitting in his office three weeks ago,
laughing and puffing on his cigar while gripping his asthma inhaler before telling me about his friend in Berlin and
how he needed an important favor from someone he could
trust.

Vita stood fixing his collar at the front door beside the
intercom; Hardy walked up holding an AK 47 in his hands
as if he were carrying a box of roses. My look told him to
'chill the fuck out' and he slipped the rifle under his jacket,
though it still stuck out. Shifting the duffel bag to my left
hand I buzzed a couple names on the intercom until a voice
answered back and I looked to Vita who spoke German into
the box.

The buzzer sounded and Vita pushed open the door, then
turned to me and whispered, 'I tell them we make delivery.'

I followed Vita into a dark spacious hall that led to a thick

16

wooden door. This opened into a cement patio where children's bicycles and plastic swings and a sandbox with pails and windmills gave me a pang of discomfort; I was hoping this one went off without any complications. We came to another building like the first, a *Hinterhaus*, Vita said, then went quietly through another spacious hall; the scrape of our shoes on the coarse granite slate made my teeth ache. To the right was a winding wooden staircase and we started up the first flight. I turned and saw the wild-beard guy watching our back; noticed a .44 Magnum *and* a 9-mm Sig Sauer semi-automatic tucked in the waistband of his pants; they weren't there when he picked us up.

The third floor was tight and claustrophobic and I found it difficult to breathe as air dropped like clay in my lungs. Vita led us to a door at the far end of the corridor, then stepped back out of the way. Hardy gripped his AK 47 and was hopping back and forth on the balls of his feet and anybody stepping out of their apartment just then was in risk of their life.

I heard voices coming from inside and silently mouthed to Vita, 'Another way out?'

Hardy whispered over my shoulder, 'Don't matter, chief. Don't wanna be standin' here all day. Let's do it.' Then he pulled a crucifix from under his shirt and kissed it and I wished the Seconals I swallowed on the ride over would kick in about now.

A bald pug with a battered face and a red-leather motorcycle jacket stepped into the hall, took one look at us and reached into his waistband. We were bunched too close for me to swing my rifle so I ripped the .44 from the wild-beard guy's waist and fired twice into the bald pug's chest. Wet splats ripped through his ribs and the far wall cracked with a metalic after-ring. The bald pug stood there, frozen upright with his head twitching spastically, as if he were

17

making a stand against what was happening to him, as if his heart were still intact and not shredded into seven separate pieces, then he crumpled to the floor like a clumsy wooden man. I spun around and kicked in the door and Hardy and I charged into the room firing. Three middle-aged men were reaching frantically into a small round safe built into the floor until their chests burst open and the wall puked blood; fleshy chunks of meat and clothing flew like tea bags tossed in the air. Hardy sprayed a tall blond guy and he slammed against the wall with his right hand rising up; the next spray ripped up the wall around him, then his wrist popped suddenly into mist, his hand flew off and spun asymmetrically to the floor like an asteroid in outer space. Hardy blasted into the furniture sending papers and patches of wood flying, while the wild-beard guy shot out the blond guy's cheeks and left his face a splattered pie of gore.

Something blurred past a back doorway and I took off after it, caught her trying to climb out the window. Behind me Hardy and the wild-beard guy still fired their guns, but sporadically now.

She couldn't have been older than sixteen with eyes black as night and simple features on milky white skin. Jet-black hair fell like silk onto her shoulders. What she was doing here I couldn't guess but she had to be somebody's daughter and shit, these people should know better than to mix their family with their business. Now she stood staring at me, not at me really but at the barrel of my weapon, as if it were the only thing that mattered in the whole wide world to her, as if everything that she ever hoped for or dreamed about was tucked inside this fickle metal tube. And I couldn't tell who was more terrified by that fact, her or me. As the gunfire ended behind me Hardy called my name.

'I'm here. Everything's cool. Let's check out. No loose ends.' Then I went into the other room.

18

Hardy had opened a window, somehow unbroken in the mayhem, and smoke poured out of it like souls escaping Hell. As Hardy poked the bodies with the end of his rifle Vita searched through the file cabinets, pulling out papers and contracts and trying at the same time not to get any blood on his shoes, his face squeezed tight as chunks of brain and skin dripped down the walls and one guy slumped back on the tabletop emptied onto the floor like a toilet overflowing. Hardy kicked the smoldering severed hand over towards the wild-beard guy.

'Hey Groucho, here's a souvenir.'

The wild-beard guy laughed coldly and kicked it into the corner, then walked out of the room like a fed cat.

'Okay,' I said. 'Let's get outta here.'

Hardy started for the door while Vita grabbed frantically through the cabinets for more papers. I went around and pulled him up by the collar, 'Let's go! We didn't come here to rob the place.'

Vita snatched one last bundle of papers and rushed toward the door as Hardy yelled out from the back room, 'Hey you!' followed by a burst of automatic fire.

I came in to see the girl crumpled on the floor gasping for air through punctured lungs, like a fish pulled out of water. Hardy stood next to me, looking down at her body.

'I heard a sound back here,' he said. 'She must'a been hidin'. Guess you missed her.'

I couldn't speak as her eyes held me firm, boring in with terror and confusion; with betrayal, as if I'd broken some secret pact between us. And as Vita came up behind me I felt his heart pounding furiously in its cage; heard it over the thumping of my own. It seemed like an hour had passed before I said, 'Come on, we gotta get outta here.'

'What about her?' Hardy said. 'Shame we can't take her with us, huh?'

I fired one clean shot into her heart and she was still. Hardy watched me with twisted respect, something just west of admiration. Then he gave her one final blast in the face that left her unrecognizable. He chuckled and remarked, 'Shit, these Russian guns ain't so bad after all.'

2

'Welcome to Berlin.'

He handed me a Crown Royal with ice and Hardy got a vodka Martini with a small white onion. This guy did his homework.

'Your first trip to Germany?' he asked.

'First trip anywhere,' I answered with pride, though I don't know why. Yossario motioned us both to sit on the plush brown leather couch against the far wall underneath a black velvet painting of a conquistador riding a white horse and holding a lance with a splash of blood on the tip. He was nothing like what I expected, Yossario. For one thing, he was pure blue-collar criminal; short and squat with a ruddy complexion and thick, hard features on a round impish face, stubby callused hands and a portly gut splashing over his worn brown leather belt; he looked more like a union delegate at the Fulton Fish Market – at least before the cleanup last year – than one of Riccardo Montefiore's business associates. But then, I wasn't here to question Riccardo Montefiore's taste in friends; I also had to consider the steady supply of cocaine and heroin that turned up regularly on the streets of Newark smuggled in from Turkey. Yossario had to be connected to that somehow.

No, what did bother me was the fact that Hardy was forced on me for this job. I prided myself on discretion, always a clean job, in and out, no clues; police write it off as an internal matter settled between criminal elements. But Hardy played by a different set of rules, which were no rules at all. He didn't care who got hurt, and he cast an awful wide net. He enjoyed raising the stakes to an obscene level; that was his signature. The last contract I did with

Hardy was a simple affair; we took out Alphonse Lettieri at sunrise in his garage with two shots to the back of the head, clean, professional, we go home. But Hardy gets it into his head that he wants to check out the furniture in the house, so he takes the keys from Alphonse's pocket and goes inside where he finds Alphonse's wife sleeping on the couch in the living room. At gunpoint Hardy shook her awake and made her cook him breakfast. I came in to find him sitting at the kitchen table with a plate of eggs and bacon in front of him while Alphonse's wife was on her knees giving him a blow job. She was whimpering and gagging and Hardy ripped out clumps of her hair then pulled her down on his cock as if he wanted to choke her to death. I told him to stop, that this wasn't part of the job, but before I could say another word he put a .32 in her ear and told me if I said another word he'd blast her eyes out. I knew he meant it. When he was finished he made her get dressed and took her with him, walked her past her husband slumped over his steering wheel like a rotten sack of fruit, laughed as she let out an anguished sob, then forced her to kiss the corpse goodbye. By the time he shoved her trembling frame into the trunk of his car she was gone, as a woman, as a person, as anything human. Hardy hopped behind the wheel and took off into the quiet South Shore morning, and Alphonse's wife was never seen or heard from again. For several weeks during the investigation, the police considered her the main suspect in her husband's murder.

Yossario pulled up a chair from behind his desk and sat in front of us, leaned forward and lowered his voice as if the room were bugged with recording devices; and for all I knew, it just might have been. His English was nearly perfect, much better than his son's, who was sent home to wash the blood off his shoes.

'I think you've made quite an impresssion on Premig,' he

said and I now noticed a slight lisp when he spoke, his s's somehow fluttered out of his mouth like feathers, a totally incongruous sound coming from this spark plug of a man. Yossario went on, 'I've never ssseen him sssmile before. Not in ten years.'

'Premig doesn't look like much of a smiler,' I answered, hoping the sound of another voice might make Yossario's voice seem less comical. Hardy still had specks of blood freckling his face and Yossario offered him a white silk handkerchief. Hardy took it and wiped his cheeks but the specks were dry and nothing came off. Yossario told him to keep the handkerchief.

'A messsy business this afternoon, eh? We're not used to this kind of violence in Berlin.'

Hardy took instant offense, 'What kind of violence are you used to?'

'Well . . . one needs to be more discreet here in Berlin. We can't make public acts of retribution. This isn't America.'

'You have to trust in Riccardo Montefiore's judgment,' I said.

'I do, but I was expecting more of a defensive posture.'

'Hey, chief, American violence is based on offense, not defense. We been doin' it for over two hundred years of bloody conflict. So, you gotta problem with our methods then give us the word and we're outta here. I don't need this shit.'

'Hardy . . .'

'No, please, you misunderstand,' Yossario said. 'I'm not criticizing. I'm just saying it was unexpected, is all. When they come back at us, which they will, it will be swift and brutal. I would have liked to have prepared for retaliation. In the future I'd like to be informed. Is that an unreasonable request?' He looked at me.

'No, it isn't.'

23

He went on, 'We'll have to be on our highest guard from now on. Quite frankly, I wouldn't mind if you wiped out the whole company and their families. But that didn't happen, ssso we have to be ready.'

'There was a young girl, about sixteen years old. She may have gotten hit in the crossfire. Do you have any idea who she might be?'

'Was ssshe very pretty?'

'Not anymore,' Hardy interjected with a grin and Yossario smiled wanly. 'It may have been Victor Rudiyov's daughter. How old did you say ssshe was?'

'She was about sixteen. Black hair, black eyes, smooth complexion.'

Hardy looked at me as Yossario said, 'Rudiyov's daughter is fourteen. Could she have been fourteen?'

Hardy shrugged and chuckled, 'I saw her for a second, then she was meat.'

There was a knock on the door and Vita slipped quietly into the room wearing an ash-gray double-breasted suit and shiny black leather shoes. He smiled crookedly at Hardy and me.

Yossario sighed, 'I guess it doesn't matter now; the dead are dead. We move on.'

'What can we expect from the police?' I asked and Vita let out a grunt. Yossario glanced up at his son, then back to me.

'The police are really no presence here. Especially in *Kreuzberg*. The other side will clean up as much as they can. There might be an official investigation, but it will pass.'

'What are you doing to protect your places?' I asked.

'I've made arrangements. We'll have enough men to handle it.'

'First thing tomorrow morning I'd like to see the setup. The building sites and the warehouses, any potential targets.'

'Yes, of courssse.' Then Yossario sat back and started going on about his appreciation for our coming out to help him and how lucky he is to have a friend like Riccardo Montefiore and how sorry he is that it had to come down to this and that anything he can do to make our stay more comfortable blah blah blah and my eyes began to glaze over until I noticed a thin line of blood appear on his upper lip; it dripped past both lips and landed on his knee. Yossario was quite unaware of it until Hardy leaned forward and interrupted, 'Excuse me, but you're bleedin'.'

Then he offered him the handkerchief back.

Yossario touched his nose and the warm juice easing out of it and Vita grabbed the handkerchief and put it to his father's face, spoke urgently to him, but Yossario seemed more concerned with the drops of blood staining his pants.

Yossario explained to us, 'It's a condition I've had from when I was a child; there's nothing I can do about it. Some days it bleeds, some days it doesn't.'

Vita didn't seem to agree, but not in any language I could recognize. Yossario brushed him off. 'Anyway, you gentlemen must be exhausted. Why don't you settle into your flat now, clean up, get some rest?'

'Yeah, that's a good idea. We'd like to wash up.' And glancing at Hardy with the specks of blood on his cheeks and Yossario with a red Hitler mustache, I had to wonder what the fuck I had gotten myself into.

3

Vita motioned for Premig and four other guys to join us. Two of them carried our bags and together they led us around the corner keeping a constant circle of bodies around us at all times; we looked like the President and Vice President of the United States; it was kind of cool.

We walked past a social club and a pub and restaurant and a quaint Turkish bakery where a sad-looking girl with long black hair stood in the doorway holding a crying baby and calling out to one of the bodyguards. I caught a glance at Hardy checking her out and hoped for her sake that she wasn't his type.

Vita led us into a green park along a cobblestone walkway where groups of men and women wearing faded paisley robes sat around portable barbecues grilling lamb while their kids played soccer in a dried-out dug-out pool. Several kids called out to the bodyguards and the one to my left with a long gray ponytail yelled back until Vita glared at him and he shut up. We walked past a row of tall shrubs and trees and at the end of the row was a clearing where a huge rectangular building with six large windows overlooked the park; its brick walls were chipped and crumbling and stepping up the narrow walkway I saw a young woman with a black scarf on her head wheeling a baby carriage and when she looked up her eyes were the black eyes of the girl killed in the office. My knees buckled suddenly and all the bodyguards dove to the ground and pulled their guns as mothers clutched their children and husbands clutched their wives and people cried and yelled and hid behind trees and it seemed like the whole fucking place just went nuts for a minute. Hardy stood there watching it all with an amused grin; he didn't even flinch. Hardy wasn't gonna kiss dirt over some poor kid's popped balloon. Vita was the first one up barking orders as the bodyguards regrouped and rushed us into the building and seeing the fear and caution on everyone's face made me think that Hardy and I would probably be here longer than the weekend.

The inside stairs were warped and graffiti covered the walls and there was a large wooden ladder leaning against a wire-glass window with a bucket of black water underneath it; as we climbed up the stairs to the second floor, Hardy pointed out some carving in the wall that read 'Fuck the Police'.

'Hey, Tony, check it out. Different things are the same all over.' He ran his finger into the groove of gouged-out plaster. At the second floor Vita took out a set of keys and unlocked several locks that led through a cement hallway at the end of which was our flat. He opened the door and behind it were five huge rooms of brand new furniture and wall-to-wall plush carpeting; there was a large-screen TV and VCR and a stereo system and couches and glass coffee tables and two of the rooms had large fluffy beds with night tables beside them.

Hardy stood in the doorway with a satisfied grin. 'I think I'm gonna like this job,' he said and Vita gave him a smile before telling him, 'There is the phone. *Telefonieren* where you like in the world. What you need, you ask me. I get it.'

Vita stepped over to the tall picture windows overlooking the park and pointed to the view and I rushed up and shoved him against the wall and all the bodyguards froze for a moment; nobody knew what to do. Vita looked at me hurt and confused.

'Vita, after this afternoon, we're at war. Everyone is a target. No view. No windows. Nobody walks past an uncovered window anymore. Anybody in that park could get a clear shot at one of us; they could chuck a gasoline cocktail through the fucking window and take out all of us. Understand?'

He nodded.

'I want long black curtains over every window. Make sure they're thick. I don't want anyone to be able to see inside. Whose place is this?'

'My father is owner.' Vita turned to the guy with the long gray ponytail and spoke to him while pointing to the windows. I followed Hardy into the kitchen where the counters and cabinets were hospital white and sparkling with cleanliness and opening up the refrigerator Hardy let out a sigh. It was filled with packages of meat and beer and cheese and cake and candy and juice and milk and vegetables and breads and condiments and Hardy pulled a bottle of ketchup out of the door.

'Hey Tony, look, they got Heinz!'

I started checking out the security of the place. There was only one entrance and luckily the windows had been newly installed with working locks and peeking over the windowsill it looked like fucking hunting season outside with the trees and shrubs offering easy cover to anyone wanting revenge.

In the kitchen Hardy opened a bottle of liquor and I heard the soft metal crack of the cap followed by the sound of liquid chugging down his cavernous throat. 'Any of you guys speak English?'

'*Ein bisschen*,' someone replied.

'What? . . . You know, English?'

Vita stepped in, 'He say he speaks a little English.' Vita turned back to me and said, 'The black for windows comes soon. You sleep. I have two men watch outside, for you. Okay?'

Vita slapped the keys into my palm and left with the

bodyguards as Hardy stepped out of the kitchen sniffing his blackened hands.

'I love the smell of cordite. But those Russian guns are a fuckin' mess.'

He walked into the bathroom and turned on the water. Looking at himself in the mirror, he called, 'Hey! I got freckles. Why didn't you tell me I had so much blood on my face?!'

'It looks good on you. You look like Huckleberry Finn.'

Hardy washed his hands and face in the sink while I put my suitcase on the bed and opened it. I took out several Chapman locks and a portable tool kit with accessories and Hardy went to the door and fumbled around with the doorknob, shook his head and told me to use the Amsterdam.

He went into the larger bedroom and laid his long frame flat out on the bed, clothes and shoes included, and a minute later he was snoring like a soggy wet blanket being torn in half.

Premig and the long-ponytail guy came back with a bundle of thick black material that looked like theater curtains and proceeded to hang the cloth over the windows. Two other guys stood guard outside our door while several others stood watch in the park.

I went into the bathroom, popped four Seconals and sucked down a handful of water, rinsed my face then came out to see the apartment looking like a funeral parlor. Premig had a box cutter and proceeded to slice long slits in the curtains so that I or Hardy could look out without being detected. I gave him a nod of approval; then when he left I went to bed.

I dreamed of happy times when I was a kid and playing stickball in the street with my sister Carrie. But then the world turned upside down and I was walking with my sister in a hospital corridor where the walls seemed to go on forever until we came to a tall counter where a nurse stood talking on a telephone. My sister turned to me and said, 'Daddy tried to kill himself.'

'No he didn't.'

'I heard Mommy and Aunt Diane talking about it. He took poison.'

'He wouldn't do that.'

'Yes, he would.'

'Is he gonna die?'

My mother appeared beside me. 'Don't be telling your brother stories like that,' she gently reprimanded my sister. 'Of course your father will live.'

'Why did Daddy try to kill himself?'

'Because he's unhappy.'

My mother led us to the counter and it rippled like blurry gray water and my father appeared lying in his bed with a tube in his arm and a smile on his face, but he seemed in a trance, as if whatever he was seeing was in a different room or on another planet. I watched him silently work out equations of reason and sanity in the back recesses of his troubled mind, while on the cold tile floor my sister slept in her blue cotton dress that was faded from years of wash and wearing. She wasn't wearing any panties.

'What do you see, Daddy?'

My father's expression never changed; his eyes didn't focus on anything except the mysterious film clips playing on the inside of his brain. With a lavender whisper he told me, 'I've seen the end of the world, Anthony. It's not a pretty sight.' Tears leaked from his eyes and flew like dragonflies into the air and one came straight at my heart like a baseball thrown right down the middle and I creamed it with the green cut-off broom handle we used as a bat. The new pink Spaulding went soaring over the pavement until it bounced off Dougie Schwick's father's gray Impala and rolled into Mrs Henry's rosebush and by that time I was on my way to third base and Carrie was cheering me to go home because she wanted to see me get my first home run. As the ball was retrieved and thrown towards home plate I had already crossed the blue chalk-drawn pentagon to the joyous screams of my sister, Carrie, who was the pitcher on the opposing team.

By the time I awoke to Vita's knocking on the door it was nighttime. We rode over to Yossario's apartment with Premig driving and Vita in the passenger seat and four other guys following in a car behind us. Colored neon lights flashed on restaurant windows and a pack of dogs roamed through an alley like a gang of kids hell-bent on felony; people on the street were jittery and suspicious, they stopped what they were doing and stared at our car as it drove by.

'What's up?' I asked Vita.

'It seems to have made quite a problem. The girl especially.'

Hardy piped up, 'Good. That was the point.'

'Yes. I am afraid you are right. They killed two of my cousins this afternoon. Cut them to . . . pieces.'

'Why weren't they armed and on their guard?' I asked.

'School children do not carry guns in Berlin.'

That was a good answer.

'When did this happen?' I asked.

'After three o'clock. It will be on TV not. We take care of it . . . I just come from talk to their *Eltern*.' Vita said this with anger. Premig didn't have any reaction and I couldn't tell what he was thinking, his face could have been made of smoke. Hardy took out the 9-mm Glock that Vita had given him at the apartment and released the safety, stood the gun on his knee. I sat back on the seat and enjoyed the fear in everyone else.

Riccardo Montefiore stood in front of the wine rack playing with the dozen or so poker chips he kept on his desk for occasions like this. The dark red bottles of wine laying on their sides and pointing like gun barrels only added to the effect for Angel Mariano Ebbens. Angel ran cocaine and crack for the Franchise and though he wasn't caught stealing money from the Franchise, he was caught selling his own private supply in competition with the Franchise, which was the same as stealing from the Franchise. For that he now sat cuffed to a chair, his mouth hanging open in astonishment, eyes swollen and bloodshot, the pupils darting in denial. Riccardo Montefiore asked him one last time to tell him exactly what transpired. Angel swore on his mother's grave and his sister's honor, babbling incoherently about loyalty and friendship and years of devoted service and when Riccardo Montefiore let the fist of chips drop single-file into his palm with a sound not unlike someone clearing their throat, I cracked Angel on the ear with a cast-iron frying pan. He shrieked and jerked his head and a second later blood began to fill in his ear, but at least he wasn't babbling anymore. I leaned in to his face, tried to reason with him, gently, in his good ear – I liked Angel and had nothing against him.

'Angel, I want you to listen to me. Nobody wants to do anything to you. This is a lot of trouble, and a lot of effort. We just want to understand the problem. That way we can fix it.'

Angel looked at me with a cross of pain, fear and hatred, but he was listening.

'You were a good worker; nobody had any complaints with you, until recently, and no matter who we might get to replace you, the same problem might come up again, right? So let's fix the thing and get it over with. We got a good thing going here, everybody's making a ton of fucking money and nobody wants to fuck up a good thing.'

Angel swallowed hard and with it went some of the hatred. He looked at me with pleading, sorry eyes; he was going to talk.

When he was finished Riccardo Montefiore nodded his head and I began putting on my industrial rubber gloves, slipped on my plastic face-shield – I was working with acids at the time. Angel looked first at Riccardo Montefiore then at me, 'You're gonna let me go now, right? We're gonna fix the problem and move on, right?'

I carefully took out the different bottles and stood them on the table next to Angel, lined up according to caustic characteristics. Angel watched me in horror, his lower lip swelled and began to quiver, his eyes became dripping cherries. Before he could find the words to begin the plea for his life, I leaned in and told him, 'Angel, you stole from the Franchise, that's the same as stealing from everyone's pockets. Some of these people got kids, families to take care of. And you're depriving them of that. Imagine if I came into your mother's house and just stole money from her; how would you feel? That's what we're dealing with here.'

Riccardo Montefiore sipped his wine, gently bounced his chips in his manicured left hand; wore a sated, complacent smile; he liked it when I rationalized. I only felt it was fair; I didn't want there to be any misunderstandings. By the time Angel told us where his stash was hidden, his face had only three layers of skin left. That's how I met Hardy. He was the one called in to hold Angel steady while I worked on him, then drive him to the hospital, which was code for never to be seen again.

Premig stopped the car in front of a group of young Turks in designer suits standing in front of a tall orange building. Two guys in wheelchairs spun around toward the street in synchronicity as if connected by an invisible gear. The car behind us pulled up and the four guys got out and joined the group out front and now there were a dozen tough-looking guys in designer suits sneering at each other and reaching nervously into their jackets and it looked like the Turkish version of *The Godfather*. I was hoping not to become Fredo Corleone.

Hardy and I got out of the car and everyone stepped back. I looked up at the building. It was newly renovated, nestled in-between two old gray buildings of soot-covered concrete. There were colorful flowers painted on the upper floors, simple blossoms of orange and green mixed with blue and red as though painted by happy kids in kindergarten. The windows were lit up on every floor except the third floor, which was completely covered over with black curtains. Hardy gave me a nudge. Vita grabbed one of the young Turks and spoke angrily in his ear while the others stood there gaping at us. Nobody said a word or made a move, but there was an undercurrent of hostility; what had taken place here today really freaked everybody out. Vita went into the lobby and we followed him, Premig hovering constantly at my back with his handless stump in his jacket pocket. In the elevator Vita wouldn't meet my eyes; I wasn't sure if he was pissed at me or pissed at the Russians who killed his cousins, but in any event he'd better get over it real quick.

He led us through a narrow corridor where the floor was made of highly polished thin slats of wood like in a bowling alley. A tall wooden door with diamond-shaped panels carved into it opened into a spacious living room of off-white walls adorned with black-velvet paintings. Gray metal tubes shone yellow light down on naked Amazonian women carrying swords and standing victorious over defeated armies of broken, crying men. Hanging by itself on one wall was a gold-framed portrait of Elvis when he was thin.

Yossario stepped in from a side door wearing a silk paisley shirt and pressed khaki pants. 'Do you like art?' he said. His nose wasn't bleeding this time. 'Sssome of them are originals.'

'I like naked chicks in paintings,' Hardy remarked. 'They're always cool.'

'Yes, they are, aren't they. My ssson finds them distasteful.'

'Insulting to Islam,' Vita confirmed.

'Issslam is insulted! My well-intentioned, ssstudious son should enjoy the fruits of life more readily,' Yossario said with a chuckle.

Hardy pointed to one painting in particular, a naked blonde-haired, blue-eyed young child straddling a sharpened spear and standing in a battlefield of dead hacked-up bodies, her shimmering wide eyes staring out over the miles of flesh with a vacant, innocent stare. 'Is that what German girls look like?'

'They come in a wide variety,' Yossario answered dryly, then pivoted toward his son. 'Vita, if it's not insulting to Islam, would you make our guests some drinks?'

Vita left but he didn't seem offended by the request.

Near the far wall was a long table set for a formal dinner; four tall chairs had place settings of china, crystal and silver.

'I'm sorry to hear about the kids this afternoon,' I said, but Yossario behaved as if he hadn't heard me. Instead he said, 'I'd like to show you something,' and led us into a room at the rear of the house.

A glass rectangular display case took up the middle of the den; inside it was a miniature mock-up of an office complex on a painted street. There were tiny model cars at the curb and trees and bushes surrounding the buildings with wire-stick people in walking poses on the sidewalk.

Vita came in with our drinks and I looked to Yossario who started speaking.

'Thisss is the cause of all the trouble. We won a government contract to build a complex of office buildings on the Potsssdamer Platz, in the former East Berlin. A very lucrative contract, and if we deliver on time, and on budget, it getsss us more government contracts in the future. There are sssome unworthy people who would like to have this contract for themssselves.' Yossario stopped and looked at me, then at Hardy. He was stewing inside. I could see the muscles in his jaw tightening, but he tried to keep it hidden; it took a lot of effort to do so.

'My youngest brother, Dahrel, was killed by a falling steel beam, on a sssite that had no steel beams. The body of Circon, my second brother, is still not found. Several friends have been crippled. And now the two children murdered today. I want to keep my family alive, and my business intact. I don't want children murdered anymore.'

I wondered if that included the Russian girl.

Dinner was something called cous cous which was no more than ground-up rice with vegetables and lamb mixed in and when Hardy called it Turkish stew Yossario let out peels of laughter. By dessert Yossario had drank two bottles of wine while Hardy had downed five vodka Martinis; I was content to blitz out on the four Seconals I took in the bathroom before dinner. Vita drank some kind of yogurt drink that looked like puke. Yossario sat at the end of the table, his head like a giant plum leaning on the back of his chair. Over dinner he talked about how he got started in life.

Though Vita must have heard this story a thousand times before, he listened in awe as his old man recounted how he came over to Berlin as a young teenager with his father in the early sixties, an exodus of Turks pouring in by the tens of thousands for the massive construction projects taking place in the western part of the city. Thirty-five years later the Turks had formed their own pocket of home with most of them settling here in *Kreuzberg*, and they had kids and there was plenty of work and life was easier until soon Turkey was just a distant memory of hunger and poverty and joblessness. Yossario and his two brothers arrived with next to nothing and he told of how they grew up with the shadow of construction over their heads and how once they got their jobs they worked from morning till night carrying bricks and digging ditches and doing all the shit work the Germans didn't want to do, working until their backs were cracking in half. And after eleven years they scraped together enough to start their own company, doing brickwork and putting tarpaper roofs on damaged buildings. He talked of how hard it was back then and how all their friends said they were crazy because of the sacrifices they made and how their families went hungry and cold and suffered deprivation until little by little they clawed their way up but it wasn't until the fall of the Soviet Union and the collapse of the Berlin Wall that things got so good.

'In a way, your country did no favor to the world by defeating communism,' he said, leaning forward in his chair, keeping his forefingers pressed against both lips, his thumbs forming a triangle underneath them. 'It was better when we knew where the enemy was, when the wall protected us. Now they're everywhere. You unleashed the filthiessst of people, and that'sss what brings us here today.'

Hardy seemed to shake himself awake at these last sentences.

'Are these real communists we're dealin' with?'

'Former GDR officials.'

'GDR? What's that?'

'German Democratic Republic.'

'I don't understand. Are they democrats or republicans?'

'Neither. They become whatever suits their needs.'

'What does a guy hafta do to get a straight fuckin' answer around here?!'

'They're Stasi. The sssecret police. The Russians are behind them.'

'Russians. That's all I need to know. I hate the fuckin' Russians. I lost a great uncle in the Korean War. You know who killed him?'

'The North Koreans,' I answered dryly.

'Fuck no!' Hardy barked, 'The Russians were behind that.'

Yossario looked like he might respond, but instead shook his head. 'Well, anyway, that's what brings us here today. Self-preservation.'

'How did you hook up with Riccardo Montefiore?'

'I know Riccardo's wife, from when she was a little girl.'

'Lucretia Montefiore?'

'Yes. Her family name is Tigrit. Her father came from the same village as my father. Just outside Istanbul.'

Hardy asked, 'Istanbul? Turkey?'

'Yes. She was born in Turkey but raised here in Berlin.'

Hardy's face lit up wickedly. 'Hey Tony, check it out, the Countess is a sand nigger!' Vita looked like he'd been slapped, but Yossario sipped his wine, didn't acknowledge Hardy's crack in any way; sometimes with Hardy that was the best way to go.

'I don't understand something,' I said, truly curious. 'Why do you need us? Why not do the job yourself?'

Yossario chuckled; the question amused him. 'This is a family business. I'm a family man. This is for my children, and my nephews and nieces, and their children. I am not an army. You've ssseen them outside, everyone with guns. Well, no one carried a gun in their life until two weeks ago. Half of them would ssshoot themselves in the foot if they had to fire them.'

'Premig seemed pretty comfortable with a gun.'

'Premig was a colonel in the Turkish army for fifteen years. The others are ... teenagers, workers. Lambs to slaughter. That's why you're here. To let them know that we will fight back to protect what is ours. Nobody pushes around the Americans, and with Riccardo Montefiore as our partner, nobody will push us around either.'

But I wondered if he knew truly what he had bargained away, and then I wondered why Riccardo Montefiore would even want to own a dinky little family-run construction company, in a country where he had no real contacts and certainly no base of operations to work it from. The logistics alone of running a criminal organization were immense.

Just as I was about to wonder something else some well-dressed guy with bushy blond hair and wire-rimmed glasses stepped in, all smiley and cheery and goofy as if he were about to break out in song. He stopped in front of me, stuck out his hand and announced, 'Hi. I'm Heinrich.'

I lifted three tired fingers and he gripped them tightly.

Hardy shoveled cold lamb into his mouth without looking up from his plate. Hardy hated pretty boys.

Yossario put his hand out as if displaying a new car.

'Heinrich is the owner, on paper, of the company. A certain number of government contracts are awarded to German-owned companies and Heinrich, through his inss-side friends, gets these government contracts for us. Then he sssubcontracts them out to the smaller companies which I own directly, and where we can put our own labor to work. For this he ssshares in all our good fortune.'

40

'We're all working together for the same goals,' Heinrich said in perfect English, sounding not unlike a corporate spokesman.

We retired to the main living room which was separated from the dining room by three rooms in between. I hadn't seen a bedroom or anything that would lead me to believe that someone slept here.

Stepping into the main living room was to be smacked in the face again with the pornographic velvet paintings so incongruous hanging over the fine leather couches and modern coffee tables. Hardy went over to his favorite painting and Heinrich strolled up beside him. While Yossario told me he was in New York City once and that he stayed in a hotel near Central Park, I listened to Heinrich croon to Hardy.

'Pure innocence. Like a budding rose. Yet surrounded by madness and depravity. There's a sublime majesty about a young girl on the edge of sexual devastation. Don't you agree?'

'What are you? A fuckin' poet?!'

'No. A pedophile.'

Hardy threw him a sideways glance, then burst out laughing.

Vita stepped in carrying a large sterling silver service tray with a coffee-set on top. Heinrich looked Hardy square in the eyes and told him, 'My cousin owns a club in *Neukölln*; I think you'd like it. It's a private place. He specializes in the sort of things you might be interested in.' Then he slipped him a round green business card and said over his shoulder, 'Ask for Volker. He's my cousin. Of course you're my personal guest, you pay for nothing. It's all on the house.'

Hardy looked down at the green circle framed by his forefingers and thumbs, then up at Heinrich strolling over to the couch and the coffee.

41

It was a masterful performance. Heinrich knew what to be and when to be it; he pulled all the right strings, like a fucking puppeteer. And his English was incredible. I shouldn't underestimate him.

4

N ext morning, Vita and Premig took us in the car through the city while Yossario went to sit with the parents of the two cousins killed the day before. The sky was dense with gray clouds hanging just above the building tops; they painted the streets a neutral tone of despair. Graffiti covered every billboard and empty space, storefronts were plastered with layer upon layer of posters that had been glued poorly and were now peeling off. On a large crowded square sat a fruit and vegetable market, overhead an orange train roared by on an elevated platform. We drove on a narrow two-lane straightway into a traffic circle where Premig made a left turn under the overpass and a beige taxi sat in front of us up on a jack, its driver changing a flat tire in the left lane. Premig rolled down his window and yelled in Turkish and the taxi driver yelled back and Vita looked over at Premig who shut his mouth and fixed his eyes on the road. Hardy chuckled and yelled out his window, 'Go fuck your mother!'

We were headed for something called *Potsdamer Platz* and the only thing I knew about it was that it was a construction site, but when we pulled up and got out of the car, I nearly choked. It was the biggest fucking construction site I'd ever seen! It seemed to go on for twenty New York City blocks. There were cranes of every height and variety with arms crisscrossing across the gray sky like a spiderweb of steel, dump trucks poured out gravel and tractors dug out huge holes and cables swung smoothly in the air and a thousand guys in colored hard hats worked and lifted and drove vehicles and Hardy and I watched it all like little boys on Christmas Eve. There had to be a billion dollars of virgin money waiting here to be fucked. And now I saw the true majesty of the plan. Riccardo Montefiore wasn't after some dinky little family-run construction company – he was after the whole fucking bank! One piece at a time. The same way he did it back home. The way the airport to the turnpike and the public parks and housing projects including schools as well as private contractors and labor unions along with the lumber yards and the cement factories next to the brick manufacturers behind the steelworks and smelting plants all came piece by piece under his tight control; until there wasn't any part of building something on the northern seaboard that Riccardo Montefiore didn't own either in part or outright. It was a grand, epic scheme, and I realized that Hardy and I were only a small part of it; the catalyst, so to speak; the advance team sent to stir things up, and then Riccardo Montefiore would step in to bring peace and stability.

The man was a visionary.

Vita walked us through the site, pointing out the future Sony headquarters across from Daimler-Benz and something called Verlag along with other names I didn't know or try to remember. We walked for a good twenty minutes and there seemed to be no let-up to the work going on. Vita turned a corner and there at the end of the site sitting atop a dozen mounts of cinder block was a long white aluminum trailer, not unlike the shanty annex buildings next to the old high schools back home. Vita started up three mud-covered wooden steps that sagged under his weight, motioned us to follow him inside. I looked for Premig but he had disappeared into the activity behind me.

Heinrich sat behind a computer console, wearing a telephone headset and talking into the microphone in German. He saw us and smiled grandly, delighted to see us. Then he pulled off his headset and got up from the desk, coming around and shaking our hands and ending with, 'Have you seen the newspapers yet?'

'You got the *New York Post*?' Hardy asked, with a tinge of what sounded to me like hope.

'I can get it on-line for you. But first, here, I'll show you,' Heinrich scooped up several different newspapers, all of them printed in the cheap, lurid style of gossip magazines.

I went to the window, scoped out the site and the dozen ways the perimeter could be breached, while Heinrich translated the details of a mysterious disturbance somewhere deep in the East for Hardy, who asked if they mentioned a missing severed hand. When Heinrich said no, Hardy cried out, 'Fuck, Tony! They're suppressin' the news.'

Vita came up beside me, saw my concern. 'Nothing will happen here. That brings *Polizei*, and problems for all. Nobody wants that. Here is safe to be.' He said it with utter certainty and not a drop of fear. I asked him, 'Why didn't your father ever threaten to go to the police in the first place? Maybe that would have scared them off?'

'We are *Ausländer*! Do you think the *Polizei* will help us?'

I overheard Heinrich and Hardy laughing at the pictures in the papers and Hardy was ogling some naked chick on the back page when Heinrich mentioned nonchalantly, 'Last night when I got home there was a message for me on the call-answerer. They want to talk.'

'Who wants to talk?' I asked, suppressing the urge to punch his fucking face in for not telling me this sooner. My expression told him to continue.

'He didn't identify himself. It's fairly obvious, no?'

'What did he say exactly?'

'He said . . . they would like a meeting with Yossario.'

'Forget it,' I said. 'Yossario's not meeting anyone. They'll try to pop him at any meeting.'

Vita agreed.

Heinrich spoke up, 'I think this killing back and forth is

crazy; we're hurting, they're hurting. Why don't we just hear what they say? How else are we going to negotiate an agreement?'

'We're not here to negotiate agreements.'

'What are you here to do exactly, if you don't mind my asking?' The fact that he said it with curiosity and not with disrespect saved his lower jaw.

'We're here to show a presence, to keep you and everyone else alive for as long as we can; and, hopefully, with all your limbs intact. Then we're going home.'

'Aren't you staying till your Mr Talbot arrives?'

Hearing that name confirmed my suspicions. It was a done deal, the Franchise was expanding. Next to Riccardo Montefiore, Lawrence Talbot was the most important member of the Franchise, the chief financial officer and keeper of the cash. He cleansed the money, nurtured it, invested it, gave it legitimacy through a rotating chain of offshore dummy corporations strategically set up so he could shift it from one place to the next according to the current day's market fluctuations and currency rates, then he socked it away so fast and surreptitiously into secret bank accounts in Luxembourg and the Channel Islands until the tax authorities couldn't tell what the fuck was going on. I don't think anybody ever really understood how it all worked, but Lawrence Talbot had doubled everybody's shares, salaries and Christmas bonuses in the four years of consolidation, so nobody was complaining.

The door opened and a young Turkish man about twenty or twenty-one came in wearing a hard hat with worn jeans and mud-covered work boots. He had wide, squirrelly eyes and a smooth thin face and he appeared to know who Hardy and I were by the way he averted his glance; somehow his face looked familiar to me. Vita introduced us to his younger brother Mustaph, a foreman on the job, who shook our hands limply then spoke to his brother in German. Vita turned to me and explained, 'This is only building talk,' then went back to his brother while Heinrich asked Hardy, 'What do you call the call-answerer in English?'

'Secretary.'

Outside, the trail of acrid smoke from the molten tar boiling in the black spattered wagon to my right blew in my face, a truck thirty feet away was dumping a mountain of powder that swept up and out from the ground like liquid, two men in work shirts and white helmets disappeared in the nuclear cloud of gray.

'We have to think like the big boys now, Tony,' he said, putting his arm around my shoulder. We were strolling along a dirt path flanked by tall grass and weeds. He said he wanted to talk to me about something and as much as I'd done nothing to warrant such discomfort, I felt my senses pumping with caution. He continued, 'The most important thing in life is security, Tony. You know that, right? The ability to take care of yourself and your family. Financially, physically, emotionally. But as the world gets smaller, taking care of your loved ones is getting harder to do. There are only so many resources, the well eventually runs dry. That's why we have to think beyond our borders; we have to look at the world in a different way. We have to think globally. Because there are billions of dollars out there, just waiting to be plucked, like leaves on a tree. Billions! You just reach out and keep grabbing.' He grabbed the air as if billions of dollars were there waiting to be plucked. When he looked at me his eyes were smiling, greedily, as if he could actually see the money there in front of him; maybe seeing it – actually visualizing it! – was the first step to acquiring it.

'Heard you dropped a bundle last week,' he remarked.

'I've had better days.'

'What were you playing?'

'Horses, and fucking Carmine Angelino's tips. I should pop him.'

'Even when the fix is in, things can still go wrong.'

We reached the end of a hedge and turned the corner, followed a path toward a crowd of people about thirty feet in front of us.

'What d'you drop?'

'Thirty K.'

'Do you have thirty K?'

'Not yet.'

Riccardo Montefiore pulled out his cell phone and speed-dialed a number. I could only guess he was ringing Scotti Gigante.

'Scotti, this is Riccardo. I'm here with Tony the Bat. Yeah, I know. I'll tell you what . . . why don't you forget about it. Yeah, it'd be a personal favor to me. Thanks.'

He closed the phone, slipped it in his pocket and looked straight ahead. 'Now you do,' he said, and never said another word about it. I had to laugh. Whatever he called me over here to ask me to do, I just agreed to do. We reached the gravesite and everyone stepped back to make way for Riccardo Montefiore, who kissed the trembling wife of his deceased partner on the cheek and vowed revenge on the culprits responsible for this reprehensible deed. I stared at the green felt-covered mahogany box, saw the wife and teenage daughters weeping beside it. I saw his face in the rear view mirror at the moment he knew it was over, when he heard the click behind his ear, that split second when he jerked around, the gamut of emotions that ran through his eyes, his pupils jolting in shock and fear, replaced by anger at the betrayal, the fact that someone would want him gone so permanently, so traumatically;

lastly I saw defiance, the will to survive and the spark to action, but this all took place in an instant, and then he was dead. Standing now at his gravesite, catching sight of Riccardo Montefiore patting the widow's sobbing frame and nodding to me with approval in his eyes, I felt fairly confident that Sammy 'Stun Gun' Bottolieri's killer would go unidentified and unpunished.

Premig came walking out of what was now a billowing wall of dust. Marching toward me with his stump shoved deep in his pocket, he had a bounce in his step and I thought I caught the outline of a smile on his face, at least from twenty feet away. When he came up and stood beside me, I noticed it *was* a smile. He didn't say a word. He didn't ignore me; he just didn't acknowledge me either. The cuffs of his pants had blood on them; I knew from his smile that it wasn't his blood. We stood there quietly, both of us looking out over the vast expanse of anarchy in front of us, listening to the maddening roar of the machinery, engines chugging and bulldozers growling as tractors lifted huge granite boulders and dropped them onto the groaning backs of trucks. Underneath it all voices yelled and called for help like the maddening din of a prison riot.

My father pulled us by the hand and we struggled to keep up with him as he practically ran through a long corridor of green-painted cinder block. It took a lot of explaining to get past the front gate and my father talked to a tall serious man in a black suit for a long time before we were finally admitted into the ominous red building where smokestacks wept rust-colored clouds into dense, colorless sky. Inside, the sound was like being underwater, it filled every crevice and orifice, a kinetic roar of static electricity and stale air, punctuated by chilling cries for somebody named Pablo. Uniformed guards stood in front of thick steel doors eyeing us strangely as we hurried past. I caught a glimpse of my sister's face staring straight ahead with her lips pressed together in uncertainty and embarrassment, a ragged flesh-tone Bandaid swung from her scraped left knee. My father pulled us past thick steel bars cutting off one space from another. I heard him sighing urgently; he couldn't take enough air into his lungs; his eyes were wide open, staring straight ahead, yet clouded, like cataracts, and the expression on his face was the same one my sister wore but for unknown reasons. We reached a metal door-frame standing by itself in a room where a heavy-set burly guard with a coarse, stubbled face turned and stopped us from moving any further. My father handed over the slip of paper given to him at the front gate, excitedly telling the guard we had permission to enter, then he lifted both our arms, explaining that we, my sister and I, had to be admitted because it was a matter of grave urgency. The guard eyed us suspiciously, warily, picked up a phone and dialed a number while my father paced around, turning back to us and assuring us, 'Don't worry, children,' always calling us 'children' when he couldn't remember our names. 'Jesus Christ died for our sins.'

The guard hung up the phone and had us walk through the metal doorway. He waved a black metal tube around me, then around my sister and my father, sniffed the air around us and wrinkled his face in discomfort, before letting us pass into a cube-shaped room where another guard led us into another spacious room with tables and benches like a cafeteria, except there were no kitchen counters or facilities. Black families sat huddled around most of the tables and there was one empty table that the guard led us over to, my father pushing us along in front of him. My father sat us with our backs against the wall and everyone else in the room looked over with puzzlement on their faces; we were the only white people there. My father sat proudly between us, righteous superiority on his upturned chin. I noticed all the windows had metal gratings over them; they cast a hive of dim sunlight on the floor. My sister leaned over. 'Daddy, what are we doing here?'

'Shhh, sweetie, just be patient.'

'But Daddy, I want to go home. We're not supposed to be here.'

My father leaned down, whispered urgently, 'We've been called here on a very special mission.'

'Please, Daddy, I want to go home.'

'Be quiet. You'll upset the chemo-flow.'

He sat with his back straight up against the wall, his stubborn rigid profile like a statue, the lobe missing from his battered left ear. Then a huge black man stepped into the back doorway, he almost didn't fit through it, had to turn his body slightly to the side. His dull green workshirt had no sleeves, showing off arms like muscular legs and his chest was taut like a full sack of cement; I don't think I'd ever seen anyone so big and imposing. The guard pointed over to our table and the man looked over with curiosity, angry curiosity. He said something to the guard who motioned for him to return back inside but he waved it off and came towards the table. My father smiled as he towered over us.

'Yeah?' he demanded. 'Who are you? I don't know you people!'

My father watched him as he eyed my sister and I, back and forth. I couldn't take my eyes off him. I noticed faded black numbers dyed into the fabric of his shirt pocket: '899' plus three other numbers I couldn't make out.

'What is this? Some kind'a joke?' he barked in a deep rolling bass, but tried to keep the volume down. 'What the fuck you want?!'

My father asked him to sit down. He glanced behind him,

51

saw the guard leaning in the doorway, watching; then he sat down opposite us.

'I want to ask you a question.'

'What?'

My father leaned forward and folded his hands. 'Have you thought about your spiritual destiny?'

'What?!'

'Have you accepted Jesus Christ as your savior?'

'What the fuck business is that for you to know?!'

'Only Jesus Christ can save your soul.'

'I don't know what the fuck you're talkin' about!'

'I'd like you to meet my children. This is Isaiah and Sarah. They hold the keys to the kingdom of God.'

'Who gives a fuck?'

I took my father's hand and told him, 'Daddy, my name's Anthony.'

My sister gripped his other hand, squeezed it hard.

899 was looking at us, studying us; he was completely baffled by it all, playing out the different scams that might be taking place, projecting all the possible angles and using his street savvy and experience, until finally, he reached his conclusion. 'You're a fuckin' nut! You get your kicks outta bringin' your kids to jails?! Wanna give your kids somethin' to remember? Here, bring over that little piece o'chicken there. I'll show her who her savior is.'

My father pulled his hand free from her grip and put his arm around her shoulder and told her to go. 'No, Daddy,' she pleaded. 'I wanna go home.'

'Go ahead. He can't hurt you. Have faith. The power of Christ compels you.'

899 lowered his voice. 'I won't hurt you, little kitten. I wanna tell you a secret. Com'ere and sit with me for a minute.'

'Daddy, please, we're not supposed to be here,' she said

louder, with growing discomfort on her face. 899 looked back at the guard who was busy talking to a woman coming into the room, then he came around the table and sat next to my sister. He warned my father, 'You tell her to behave. I just wanna sit with her for a minute.' Then he lifted her onto his lap as if she were a foam pillow, faced her away from my father and me as she pleaded to be taken home.

I joined in, 'Daddy,' I said, 'let's go home. I feel sick.'

'You two look straight ahead,' 899 said to me and my father. 'Make like nothin's goin' on. You,' to my sister, 'shut the fuck up.'

He looked back at the guard one more time before leaning forward with his wide body blocking her from his view. I saw her shoulders arch violently and twitch as he grabbed and fondled her, whatever sound she made was muffled in his heaving chest. He started writhing up and down on his seat and my sister's hair bounced up and down with him, I heard him breathing rapidly and grunting secretly and my sister cried softly in a half-stuttering moan. He clutched her tight around the body and the veins in his arms clenched like steel cable and I thought he might crush her to death. When I looked to my father he was mumbling to himself and fingering the feces-covered rosary beads around his neck. My stomach shook, and I wet myself after 899 ordered me to look away or I would be next. A sharp crack of wood on flesh made 899 jump up and wail in pain, sending my sister tumbling to the floor underneath the table. The guard beat him repeatedly with a club until he fell to the floor and covered himself with his arms screaming that he didn't do anything, that these people are fucking nuts. He was dragged away by three other guards and my father was taken to a different room while my sister and I stayed with a nurse. By the time my mother came to pick us up my father had been taken to a hospital so she took us home and we had fried chicken for dinner.

Hardy walked awkwardly over the lumps and crevices in the soil. 'What do you make of Lawrence Talbot coming out?'

'I don't think we've been completely briefed.'

'Shit, I gotta move my watch ahead. Look at that, it's three in the morning back home.'

Hardy and I spent the rest of the day with Vita and Premig driving around to see the other places Yossario owned, several apartment buildings and two warehouses for importing and exporting and a gift shop and a bakery but nothing that was instrumentally of value or in strategic jeopardy. But every place had several guys standing guard either in the doorway or hanging out inside and I wasn't going to discourage caution.

For lunch we went to a Turkish restaurant but first stopped off at McDonald's so Hardy could get some 'real food'. The last stop we made was the place where Vita and Premig got the guns when we first arrived. It was a cellar. They took us down cement steps leading below street level to a painted green metal door. We walked through a dark wet corridor with wooden crates stacked up against the walls, the crates had colorful labels on them of smiling women with rosy cheeks and jet-black wavy hair, the kind of labels they put on packs of firecrackers.

Hardy asked, 'What's in the crates?'

'Grapes. My father makes wine.'

'This is a wine cellar?'

'It has many uses.'

The corridor had a low ceiling and we had to walk hunched over to avoid hitting our heads. At a wooden slat that was decrepit and warped, yet locked by several thick padlocks, Premig took out some keys, undid the locks and swung open the door which cried as rusted springs stretched across a rotted frame. Vita clicked on a light bulb hanging from the ceiling; one wall was lined with six big wooden barrels, all of them laying on their side two feet off the floor. One barrel hadn't been plugged and foamy pink bubbles boiled out of the hole in the top. I thought it might be acid. Hardy remarked, 'Hey, look, it's fermenting. Tony, check it out. Wine.'

Vita went with Premig into a corner and pulled away some planks covering a hole in the wall. They carried out a heavy wooden footlocker, placed it at our feet and opened the lid. It contained about a dozen automatic and semi-automatic pistols. Most of them were old but a few were brand new, still in their manufacturing boxes. Hardy crouched down and inspected them with the respect and admiration of a collector. He turned back to Vita, 'Where d'you get them?'

'In Darra. A gun bazaar. Premig has friends from the army. He can get guns you want.'

'Except Mac 10s, it seems,' Hardy added, then carefully placed the newer guns and boxes of bullets into a duffel bag on the floor.

I asked Vita, 'If I gave you a list, could he get us certain guns and silencers?'

Vita translated in Turkish to Premig who turned to me and smiled proudly.

I took that to mean yes.

'I just want somebody to tell me what the fuck's going on?!'

I was yelling into the receiver at Manny Simone, the distance of 3,000 miles gave me the courage to do so. Manny didn't take edge and tried to explain to me calmly that Riccardo Montefiore wasn't available to come to the phone right then, and that I should just hang back and not do anything until Lawrence Talbot arrived tomorrow.

'That's another thing, why didn't anybody tell us Lawrence Talbot was coming out? . . . Manny, this is bullshit! Nobody told us we were gonna be in the middle of a fucking construction war. We're all alone out here; these people don't know what the fuck they're doing. They're cutting off each other's hands. It's medieval!'

Hardy watched me pace the room. He was rather impressed with my tone of voice; even *he* never spoke to Manny Simone the way that I was now.

'Listen Tony, things are in the works that I can't talk about now, especially over the fucking phone — you know that. Riccardo has been in contact with the other side; there's a ceasefire in effect. You're not in any danger. So don't do anything. Be alert. Spend your fucking per diem and enjoy the fucking city! Keep your eye on Hardy; don't let him outta your sight.'

I looked at Hardy planted on the couch like a molten lump of depravity, aiming his new toys around the room at imaginary targets. 'That's another thing we need to discuss, Manny.'

'At the right time, kid. Now, I gotta go.'

'Yeah. Okay. Hey Manny?'

'What?!'

'Sorry about yelling before.'

'Don't make it a habit.'

The line went dead. Hardy sat up.

'Well? What's up?' After I told him, he said, 'Shit, I wanted to use these things tonight. Well . . . that's over. Let's fuckin' book. Henry the Kraut gave me his cell number; throw me the phone.'

While Hardy dialed the number, I went inside and laid down to rest for the evening's festivities: babysitting Hardy.

The screen faded to black and intermission began, singing bags of popcorn and dancing cups of soda flashed across the screen. My mother asked us if we were tired and we both said no. We'd never been to a drive-in movie before and the huge screen in front of us and the tinny green speaker hanging inside the window exulting the joys of candy, plus the big scary Japanese guy with the round black hat that flew through the air and cut off a statue's head, kept us thrilled and awake. My father sat with his arm across the back of the seat, my sister and I in-between him and my mother. I told my father I wanted ice cream and Carrie sang for Jujubees and my mother scolded that it was too late for snacks and we would probably be up all night because of the movie and she wasn't going to get up when we started screaming from nightmares. My father got out of the car and leaned back inside, 'Come on, Anthony, take a walk with me.'

I jumped out and we went toward the white wooden screen; it seemed to have no end as we stood underneath it. My father put his hand on my shoulder and whistled a song I'd heard on television. His face looked noble when he whistled. At the snack bar he bought a tray of four sodas – two cokes, two orange – a box of popcorn, a box of Jujubees for my sister and a chocolate ice-cream cone for me.

My father handed me the cone and paid the cashier. I turned around licking the ball of chocolate as a tall skinny kid with curly black hair and a pimple-scarred face rushed up and bumped into me, sending the scoop splatting to the floor but not before getting some on his patched-up dunga-ree jacket. My father heard the splat and turned around to see me holding an empty wafer cone and the kid checking out his jacket.

'Anthony, what happened?' he asked and the kid looked up with an angry scowl.

'Look at my fuckin' jacket. Why don'tcha watch what you're doin', you fuckin' klutz!'

'There's no need for that talk,' my father said gently. 'It was an accident. Let me help you.' My father took some napkins and went to wipe the ice cream, but the kid pushed his hand away.

'Get off of me, Pops! What the fuck am I gonna do about my jacket?!' Several other teens stepped up behind him to ask what happened. 'This fuckin' retard ruined my jacket!' he complained.

'Why don't you watch your language, son. He's a young boy; he didn't mean it.'

'I ain't your fuckin' son, Pops. Don't call me your fuckin' son. Stupid fuck.'

'Daddy, let's go.'

But my father raised his voice in the stern, clipped manner he used when scolding students who misbehaved in his math class.

'We're sorry for your jacket. But you should behave better than that.'

My father turned to leave but the kid jumped in front of him and shoved the tray of snacks into his chest. My father's shirt and pants got soaked and popcorn spilled everywhere and the gang of kids laughed cruelly and my father stood there looking at the mess on the floor. Everyone on line was watching but nobody said a word. The kid looked back to his friends and said in mock sincerity, 'I'm sorry, Pops, it was an accident.'

My father spoke softly, yet firmly, into the kid's face.

'You are a coward and a bully, and you should be ashamed of yourself,' then he took my hand and started for the door.

'Hey, Mr Sorry, you forgot your Jujubees.'

As the kid and his friends snickered, my father muttered

under his breath, 'Fuck you, punks.'

I'd never heard him curse before.

Without saying another word he stared straight ahead as we walked to the car. When we reached the back of the movie screen footsteps shuffled up behind us and I turned just as they jumped him. He didn't have time to react or cry out before he was pummeled to the ground. Someone grabbed me from behind and pulled me away and covered my mouth with a hard, callused hand; I smelled stale beer on salty skin. My father rolled himself into a ball as hard leather shoes rained down on his head and back and the tall skinny kid was stomping on his face with the heel of his boot. Someone grabbed a metal trash can and slammed it down twice on my father's head as the gang let out whoops of delight. I was flung to the ground and the gang gathered around his twisted beaten frame; laughing and undoing their zippers, they began peeing on him. I sat up crying 'Daddy, Daddy' and the tall skinny kid with the jacket looked over grinning; he took a step toward me when an old man came upon us and the gang took off like puffs of air into the night. My father didn't move or make a sound as he lay there with his face resting in a balloon of blood while the old man went for help.

Two weeks later when he came out of the hospital with a broken arm and his head still bandaged, his eyes bruised and blackened, his lips swollen and stitched up and a piece of his left ear missing, he seemed in a trance, as if he didn't know where he was or why, talking in riddles of places he'd never been to, and of things he'd never seen.

5

'That's the Spree to the left; you can take boat rides on the weekends. You can see the city from different angles that you don't get by walking or driving.'

'How about fishin'?'

'Fishing?'

'Yeah. You heard of fishin'? They got fish in there?'

'I don't know. It looks a bit dirty for fish.'

'Is it salt water or fresh water?'

'I would guess fresh water.'

'Too bad. No crabs then. Crabs clean themselves out, you know. They act as filters, clean out dirty water.'

'How do you know so much about it?' I asked, in parts both annoyed and genuinely curious.

'My old man used to take me crabbin' when I was a kid. Down in Belmar. But we never used crab nets; that's for pussies. We went crabbin' like men. The real way.'

'The real way?' Heinrich asked, taking his eyes from the road and looking at Hardy in the passenger seat.

'You take a string, or some fishin' line, and you tie the bait around the line. We used to use pieces of raw chicken, chicken necks work good, or you could use mackerel, cut them in half and tie them up; some people use squid.'

'Squid? What is that?' Heinrich asked.

'It's like a baby octopus.'

'*Ach so. Tintenfisch.*'

'What you do is tie the bait on the end of the line, then you drop it in the water and you keep the line in your hand, restin' across your fingers. Then when a crab starts to nibble on it, you feel the string jerk, because crabs pick at it with their claws. Then what you do is, slowly, you ever so gently pull the string in, an inch at a time, little by little, until the crab don't realize it, but he's comin' up to the surface as he's clawin' at the bait. You see, crabs are fuckin' mean but they ain't smart. So you bring him up as close as you can, then you grab a pole-net with your free hand, and in one quick scoop you scoop him into the net. Those cocksuckers are fuckin' fast so you gotta be real good to catch 'em that way. My old man could get 'em every time. He was a master at bringin' 'em up nearly to the surface, they never knew what hit 'em. Then we'd throw 'em in a pot of boilin' water and make crab sauce for spaghetti.'

'That's the most pathetic thing I've ever heard.'

'Hey, fuck you! You ever eat spaghetti with crab sauce? It's fuckin' good.'

Heinrich looked over and asked sincerely, 'Seems like an awful lot of trouble; why not just buy them at a fish market?'

'Hey, what are you fuckin' guys? Against fishin' or somethin'?! You know, the fuckin' Apostles were fishermen.'

Heinrich drove past the tower with the giant silver ball on top. 'That's the *Fernsehturm*. The TV tower,' he said. 'There's a spinning restaurant at the top, we can go up there for lunch one day.'

Hardy craned his neck to see the spinning restaurant that we would have lunch in one day.

Heinrich took us further east and pointed out certain landmarks and churches and government buildings and everywhere you turned there were cranes and construction sites and Heinrich said that soon the whole city would be transformed when the Government moved in and it was important to establish a foothold now while there was still time. I had to laugh to myself – why did he think we were here?

'Did you really kill Victor Rudiyov's daughter?' he asked after a pause of silence. Something stirred inside of me, a

62

profound ache made all the more vigorous by the fact that the Seconals weren't working yet; I'd taken five before dinner and still felt sensation.

'It's healthier not to ask a question like that,' I advised.

'There was no mention of it in the newspapers. None whatsoever.'

Hardy leaned up, 'So what does that mean?'

'The Russians removed her before the police came.'

'Why would they do that?'

'Perhaps they don't want an autopsy. They want to bury her back home without any red tape.'

'What do you know about the Russians?' I asked.

'They're behind several of the German companies. They keep a low profile. But they make themselves known. Eventually they would've taken over the whole operation.'

'What about the Turks?'

'A puzzle. They could have avoided all this mess in the beginning. Rudiyov and Kopp tried to settle with them, several times, some kind of buyout. But Yossario would have none of it. Now I'm afraid it's gotten a little out of hand.'

Hardy chuckled. 'Hey, you made a pun! Get it, a little out of hand?'

Heinrich grinned.

'What do you know about Hans Kopp?' I asked.

'Former Stasi official. Runs the daily operations; does the dirty work. I don't know why you didn't go to his office first; he's the one causing all the *wiolence*.'

'Wiolence', he said, with a 'W', that was the first slip-up in Heinrich's English; I made a note to watch for others.

'A fish stinks from the head down,' Hardy said. 'Right, Tone?'

'Where do you fit into all this?' I asked Heinrich.

'It's exactly like Yossario said. I'm a German; I have

friends in the Government; that's why we got the contract.'

'How much is this contract worth?'

Heinrich looked straight ahead and lied through his teeth. 'I don't know.' Then he changed the subject. 'I love America. I lived in Texas for two years. My cousin married an engineer, he worked for Esso—Exxon in America; I stayed with them in Austin for two years after school. That's how I learned English, from watching cartoons.'

'What's your favorite cartoon?' Hardy needed to know.

'Scooby Doo.'

Hardy nodded; that was an acceptable answer. 'What about sports?'

'Football. But not the football you think. Football is different here.'

'Chief, that shit ain't football. They play for four hours and the score is one to nothin'. What the fuck is that?'

'Watched by 40 billion people all over the world.'

'Fifty billion flies eat shit. That don't make it tasty.'

Heinrich pulled his black Mercedes over to the curb on a dark and desolate street, the kind of place I preferred when doing a contract in public. This fact didn't go unnoticed by Hardy.

'What are we doin' here? You gonna fuckin' pop us?'

'The thought had occurred to me.'

Hardy grinned. 'You ever pop anybody, Henry?'

'No. What does it feel like?'

'Depends. It feels like a lotta things . . .'

'We should probably get out now,' I said, and the edge in my voice told Hardy to drop it.

The street was narrow with broken cobblestones and mounds of sand along the side. A cold wind blew in from between charcoal-colored buildings tossing up papers and dust in a swirl of anxiety. Hardy's feet thumped dully on the cracked pavement while Heinrich's stiff shoes tapped a crisp and sterile rhythm. I stayed on the balls of my feet, quietly, cautiously. An empty bottle tipped over in the gutter and we walked past a narrow alley of secrecy and danger. I felt someone watching me, but when I turned around only the mysterious eyes of darkness looked back.

'Say Henry, I wanna meet some Nazis. You still got Nazis here?'

Heinrich considered the question. 'There are some old people who were members of the Nazi party during the war. But not many would be proud to admit it.'

'No, I mean new Nazis.'

'We have the NPD, and skinheads.'

'Yeah! Skinheads. They're Nazis, right?'

'I would say yes.'

'I wanna meet some.'

'I'm afraid they may not like to meet you.'

'Why not?'

'They hate foreigners; they blame foreigners for the problems in Germany.'

'But I'm an American!'

'I'm afraid here in Berlin that makes you a foreigner.'

'What?! You gotta be fuckin' kiddin' me. What kind'a godforsaken place is this? Tony, I'm a foreigner. Shit.'

I couldn't take it anymore. 'Hardy, I'm gonna fucking cut my throat in another minute. Please!'

That was all it took. He looked at me as if I'd stabbed him in the heart. He seemed to shrink a little, and then he bowed his head and moped along like he was the poorest man in India. Only Hardy could do that to you, make you feel bad for having a reasonable limit. I wanted to apologize but instead turned to Heinrich and said, 'So, where is this place of your cousin's?'

'It doesn't open till late. I thought we'd go someplace else first. This other place is very 'Berlin',' and Heinrich made quotation marks with his fingertips. I wished he hadn't; I hated three-dimensional quotation marks.

We turned a corner and a crowd of people waited in front of a fenced-in lot, some were drinking beer but most were smoking hand-rolled cigarettes and talking in gibberish not seeming in any rush to get wherever they wanted to go, which should have been any place but this barren war-torn street. Heinrich walked to the center of the crowd and went up to a big broad guy wearing wire-rim glasses who held a car steering wheel in his hands. Heinrich said something that made the guy laugh and we were immediately brushed inside the gate. All around us rusted metal sculptures of prehistoric creatures stood beside stacks of worn out tires and several old-fashioned bathtubs with claw-arm feet filled with dirt and barren skinny trees. Heinrich led us over to a three-story cement building with boarded up windows where a short punked-out hag with flaming red hair broke into a malignant toothless grin. She pulled out a walkie talkie and spoke into the mouthpiece and two metal gray doors opened and like magic we were blasted by bass and drums and talking voices as waves of smoke rolled at our feet. Purple spotlights mounted in the ceilings and a dozen TV monitors flashing black-and-white home movies from the 1950s lined the hallway leading to the dance floor where black-clad men and women danced in a gyrating throng. Thunder roared from the speakers as Heinrich led us over to a blue sparkled cushioned bar where some vampire chick with long black hair cut in bangs across her forehead wore a short black dress and filled huge mugs with beer from the tap. When she leaned over to retrieve a bottle of vodka and her tits nearly dropped out of their nest, I noticed the number '6' carved into her skin. Hardy checked out the dance floor and the black leather miniskirts that filled it; a field of slender thighs in fishnet stockings waiting to be assaulted. Heinrich turned around with beers in his hand and handed us each one. He leaned back proudly as Hardy yelled over the roar, 'I want to get laid tonight.'

'You will. It's early.' Then he turned to me and shouted, 'A friend of mine owns this place. He also owns a record company.'

Hardy yelled back, 'Cool.'

I checked out exits and escape routes and doorways and scanned for suspicious faces or anyone taking undue notice of our presence. At the end of the bar a piercing outrageous laugh burst from someplace odd and ridiculous and I turned to see a skin-and-bones junkie in black leather pants with no front teeth. He could barely stand up as his booze splashed out of his glass and two young sluts walked a wide arc around him to get to the bathroom. I felt someone's eyes on my back and turning around the vampire chick was watching me, studying me, while Heinrich chopped up a mound of beige powder into thin lines on the bar. He handed the vampire chick a small silver tube from his pocket and she swooped down and came up pinching her nose as if inhaling drugs were the most natural thing in the world to do. Heinrich gave the tube to Hardy who snorted four fat lines then stepped onto the dance floor disappearing in the throng of undulating black leather. Heinrich offered me the tube but I took his cigarette instead, took a deep drag off the end and felt a dizzy rush from tobacco because I never smoked cigarettes.

Heinrich yelled in my ear, 'She likes you!' then nodded behind the bar. The vampire chick gave me a hungry gap-toothed grin.

'She looks like the undead.'

'What?'

'She looks like— She's not my type!'

'What?'

67

'Nevermind!'

The music was deafening, I could barely hear my own voice. I strolled away from the bar and roamed through the crowd of jerking bodies with my hand inside the flap of my jacket just in case . . . The fog of hash-laced cigarettes and cheap perfume was giving me a headache, but then I felt a sudden kick from the Seconals and thought, 'It's about fucking time!'

At the back of the club was a crowded hallway leading to a cement stairway where a group of guys hung out drinking beer while one of them pissed on the wall. Behind the stairwell a red-haired chick was giving head to some guy in blue velvet pants; as her head jerked in and out in rhythm to the riot of music permeating every pore of my being, everything got slow, like in water. It all became a ballet of depravity with arms and legs floating in a milky sea of ink. Upstairs were several rooms with couches and chairs and people smoking dope and sitting on the floor in a pool of liquid was some guy wearing a porkpie hat and playing an accordion, crying his eyes out over some recent heartbreak real or imagined. I stood at the upstairs bar when a six-foot blonde chick wearing clear-framed glasses leaned into my face. She wasn't great-looking, but she wasn't bad-looking either. The gleam of desperation in her eyes perked my interest.

She mumbled something in German, saw immediately that I didn't understand, then started firing words at me in English.

'Where are you from?'

'America.'

'What are you doing here?'

'Visiting.'

'Do you like it?'

'It's okay.'

'Your first time to Berlin?'

'Yeah.'

'Stay you long?'

'I don't know.'

'Where are you from America?'

'Newark, New Jersey.'

'I have not heard of it.'

'A lot of people haven't.'

'What do you do there?'

'I kill people.'

'Do you like it?'

'Sometimes.'

'I'm in school. I study architecture.'

'That's nice.'

'I go to Humboldt University.'

'Oh, I'm sorry.'

'Would you like to dance?'

'No.'

'Would you like a drink?'

'No, thank you.'

'Do you find me attractive?'

'Yes.'

'Would you like to come back to my flat?'

'No.'

'Why not?'

'You scare the hell out of me.'

She stopped, studied my face, then kissed me clumsily on the mouth; her tongue darted through my lips and with it came the pungent tang of beer and cigarettes. She held me with utter starvation, wrapped her arms around me and thrust her pelvic bone solidly into my groin. She was sucking the saliva out of my mouth like a pump; her glasses pushed up against my eyes as cool plastic played contrast to her warm, sloppy lips. I put my hands on her throat, firmly, felt her Adam's apple bobbing with the movements of her tongue wrestling furiously with my own, when a fire raged inside me and the only thing I could think to do next was snap her neck like a twig.

I released her and stepped back, told her I had to go. She looked at me crossly. 'What is wrong?'

'Nothing, I just gotta go.'

For a second I thought she might slap me, she had that sort of look on her face, but then she thought better of it and walked away.

I swam through the room with my head as light as Styrofoam, moving through the smoke the way a shark moves through water, watching, always watching. Near the bathrooms I saw the crazy blonde with the clear glasses but she was talking to some other guy. As I came down the stairs there was a commotion on the floor; the fucked-up junkie in the black leather pants was lying on the floor twitching and writhing around as if he were on fire. Everybody stepped back as he flailed his arms and screamed in agony but his voice was drowned out by the pounding bass of music. I kept my hand on my gun and scoped out the surroundings as Hardy came up behind me, leaning against my back so nobody could sneak up on us. A plain-looking chick with wire-rim glasses came pushing out of the crowd and nearly dove to the floor, gripping the junkie's hands and pulling them away from his face. She grabbed a piece of cloth and wedged it between his teeth as he slammed his head hard against the wet cement floor, then she cradled his head in her arms so he wouldn't smash it to pieces. His body ceased up suddenly, stopped moving, then he crumpled flat on his back as if he were liquid. There was a flash of panic in her face, just for an instant, then she put her ear on his chest and two fingers to his neck and put her mouth over his and the music stopped abruptly and everything got a hundred pounds lighter, except for the cheering and laughter of everyone around me. Hardy chuckled over my shoulder, 'Shit, she's wastin' her time, that bastard's gone.'

She glanced around at the grinning faces; maybe she was looking for a friend or someone to help her. Her eyes caught mine and I was struck for an instant, frozen with shame. She raised a closed fist and pounded it on the junkie's chest, listened for his heart then pinched his nostrils and blew air into his mouth; sweat poured down her cheeks as she again pounded his chest and blew air into his mouth then yelled at him in German, her voice slightly scratched as she shook him by the shoulders and ordered him to live. Her face was flushed red and her eyes were furious hot daggers; she would not be defied, this woman. Hardy leaned into my ear. 'Come on, let's get outta here.'

'I agree,' Heinrich added. 'We should leave.'

'Wait a minute,' I said.

She blew air into his mouth and I could see his chest heave up and down, but only from her effort. Her fingers clung to his arms strongly, desperately, until the junkie choked unexpectedly and heaved puke into her mouth and she fell back as everyone laughed and applauded. She rolled the junkie over on his stomach so he wouldn't choke to death on his own vomit. His dinner emptied onto the floor and she pulled his hair back out of his face, patted his head. She looked up and found me out of the crowd again, and again I was jolted by nakedness and shame. Sirens pulled up outside and Heinrich and Hardy were on me to leave, so I started backing out into the crowd as two guys dressed in green overalls rushed in with a stretcher. They went to the junkie now trying to lift his head up out of his own puke. She said something to the overalls guys and they said something back, loudly; they didn't sound too

71

grateful for what she'd just done; then they heaved the junkie onto the stretcher. She eased back into the crowd, but couldn't blend in. Her face was bleached white and in shock; she looked as lonely as a person could be. I caught one last look at her before stepping out the door.

In the car Hardy told me I was reckless for hanging around in the club back there and I had to laugh to myself; he was right.

Heinrich took us to his cousin's club, which, he reminded us, was in *Neukölln*.

Lying in bed I couldn't sleep, couldn't stop thinking about her. When she looked at me, it was as if she recognized me, or something inside me, something I didn't recognize in myself. I lay awake until it was light outside, until the bruise of morning swelled in through the slits in the black curtain covering the windows of my room.

6

'You have to train a glove, work some oil into it so it forms to your hand. All the professional players do it. Works the leather and makes it softer.' He pounded his fist into the pocket, then rubbed the inside palm. I could see the light tan leather changing dark brown as he rubbed a rag of motor oil all along the inside.

'Here, give me that ball. No, the softball.'

I tossed him the grapefruit-sized ball and he slammed it inside the glove, pulled on the weavings, opened and closed the fingers a few times.

'How is it?' I asked. 'Can I try?'

'Sure,' and he handed me the glove and it *did* feel softer, more pliable to my hand, not stiff and resistant like it did when he first bought it for me.

'Okay, now we have to tie it up overnight, let it get used to having a pocket. Watch.' He took the softball and put it deep in the palm of the glove, then took a thin leather belt and wrapped it around the outer fingers, squeezing the whole thing closed into a tight pouch. He rubbed some more oil on the outside, then told me to leave it alone overnight. We played catch the rest of the afternoon with my old glove and he taught me how to throw a split-fingered curveball, crouching down behind home plate and giving me signals as if we were in a real game.

The ball was high and outside but he always made it crack in his glove. 'Beautiful!' he said. 'You're getting the hang of it.'

'You really think so?'

'Sure! You have natural talent. Nobody's gonna be able to hit your stuff. Come on, put a little mustard on that ball.'

My father always made me feel like I was pitching a no-hitter at Yankee Stadium.

The second we reached the site, I knew they were here. The sterile stench of criminality hung over the place; it was a presence, like the sickening sweet fragrance of wilting flowers at a friend's wake, or the pungent aftershave worn by Tito and Ernie Pasquale, identical twins, Lawrence Talbot's private soldiers, two hunks of simplicity now standing guard outside the trailer door like matching refrigerators. Hardy let out a derisive snort. 'You guys look a little obvious. Shouldn't you be wearin' shorts and suspenders, or somethin'?'

'Why don't you shut your mouth,' Tito or Ernie said. The other one said, 'He's waitin' for you. You're late.'

'I'd say his wait is over.'

Yossario and Vita looked up nervously when the door opened. Lawrence Talbot sat behind Heinrich's desk, bespectacled eyes fixed steadily on the computer screen, jotting numbers into a black composition book with his forehead creased, too engrossed in the figures in front of him to acknowledge our entrance. He wore an immaculate black pinstriped suit, the kind of suit a crippled uncle might wear to a funeral. Sticking out from under the desk were size ten-and-a-half lustrous black shoes with tiny fancy circles cut into the leather around the toes; on his head short gray hair stood up in thick clumps like primitive stones, and the monogrammed white cotton handkerchief crumpled permanently in his left hand was kept never more than a foot away from his nose, which had been clogged and running for the last seventeen years; he regularly scraped up pulp from his lungs with a sound not unlike the moist thud of a body hitting pavement.

Nobody said a word as Hardy and I stopped a few feet from the desk, waiting. Vita stood irritably with his arms folded in front of him while his father sat in the chair across the room holding a bloody handkerchief to his nose. Heinrich was missing today. Lawrence Talbot opened a German–English dictionary on his lap, looked up a word and scanned his finger along the computer screen, let out a groan. Not a good sound. The figures weren't adding up, or something wasn't making sense; I'd heard this groan before, when the Franchise had taken over other businesses and the books didn't add up. It usually meant that someone was skimming, or being careless, and even though it had taken place before the Franchise had a vested interest, Lawrence Talbot took it as a grave offense.

Hardy began to slouch and would soon begin to pace and let out audible sighs of impatience; he wasn't afraid of Lawrence Talbot, though he should have been. Lawrence Talbot was not somebody to fuck with. His manner was studious, implacably harmless, closer to that of a nineteenth-century accountant in a Dickens novel than a financial, albeit criminal, mastermind. But he could have you crushed with the wave of his hand. Riccardo Montefiore would do anything to accommodate him – and often did. If Hardy knew how close he'd come several times to getting popped if not for Lawrence Talbot's loyalty to his father, he might be showing a little more respect and appreciation right now.

Lawrence Talbot finally took his eyes from the screen and sank back in his chair, looked at us for the first time. When he wasn't working the numbers he seemed to withdraw into himself, to shrink in stature, his body took on a pliant, almost fragile fickleness. He turned to Vita and Yossario and wiping his glasses asked them to please leave us alone for a few minutes; if dust had sound it would be his voice. Once they left he asked us, pointedly, 'Have you kept all your receipts?'

'What?'

'Receipts. Do you have receipts for everything you've bought since you've been here?'

'We haven't bought anything.'

'From now on keep receipts for everything, understand?'

'Why weren't we told the size of this thing?'

'There wasn't any reason to tell you,' he answered, somewhat puzzled by the question.

'It helps if I'm more informed, that's all.'

'Who does it help?'

I didn't know what to say to that. He always threw things like that at me and I could never tell if he was fucking with me or not. All I could think to answer was, 'The other side's pretty good. They hit back fast and they're brutal.'

'That's why you're here.' He shifted slowly in his chair; any movement caused him physical discomfort of some sort.

'Congratulations on your arrival,' he added. 'That was good work.'

'We killed a young girl. She might have been only fourteen years old.'

Lawrence Talbot peered over the rims of his glasses, no expression on his face, eyes like sand-beaten seashells. 'She shouldn't have been there,' he said. 'She was a witness and could have implicated us later on. You did the right thing.'

'It doesn't feel like the right thing.'

'You're paid not to feel.'

And that right there was the problem, it seemed. Ever since I'd arrived, I'd been thinking thoughts and dreaming dreams and for the first time in many years I was feeling feelings. For the life of me I couldn't understand why.

Lawrence Talbot fixed me with a penetrating stare, as if he heard the uncertainty playing out in my mind. Then he glanced to Hardy who was slouching and yawning and looked like shit from the night before. 'And what's with

Dumpy over there? What's the matter? Too busy with the girlies; didn't get no sleep?'

'I ain't complainin'.'

Lawrence dismissed him with a shake of his head, then glanced again at the computer screen. 'This is going to be more work than we anticipated. The company's a mess. They're spending money like it's raining piss.'

A familiar voice barked outside and it was like being back home in Newark, where I'd stood in dozens of trailers at dozens of building sites and lived this same scene dozens of times before. Manny Simone barged into the room, his presence like a winter wind until he saw me and broke into a sinister autumn smile.

'Well, look who's here!' His face was tanned and pressed tight around his skull like leather, his body taut, wiry, poised to spring at any moment, all energy and power packaged in a loose-fitting shiny gray suit.

'I didn't know you were coming out.'

'You can't know everything, kid,' he grinned. 'It's healthier that way.'

Lawrence Talbot chuckled at that, then Manny turned to Lawrence and complained, 'You should see all the gravel they're wasting out there, I nearly had a conniption! We gotta get our guys out here quick before there's nothing left to skim.'

'I agree. It's out of control. They're overpaying for supplies, their wages are too high, they have more workers than they need. They're not even unionized; nothing gets kicked back upstairs.'

Manny turned to me with a grin. 'See, kid? We're like missionaries, spreading the word to the unenlightened.'

'That's a charitable way to put it,' I said.

'We're like priests,' Hardy chuckled, but no one acknowledged his remark. Manny had given him a silent nod when

77

he entered the room and that was it.

Lawrence turned to Manny, 'Why don't you take Tony outside and show him around.'

'I've seen the site,' I said.

'See it again,' Lawrence snapped. Then he looked at Hardy. 'Sleepy, why don't you sit down, you're making me nervous.'

Hardy sat on the chair, hurt and insulted by the snub. Manny opened the door and I followed him outside. We went behind the trailer and walked along the construction site where the foundation had already been dug out and was now supported by wood beams all around. Manny asked me how things were going and I told him it was too early to tell. He asked about Hardy but there was nothing bad to report so far.

'These fucking Krauts really know how to throw a party,' he said, marveling at the huge football-field sized craters in the distance and the hundreds of men working in them. 'I never seen anything like it. Riccardo Montefiore really hit pay dirt with this one, gotta say. Once we set ourselves up out here, forget it, we're taking over the world!'

We walked along the perimeter of the next foundation, a dozen brown-skinned men in hard hats dug out huge rocks with gas-powered drills while others drove small yellow forklifts precariously carrying planks of lumber over the hills of dirt and stone.

'When did you come in?' I asked, during a break in the drilling.

'Early this morning.'

'You must be tired.'

'It hasn't hit me yet. But your concern is touching.'

'I don't give a fuck. I'm just making conversation.'

Manny stopped and gave me a cruel smile; he sometimes got a kick out of me. 'What's the food like out here? They got Italian? I could go for a good linguine with clam sauce.'

'Good luck. I've only had Turkish so far, something called cous cous and something else I can't pronounce.'

'Cous cous is North African.'

'Whatever. They got McDonald's, that's where Hardy eats.'

'I'd rather eat dirt.'

'Well, ask Heinrich about restaurants. He seems to know the city pretty well.'

'I hear he's been hanging around with Hardy.'

'They have some mutual interests.'

'Watch him. I don't like him.'

'I don't like him either.'

'I can tell in an instant. It's a feeling I get, in the back of my spine. Like a little man, tapping me, telling me, "Watch the fuck out."'

'Sounds like Scoliosis.'

'You're gonna get Scoliosis, you keep it up.'

We continued walking and Premig appeared in the distance. Manny said, 'What's with Captain Hook – the one-armed bandit?'

'That's Premig. I told you over the phone, they're cutting off limbs out here. But he carries big-time steel and he ain't afraid to use it. He was with us on the hit and he may be the only one we can count on when the shit comes down.'

'Why? You think it's gonna come to that?'

'No. It's all gonna go without a hitch.'

Manny grinned meanly and pinched my cheek hard.

'Ow! I hate when you fucking do that.'

'Then don't fuck with me. I asked you a straight fucking question. I want a straight fucking answer. Tell me the fucking truth!'

I wanted to tell him that it was fucking nuts for us to be here. We don't speak the language, we don't know the streets or the people on them, the culture. The Russians have been here since World War II, this is their back yard, they know every inch of the place and they are completely entrenched. We might as well be on another planet. Instead I told him, 'This could be our Vietnam.'

'What do you know about Vietnam?'

'What everybody knows. I seen the movies.'

Manny creased his brow; he served two tours in Vietnam and knew better than anybody what that was like. He spit a gnat out of his mouth and leaned in close. 'I need you to do something for me tonight. The old-fashioned way. Things ain't going so good with the negotiations. We need to push it along a little bit.'

'What about the ceasefire?'

'Hey kid, I'm telling you things ain't going so good and you're telling me about ceasefires.'

'What I meant to say was, "How can I help?"'

'That's what I thought you said.'

I heard their feet coming down the hall and I slid in deeper under the bed. Carrie was the first one through, her white and black shoes topped with red and blue pompoms turned as the door closed behind his clumsy, worn sneakers with the laces undone. He lumbered toward the bed, turned around and the mattress plunged down threatening to crush me. I didn't move or take a breath, gazing out between the canvas spine of Converse All Stars as Carrie's shoes approached and stopped in between his. I heard their lips smacking and a quiet moaning as Carrie's cheerleading dress crumpled under the dull embrace of her football-playing paramour.

'When are they coming back?' he asked.

'My mother won't be home for another hour.'

'Great.'

'But we can't fuck today.'

'Why not?'

'I'm having my period. I'm bleeding like a pig.'

'Shit.'

'I'll give you a blow job.'

A breathless, 'Yeah great.'

Carrie sank to her knees and I saw them pointing at me under the bed. I was terrified of being caught; this was the stupidest thing I'd ever done but my curiosity as to what took place here several afternoons after school each week finally ate me alive. She spread her thighs apart on the floor and I caught sight of her orange cotton panties with several strands of curly black hair twisting out from underneath the elastic. His zipper unzipped but I couldn't tell if he unzipped it or she did. I heard him let out a moan followed by the wet slurp of willing surrender. The bed began to creak in a steady rhythm and his feet wrapped around her back and he panted and clutched her head and told her, 'Deeper Carrie, suck it deeper,' and she didn't answer but must have sucked it deeper as he let out a high-pitched piggish squeal. Her arm began to stroke up and down in counterpoint to the bouncing bed and her plunges became more powerful and she gulped twice and gagged and then withdrew, yet still stroked her arm up and down.

'Not so hard, you're choking me.'

'I'm sorry, I like it sucked deeper.'

'I'm sucking as deep as I can.'

'Okay, I'm sorry. Maybe you could relax your throat a little more.'

'Are you going to cum soon?'

'You're not finished yet, are you?'

'No, but just let me know before you cum.'

'I always dooooooooo!'

Carrie was on him again, feverishly gulping and slurping and I stared at the crevice between her thighs which ended now in a dark mysterious triangle. He started grunting, a series of snorts in syncopation to her sucking plunges until his feet shot straight out and he stopped moving.

'Oh, oh, God!'

He let out his breath and gripped Carrie's head and wrapped his feet again around her but she twisted and jerked and pulled herself free, sitting back on her haunches. If she leaned back another foot she'd be able to see me, but I didn't dare move. The bed trembled above my face and a streak of glue landed on her neck and she slid herself back and complained, 'Watch it, my dress! Here, use a tissue.'

Carrie reached back and grabbed a tissue from a box on her desk and handed it to him. He sighed and the bed shook a few times then came to a gradual, tired stop. He stood up and buckled his pants. Carrie sat there looking up. I couldn't see her face, only the drops around her neck like a string of liquid pearls. He zipped his pants and began, 'You know, can I ask you a question?'

'What?'

'You know, I'm not complaining or anything. It's really good and all, but . . . why don't you ever finish?'

'What do you mean?'

'You never swallow.'

'I don't like to swallow.'

'But why not?'

'I told you why.'

'But I don't understand. If you swallowed you wouldn't have to worry about your dress.'

'Do we have to talk about this now?'

'It just makes no sense to me. It's frustrating, is all.'

'I still make you cum.'

'It's not the same. If I don't cum in your mouth, it's like . . . a wasted blow job; it's ruined.'

'You consider that a wasted blow job?'

'No. But . . . it just would be better. Look, if you really love me like you say you do, then you'd swallow. That's all. I don't see what the big fucking deal is.'

'The deal is that it's alive, it's got a million little creatures in it. I don't want to have living things in my stomach.'

'You make it sound like a horror movie.'

'I'm sorry; that's how I feel.'

'You're the only girl I know who feels that way.'

'C'mon, do we have to talk about this now? Can't we just be together?'

She moved to hold him and he crossed his feet but she held him anyway and there was silence. The box spring creaked and there was movement, then Carrie sat back on the floor, the muscles in her neck tightened. She was revolted as she said, 'You're an asshole.'

'And you're a fucking prick-tease!'

He got up and fastened his pants; a crumpled tissue flew down at her knees and he stepped over her to the door and undid the lock, turned the knob and left. Carrie sat on the floor for a moment, straightened her dress with the palms of her hands, picked up the tissue and wiped off her neck, then got up and went into the kitchen.

7

Vita directed Premig to pull into a long narrow drive-way in the middle of the block. It was dark and des-olate and I couldn't believe there'd be any kind of public business here, let alone a movie theater. But thirty yards later we were in a parking lot where floodlights lit up a doorway to our right. Several people moved about in the lighted ground-floor windows.

Vita pointed to a large metal door not unlike the steel reinforced doors of the after-hours clubs in New York City.

'*Nur* one door, in *oder* out. The film *beginnt* in fifteen *Minuten.*'

Premig turned the car around and parked far off in the back so he could face the entrance. Getting out, Vita told me that nobody here spoke English, that they weren't used to Americans coming in. He said I should just keep my mouth shut or they'd know I didn't belong. I felt like a hornet in a hive of worker bees.

The plan was for Vita to get me inside and then split once I'm settled in. Premig would wait in the car to drive me home afterwards. I was to follow the cog out into the park-ing lot and pop him as he got in his car. Tonight I had a chrome-plated Baretta .32 Alley Cat with a silencer. True to his word, Premig had gotten Hardy and I our wish list of guns and accessories, enough to start a small war, which was the point of it all, I guessed.

Vita approached the entrance and it occurred to me, get-ting my first good look at his elegant double-breasted wal-nut pinstriped suit, that he must have been the best-dressed man I'd ever seen. The interior looked like a French café with small tables and chairs. At the far wall was a huge movie projector from the early days of movies. Old posters

hung from rusted nails; to the right was a chest-high counter with a display of assorted candy bars and magazines,
and lined up on the top shelf were different bottles of beer
and liquor and shit! I thought, 'They sell beer and liquor at
the movies.' I noticed three separate doors for three different movies currently playing, none of which I knew or
cared to know. Vita stepped to the counter and bought two
tickets as I went to an empty table and sat down, faced the
one and only entrance. Vita sat down beside me and handed me a bottle of mineral water, took a short sip from his
own. He wouldn't even look at me; that bugged the shit out
of me.

I leaned over, 'You don't have to wait with me. I'll see
Premig outside after it's done.'

'I stay till you go *ins Kino*,' he said dryly.

Several people came in but the cog wasn't one of them.
The movie was about to begin and I wondered if I should
wait here for the cog or go inside. Thirty seconds later he
came in wearing a black leather jacket and a grin on his
face; the grin seemed perpetual; it was one of those faces
that grinned even when it wasn't grinning. Behind him
came another guy in a tan corduroy jacket and long blond
hair who put his hand on the back of the cog's neck. The
cog pushed his hand away and whispered in his ear and
they giggled like slutty teenage girls. I began to have my
doubts if he was the right guy; he looked nothing like a
player. His flushed cheeks and wire-rimmed glasses made
him look younger than he did in the photograph, no older
than twenty-five, a few years younger than me in fact. Vita
leaned over and whispered, 'Are you here to see him?'

'No. The guy didn't come in yet.'

But this was the guy. There was no mistaking that.

Manny stood peering into the huge hole dug out for the
foundation, the wind flapping the tail of his jacket and toss-

ing sand in his face. When I pulled the black-and-white photo out of the envelope he began, 'He's a cog in the fucking wheel of progress, if you know what I mean. We want to give the Krauts something to think about, so do this one with juice. I want a closed coffin at the wake.' Manny looked at me for effect; he wanted confirmation.

'I'd iron my black suit if I were you.'

Manny grinned and slapped my back and we both had to laugh.

Vita scolded under his breath; his lips barely moved, 'He is Ulf Kopp, Hans Kopp's son. He is innocent. Not part of business. He is student.'

'I told you he's not the guy.'

But when Ulf Kopp and his friend took their tickets and waited near the second theater, I watched them closely and Vita watched me watch them closely. A quiver of hatred rippled through the air as he got up and threw his coat over his forearm, shot me a glare and said, 'I go out for cigarette.' That was his cue for taking off.

I followed Ulf Kopp and his friend past a slinky red-haired babe with absolutely no breasts whatsoever and wearing orange Elton John glasses who took my ticket and ripped off a tiny portion of the end. Everyone here wore glasses it seemed; it was a country of bad eyesight. I sat in the last row, on the end away from the door, as I could then see every seat in the theater. The cog and his friend slouched down in one of the middle rows, their heads perilously close to touching. The movie began and it was a wild romp through the wilderness of Germany with five guys having a picnic. A minute later they were having sex. I stared at the cog's head; in the dark it was easier to play the hate game.

The door to my left opened and I shifted in my seat to see who came in. She took several steps down the aisle and stopped, her eyes riveted to the screen where two guys were tongue-kissing against a tree, really going at it too. I studied her profile. I hadn't really seen her from the side that first time at the club. Now I noticed her straight stubborn nose, pale round cheeks with the coarse complexion of life experience on them, lips that told me she was fragile. She held a paper bag of popcorn and a single-serving bottle of wine; blue light from the screen danced in the convex lenses of her glasses. By the amused look of outright curiosity on her face, I knew she'd stepped into the wrong theater by mistake. As she turned to leave a guy bumped into her going to his seat, knocking her popcorn to the floor. She crouched to pick it up; then she saw me sitting there, in the last row. Alone. I ducked down and scratched my head, watched her surreptitiously through my fingers. It felt like an hour had passed before she picked up her popcorn and walked out, but it took only a few seconds. I wanted to go after her, to make some kind of contact, but the cog and his friend told me I had to stay put, that to do anything else was insanity, that any action that would draw attention to myself was life-threatening – to her, to me, to everyone. So I sat back as Klaus, Olli and Tupac did a three-way by the waterfall.

Eighty-six minutes later I ambled out with the other viewers, maybe a dozen. The cog and his friend were the last ones to leave, choosing to stay on to see the final end credits. In the lobby I buttoned my jacket and read the upcoming schedule. I was facing the wall but could also see the exit of the theater. A group of people came out of the far theater and she was one of them. She buttoned a thick navy-blue jacket, spoke to the guy behind the counter. Her voice was hoarse, scratchy, like she had a cold, the way it sounded that first night I saw her; a sound that both tickled and irritated me. She smiled and waved goodbye to the counter guy, then left the theater alone without glancing in my direction.

The cog and his friend came out laughing. They really got a kick out of each other. There were pockets of people hanging out in the lobby, smoking, talking, drinking; it was that kind of place. The cog lit a cigarette and held it flimsily at the ends of his fingertips like Heinrich had the night before. I continued reading the schedule until he finally snubbed it out in the standing sand-filled ashtray.

In the parking lot Premig's car sat way off in the corner; it looked like a slimy black fish. The cog and his friend walked arm in arm toward a dark part of the lot and I crept after them, keeping in the next row of cars; the friend was a problem, but I figured I'd come up out of the darkness, blast the cog twice in the face and disappear before anyone knew what happened.

They stopped at a rundown white Mazda sedan parked beside a cement wall, the friend kissed the cog lightly on the lips, then got in alone behind the steering wheel; I let out a sigh of thanks. The Mazda sputtered and choked before revving up with an angry whine and driving away, leaving the cog waving goodbye. The lot was now deserted and I sprang forward, the gun gripped tightly in my hand. As the cog stepped to a brand new black Porsche 911 and pulled out a jingling ring of keys, it was perfect, I thought. I could shove his body in the car without breaking stride; he might not be found till the next morning. I came up behind him, close enough to smell his cologne and hear his key fuck the lock. But at the moment of truth, that instant when what's about to be done can't be undone, something stopped me. I couldn't raise my weapon, couldn't lift my arm. I stood there, frozen, scared, not knowing what to do. But knowing one thing for absolute certain. I didn't want to do this anymore. Until he turned around.

'*Entschuldigung*?' he said, a puzzled look in his eyes. He keyed on my hand and his face cracked with fear. He clumsily reached into his jacket and I fired instinctively into his gut and he crumpled like a sack of wet meat. I took his gun, a small-caliber pocket model, and shoved it into my pocket. I looked over at Premig and the BMW rocked slightly as the engine revved. All I had to do was fire a few more plugs into the cog and be on my way. He was curled in a ball, crying softly and clutching his gut.

'Let me see,' I said and tried to pull his hands free from the wound. He struggled to keep them there and I whispered urgently, 'Let me see where you're hit!'

He looked at me through crazed, tear-filled eyes. The hole in his belly was tiny and round, oozing blood in a steady ribbon; he was lucky I wasn't using exploding heads. I tried to lift him up from the ground but he stiffened and cried out in pain.

'I wanna take you to a hospital. Do you speak English?'

'Who . . . who are you?'

'Don't worry about who I am. Can you get up?'

'I don't know. It burns.'

I grabbed him under the shoulders and with great effort dragged him around to the passenger seat. He nearly passed out when I lifted him into the car. Searching for his keys on the ground I found them under the oil pan and got behind the wheel. He leaned his head against the window and sobbed something in German. I told him to shut up.

'Who are you?' he asked again.

'I'm fucked, that's who I am. Where's the nearest hospital?'

'I don't know,' he groaned. '*Friedrichshain*.'

'Where's that?' I asked, pulling out of the parking space and speeding down the narrow driveway. He didn't answer, but grinned in pain. A bicycle darted across my path and I slammed on the brakes but not before sending a body to the ground. The cog bounced off the dashboard with a sharp cry.

'Shit! I'm sorry.'

I saw the headlights of Premig's car stop about twenty feet behind me. I thought of taking off, of driving over the bicycle and whoever else was in my path, but instead I got out of the car and ran to the front bumper. She sat sprawled out on the ground, rubbing her shins and cursing me in German. I leaned into the darkness. 'Are you okay?'

She continued with a string of harsh-sounding words but I said, 'Look, my friend is really sick and I gotta get him to a hospital. Where's the nearest one?'

She squinted at me, tried to focus on my face. Hard anger replaced by soft curiosity. 'What is wrong with friend?' she said in simple, broken English, then felt around the ground for her glasses.

'He's sick. Where's the nearest hospital?'

'*Fröbelstrasse*. I work there.'

'Are you a nurse?'

'*Nein, nein.*'

'How do I get there?'

'Is *besser* I show you, the *Weg ist kompliziert*.' She patted the gravel for her glasses but I snatched them up and chucked them out of reach.

'Please, just tell me. I'll find it.'

'Go to street, drive right then *links* . . .' As she spoke I lifted her bike out of my way and leaned it against the wall.

'I can find not my *Brille*.'

I stopped by the door, told her, 'They're to your right.'

I threw the shift into first and raced away. Ulf looked at me in wild disbelief.

'Don't look at me,' I snapped and he looked out the windshield. 'Where the fuck is Frisbee-*strassa*, or some shit like that?'

The cog just stared out the windshield, the corners of his mouth rising helplessly close to grinning.

'Hey, did you hear me?'

'Fuck you,' he spat without moving his head.

'Yeah, that's right. Fuck me. But where is it?'

'Fuck you.'

'Hey, you wanna play games or you wanna tell me where this place is.'

'Fuck you.'

'There's a hospital there.'

'Drive left here.'

I turned down a dark narrow alley. It sunk in the middle and was lined with boxes and bags of trash, piles of cement sacks and scaffolding supplies. I nearly hit a ladder leaning against the wall and a gray cat scooting across my path before shooting onto a sidestreet with the front bumper scraping on the pavement and Ulf howling in the passenger seat.

After a moment of quiet he said, 'Who are you?'

'Don't talk to me and don't look at me. Look at the fucking street and tell me where the fuck I am.'

'Why do you want to kill me?'

'Don't fuck with me, Ulf. 'Cause I'll put another slug in you, and then this trip will be moot. I'm in enough trouble without taking any shit from you.'

Ulf sank back against the passenger door, thought about what I'd said for a second. His pain turned into a difficult grin. Then he looked up and told me to fuck myself. He was proud after he said it, as if he'd just beaten some sort of dangerous test. And I had to laugh to myself, because maybe he had.

'I'll just keep driving till you bleed to death, ya crazy fuck.'

Ulf's head slumped against the side window, his face

was pale, nearly jaundiced, blood still dripped between his fingers but a lot slower now. His eyes caught a street sign and followed it past the window, then he groaned, 'Drive left . . . next *Strasse*.'

In the middle of the block was a dark brick building with an awning over the sidewalk; written in white block letters was the word *Krankenhaus*. I pulled up to two immense wooden doors right out of a Frankenstein movie. The street was deserted, not a soul around, until Premig's car appeared in the rear-view mirror, the interior a black void of anything human. I leaned over and touched Ulf's cheek; it was hardly warm.

'Come on, Ulf. Hold on. We're here. We made it, you fuck. Come on. You made it! Just fight it. Tell me to fuck myself!'

He looked flat, as if all of his insides had been squeezed out, leaving just a suit of skin and hair. I jumped out of the car and pulled my jacket up over my head, leaned over the steering wheel and jammed down on the horn. A burly guard in a gray uniform stepped out barking like a pit bull and I took off across the street as he skipped toward the car. He yelled urgently back toward the building, then Premig's car roared past, made a screeching left turn at the corner and disappeared in a cloud of exhaust. I watched from a narrow alley as two large nurses rushed out with a stretcher, opened the car door and Ulf's head dropped out of view. Frantically, they lifted him onto the stretcher and rushed him inside while the guard stayed behind, checking out the interior of the Porsche and glancing into the alley across the street. I pressed flat against the brick wall until the guard spoke into a walkie talkie and went back inside the hospital.

At the rear of the alley was a square cement patio with grass and weeds growing up through numerous cracks;

seven small refrigerators lay on their sides with the doors ripped off; on the other side of the patio was a back street of crumbling apartment buildings and tall and foreboding doorways, brick faded past any recognizable color; the cobblestone seemed to tilt unevenly to the left, the whole place was twisted and deformed, cruelly angular – as if Dr Seuss had dropped acid and tried to kill himself. On top of that I had no idea where I was or how to get back. And with that thought, it struck me like a crowbar . . . Back to where? I had crossed a line tonight, a line I didn't know how to cross back over. What was I thinking? Why didn't I pop him? When I had the chance, why didn't I do it? I didn't even like him, that stupid grin even after I shot him and he was bleeding to death. It would have been the easiest thing to do, and yet, why didn't I do it? I wracked my brain trying to figure it out and all I came up with was:

No . . . fucking . . . idea.

Whispery wind howled ghost-like in the alleys and the blue fumes of night burned sharply through my sinuses. Someone came toward me riding a bike, a shadow coasting on momentum. I reached into my jacket and that jerky movement frightened her and she bounced off the curb and wobbled into the street. I leaned back in shadow as she pedaled past; her profile gave her away.

He tied the hook on my line, showed me the special way it had to be done, with three different knots, but I could never get it right, or remember it exactly. Next he opened the box of bloodworms, squirming and writhing around on noodle-like twigs. This was the part of fishing I hated the most; I never truly believed they didn't bite. My father lifted one out by the tail and it question-marked toward his hand.

'Look, see? They're completely harmless. Take one.' But I cringed. He chuckled lightly and said, 'Okay, here, I'll bait yours. But watch me, okay? You may want to do your own after a while.'

All I really wanted to do was go home. 'Daddy, I'm not feeling good.'

'Well . . . I'll tell you what. How about we sit here for a few minutes and fish, and if you're still feeling sick in a little while we'll go? Is that okay?'

'Yeah, I guess.'

Then he baited my hook with the twisting, fighting worm, impaling it four and five times until it became a hook of crumpled flesh. He turned to me; let out a grin.

'I know it looks unpleasant. But rubber worms don't work as well. Okay, you're ready to cast out.'

'Where should I do it?'

'Right there,' he said and pointed out about thirty feet to his right. 'And be careful with the hook.' I reared back and cast my line with hook and float and crumpled worm about twenty feet away.

'Yeah, that's a nice cast. You just let it sit out there for a bit and you'll have a fish in no time.'

My father baited his own hook and cast out in the opposite direction from where I had cast. We sat there watching our floats.

'My father used to take me fishing when I was your age, Anthony. He once took me on a boat and we went way out in the ocean. I couldn't see anything but the water all around me. I thought we'd never see land again. Someday I'll take you out on a boat; we'll go way out. Would you like that, son?'

'I'm still not feeling good. Can we go now?'

'It's not ten minutes yet. Did you know that if you pray to Saint Christopher you always catch a fish?'

We sat there in the waning orange haze of chemical vapors burning in the sunset, the pavement still warm from a sizzling summer day. My fishing line sat still in the middle of the factory parking lot. I was trembling at the thought of someone from school coming by and seeing me here. I would tell them I was playing a joke. My father reeled in his line and checked his bait, recast it out to the seventh parking space where his float bounced twice and rolled onto its side. I wanted to run, to get as far away from here as possible. But my father smiled vaguely and patted my head. In spite of Saint Christopher we didn't catch anything that night.

I hopped down the steps to find a subway station, just like the PATH back home. Except there were no turnstiles. It seemed you could just get on the train without having to go through any gate. It couldn't be true. I read a subway map on a big square token machine, found a train that would take me into *Kreuzberg*, and when the train pulled in I got right on without a token or a ticket – it was bizarre! I laughed to myself, imagined the 'honor system' back home. For all the trouble I was in I felt remarkably light-headed, almost transcendent. I had worked for the Franchise for too long to have one fuck-up ruin me. Sure, there'd be some sanctions and maybe probation, but they wouldn't pop me, not over this.

The train rumbled along and I was surprised by the compactness of the cars, the booths could barely fit two people. The foam cushions were a horrid pink leopard-skin design, none of which had been sliced open or defaced by graffiti. Except for an overturned can of beer peeing on the floor, the car was, by New York standards, immaculate. A big black dog on a leash slept by the feet of a middle-aged gypsy woman wearing beads and a bandana, a heavy-set biker-type clutched a small furry rat-like animal inside his dungaree jacket, the cone-shaped face peering out and sniffing at the dog before going back inside its denim cocoon. At every station a woman's sultry voice came over the loudspeakers telling me which *Strasse* or *Platz* I was at.

The TV tower at *Alexanderplatz* stood huge in front of me and I tried to use it as a guidepost. I walked past shuttered clothing stores and fast-food restaurants and small taverns with laughter and pop music coming from inside; people hung out talking in the street and laughing in the gutter, smoking cigarettes and debating issues of debatable importance. I walked by them as if I were dust.

I came to the steps of a green-domed church and rested for a bit, watched the lights of the city flicker in front of me. I felt the tragic eyes of the Russian girl watching me from the clouds. I played with my gun, the cool, polished metal solid in my hand; substantial; fired an angry shot into her chest. A side window burst on a parked car. I emptied the clip around the street and hot shells tinkled harmlessly down the steps; the barrel smoldered with the sharp, seductive scent of cordite, not unlike the alluring tang of gasoline, only now it made me sick with shame and revulsion, the flatulence of death. I heaved onto my shoes and the gun dropped from my hand and clanked on the cement.

'We're better off without him, Ma.'

She was a wreck, sitting at the dining room table and wiping her eyes, puffy and red from too little sleep and too much hardship rubbed in. My father had been missing for three days; he disappeared on Wednesday night and hadn't been seen or heard from since. She was worried that he might hurt himself, or get himself into a bad situation. She still loved him, in spite of the way he destroyed our lives. I told her he'd be back, but that we all might be better off if he didn't return. Whenever she'd had him committed to a hospital he threatened to kill himself, and several times tried to do so, no matter what medications they pumped him with. My mother felt that to keep him there was the same as killing him, so he always came home with us until the next episode. The local police were no strangers to our house; there were countless visits and warnings and several times the authorities tried to put him away legally. The last big incident, last summer, nearly got him killed by an irate neighbor. My father had got it into his head that the cars of the neighborhood were talking to him; some were recording him and altering the tapes to incriminate him in the eyes of the Lord. He claimed they were sneaking into the house late at night and hammering small nails into his shoes. He took to hiding his shoes late at night before going to bed, secret places in the house no one, not even my mother, knew; then the next morning when he retrieved them and put them on, he would cry out that the cars had found them. On July 3rd, he went out very early in the morning, before anyone else was up. By the time he was jumped and beaten to the ground, seven cars on our block had been sent exploding into fireballs. With the red five-gallon gasoline can he bought the night before at Rickles, he calmly doused each car before setting it off with a match. He was chanting from the Bible when Tim Rialy came out of his house just in time to see his '67 rebuilt Mustang die a slow and agonizing death. My mother got there as Tim Rialy was dousing my father with gasoline; by then my father's wrist had been broken and his head was bleeding and my mother covered him with her body and begged Tim not to light the match. My father was arrested and taken away in an ambulance. Later that day my mother went to all the houses of the car owners and begged them to drop the charges. None of them would do so, including Tim Rialy, but he promised he would after my mother scraped together – and he accepted – three thousand dollars as a down payment on his new car. Seven years later I beat the living shit out of him for that.

Now when I looked at my mother I saw someone old, and ragged. The first time you see your mother that way,

98

weak and feeble, helpless, and the roles between parent and child start that slow dip into reverse, it jars you a little bit. And I hated my father for that.

The cab took me to the end of the park, the driver didn't know how to get in. He spoke a little English, enough to let me know he wasn't going any further. It was nearly four in the morning by the time I started along the cobblestone walkway leading to the apartment. The church spires stood out in twin silhouettes, a big black bird flew overhead, its wingspan spread like a cape. I heard movement behind the bushes and immediately grabbed my gun, crept up softly and slowly and leaned in simply until I felt the chilled moist leaves brush my face. Behind the bush a young couple kissed on a bench. The guy had his arm around her shoulders and held her close and their lips smacked with saliva and passion and she moaned like the wind and these people were as foreign to me as aliens from a distant planet. The gun weighed a ton in my hand.

I turned on the light and the entire place had been trashed. Everything was smashed or overturned; the wall unit was lying cracked on the floor amongst the stereo and TV and glasses and ceramic lamps and the glass-topped coffee tables and the only thing not tossed was the couch which held up Hardy laying there with the frightened look of a beaten bully on his face.

'I'm in deep shit!'

I laughed out loud, relieved that Manny and Lawrence Talbot hadn't already paid a visit.

'I went berserk! Just fuckin' lost it. Bein' kept out of the job tonight . . . I cracked. Smashed a few things.'

'A few things,' I repeated, scanning the damage. It was a typically thorough Hardy operation, the one thing he did with any amount of skill.

'I don't even remember doin' it! I must'a blacked out.'

'The kitchen?' I asked. He nodded gravely.

'And my room?'

'I'm really sorry, man. It wasn't nothin' personal.'

I chuckled at the truth of that.

'It's not funny. What am I gonna do?!' he moaned. 'If they see this they're gonna fuckin' pop me! I'm on probation as it is.'

'Probation?'

'It's a long story.'

'Make it short.'

'I popped a civilian.'

'You've popped civilians before. Your uncle always took care of it.'

'This guy was somebody's brother, a councilman.'

'Ouch.'

'All right, what do you think, councilmen wear signs?!'

'I'm sorry. I gotta get some sleep.'

'Tony, man, help me clean this fuckin' place up!'

'Tomorrow.'

'Tomorrow's too late. What if they come over tonight?!'

'They're not gonna come over tonight.'

'Manny's been callin' here every twenty minutes! He says you should give him a call as soon as you get in.'

'I'll call him tomorrow.'

'Come on, Tony, help me, man. I'm freakin' out over here! They been lookin' for a reason to fuck me and this is it. They hate me, you know that!'

'Riccardo Montefiore doesn't hate you,' I said, which was true because the mere mention of Hardy's name got most people paying up without a fuss. Riccardo Montefiore liked that, and he used it the way a carpenter uses a buzz saw. Now this buzz saw sat there whining with red eyes and swollen lips; the only thing missing was a soundtrack of violins.

'Tony, the Franchise is the only thing I got in my life, and if I lose that I'm over, man. I'm fuckin' over.'

'Hardy, don't jump to conclusions,' but he was off and jumping and there was no stopping him.

'I give my heart and soul to this fuckin' Franchise and all I get back is the shit end of the stick. I don't fuckin' understand it. The sacrifices I made! They forget . . . I was fifteen years old when they popped my old man, sent him to Florida on a job and popped him once he got there. Did I hold a grudge? Did I go lookin' for the responsible parties? Fuck no, my old man knew the rules and got caught in a turf war.'

'I thought your father was killed over a woman.'

'Well, that don't explain why they treat you like the golden boy and me, who's really connected by blood, they treat like a fuckin' mook!'

Several dozen reasons immediately came to mind. Instead I told him, 'I don't know. I'm sorry.'

'I know. It's not your fault or anythin'. I ain't blamin' you. It's just fuckin' curious, is all. I mean, I never betrayed anybody that didn't have it comin', and I never stole a dime from the Franchise.'

'Hardy, I'm nearly unconscious. I gotta get some sleep.'

'What about the apartment?'

'I'll help you tomorrow, first thing in the morning.'

I started down the hall and Hardy took his parting shot, 'You know, Tony, in the past you wouldn't'a left me hangin' on a fuckin' hook. You wouldn't'a done that.'

My room was as he said it would be. Nothing personal. I laid on the mattress tossed halfway off the box spring and fell asleep to the sounds of Hardy cursing under his breath and cleaning up the kitchen.

I woke up at sunrise to knocking on the front door. I got up, still dressed from my nearly two hours of sleep. Hardy came rushing into the hallway in his underpants carrying a Browning .45.

'Put that away. It's Manny.'

'How could they fuckin' know so soon?! Did you tell them anything?'

'They're here to see me.'

'You?'

I unlocked the door, removed the chain. Manny peeked through the crack and said, 'Morning, kid. Mind if we come in for a minute.'

'Suit yourself,' and I stepped back as Manny Simone and Lawrence Talbot came in with Tito and Ernie behind; Vita, Premig and several young Turkish guys stayed back in the hall. No one looked happy to be up so early.

Hardy came out from his room buckling up his pants and looking spooked. 'Hey, guys. What brings you here?'

Lawrence Talbot spoke dryly, 'We got some business with Tony. Why don't you go back to sleep?'

'Oh, uh, sure, okay. Hey, Tony, why don't you take everybody into the kitchen and make 'em some coffee?' he nodded toward the kitchen while I followed Manny and Lawrence Talbot into the living room. Tito and Ernie stayed near the door. Lawrence looked at the damage around him with pain on his face; I could see him already tallying up the cost in his mind. Manny's snarl wouldn't betray his thoughts; he was always angry, even when he was happy.

'Looks like there's been a hurricane in here,' he sniped.

'Yeah, it gets windy in these old apartments.'

Hardy shuddered in the doorway. Manny Simone was one of the few people in the world who truly frightened him, and when Manny looked over and said, 'You still here?' Hardy dashed off to his room and closed the door. Manny stood in the middle of the mess.

'Did you get my message,' he said, 'about calling when you got in?'

'Yeah. I was gonna come in first thing in the morning and see you both.'

'We're here now; save yourself the trip. So . . . How'd it go last night?'

'Not so good.'

'Why don't you tell us what happened?'

'Well . . . I really can't say for sure. It just seemed like the wrong thing to do. So I didn't do it.'

This got no response from either one of them, not surprise, not anger, nothing. Manny pondered the issue. 'Seemed like the wrong thing to do . . . so you didn't do it. Maybe there were police around? . . . Too many witnesses? Or maybe your gun misfired?'

'No, I can't say anything like that happened.'

Lawrence Talbot spoke. 'Why don't you just walk us through it.'

'Well, I waited in the theater like I was supposed to do. The guy came in with his boyfriend. It was a gay movie; guys were sucking each other off all over the place, unbelievable. After the movie I followed them out into the parking lot. The boyfriend drove away and Ulf went to his car.'

'Ulf?'

'The cog. I came up behind him. But at the last instant I didn't pull the trigger.'

'But you shot him?'

'He pulled a gun on me, a Jennings 380.' After I told them the rest, leaving out the part about the girl on the bike, Manny summed it up so there'd be no misunderstanding.

'So you shot him, put him in his own car and drove him to the hospital?'

'Yeah, pretty much.'

'Why didn't you take him out for dinner first? Maybe go dancing afterward?'

'Manny, you told me he was a buttonman. He's not even in the business. He's a student, a civilian.'

'The fucking guy was carrying a piece! How many students you know who carry pieces?!'

I knew if I answered that question I'd be shot right there and then. Manny wasn't finished.

'Who the fuck are you to decide who lives? What are you? . . . God!? When I give you a fucking order your fucking job is to do it. And you didn't! You broke the fucking chain of command. You fucked us tonight! Now they're gonna think we're a bunch of fucking incompetent pussies! People saw you! At the hospital; running through the streets. Your fucking face is gonna be everywhere tomorrow morning. You're a fucking liability to us now!'

'No one saw me. It was really dark and I was careful.'

'What about the so-called fucking student? Didn't he see you as you were driving him around town?'

'He had other things on his mind. By the way, did he live? He was in pretty bad shape when I dropped him off.'

Lawrence Talbot's voice poured in my ears like syrup laced with razor blades. 'I don't think you appreciate the grave seriousness of what you haven't done. You've been acting strange lately. We've all noticed it. What is it? Those pills you eat like candy?'

'Seconals. I have a prescription for them. I haven't taken any tonight.' And maybe that was the problem, I thought; though I'd never needed pills before to commit horrific acts of violence; in fact, the only reason I stopped taking them at all was because they stopped working.

Lawrence Talbot bored into my eyes with a Bela Lugosi intensity as he asked the next question.

'Lawrence, it ain't like that,' I said, with genuine hurt.

Manny jumped in, 'Where'd they get to you? In the theater?'

'I told you, it ain't like that. Nobody approached me. I ain't no fucking traitor!'

Manny said, 'You ain't no fucking patriot either. You lost your nerve tonight, didn't you?'

'I had it two days ago.'

Lawrence Talbot looked at Manny. They were both frustrated, confused; they wanted to understand. Unfortunately, I couldn't help them; I didn't understand myself.

'And what about the girl?'

'What girl?'

'Primo told us you stopped to talk to a girl.'

'You mean Premig?'

'Don't fuck with me, kid. I ain't in the mood. Who's the fucking girl?'

'She's nobody. She was riding her bike and I hit her with the car. Got out to see if she was all right.'

'Did she get a good look at you?'

'No. She wore glasses and they got knocked off in the fall. She didn't see a thing.'

'How do you know what she couldn't see?'

I shuddered as his train of thought barreled through my mind.

'She was squinting all over the place, and I kept my face turned away. Believe me, she didn't see anything.'

'What did she say to you? Where is she from?'

'She didn't speak English. I didn't even get a good look at her. What are we gonna do, search the city for some strange girl on a bicycle?!'

'Don't fucking pooh pooh me, kid! These Russian bastards use women all the time to infiltrate and turn people over, so don't fucking play dumb!'

'I hit her, I asked her where a hospital was, she didn't understand and I drove off. That's it.'

They both studied me cautiously, suspiciously. Finally Manny snapped, 'Fuck! This is a fucking nightmare! We could always count on you. You were a fucking star! The boy wonder! Then when we need you the most, when we gotta be tighter than a nun's cunt, you ram a fucking tree stump through it.'

'I'm sorry.'

'You're worse than sorry. Maybe I've been leaning on the wrong guy all this time. Hardy! Get your ass out here.'

Hardy appeared in the doorway. He'd been listening the whole time and could barely contain his glee as he hopped back and forth on the balls of his feet until Lawrence told him, 'Watch it, you're gonna . . .'

'Ow! Fuck!'

Manny barked, 'Be careful! You fucking klutz.'

As Hardy bounced on one foot, Lawrence turned to me, back on track. 'Did you have to break everything in the apartment? What sense did that make?'

Hardy's eyes burned a hole in my chest, pleading.

'I was angry. I knew I fucked up and was just letting off some steam.'

Manny said, 'That's the only bright spot on the whole fucking horizon, kid.'

Lawrence watched me out of the side of his head. He still had questions, but for now he was done. 'This is Franchise property,' he said. 'You're paying for the replacement of everything here. Is that understood?'

'Yes.'

'And you're on probation from now on.' Then he pointed a crooked finger at Hardy. 'You, you're off probation.'

Hardy nearly cried out in joy, but held himself back and instead let his foot paint joyful red splotches on the carpet.

Lawrence Talbot buttoned his jacket. They were ready to leave. Manny stopped in the doorway and pointed at me. 'I want you in the office in two hours. Hardy, I want him in the office in two hours. No excuses – you got that?' When Hardy's brow sank like the handle on a toilet bowl, I knew if they told him to he'd pop me on the way. But it wouldn't come to that, not yet; they needed more information first. Nobody got popped until all the questions were answered.

They stepped to the foyer, treading cautiously on the glass crunching under their feet. Lawrence picked up a small headless statuette, 'Look at this,' he said and studied it in his hand.

'Emily collects these. Limited edition. That's about three hundred and fifty dollars.'

Manny turned to me with disgust, 'That's a fucking Lladro, kid.'

8

The next morning, only two hours later, I was sitting in the trailer with Lawrence Talbot, Manny Simone, Heinrich and Yossario. Nobody said a word to me or even looked at me, it was as though they felt whatever transgression I'd committed was contagious through direct interpersonal contact. Lawrence questioned Yossario over the number of men working on the site.

'Who are these mystery people? They don't show time-cards yet they're being paid by the company!'

'Some are ssstill in hospital, others can't work, their knees were broke.'

'What do you mean their knees were broke?'

'They were hurt by Hans Kopp. His men grabbed them after work, sssmashed their knees with pipes.'

'So, they're unable to work?'

'Yesss.'

'Why are we still paying them?'

'They have families, children to feed. We have to help them.'

'We're not a charity organization. If they can't work, let the Government take care of them. You got a social system here, don't you?'

'It's not enough. Thessse are our workers. Sssome are here illegal.'

'If they're not working, they're not workers.'

'Thessse are my people!'

'Then pay them out of your own pocket. We're running a business; we can't support every cripple that limps onto the site. That may seem cruel but we have a responsibility to our shareholders, to our legitimate employees. In business, compassion is like a hemorrhoid, and nobody wants hemorrhoids. From now on nobody gets paid from the company that ain't contributing.'

The color drained from Yossario's cheeks and his eyes began to flood. I knew any second the trickle would come dripping from his nose. Lawrence continued, 'There's gonna be some drastic changes in the way things are done around here. We're slashing the workforce by ten per cent on Monday, and starting tomorrow there will be an across-the-board seven per cent cut in wages.'

Yossario turned to Heinrich and stammered in German and when Heinrich spoke back in kind Manny stepped up and silenced them both with a wave of his hands. 'No more Kraut talk in the office! I wanna know what is said around here and I wanna know it in English.'

Yossario looked to Heinrich, who took a breath, 'Yossario is concerned that if these changes take place there'll be a revolt on the work site.'

'Why don't you let me worry about the work site? That's what I'm here for.'

Yossario said, 'But if we cut the workforce by ten per cent we won't make the completion date!'

'Exactly!' Manny shouted to the heavens. 'He finally gets it!' But the confused, rattled look on Yossario's face betrayed that conclusion.

'But . . . why do you want to fall behind the completion date?'

'Because the job was underbid, of course. Now we have to bring it more in line with the actual costs of a project this size. We go to them and tell them we need more money for unforeseen overages, to replace supplies that got lost or damaged in transport, unexpected problems that come up naturally on all projects.'

'But the Government will investigate if we ask for more money.'

Manny chuckled lightly and took a step back. 'Lawrence, enlighten the masses.'

Lawrence Talbot leaned away from the computer screen and polished his glasses, scraped up a heave of phlegm before speaking. 'Let me tell you something about government contracts, because I know a little bit about them. I've rigged over two hundred government contracts in my lifetime. Nobody wants an investigation, the project gets stalled, people lose money. Or worse. People become . . . exposed. Everyone, from the mailroom clerks to the president, has his hand in the pie. Believe me, they'll pay the extra money and let the project move forward. It's in everyone's best interests.'

Yossario cried in exasperation, 'But this isn't America! We do it differently here! We can't fire workers and drop their pay.'

Manny quipped, 'We can do whatever the fuck we want, and anybody that has a problem, well, we can always order up some more wheelchairs. Right kid?'

I answered like an idiot, 'Whatever you say, Manny.' But seeing the look of abject fear and disappointment on Yossario's face was like watching children learn the truth about sex.

'What are you doing in there for so long?'

'I'm busy.'

'Come on, what's the big mystery?'

'It's private.'

'Can I watch?'

'No, because then it wouldn't be private.'

'Come on, Carrie, let me in. I don't want to be alone.'

'Where's Daddy?'

'In his room. He's sleeping.'

I pressed my ear against the door. Water ran in the sink and a glass jar tinkled on porcelain.

'Come on, let me in. I showed you how I pee.'

'I didn't ask to see it.'

'Please.'

A moment later the door unlocked and opened. She gave me a weary, big-sister smile and stepped back so I could enter. I sat on the toilet lid and watched as she studied her eyelashes in the mirror. On the counter in front of her stood a dozen bottles and tubes with colored creams and liquids inside them.

'What is all this stuff?'

'I knew you were going to ask a million questions,' she scolded.

'I'm sorry.'

'Every tube and bottle has a specific purpose and function. The creams are for skin treatment and complexion maintenance, the lotions are for color and tone, texture and porosity. The powders are for finishing and laying down a solid foundation to build upon one's natural beauty. The key is to maintain the natural qualities of each face's uniqueness. The way no two apples are exactly alike, neither are any two faces. See?'

'Oh.'

I'd never heard her sound so grown-up before. The modeling books and magazines she'd been reading were having a profound effect. She wanted to play with me less and less and her body started changing in not so subtle ways. She wore dresses with flowers and birds on them while her ripped jeans and tee shirts sat crushed on her chair under her NY Yankees baseball cap, all of them unworn for weeks. She spent hours in the bathroom with the door locked and on the phone she giggled demurely where in the past she had cackled loud and boisterously. I was confused by it all, watching her teeter between childhood and adulthood, wondering why she'd ever prefer that life of hospitals and hysteria and gray-haired hand-wringing worry to the cozy comfort of our secret fort in the woods. Watching her transform herself from my partner-in-crime into a person I didn't know any longer, I felt myself slipping from the only perch of security I'd ever known.

Hardy came in about noon with Premig, walked past me without glancing my way and stepped up to Lawrence still planted intractably at the computer. On the drive over to the trailer this morning he asked me but one question.

When I told him exactly what happened the night before, he simply shook his head in disgust and said I was a disgrace to killers everywhere. Then he stared at the road in front of him and didn't utter another word.

Lawrence Talbot finally sat back from the computer screen and Hardy told him, 'He's on the third floor, but it's crawlin' with guys. Nobody can get in or out without bein' checked out. For now, we can't get near him.'

Manny looked at me with disdain. 'Thanks kid. Hell of a job last night. Hell of a job!'

Hardy glared at me and I met his glare with one of my own. Manny keyed on Premig keeping his stump deep in his jacket pocket, then turned to Yossario and griped, 'We gotta do something about that guy. He stands out like a fucking sore thumb, pardon the expression. Can't he get a rubber hand or something?'

'It's too sssoon. The wound is not properly healed yet.'

'Well, he can't go around like that. He looks guilty of every crime ever committed.'

Yossario spoke to Premig in Turkish, but before Manny could protest, Yossario turned to him and said, 'We'll get something to cover his hand.'

Hardy offered, 'Hey Manny, why don't we just get those Russian assault rifles and blast our way into that fuckin' hospital? Pop anybody that gets in our way?'

'Because we ain't fucking idiots, that's why.'

Hardy shrunk down like a beaten mime. Manny explained, 'Hardy, we gotta sit tight for now. We gotta use our heads, Gabeesh?'

'Sure, it was just an idea.'

'Take Primo outside and make sure nobody's stealing our lumber.'

Hardy left and Manny stepped over to Lawrence and whispered in his ear while Heinrich clicked a button on his computer mouse and a row of playing cards appeared on the screen. I looked through the magazines on a small table to my left but there was nothing I could read except a map of Berlin folded inside a travel magazine. I found the park in *Kreuzberg* where the apartment sat and followed lines representing each street trying to find the bakery and the wine cellar and Yossario's place and then streets leading to the construction site. Then turning the map over I searched through the listing of street names beginning with the letter 'F'. Nothing looked familiar until halfway down I found it, G-14. The hospital was situated on the corner of *Diesterwegstr.* and *Fröbelstr.* Manny turned and asked me what the fuck I was reading.

I clapped the map closed and told him nothing.

The door swung open and Vita rushed in followed by three Turkish workers and Tito and Ernie. Vita looked flushed and frightened with his hair messed and his suit wrinkled and fresh mud on his polished shoes. He marched up to his father and cried out in Turkish and his father cried back in kind and Heinrich yelled in German and they all began screaming at each other as Lawrence growled to keep it down. Manny barked that he wanted English spoken but nobody heard him until he slammed his fist down on the rattling metal desk. Vita turned to him and breathlessly explained, 'My brother is missing! He come not to work. He is not *Zuhause*! I can not find him!'

'Well, maybe he overslept.'

Yossario protested, 'He doesn't oversleep, and when he does he calls to tell us. He's been taken by Hans Kopp!'

Vita snarled at Manny, 'This is *wegen* last night!'

'Don't jump to conclusions. The kid could be anywhere so don't go losing your head until we know what the fuck happened.'

Vita started yelling at his father and the Turkish guys were mumbling to each other and Yossario yelled back with blood running out of his nose and Heinrich tried to calm everyone down in German, Turkish and English as Lawrence let out a loud grunt of phlegm which Tito and Ernie took as their cue to rush to his flank. Manny shot me a look and I reached into my jacket just as the door swung open with Vita's younger brother standing behind it. Everyone got quiet and then Vita and Yossario rushed up and grabbed him by the collar and barked at him in Turkish and the kid answered with a bewildered sheepish grin. Vita slapped him hard across the cheek and throttled him by the neck and Yossario tried to pull him away as the kid started bawling and I thought Vita would kill him. Manny stood there completely perplexed until Heinrich told him Mustapha had stayed at some girl's flat where he overslept and had just come in. Now Manny started flipping out and demanding to know who this girl was and where did she live and asking if she was Russian and looking at me he reminded everyone of the Russian trick to get girls fucking with everyone's heads. Manny warned, 'From now on nobody goes out with Russian girls or drinks Russian vodka, and anybody coming in contact with anything Russian has to report it immediately and be debriefed. Is that clear?'

I was tempted to ask him if this included Polish girls too, but I wasn't feeling suicidal just yet.

After lunchtime when the day settled down a bit and the trailer was empty except for Lawrence Talbot, Yossario and myself, Lawrence moved away from the computer and sat with Yossario asking him friendly questions about his life. I listened with curiosity as he segued into other topics, sliding smoothly from family and culture into business and other companies on the site, which ones Yossario knew and was friendly with and if any of the others showed signs of financial need. Like a serpent in Eden he was searching for Eve but Yossario wasn't taking the fruit, denying knowledge of anyone outside his own company and I could tell Lawrence didn't believe a word of it by the way he scraped up phlegm with a groan not unlike the sound of longshoremen losing overtime.

Near six o'clock the door burst open and Manny came in like a tornado, kicking my feet off a chair and telling me to straighten up and barking for Tito and Ernie to start cleaning the place as Yossario looked up worried over this new assault of activity. Lawrence Talbot didn't budge from his numbers while around him dust was swept into the air and chairs were placed behind desks and the desks fixed at perfect geometric angles with the walls. It could only foretell the sudden arrival of Riccardo Montefiore, who demanded order and cleanliness and desks fixed at perfect geometric angles with the walls. Manny ordered Tito and Ernie to stand guard outside while he made several last adjustments to the ashtrays and magazines and other minutiae in the trailer.

A hush fell over the trailer as Yossario, Vita and Heinrich looked over at the door with apprehension. Manny quickly inspected each desktop for clutter, runaway pens or crooked papers. Lawrence Talbot continued typing numbers into the computer, altering figures and inflating expenses and wiping out any hint of legitimate earnings.

It was quiet outside, no sound of work or machinery or voices, nothing, just the cruel wind blowing sand and dirt against the outer aluminum walls. Out of the wind came the shuffle of leather shoes on hard dirt, a group of feet walking heavily in steady, percussive cadence. Manny stood in the center of the room waiting. Yossario and Heinrich stood up and Vita leaned on the desk causing it to scrape along the floor. Manny scowled at the uneven angle of the newly moved desk. He turned to me and said, 'Get up, kid.'

I didn't budge and he didn't push it.

Tito or Ernie stuck their head in the doorway and whispered, 'He's here.'

9

We sat at the back booth, a raised platform with a round table and a cushioned red metal-flake semi-circular bench two feet above the dance floor. Murray hadn't come in yet, but he was expected any minute. Rodney sipped his Scotch and drummed his fingers in military rhythm on the table top, but it wasn't because he was nervous. Rodney used to play for the Newark All Star Marching Band on holidays until Manny Simone was sitting home one Thanksgiving afternoon watching television and his wife casually remarked,

'Say, isn't that Rodney Hamilton?'

Manny sat in shit-defying horror as one of his soldiers responsible for thirteen contract hits marched across the TV screen wearing a red feathered hat and playing a big wooden drum. Manny had to be talked out of going out that very afternoon and popping Rodney himself. The next day the Franchise enacted a law barring any members from appearing on television. Rodney now confined his drumming to neighborhood table tops.

This job was handed to me personally by Riccardo Montefiore, who asked for delicacy and discretion because Murray was one of his oldest, dearest friends. He said it was with deep regret that it had come to this, but after Murray had taken over a downtown messenger service from someone who owed a lot of money to the Franchise, instead of collecting the overdue vig in cash or someone's health, Murray had invested a lot more money into the service in the belief that it was about to land a major contract with a huge insurance company. After several months that contract had not materialized and for that miscalculation someone had to pay. Naturally that someone was

Murray. Riccardo Montefiore asked me to take Rodney Hamilton along because Murray and Rodney were first cousins.

Murray came an hour later with his wife, Estelle, hanging onto his arm, which surprised us both because Murray was supposed to meet us alone for drinks. Murray went to the bar and greeted Jimmy the bartender and his waitresses and all the regulars because he was well liked by everyone who knew him. As he joked with two old boozers Estelle took a glance over her shoulder and clutched tightly onto Murray's biceps; that's when I had my first pang of discomfort. I nodded to Rodney to play it cool. Murray came over laughing and shaking our hands and he seemed in a particularly grander mood than usual and he joked with his cousin and gave him a hug while his wife held onto his arm and eyed me with profound distrust; as long as she was attached like that we couldn't touch him. When Murray and Estelle went into the kitchen, Rodney leaned over and whispered, 'She knows! We gotta do them both.'

'That's not the job.'

'But she won't leave him alone.'

'Then it's off.'

'No fuckin' way!'

'I'd like you to reconsider.' It must have been the whisper in my voice that frightened him, because he looked up, saw his own death, then sat back with failed ambition creasing his brow like pressed clay; I was ruining his big chance to move up in the eyes of Riccardo Montefiore. But I had a sense for things like this and I never rushed a job or forced the issue because if you wanted somebody bad enough you could always get them. Where could they go? This was all they ever knew. It was their home and their universe and to call it provincial was to call a gunshot wound a bruise. Take your time and get it right; that was the point.

Murray and Estelle sat with us at the booth and we drank two bottles of wine and Murray kept talking about the messenger service and how much money it would make and what a sweet deal it is and Estelle played real nice but wouldn't meet my eyes. Murray stood up and Estelle got up too and he laughed and told her to sit down, that he was only going to pee. I poured her another glass of wine and Rodney slid out of the booth.

'Where you going?' I said. 'You didn't finish your drink.'

'I gotta pee too.'

Estelle looked up with torture on her face. 'I have to go to the ladies' room, Murray.'

'Sweetheart, sit with Tony till we come back. I'll be a minute.'

Murray put his hand on her shoulder and eased her down onto her seat. Rodney wouldn't meet my eyes, then he and Murray strolled to the men's room. Estelle sniffled and tears dropped from her cheeks.

'Estelle, I'm not here to do what you think.'

'Don't fucking lie to me, Tony.'

'Listen to me. I promise you, it's not what you think.' The bathroom door clanged shut and I stood up.

'I want you to wait here. Trust me. If you wait here everything will be okay, I promise.'

I don't know if she trusted me or not, but she stayed at the table as I went to the men's room. Murray and Rodney stood at adjacent urinals until Rodney took a step back and Murray let out a bray of relief. Rodney reached into his jacket and I stepped up and fired a silenced slug into the back of his head. His eyes puked out of his skull and hung by cords on his cheeks. Murray swung around as the body slapped the floor and I snatched his gun from its holster. He looked at me with fear, then defiance.

'Go ahead, do it,' he said. 'But let Estelle go.'

Estelle ran crying to his side and wrapped herself around his neck and if I was gonna pop Murray it wouldn't be singular. I lowered my gun.

'I'm not here for you, Murray. Rodney got caught skimming from Bobby the Shark.'

Murray spat in a urinal. 'What the fuck do you take me for? I don't believe that for a Goddamn second. But if Riccardo was a little more fuckin' patient, he would'a found out after he returned my call from this afternoon, that the insurance company came through. We got the contract. It's good for about seven-hundred and fifty K the first year alone. I just increased the Franchise's money ten times. That's a good reason not to be popped, don't you think?'

'I would have to say yes.' I gave Murray back his gun.

'You know, Riccardo was best man at my wedding.'

'Yeah, I know.'

The next day Riccardo Montefiore let out a laugh and patted my back and thanked me for sizing up a situation and being able to think on my feet. Then he handed me a thick envelope of cash and the disappearance of Rodney Hamilton was never mentioned by anyone. The Franchise made over three million dollars before the messenger service had been run into the ground. Two months after the building was set on fire I popped Murray out behind the Chinese takeout on direct orders from Riccardo Montefiore for reasons that to this day remain unknown.

Riccardo Montefiore greeted the room and immediately Yossario, Heinrich and Vita relaxed; Riccardo was nothing like what they expected. At six-foot-five he was an imposing figure, but his warm smile and delicate features put most people at ease. He was bigger than life, but in a friendly, non-threatening way. Wearing a charcoal-gray hand-tailored Versace suit and polished black Italian leather shoes and with silky graying hair framing a smooth

Caribbean complexion courtesy of his tanning salon on South Elizabeth Street, he could have passed for a mature fashion model in a men's magazine.

He stepped up to Lawrence Talbot who sat back from the computer screen and shook his hand.

'What's it looking like, Lawrence?'

'It's a mess, but we'll straighten it out.'

'You got everything you need?'

'I'm fine.'

'You have a good flight out?'

'Yes, actually I did.'

'Good.'

'What's the weather back home?'

'It's warm. Sunny.'

'It's cold here.'

'You bring enough clothes? I'll get you some coats and blankets.'

'I got Ernie already checking out the discount stores.'

'You get what you need; don't worry about cost.'

'I want value for my *Deutsche Mark*.'

'What's the exchange rate today?'

Listening to this stilted exchange of drivel I had to laugh to myself. For all their criminal intercourse and diabolic synergy together, they could never quite mesh personally. Like two halves of a magnet, at once attracted to and yet repelled by the other, they needed each other, respected each other – in some ways even trusted each other – but I don't think in fifteen years they'd ever once socialized outside of Franchise business. Being in the same room with them was like watching Escher's lizards gnaw on each other's tail.

Riccardo turned to Manny Simone and kissed his cheek and thanked him for some private favor successfully performed. Then he turned to sit on a chair that had been wheeled out into the center of the room. He spoke in a quiet baritone and said how good it was to finally be out here and how sorry he was it took so long but there were other matters that needed to be settled first.

I was the Invisible Man, no one gave me a second glance as I sat on the end of the couch.

Yossario leaned forward and asked about Riccardo's wife, Lucretia, and to pass along his good wishes and what a lovely little girl she had been growing up in the neighborhood and how proud they all are that she had the good sense to marry a cold-blooded wealthy criminal mastermind; actually, I interpreted that last part. Vita sat beside him quietly seething because his father seemed to be groveling, but then Yossario said there was something of great importance on his mind and Riccardo leaned forward to hear it. Yossario spoke of the crippled workers who had no support and that it wouldn't be right to leave them and their families out in the cold especially after they suffered because of no fault of their own and what kind of people would we be to abandon them in this their hour of need. Vita looked at his father with genuine admiration and even I had to admit that Yossario was an eloquent man when he wanted to be. Riccardo rubbed his chin, nodded his head.

'You're absolutely right,' he said. 'Absolutely right. What kind of people would we be? I bear no tolerance for disloyalty or treachery among my friends.' Manny shot me a look that bore no tolerance for disloyalty or treachery. Riccardo continued, 'Of course all the crippled workers will be taken care of. In fact, I suggest we start up a fund immediately to help support these less fortunate workers. Manny, get on that right away.' And as sure as death and taxes, I knew that not one cent of that fund would ever see the light of day, unless that light was in Riccardo Montefiore's pocket. But Yossario let out a sigh of appreciation and shook

Riccardo's hand, then sat back and patted his son's knee.

Riccardo Montefiore asked for a moment alone with his associates as there was a private matter that needed to be urgently addressed. Yossario got up with Vita and Heinrich and invited us all to dinner at his home later that night.

When the room was cleared, the smile fell from Riccardo's face and he stood up. His head seemed to brush the ceiling. He whirled around as if seeing me for the first time. 'Now, what the fuck happened last night?'

10

Yossario's apartment had been fixed up with a long buffet table covered with silver trays of rice and noodles and strange-shaped pasta surrounded by bowls of red, green and white sauces; salads and breads and chips sat beside two tall stacks of glass plates and sterling silverware; a wet bar had been wheeled into a corner where a lean Turk in a red vest mixed drinks. The room was filled with Turkish workers and New Jersey soldiers and Riccardo Montefiore worked the crowd like a visiting politician; Yossario translated in Turkish and German when necessary. Heinrich stood with Hardy holding a bottle of beer and facing the pictures of naked women as they debated the merits of German versus American hookers. Manny Simone and Lawrence Talbot talked to a circle of men that included Tito and Ernie and Vita watched us all with a scowl of distaste and I wondered how long it would take before that scowl gets beaten out of his head. I went to the bar for another Crown Royal with ice and put twenty Marks in an empty glass on the bar. The bartender looked at me puzzled, then he smiled. Vita stood in my path sipping a glass of what I assumed to be fruit juice.

'I want to ask you question,' he said.

'What?'

'Why did you do last night?'

'Do what?'

'Let the son live.'

'It was a big misunderstanding.'

'You drove him to hospital?'

'He wasn't feeling too well.' Vita shifted his gaze and I went to move past him, but then stopped and turned around. 'Hey, can you get me a map?'

'A map?'

'Yeah. Something that shows the streets, the subway. Hospitals. Without telling anyone?'

He eyed me, not sure what to make of that last part. 'Here wait,' he said, and went into the hallway.

Manny called me over and slapped my back nearly spilling my drink as we were now best of friends again. Through the stale wine and cigar smoke on his breath he asked, 'How you feeling, kid?'

'Fine. How about you?'

Manny turned to Lawrence, 'The kid's got balls of steel, don't he, Lawrence?'

Lawrence Talbot thought about it, a half smile creased his lips. 'He's got something. I don't know what. Luck, I guess.'

'Yeah, he's got plenty of that too.'

I remarked, 'You were pretty lucky yourself today, Manny.'

He grinned and pinched my cheek hard. 'Luck runs out, kid. I hope I don't hafta be the one to show you that some-day.'

When Riccardo Montefiore found me in the narrow scope of his dark green eyes, like twin barrels of a sawed off 12 gauge, I felt the expiration date of my life flash forward. The last thing to show him or anyone else in this room was that I was aware of that fact or concerned either way.

'I was supposed to pop a kid and I didn't,' I answered.

'And who ordered you to pop this kid?'

The question struck me as unusual. I wasn't sure where this was going. 'The usual channels,' I answered.

'Why didn't you do as you were told?'

'It was a judgment call.'

'I see,' he said. 'What was this judgment call based on?'

'Just a feeling. It didn't feel right.'

Out of the corner of my eye I caught Hardy grinning, relishing his new position as the guy who didn't fuck up for once. Riccardo shifted his gaze around the room.

'What are you laughing at?'

Before Hardy could answer Riccardo told the room, 'Tony saved our asses last night. He's a fucking hero as far as I'm concerned.'

The smile ripped itself from Hardy's face, Manny Simone's jaw hung open, and I nearly peed my pants. Riccardo turned to Manny Simone, 'It was a mistake to try and pop the guy's son, Manny.'

'But . . . you told me to check the kid out. Our guy inside, what's his name? Timmo! He told me the kid was gonna be at that theater.'

'I said to establish a list of possible targets. I didn't say to pop the kid!'

'I thought you were talking code because of the phone!'

'He's a fucking film student, Manny. What's he gonna do, make a movie about us?!'

Manny looked down at his feet, shook his head in frustration; he had the same look I'd seen on Hardy's face a hundred times before. But Riccardo needed Manny and wouldn't keep him on a hook for too long. He explained, 'Look, this is an unusual situation; things are bound to get a little strange, granted. But until we get more of our guys out here, we all gotta be on the same page. We can't make these kinds of mistakes anymore.'

Lawrence Talbot coughed, 'When are the others coming out?'

'Six tonight, six more tomorrow. I'll have thirty guys out here by next week.'

Manny asked, 'Why the delay? Why not just bring everybody out at once?'

'If all of a sudden a crew of guys come out from Newark,

that could raise a few eyebrows, no?'

'And what's to stop the Russians from hitting us now, while we're not up to force?'

Riccardo grinned. 'The fact of the matter is, thanks to Tony, the Russians are scared to death of us. They think we're crazy!'

Chuckles floated around the room like dirty water bubbles.

But Lawrence Talbot, all business, asked, 'What happens now?'

'We have a meeting with Victor Rudiyov and Hans Kopp on Friday, to settle on terms.'

Hardy nearly screamed; he couldn't help himself. 'Terms!? With fuckin' communists!?'

Manny added, 'He's right. We can't trust them.'

'Trust?' Riccardo raised his eyebrows in amusement, as if the word itself tickled him. 'Gentlemen, have we ever conducted business on the basis of trust?'

No one answered, there was no need to.

'The Cold War is over. We're gonna sit down and form a partnership. Soon, in good time, that partnership will become restrictive, and distasteful, as all partnerships are wont to become. And like all partnerships, it will eventually end. Then we'll show them what capitalism is really about. The American way!'

Manny and Hardy chortled – imagine pigs laughing.

Riccardo warned, 'But for now, we're a peace-loving organization. Let's put the big bear to sleep. Is that clear?'

Manny spoke first, 'Clear.' Riccardo turned next to Hardy.

'Yeah, sure. I got it.'

Riccardo turned to me, 'Can I count on your intuition? Once again?'

I raised a 'V' with my fingers and said, 'Peace.'

Riccardo Montefiore smiled like he'd eaten a big steak. 'Tell me something,' he said, 'what made you drive him to the hospital?'

'He had a Porsche 911. I'd never driven a 911 before.'

As Riccardo Montefiore and the others laughed darkly, I wondered how many more bullets I could dodge; the odds were shifting way against me.

I slipped out of Yossario's and rode the elevator down to the ground floor. Standing in the lobby, guarding the front entrance of the building, was Premig, as well as two young guards from the Franchise, new talent, faces I'd seen once or twice before but didn't know personally. By the look of recognition and respect on their faces they clearly knew who I was. Premig gave me a nod and I noticed something sticking out from his left sleeve, it was bright pink and unnaturally large and looked like a rubber toy bought at a novelty shop, much more conspicuous than keeping his stump in his pocket, but Manny Simone wanted a fake hand and now Premig had one.

Walking around the corner I took out the map and tried to find my destination. The nearest subway station was a few blocks away and I started for it, passing cafés and pubs with wooden benches out front and seeing everyone wearing old jeans and tee shirts it occurred to me how much they dressed like downtown New York City denizens. I took off my tie and shoved it in my pocket; realized I'd better dress a little less criminally. The subway lines went by color and I found the long purple line that would take me where I had been the night before. In the station I pressed some buttons on the ticket machine and a green light popped on. I slipped a ten Mark bill in the slot and got a printed ticket and some coins back. The train came in and I got on.

Though it hadn't helped me the night before, I used the

TV tower at *Alexanderplatz* as an anchor to keep my direction. I passed the green-domed church as a streetcar came by. When it stopped I hopped on and rode for a while, checking the map and trying to find the stops along the way. Forty minutes later I was on the block where the hospital sat. Looking up at the lighted windows I wondered if she was in there somewhere. Would she recognize me? Or remember my voice? Had she checked in on Ulf and realized how close she might have come to getting herself killed?

I ditched my jacket and unbuttoned my shirt halfway, pulled it out of my pants and pushed on the heavy wooden door. Inside was a plate window to the right. Behind it sat a middle-aged woman with honey-colored hair tied up in a beehive. She wore a gray security guard's uniform and her eyebrows were drawn on with pencil; the left one had smeared. I asked if she spoke English and she answered back in German. I didn't know what else to say. I really had no set plan of action and the foolishness of the whole thing became suddenly apparent as I stood there looking suspicious. She called to a co-worker, another woman, younger by about twenty years, who also wore a gray uniform but without the beehive hairdo.

'Do you speak English?'

'A little.'

'I'm, uh, looking for a friend who works here. She's got red hair and wears glasses. Do you know if she's working now?'

'*Was*? What is *ihr Name*?'

'Her what?'

'*Ihr Name* . . . name?'

'Oh, I don't know.' The two women looked at each other.

'But she's tall, and slender, with long red hair. She wears glasses and likes movies; I'm sure she works here. I was in the neighborhood and wanted to say hello.'

'Red hair,' the older woman said as if counting numbers on the top of her forehead. The younger woman turned to her and they started arguing in blunt, foreign counterpoint, until the young one turned to me and said, '*Jibt's hier nich*'!' followed by a bunch of other things I took to mean get the hell out of here.

It was a foolish thing to do; you never went back to the scene, not so soon afterwards, for a number of reasons that any high-school dropout could guess. But there I was an hour later sitting in the lobby looking out-of-place and guilty. What did I expect? That she would come and see the same movie the next night? Fortunately, the guy behind the counter was new, as was the ticket taker.

I walked for an hour down dark deserted streets with a hunger for something I couldn't quite describe. I ached and I didn't know why.

The bar was dark and packed with young people, my contemporaries, but looking at their carefree smiles and shining eyes, hearing laughter that wasn't bought with someone else's misery or pain, I felt old. Out of place. The room was an 'L' shape. To the right two women played a game of pool with balls I'd never seen before, solid colors without any numbers. To the left were occupied tables and a platform at the rear. Old rusty pipes ran along the ceiling and dead fish hung on plaques on the walls; from the juke-box Nick Drake crooned a song of flowing despair. I went to the bar and asked for a Crown Royal with ice. When the bartender leaned forward in confusion I simply said, 'Beer.' He went to the tap.

By my third beer I heard something that caught my attention. English. More than English, it was American English! I recognized the east-coast accents, proper, well-schooled; they could have been from Connecticut. Two couples, mid-thirties, very well dressed, lawyer types and their wives, completely out of place here, yet talking and laughing about a mutual friend who had a comical time on her last vacation to Spain. There was something inside me that wanted to talk to them.

'American?' he asked.

The look of anticipation in his face spooked me for a second. 'Who are you?' I said, targeting the vital spots.

He chuckled and spoke confidently, 'I saw you looking at those people, the same way I was looking at them. When you hear it, it kind of . . . snaps you back.'

'Yeah, I guess it does.'

'My name's Jonathan.'

'Tony.' The first rule broken.

He was in his late twenties and had longish hair and large, dull features, wore corduroy jeans and a wrinkled shirt; his accent was similar to mine, but there was something strangely foreign about it also.

He introduced me to his friends Wolfgang and Zep who hadn't said a word, but by their wire-rim glasses, hand-rolled cigarettes and frizzy *Eraserhead* haircuts I knew they were German. I called over the bartender and bought a round of beers, gesturing with my hands until he got it. I slipped him a fifty Mark bill and told him to keep it; once he understood he looked like he might kiss me. Wolfgang and Zep took their beers and thanked me in English. Jonathan raised his glass and said, '*Prost*!', then we all drank.

'So . . . where you from?'

'New Jersey.'

'I'm from Pennsylvania.'

'Yeah? Where about?'

'A little place you never heard of.'

'Try me.'

'Wilkes-Barre.'

'Sure, Wilkes-Barre, four hours from Newark,' I said.

'That's right,' he said surprised.

'They cut their pizza in thin square cuts instead of slices. Very strange.'

'I can't believe it. You were really there! Shit, what were you doing in Wilkes-Barre?'

Three years ago I drove up with Hardy to collect on an overdue debt from a contractor who'd won a carting bid through the Franchise and then refused to pay the kick-back. Hardy cut off the tip of his left index finger and with a gun to his head made him eat it. The guy nearly choked to death before swallowing it, then he paid us the tribute and we drove home.

'Just passing through,' I said.

'What's your name again?'

'Tony.'

'Hey, there's a free table; you wanna sit down?' He turned to his friends who downed their beers in long gulps. Then Zep, or was it Wolfgang, shook my hand and said, 'We go now. Thank you for the beer.'

Jonathan grabbed up a cardboard shoebox sitting on the bar and we went to a table on the platform in the back of the room. He slid the shoebox on the chair beside him.

'What brings you to Berlin?'

I told him I was working with a construction firm, sort of a union exchange program between Germany and America. He bought it, then told me he'd been here for eleven years.

'Eleven years?!'

'I came out for a woman,' he grinned and his chipped front tooth created a small black triangle with the back of his throat.

'I was just about to start college, Penn State, you know?

135

Figured I'd take one last trip overseas before buckling down, two weeks in London. When I got there I met this older German woman – she was 42, I was 19 – and we fell in love. I moved here with her and that was that. Never left.'

'Shit. That beats anything I could tell you.'

Two punked-out chicks with short hair and dirty ripped jeans came up to the table. One was tall and pretty, the other a little overweight and wearing really thick glasses; both had studs in their noses. The blind one spoke to Jonathan in German and he opened the box and took out two round disks wrapped in tin foil. She took out two five-Mark coins. An exchange was made, then she and her pal disappeared into the crowd.

'What's in there?'

'Hashish. Here, try one.' He slid a disk across the table and I reached into my pocket for five Marks.

'No. On the house,' he said.

I unwrapped it and it was a chocolate chip cookie with bits of walnut on top. He unwrapped one for himself and took a chomp out of it. We sat there without talking, chomping on our cookies, checking out the room. The chatter of voices was a presence, as was the smoke hovering under the ceiling.

'Did you speak German when you came here?'

'Not a word. Me and Ilka spoke English for the first two years, then I realized, "I'm living here, I gotta learn the language." So she started speaking to me in German. After a couple years I could speak it back. By the time we split up I was completely fluent.'

A waitress walked past and he called her over and ordered two more beers and said something in German that made her smile.

'Where you staying?' he asked me. 'What part of the city?'

'*Kreuzberg.*'

'How do you like it?'

'I don't know. It's not what I expected. I thought there'd be more Germans.'

He laughed and the pure amusement he got from it made me grin. 'You must be staying in 36,' he said. 'The old *Kreuzberg.*'

A short fat guy wearing a black leather vest and smelling of vinegar came up to the table and Jonathan reached into the box and sold him a cookie. This went on until there weren't any cookies left. He asked me what's going on in the States these days. 'I don't keep up with the news back home.'

I told him as much as I knew, about the President and sports and different changes in New York City like Times Square shutting down and getting cleaned up and about certain famous murderers like the guy who cut off his girl-friend's head and boiled it in a pot of water on the Lower East Side. He liked that story, as did I.

Something grabbed his attention. Tall, blonde, voluptuous, but not really my type. 'Damn, if her dress was any shorter it'd be a belt,' he said.

'She seems to be alone. Why don't you go for it?'

'I wish I could. I been seeing this girl for about a year; it's kind of serious. I can't cheat on her.'

He watched the tall blonde strut across the floor and disappear into the side room. 'Lately my girlfriend's been talking about living together. I don't know. That's a big step. I'm not sure.'

'Do you love this girl?'

He answered without hesitation, 'Yes.'

'Then you're completely fucked.'

He laughed and told me I was fucking crazy.

I began to feel tingles in my arms and legs, my stomach

unwound and my head got light. The hash crept up on me like attacking red ants.

A clear tube poured saline solution into her arm and her skin hadn't yet lost its jaundice pallor. She sat up in bed and checked the door. We were alone.

'You got anything?'

'I copped some hash at school.'

'Light it up.'

'Carrie, we're in a fucking hospital. You get caught and they'll have you arrested.'

'Open the window. We'll blow the smoke out. I'm gonna go crazy without something.'

'Aren't they giving you anything for pain?'

'Nothing. I been complaining since I got here. All they give me is Tylenol – without codeine!'

'Well, they had to pump your stomach. If they didn't do that you might not have lived.'

'Oh please. Everyone overreacted. I was drunk. We were drinking Tequila. Every time the pills came around I took a couple. They were only diet pills. That's all. I simply lost count of how many I'd taken. If I really wanted to kill myself I would have, believe me. Besides I don't want to kill myself, I got plenty of reasons to live. One of them is that hash in your pocket. Come on, light it up.'

I took out my pipe and broke the hash into flaky bits and filled the bowl, opened the window. Carrie slid out of bed and stood by the window. She pulled on the tube connecting her arm to the clear bottle hanging from a stand. Handing her the pipe I lit the bowl as she toked on the stem.

'When is Andy coming?'

'I don't know.'

'Hasn't he called for me at the house?'

'No.'

'I left him two messages; you sure he didn't call?'

'Not when I've been there. No messages on the machine.'

Carrie took another long pull on the pipe, blew the spicy ghost into the springtime air.

'Where's Mom?'

'She's home with the lunatic.'

'Does he know I'm here?'

'Mom told him last night.'

'What did he say about it?'

'He called it Satan's work then slept for fifteen hours.'

'I wish I could sleep for fifteen hours.'

'You almost got your wish!'

'Did you come here to lecture me?'

'No. But I was wondering something.'

'What?'

'Did you see a white light or anything? When you were out? I've heard that you're supposed to see a white light.'

'I didn't see anything. Just darkness. I could hear the ambulance guys talking on the way to the hospital. That was it.'

'What were they saying?'

'They were talking about anal sex. One of them wanted to pork his girlfriend up the butt, but she wouldn't let him. You sure Andy didn't call?'

'Positive. Is there anything else you can tell me?'

'Why this sudden fascination with my death?'

'I wouldn't call it a fascination.'

'Are you absolutely sure Andy knows I'm here?'

'Look Carrie, forget Andy. You got other things to worry about. The cops are gonna be back. They wanna know where you got the pills.'

Her face went blank like a zombie's, frozen, vacant. 'I can't remember a thing, officer. It's all a gray fog.'

'Good. Amnesia's the way to go. Go ahead, finish that.'

139

I refilled the bowl and we spent the rest of the afternoon smoking hash and watching soap operas on TV.

Four hours later the bar was empty and two waiters were standing chairs up on the tables. Jonathan and I were the last ones to leave. I paid for the dozen beers we drank and the food we ate, one-hundred and thirty Marks including tip, refusing Jonathan's offer to pay half, then we headed for the street. Jonathan went to a bicycle locked to a pole; I asked him for the nearest subway station.

'There aren't any trains up this far. You gotta take a night bus, or else a taxi.'

'I took a streetcar to get here.'

'Trams stop running around twelve-thirty.'

'How do people get around late at night?'

Jonathan pulled his bike loose from the pole and bounced it a few times on its wheels, came up beside me and flagged down a passing cab.

'Let me give you some money for the taxi.'

'Don't even try it.'

'Hey, you didn't give me your number.'

'Next time.'

'But how am I gonna let you know about . . .'

I hopped in the back seat and told the driver *'Mariannenplatz'* and he pulled away. It was nearly five o'clock in the morning and the streets were alive with people and restaurants and bars still open, plate-glass windows revealed couples at candlelit tables sipping coffee and laughing. I tried to imagine what my life would have been like if I had just picked up and moved away eleven years ago, like Jonathan had done. Left everything behind and started anew. No looking back. It made me angry to think about it, because I never had the courage to do something like that, to take that kind of chance. I took the easy way out and now it was too late to do anything about it.

Certain acts, certain things you do in your life mark you, scar who and what you are, what you could ever hope to become, and I was one hell of a marked scar. It seemed that the gut instinct that kept me alive in the Franchise, what Riccardo Montefiore called my 'intuition', had failed me grossly in the franchise of my life. It was a betrayal that haunted me now, because I cheated myself out of something, and there was no way to get it back.

My legs began to tremble, slight quivers in the tendons like pins and needles from sitting in an uncomfortable position for too long. I wasn't sure I could walk if I had to, and any second the door would open and I'd be asked to do so. I practiced in my mind what I would say, the way I would say it, but the best thing was to not be too prepared, they'd see through that. For two years I'd been delivering stolen liquor and restaurant supplies to private clubs around the city, never with incident, and no one ever complained; in fact, everyone seemed to like me. I was never late and I worked like a machine, usually the van was unloaded and the crates stacked before anyone else could lift a finger to help. I had no ambitions other than paying my rent as I had finally moved out of the house, leaving my mother and the lunatic to fend for themselves. Minus any kind of real schooling and with severely limited resources I naturally jumped at the opportunity to drive a van for six hundred dollars a week with no questions asked. I was not completely unaware of who I worked for, a colorful group of men with endearing names like Jerry the Fixer and Bottle Rocket Al and Meat Hook Maglio, but I was so far down the totem pole of importance I never dreamed I would, or could, be in any peril. Until Gary Hudson came into my life.

Gary had gotten it in his head that he didn't like me. Maybe it was something in my face or a look he imagined in

141

my eyes, maybe it was the way my lungs inflated with air when I breathed, but no matter what it was, nothing could remove that festering scab from his mind. I would see Gary once a week on my delivery of merchandise to a cheap strip joint called the Dream Room, a nightmare owned by crew chief Bobby the Shark. Bobby the Shark made loans to union workers and gamblers out of the back office while Gary Hudson was newly demoted to run the nightclub operations. Gary started in on me his first day on the job when he told me I shortchanged him two cases of vodka, demanded I cough up the missing cases, then threatened to kick my ass after I showed him the invoice and counted the boxes, which all added up properly. Gary threw the invoice to the floor and dared me to take a step toward him. I turned around and left without further incident.

The door opened and a neckless brute in a loose-fitting blue silk running suit ordered me inside. A group of men sat behind a long table; I was to learn later those men were Riccardo Montefiore and Lawrence Talbot and Manny Simone and Dom Calabrato and Tommy York – Hardy's uncle – and two ancient men sitting at the end of the table whose names to this day remain unknown to me. Riccardo asked me to sit in the single metal folding chair placed ten feet in front of the table. I don't recall who spoke next but I was told the council had been convened to pass judgment on the unfortunate incident of two days before. Riccardo Montefiore leaned forward and asked me to recap what happened, exactly as I remembered it.

When I finished no one spoke. A full minute of silence had passed and I wanted to fill it with a plea for understanding but knew enough to keep my mouth shut.

Manny Simone was the first one to speak up. 'Why didn't you stop once he stopped moving? He was no longer a threat.'

'I thought it was a trick.'

'His legs were shattered in ten places.'

'I'm not a doctor.'

Riccardo let out a silent chuckle but Manny took offense.

'You being a fucking wise guy with me?'

'No, sir. Absolutely not.'

He sat back and folded his arms.

Lawrence Talbot asked me to wait outside and the big brute in the blue running suit escorted me to the waiting room. He seemed less threatening now as he stood in the doorway. I sat on the chair while the council decided my fate.

Gary Hudson was screaming into the phone as I stacked the crates against the wall. I had never heard anyone assault the mouthpiece of a telephone so ferociously before. I decided against presenting him with the invoice, which he usually sliced in half with his violent scrawl, and went outside to the van. Gary came after me like a wild boar, accusing me of disrespecting him behind his back. I opened the van door but he grabbed my arm and spun me around. Before I could do anything he creamed me in the stomach and kneed me in the face. He began pounding on my back in a tornado of rage; I thought he might crack my spine. He threw me up against the van with enough force to dent the side, then grabbed me around the neck and dug his nails into my skin. His face was a crush of oily wrinkles and his breath smelled of fish. I shoved my thumbs into his eyes and pushed him off and he fell back clutching his brow; I hopped in the van and tried to start the engine. The passenger window exploded and a hail of glass cubes struck me in the face, the windshield coughed in a blue-green web. Gary went around the van smashing every window with a baseball bat. The engine whined but wouldn't kick over. Then something caught my eye in the rear-view mirror, a flash of light that kicked the air out of my lungs. The van was filled with crates of firecrackers and Roman Candles and Flaming Fountains and Cherry Bombs and Aerial Bombs and M-80s and Ash-cans and every kind of rocket you can imagine, all for the Fourth of July weekend next week, and as Gary struck another match the engine kicked over. I could have just screeched away, I was facing the driveway exit, all I had to do was floor the gas and I was free; instead I slammed the van into reverse and sent Gary tumbling back into a row of tall metal trash cans. He gasped as his legs were crushed by the bumper of the van, then he started screaming and flailing his arms against the back doors making a terrible racket, until I got out and told him to shut the fuck up. Stuck there like a mouse in a trap he threatened to kill me, to make it slow and painful, to go after my family; I knew he meant every word of it. He tried to lift himself free but couldn't budge; the cans had bent an arc around his torso, a ring of red colored his shirt where the cracked metal rims bit into his flesh. Gary began to slobber, his eyes blazed with perplexity, embarrassment; it was a look I'd seen before, the helpless, destructive face of insanity. The baseball bat, as if on cue, rolled from underneath the van and stopped against my foot. In the circular grain in the wood, the burned-in black logo, stated simply, eloquently, 'Louisville Slugger, Hank Aaron Model' – I remembered my father tossing Eileen Pine's kittens to me one at a time and ordering me to swing for the bleachers. Gary stopped moving after the fourth bash but by then I had lost my soul; I didn't stop until his face was a mass of jelly. Once it all sank in, what had taken place and what I'd done, I threw up on my shirt.

I didn't know what to do or how to do it. I had taken out a made member of the Franchise, without permission; nobody had ever done that before. And lived. I thought of ditching the body somewhere, dumping it in the bay or burning it in a field, like I'd seen countless gangsters do in the movies. Instead I went inside and called my boss, Marty Oppenheimer, who told me to bring the body inside and wait for him to get there.

The door opened and Manny Simone stepped out. He sent the big brute inside and stood before me. His face revealed nothing. I was covered in sweat, wondering how they would do it. Would they bring me out back and put a bullet in my head? Or beat me with a bat like I had done to Gary. Manny asked if I had any regrets about killing Gary Hudson and the sound of that name dropped like a dead cat in my lap. I said none whatsoever. He grinned, told me after careful consideration the council had decided that everyone has a right to defend himself. Then he said he wanted to talk to me about something. I got up and followed him into his office down the hall. I was to learn a year later that Riccardo Montefiore told Manny to take me under his wing; anyone who could pin somebody to a wall with a van and then beat them to death with a baseball bat, was someone he wanted close by.

It was nearly sunrise when I entered the apartment. A woman was crying in Hardy's bedroom. I tapped on the door and Hardy appeared in the crack. His eyes darted beyond me. 'You alone?' he asked, hopping back and forth on the balls of his feet, his face pale and covered in sweat.

'Yeah. Everything all right in there?'

'I'm with a friend.'

'She's crying.'

'I know.'

'What are you doing to her?'

'Nothin'! She's upset over somethin'.'

'Over what?'

'It's personal! Just go to bed; I got things under control.

145

Don't worry, she'll be quiet.' He slammed the door and whispered harshly behind it.

The bathroom sink was stained with red syrup and a small fleshy mass sat in the drain. A female nipple. I threw up, turned off the light and went to bed.

11

Whenen I got up the bathroom had been cleaned and
the apartment was empty. Hardy's room had
been made up, the bed was snugly covered with
a thick blue spread and all his clothes were neatly hung,
shoes lined in a perfect row under the dresser; the room
showed no trace of whatever dark revelry took place the
night before. I went into the kitchen and ate a bowl of corn-
flakes. Hardy came in carrying a dirt-encrusted shovel with
his shoelaces flopping around his feet. He stood the shovel
against the wall and leaned against the counter with a sour
sheepish grin. I got up and told him to hurry or we'd be late
to the office.

When we arrived there was a crowd around the main
foundation. All the workers had congregated where Manny
stood with Tito and Ernie and seven other Franchise
enforcers, along with Heinrich, Yossario and Vita. They
were arguing back and forth and Yossario tried to speak but
was yelled down by a short bulldog of a man with a curly
beard and tarnished gold skin. Manny grabbed Heinrich by
the shirt and pulled him close to his side.

'Explain to this guy that we're saving his fucking job, that
the only way this thing works is if we all pull together and
make some sacrifices.'

Heinrich tried to speak but the bulldog guy screamed in
his face and Yossario tried to intervene and soon all the
workers were grumbling amongst themselves. Manny held
his hands up for a silence that never came and as the anger
flared in his face it became ominously clear to me: The system here was all wrong. There were no union delegates to
keep the workers in line and no friendly politicians to bend
the laws, no cops to look the other way, no long-time rela-

147

tionships to call upon for favors and as the Franchise had
no history or reputation here, nobody feared it. Watching
the bulldog guy argue himself into an early grave I saw that
these workers weren't at all like the workers back home
who were routinely overpaid so that even after skimming
from their paychecks they still had plenty left over. These
men had a hunger and a desperation in their eyes and I
knew that anything we took from their pockets meant less
food and more hardship on the table. I was hoping Manny
wouldn't assign me the bulldog guy because I didn't think
I could carry it out and then I hoped he wouldn't assign it
to Hardy because I knew that he could.

I ate lunch in the trailer with Lawrence Talbot and Manny
Simone and Riccardo Montefiore was nowhere to be seen
and nobody said a word about it so I didn't ask. The office
phone rang and we sat there eating our lunch; no one made
a move to answer it. Seventeen excruciating rings later it
stopped. At five o'clock Hardy drove me to the park and
said he had something to do and let me out by the fountain.
I walked to the apartment as he sped off.

I picked up the phone on the fourth ring.

'Hello Tony?' The familiarity in the greeting jarred me for
a second and I didn't answer.

'Hello? . . .' he repeated, then said something in German.

'How did you get this number?'

I waited in the alley across the street, the smell of burning
charcoal hung heavy in the air and my clothes were still
wet from the violent downpour ten minutes earlier. A tall
thin figure stepped out of the huge wooden door and the
streetlight bounced a reflection off her glasses. But I was too
far away to be sure. She went to a bike and unchained it
from a pole, then went around the building into darkness.

'How the hell did you get this number?' I snapped, angry
and puzzled. I'd opened up to him way too much, like a

fool, and now it had come back to kick me in the balls.

'A friend of mine works for *Deutsche Telecom*. I got him to track your number through your address.'

'But I didn't tell you my address.'

'You told the taxi driver last night '*Mariannenplatz*,' this is the only number activated in *Mariannenplatz* in the past week. Hey, I hope that was okay.'

'You shouldn't have done that,' I said, as the various ways to pop Jonathan played out in my mind.

He said, 'I got some info on that girl you were asking about. From the hospital.'

I took off toward the side of the building, darting between parked cars and trying to be quiet on my feet. As I reached a block of shadow where the sidewalk met the alleyway I smashed into something and tumbled to the ground. She landed on her back with her bike bouncing on the pavement and a groan pushed out of her lungs. She didn't move for a moment, then she sat up slowly and felt the ground for her glasses. I saw them under the bike's front tire and got them.

'I'm sorry, are you okay?'

She scolded me in German, slipped her glasses over her ears and blinked her eyes twice.

'Are you hurt?'

She looked at her hands, patted her legs, and said with hesitation, '*Nein*.'

I picked up her bicycle and she got up, brushing the dirt off her jeans; her eyes were hidden by glass and shadow.

'It's really dark over here. They should put some lights up.'

'*Spricht's du kein Deutsch*?'

'I don't know what that is.'

She gave me a crooked pained expression and said, 'You are . . . *Amerikaner*?'

149

'Yes, but a sorry one.'

'I speak not good English.'

'You speak good enough.'

'I go now,' she said dryly, then started toward the street with her bike. As she swung her leg over the seat I ran up beside her, told her I was lost, and that I needed help.

'Do you feel it moving?'

She waddled over and sat on the couch, placed her legs up under her. I laid my head on her belly and she stroked my hair. Her skin smelled of sweet berry-scented powder; underneath her swollen breast I felt the soft, thumping of a heart. Becky sat back and moaned as I took her nipple in my mouth, pulled on it with my teeth.

'Go easy, they're very sore.'

'Sorry.'

I pushed her down and began dry-humping her, took her nipple again in my mouth and it stiffened and started dripping warm bitter milk.

Becky sat back annoyed as I went to answer the phone.

'I have to take it; I'm on call.'

While she propped a pillow up behind her back Manny Simone told me that Becky's brother had gotten busted again and I had to bail him out and bring him in. I asked Manny if Barry was in any trouble over this and Manny assured me he wasn't, which was true, because Barry would live for another four years.

Walking through the door I followed Monica to the same table I'd sat with Jonathan the night before. She took long strides across the wood-plank floor on legs that were slender and tall. She wore black leather shoes and her jeans were loose fitting, faded; her hair roared down her back in a riot of crimson confusion. She sat with her back against the wall and turned to me, her look was stubborn, almost hostile. We didn't speak for a minute; it was an uncomfortable minute. A waitress came to the table and Monica ordered a glass of red wine and I asked for a beer.

Monica glanced around the room. Two guys talked loudly at the pool table, the bar was half empty and the bartender rolled a cigarette on top of it, a pair of dirty brown shoes sat alone on a chair in the corner. Monica gazed at something through the window, her forehead creased and she phased out for a moment. I noticed tiny freckles on her cheeks, wondered if she could hear my stomach rumbling because of them. I didn't know what to say to her, afraid to say or do the wrong thing; it had been so long since I'd been with anyone who hadn't killed somebody.

'So . . . my first trip to Europe, pretty cool so far.'

She smiled uncomfortably and sipped her wine. Didn't say a word. I began to wonder if she had any intention of speaking back. She shifted on the hard wooden chair and met my eyes, held them firm.

'Is something wrong? You're staring at me.'

'You are different . . . from what I expect.' Her voice had that same rip in it from the night at the club.

'What were you expecting?'

'In the school . . . I learn Americans are fat and lazy, and want to rule the world.'

'You learn that in the school, do you?'

'Yes.'

'Well . . . I'm not fat and lazy.'

There might have been a hint of a smile, but I couldn't be sure. I asked a direct question.

'*Ja*. But not in half . . .' she lifted her finger and drew a squiggly line in the air. '*So das . . .*'

'So, it curved around, it wasn't a straight line.'

'*Richtig*. Curved.'

'Did you ever try to climb over?'

'No. It was not safe to do that.'

151

'What was it like? To live like that?'

'Like *was*?'

'Under communism.'

'It was good.'

She glanced toward the kitchen behind the bar, keeping track of where everything was, like a cat. Like me.

'So . . . what were you doing in the hospital tonight? Visiting a friend?'

'I work.'

'Are you a doctor?'

She grinned shyly and showed a gap between her front teeth.

'*Noch nicht*,' she said. 'Perhaps, one day. I study in *die Universität*.'

'I see. So you wanna become a doctor?'

'*Genau*.'

'When would this happen?'

'Two years, when I pass test.'

'You're pretty young to be a doctor.'

'*Wie bitte*?'

'What?'

'*Was*?'

'I said you are young, to be a doctor. Young . . .'

'*Ach so, verstehe*.'

'That's a cool thing to be. You'll make lots of money.'

'Here is not the USA. Doctors in *Deutschland* make not much money.'

'Really? Then why do it?'

She grinned, the question genuinely amused her. 'To help people.'

'Oh. Yeah. I guess that's a good reason. It's good to help people. Most people sure do need help; they're fucked up enough. I don't really like people.'

She found that amusing too, but I couldn't tell if it

was in a good way or not. I asked her if she had any family.

'I have a brother.'

'What does he do?'

'He is a music player.'

'What does he play?'

'Music.'

'I see.'

'And *du*? What makes you here?'

'I work in construction.'

'*Ach so.*' Something sparked in her eyes and it shot me back to the other night at the movie theater. I sipped my beer and checked out the couple sitting at the table to our right; two old dykes holding hands and pining into each other's eyes over the votive candle between them. When I looked back she was eyeing me strangely.

'You're staring again.'

'You remember me of someone.'

'Who?'

'A friend. When you laugh.'

'But I wasn't laughing.'

She chuckled warmly and her eyes caught the candlelight. Two hours later we left the *Kneipe* and she walked me to the tram stop, which was just down the street. I took her hand and thanked her for a wonderful evening. Her cheeks were flush and her eyes glassy from five glasses of cheap Cabernet, then I leaned in and kissed her softly on the lips. She watched me from the platform until the tram took me out of her sight.

12

Marzahn. Deep in the former East Berlin. We drove out in an armed caravan of four BMWs with Yossario's Turks planted along the route just in case. The buildings here looked like towers made of Lego blocks, tall white structures all identical in design with the only difference being a red, blue or yellow stripe on the top of each one. Vita told me the GDR wanted the whole city to look this way.

Old ladies wore gray cloth coats and carried canvas bags of fruit and vegetables. Street kids with shaved heads roamed in packs; they wore ripped leather jackets and military boots and several had pit bulls tugging on thick leather leashes. Hardy gave me a nudge and nodded out the window, asked over the front seat, 'What's this place called?'

Vita answered, '*Tierpark*.'

I leafed through my pocket dictionary. 'Animal park.' Hardy looked at me with question marks.

'I wanna know what people are saying,' I said.

'Shit! What the fuck is that?!'

Huge brown bears climbed on large boulders on the left side of the road. Vita turned around and told us, 'It is zoo. In the East. *Tierpark* is zoo.'

'Fuck me with an umbrella!' Hardy added for color.

We rode in the second car past an island of bears separated from us by only a deep moat. Exotic long-legged birds roamed wild through tall grass while across the way two baby elephants disappeared around a hill, hyenas screeched from trees and a herd of long-horned goats trotted off as we approached. There were no bars or cages anywhere; every species had its own island surrounded by a moat. We stopped at a wide white building, built like the tall Lego apartment buildings except this one lay on its side, next to the monkey house. Vita told me it was an office in former times for the *Stasi*. He said the *Stasi* were the secret police who turned children against their parents and tortured people to get information out of them and Hardy spit on the ground in disgust. I told Premig to be alert and he shot me a glare that told me he knew that already. Robert Herrencamp and Miles Benowitz stood beside the third car gaping in astonishment at a crocodile moving through the brush. Known affectionately as 'the Killer Cousins' by virtue of their mothers being sisters and the lingering notoriety of a rather impressive killing spree they'd committed single-handedly three years ago, I knew they could be counted on when needed, in spite of the fact that at this moment they looked like Boy Scouts on their first trip away from home, which wasn't so far from the truth, I guessed. I straightened Miles's tie and told him he was now representing his country and that he had to look good.

Robert Herrencamp snickered, 'What are you, his father?'

I answered, 'It's possible.' The cousins laughed out loud but it was a nervous laugh, too loud for the situation. Riccardo Montefiore threw me a glance, then tugged on his sleeve.

'Okay, let's book.'

We entered a red brick building with a rounded front; it brought us into a house of white tile walls and cages with various tigers inside them. Brown tigers and gray tigers and tigers that looked like shaved dogs and in the biggest cage was the traditional orange tiger with stripes, all of them eating limbs of meat; the orange one looked like it was chomping on a human leg. We entered a corridor of green-painted cinder block that curved sharply to the right, rust-colored water stains dripped down from the ceiling like tears of blood. I walked beside Hardy, first position in front of Riccardo Montefiore and Manny Simone; Robert Herrencamp and Miles Benowitz took up the rear. Lawrence Talbot stayed back at his apartment with Tito and Ernie as Riccardo always kept him out of the less numerical parts of Franchise business.

Around the bend we came to a pair of swinging metal doors, the kind you see in cafeterias, and stopped; if betrayal was on the menu, this was where it would be served. No one said a word, but the air around us buzzed like a low-grade electrical current. Hardy shifted his weight lightly on the balls of his feet, a subtler version of 'The Hardy Shuffle'; the Killer Cousins were grim-faced, serious, they looked fifteen years older than they did two minutes ago; and Manny, cool as sea air, gave me a nod to proceed.

We barged through the doors and stopped in our tracks. The room was immense, made totally of cement, and empty. Except for two old men sitting at a long table talking. I checked for hidden doors or hinges on the walls, all made of cinder block, the ceiling had no breaks in the paint, the floor was solid concrete, there were no windows; there was nothing here, it seemed, other than two old men sitting at a long table talking. I recognized Hans Kopp immediately; he had the same perpetual grin that his son had, but his was cruel, threatening, topped by a battered, misshapen nose. The other guy got up from his chair, a craggy, leather-skinned bastard about sixty years old with milky-blue eyes and bones under his skin where most people had none. Victor Rudiyov bore no resemblance whatever to his daughter and I began to wonder if the young girl was even his. But then, she belonged to someone. To herself. Riccardo and Victor studied each other across the aged wood of the table. Everything here was aged; even the air felt old. Victor nodded to Riccardo and motioned to a chair, and Riccardo and Manny sat across from the two old-timers. I, Hardy and the Killer Cousins stood guard behind Riccardo and Manny, our nerves on ultra-high alert, prepared for the unexpected.

Until Riccardo Montefiore spoke in German!

Hans Kopp looked offended by the surprise. Victor Rudiyov sat back in his chair, grinned harshly and returned some words in German. They talked like this for a minute, politely, conversationally, until Riccardo asked a question that Victor Rudiyov answered with a heavy accented 'Okay.' Then Riccardo Montefiore spoke English again and my stomach untwisted.

Victor Rudiyov and Hans Kopp listened smugly as Riccardo Montefiore went into his standard plea for peace and co-operation and of putting the past behind us and how did it ever get this far out of control and that together we are stronger and think of all the money there is to share if we all play nice.

'Comrades,' he added for emphasis, or mockery, 'we could lose it all if we continue on like this. Surely there's enough for everyone. I know you're no strangers to the concept of sharing the wealth.'

Victor Rudiyov didn't move a pore, nothing. He was like a frozen lake, but Hans Kopp boiled over like burnt milk. 'This is not a *Markt*. You have no place here! You do not belong. Go home! *Ausländer*.'

'Do you want to debate whether we should be here or not, or do you want to try and stop the killing?'

Hans Kopp snarled to Rudiyov, but in English so we'd understand, 'The Americans want again to be an occupying force.'

Manny Simone leaned forward and said, 'The Americans are protecting their own interests. And we're not leaving.'

'So you kill children! Victor's *Tochter* . . .'

'And you kill children too! The Turkish kids!'

Hans Kopp and Manny Simone barked at each other like rabid dogs, each in their own respective language, until Riccardo Montefiore said softly, 'That's enough,' and Manny shut up. Riccardo spoke directly to Hans Kopp in German. His voice was calm, reasonable, beseeching. Hans Kopp answered curtly, then got silent, scanned the faces above Riccardo's head.

'Who is the one drove my son to hospital?' he muttered.

His eyes stopped on me, revealing nothing, then moved on to Hardy and the others. Riccardo Montefiore asked, 'Do you want to look at your ass, or look at your future?'

'Are you making joke of me?'

'No, I'm asking you to look ahead. We've suffered tragedy too. My friend was under attack; members of his family were killed and are missing. I say let's end it. It's not worth losing loved ones over, is it? I want to stop the killing, stop the violence. Let's start anew, establish ground rules so everything runs smoothly. It's the smart thing to do. Like I said ... share the wealth.' Victor Rudiyov chuckled at that, he didn't seem like a guy who chuckled very often. When he spoke his right cheek caved in.

'How do you plan on sharing the *Geld*?'

As Hardy drove home I thought about Riccardo Montefiore speaking German. Considering that his wife grew up in Berlin, it made sense. It was a cool trump card to be holding, he threw them off their game with it. He walked in and took half their city without having lost any guys so far. How he would keep it was another matter entirely, one which concerned Hardy not in the slightest.

'Don't they believe in soap?' he bitched, his breath filling the car with fumes from strong menthol throat lozenges. Manny's car in front of us made a left-hand turn onto the *Oberbaumbrücke* towards *Kreuzberg* and Hardy ran a red light to follow close behind.

'I smelt 'em from across the room,' he continued. 'Like old fish, those fuckin' commies. I almost wish they didn't take the deal, because I wanted to pop 'em right then and there. Imagine, sittin' there alone like that, nobody to protect 'em. Know why they ain't afraid of death, Tony? 'Cause they got no fuckin' souls.'

'Hardy, you don't even know these people.'

'I know 'em better than you think. Don't be fooled by the Old World charm and bullshit, chief. Remember what Riccardo said the other day.'

'He said a lot of things.'

'About the big bear.'

'The big bear?'

'That's right. The big bear. And Riccardo's not the only one. Nostradamus wrote about this shit over a hundred years ago. And nobody fucks with Nostradamus.'

'Nostradamus?'

'The guy who predicted Hitler!'

'I know who Nostradamus is.'

'Then you know what I'm talkin' about.'

But I had no idea, and in a cruelly amused way I was curious to find out. Hardy looked at me before answering.

'Tony, what took place here today, between us and the fuckin' Russians, ain't what you think it's about. I know you think it's about one thing, but it's about something that ain't that.'

'You're losing me.'

'All I'm tryin' to say is . . . it ain't about business, or the Franchise, or other worldly things. It's so much bigger than that, you can't imagine.'

Here, he paused for effect and lowered his voice. I went with it.

'This is the beginning of Armageddon.'

It was better than I thought it'd be.

'Armageddon,' he continued. 'Right fuckin' here! This is it, the whole fuckin' casino, chief! Can't you see it? The Russians are Satan's minions. They're evil and desperate, a pestilence on earth. Their system is crumblin' all over the world, they're bein' chased outta every country they try to take over, they're hurtin' and dyin' off! But the big bear ain't gonna go quietly. He's gonna rise up for one final confrontation. One final battle between Heaven and Hell and this is it! Armageddon. And Tony, check it out; don't just take my word for it. All this shit is written in the fuckin' Bible. In Revolutions.'

I let it pass. Instead I asked him, 'When did you get so religious?'

His voice rose an octave as he said, 'Ain't got nothin' to do with religion, chief. I'm just readin' the signs around me, that's all. Open your eyes, you'll see them too. There's some evil motherfuckin' shit goin' on over here, and I wouldn't be surprised if the fuckin' anti-Christ himself is directly behind it.'

'I think you're taking your work a little too seriously, Hardy.'

'You think I'm fuckin' nuts, don't you?'

'Well . . . Yeah, I do.'

He thought about it, then cracked up. We both had to laugh.

Hardy jammed on the brakes and we stopped short behind Manny's car in front of Riccardo Montefiore's house. After we made sure Riccardo was settled in safe with six seasoned soldiers watching his back, Hardy drove back to our apartment. On the ride he explained to me the secret way he knew to finger-fuck virgins without breaking their hymen. He seemed to know *Kreuzberg* quite well, making sharp turns down mysterious side streets until a cobblestone road led directly into the park and he let me out and drove off by himself. I went inside and picked up the phone. An hour later I dialed Monica's number. Her voice on the machine made me grin; I pictured her pursed lips and creased brow; she seemed to be in a constant state of pondering. I drank a pint of Scotch straight from the bottle and laid in bed with my clothes on.

Becky sat at the table with Clarissa on her lap, rocking her up and down on her knee. When Becky looked up at me I knew this wasn't over yet.

'I'm powerless in this situation,' I pleaded. 'What do you want me to do?'

'I asked you to look out for him! He needs help and all you do is enable him!'

'I've tried to help him; he doesn't listen to me. He does whatever the fuck he wants. How do I stop him?! I'm not his father!'

Clarissa started humming loudly. It was something she did whenever her parents fought, which was always. Becky slid her to the floor and told her to go inside.

I woke up to pounding on the door. I jumped out of bed and grabbed the .32, went to the door. I nearly shot Adam Gottlieb when he rushed into the apartment. He was jumpy and nervous and couldn't stop moving; grabbing my jacket I didn't like what he told me.

Lawrence Talbot's building was about ten minutes away. The sky opened its swollen bruised eye when we pulled up. Manny Simone met me outside the living room. I'd never seen him so spooked before.

'Where the fuck were you tonight?'

'My apartment.'

'I tried calling a dozen times.'

'I turned the phone down. I was sleeping.'

'Where's Hardy?'

'He went out.'

'Where did he go?'

'I don't know.'

'I told you to keep your eye on him.'

'I can't watch him all the time, Manny. He's crazy, you know that. Now what the fuck's going on?'

Manny clenched his jaw and led me inside. I was struck by the color. Lawrence Talbot had simple tastes and hated ostentation, yet all the walls were dark red. I noticed they were still wet and dripping; there were fresh brushstrokes on them. The ceiling too. Pools of blood formed along the floorboards, all the furniture was speckled in crimson. It was the bloodiest thing I'd ever seen in my life. Worse than the sight was the smell, the sickening sour tang seeping into my clothes and hair like cheap cigar smoke. A nauseating glue had formed in my stomach. I began to sweat, the room was warm, nearly body temperature, as if the walls were hot and pulsing with life. Manny stepped into a back hall and I followed with a lump in my throat. He stood outside the bathroom, motioned me to look inside. The first thing I saw was a massacre of red footprints on the white tile floor, and several red rings from where buckets sat underneath the sink. The tub was coated with coagulating plasma and the drain was clogged by a coiled snake of intestines. Near the ceiling were newly drilled hooks and chains to hang the bodies while they were being emptied. Manny snorted over my shoulder.

'They scooped it all into buckets and carried it into the living room, painted the fucking walls.'

'Where are the bodies?' I said.

'They took everything else with them.'

'Nobody heard anything?'

'The building's empty. Except for Lawrence and the twins.'

I played out the details of what took place here, the physicality of the deed. It was one thing to plan a horrific act; it was another thing entirely to carry it out. That's when the scope of it all hit me; that's when I knew we couldn't win. I didn't think we could top them on this one, and I didn't want to try. Manny leaned over and lifted the toilet lid. Swimming at the bottom of the toilet was a small black fish. Manny looked as puzzled as I did. 'These Russian bastards are fucking demented, what can I tell ya?'

Someone came in from outside; I was glad to have something to distract my attention. He took a step in and scanned the room. His face betrayed nothing, but I saw a slight crack in his eyes; he was impressed. He looked to Manny and spoke barely above a whisper.

'Any sign of Lawrence?'

'None. Tito and Ernie are gone too.'

Riccardo glanced at the walls around him, thirteen-feet tall and dripping with thick fresh blood. His eyes told me Lawrence, Tito and Ernie were very close at hand.

Manny mumbled under his breath, 'This was an inside job. How else could they know he was here?'

Riccardo Montefiore steeled himself. 'Is everybody accounted for?'

'Everyone except for Hardy and the slimy kraut.'

'Heinrich,' I said.

'Whatever the fuck!' Manny snapped.

Riccardo asked, 'What do you think?'

'I think we're in deep fucking shit. I got the cousins out with Primo tracking down Hardy.'

'Heinrich has a cousin who runs a whorehouse,' I offered. 'That might be where he is.'

Manny turned to Riccardo as if he hadn't heard me. 'If they turned Hardy over, we're in more than deep fucking shit.'

'Let's not jump to conclusions.'

Riccardo turned to me calmly and asked, 'Where is this whorehouse?'

Hardy sat back as a parade of teenage hookers one by one flashed him their genitalia, some with barely anything to flash at all. He gulped the rest of his Martini, chewed the soggy onion and turned to Heinrich with a yawn.

'This is bullshit.'

'Come with me.'

They went up the main staircase at the front of the house while an auburn-haired babe with pointy breasts knelt before me and rubbed my cock through my pants. A minute later she sat back annoyed as I was more concerned with what was taking place upstairs; so far I hadn't heard any screaming yet. At the top landing was a long candlelit hallway with elaborately carved wooden doors on each side. I listened for voices behind them but there was nothing except the creak of the floorboards under my feet, muffled by the mildewed carpet. A toilet flushed behind the last door and a young Vietnamese girl came out wearing a Bart Simpson tee shirt and nothing else. She had straight black hair and eyes like burnt almonds; life had already carved frown lines around her mouth. She had the slightest hint of breasts and couldn't have been older than ten. Hardy called out from a side room, 'Hey, where the fuck d'you go? Come on back!'

I gently took her arm and pulled her toward the staircase.

'It's okay, I'm not gonna hurt you. Let's find you some clothes and get you outta here. Do you speak English?'

She pulled her arm away, frightened, and I turned to see Heinrich coming toward me carrying a bundle in his arms.

He spoke to the girl in cold, harsh German, as if ordering a disobedient dog; called her La Fontaine, then she quickly scurried into the side room where Hardy scolded her for leaving him alone. The door closed and Heinrich leaned forward, the bundle in his arms was a young child, younger than the one he'd just sent away.

He told me, 'You can have this one if you like. She just turned four, and she's *wery, wery* affectionate.'

No one questioned Hardy's loyalty after he saw Lawrence Talbot's apartment. He punched his own face and tore at his skin, cried in pain and loss from someplace deep in his gut; it was like watching a house burn down. And it was no act. He and Lawrence had an unusual relationship; it was great affection based on great antagonism with a sickly dose of dysfunctionality thrown in, but for them, it seemed to work. Now that Lawrence was gone Hardy lost his safety net and that fact did not go unnoticed by any of us. Adam Gottlieb and Robert Herrencamp blocked the side doors and I covered the front in case Hardy tried to do something stupid. Instead he pulled his gun and dove for a window. I caught him and we tried to wrestle him to the ground but he nearly threw us off until Manny popped him clean in the mouth and he splashed to the floor like ink. Manny stood over him yelling to calm the fuck down as Hardy kicked and bucked like a wild mule. Manny pulled out a bottle of Vicodan and took a bunch in his fist, ordered us to hold him still while he shoved the pills into Hardy's mouth.

'This is gonna calm you down, you crazy fuck! So swallow 'em!'

Manny took a flower vase from a coffee table and dumped the water into Hardy's face but Hardy continued struggling against our arms. I leaned over and spoke quietly into his ear.

'Hardy, listen to me. We have to be cool now, more than ever. We have to be clear-headed, and strong, and we have to stick together. All of us. Armageddon, remember? What good is it to run off like a maniac into their arms? How does that help?'

Riccardo spoke over my shoulder, 'Hardy, listen to Tony. He's talking sense. This will not go unpunished. I promise you that.'

Manny added, cruelly, 'Swallow those fucking pills or I'll shove 'em up the other end! You hear me?!'

Hardy choked, gasped, then with several loud, difficult gulps swallowed the pills; lastly he broke down crying like a baby. Riccardo Montefiore told us that no one else must know what took place here tonight; he threatened severe punishment if anybody broke that pact. He said that if anybody asks, Lawrence and the twins were sent out on a secret job under his direction. Then he looked at the walls and said he had a plan. But for the first time since I'd met him, that didn't reassure me.

A few hours later we were painting over Lawrence Talbot's apartment with dark green paint; there were four of us, me, Adam Gottlieb, and the cousins Robert Herrencamp and Miles Benowitz. Manny took Hardy back to the apartment and put him to bed as he was nearly unconscious five minutes after swallowing the Vicodan. While we worked nobody said a word, the silence felt like something tangible, like the smell of rubbing alcohol, except for the haphazard slaps of wet paint on moist walls; they sounded like what they were. Adam and the cousins splattered paint everywhere; they didn't care where it went so long as it got them out of the apartment sooner. I tried to stay within the floor and ceiling trims. I flushed the intestines down the toilet, along with the fish, then splashed down the entire bathroom with water. When we finished, we nailed shut the windows and I filled the locks with Superglue. Later at the construction site a few soldiers asked me where Tito and Ernie were and I told them they were sent out on a secret job under Riccardo's direction. During the day Riccardo huddled with Manny in the office, plotting how to approach the construction company adjacent to our site, first to infiltrate and form a bond of co-operation, then to take over and swallow the organism whole, thus increasing our territory and our power. Earlier that evening Manny Simone gave me an envelope with instructions inside it.

Premig drove us deep into a part of the city called *Köpenick*. It was further east than *Marzahn* and it looked like Beirut on a downcast day, burned-out buildings and shuttered stores, cobblestone streets with bumps and craters, everything seemed dirty, gray; a mushroom cloud of misery hung overhead. I felt ten pounds heavier just being there. Premig parked around the corner and we got out; me, Hardy, Adam Gottlieb and Miles Benowitz. When Premig began to get out of the car Adam Gottlieb whispered harshly, 'No! You stay here. With the car! You stay!' and Premig looked angry but got back in the car. We stayed close to the buildings, moving from shadow to shadow. At number 23 I felt fear and potency boil up in my gut. Bags of rotting trash were piled high against a brick wall and long rusted pipes lay underneath them. We came around to a green metal door. I hoped there'd be no civilians behind it. Adam Gottlieb knelt by the lock and opened his leather satchel of instruments. He looked up and it gave me a start; Adam was thirty-four but looked sixteen, he could have been an altar boy with his blushing cheeks and young doe eyes and it was always a little unsettling to see him pop somebody or beat them to a bloody pulp. He probed and poked around with the lock until it clicked, then he closed the satchel and stood up, took out his silenced pistol. Hardy stepped up bouncing on the balls of his feet and I noticed he was hiding something under his coat; when I pulled aside the flap two hand grenades were clipped inside.

'What the fuck is this?!' I whispered harshly.

'What the fuck is what?'

'This!' I tugged at one of the grenades.

'It's a fuckin' grenade.'

'I know what it is. What is it doing here?'

'Don't fuckin' start with me, okay?'

'This is not what we were ordered to do!'

'Did you see what they did to Lawrence? No fuckin' way! I'm gonna fuckin' kill 'em. I'm gonna fuckin' send their Goddamn fuckin' black souls to the burnin' pits of Hell.'

'No, you're not. We're doing this like we were told.'

'You're not gonna fuckin' tell me what to do!' Hardy whipped out his silenced .44 and jammed the barrel hard under my chin. I didn't flinch. Not for Hardy.

'Yeah, now what,' I said. 'Go ahead. Do me the fucking favor. Because if you let off a hand grenade, I'd rather be dead than face Riccardo and Manny when we get back.'

A click was heard and Hardy's eyes widened. Miles Benowitz had his .45 to Hardy's ear. Miles spoke in a soft, melodic whisper, the way a spider talks to a fly. 'Hardy, Tony's the chief tonight. So put the fucking gun down. Now.'

Hardy didn't move; no one did. Adam Gottlieb began looking nervously at the buildings behind us, an open patio of windows facing the green door. 'Come on, guys. Let's quit fucking around. Anybody could look outta their window and see us!'

'Make a decision, Hardy,' I said to him dead in the eyes, his silencer dug hard into my skin. Adam Gottlieb stood in Hardy's face and pleaded, 'C'mon, Hardy, let's do it like we were told. We can still do a lot of damage in there. We won't leave until you're satisfied everybody's been fucked up enough.'

Hardy thought about it for all of two seconds, then fear slapped his face.

'What's the matter?'

'I can't give it up.'

'Why not?'

'Tony's gonna pop me!'

'I'm not gonna pop you.'

'Man, you're gonna fuckin' pop me! Nobody pulls a gun on you.'

'Look, I know you're upset about Lawrence. I'll take that into consideration.'

'You're gonna pop me anyway.'

'No, I'm not.'

Adam piped in, 'C'mon, we're gonna get fucked if we don't start moving.'

'Promise me you're not gonna pop me.'

'I promise you I'm not gonna pop you. Now get the fucking gun out of my face.'

Hardy looked at the others, unsure, then conviction flashed in his eyes. 'I can't do it! He's gonna fuckin' pop me!'

'Hardy . . .' Adam pleaded, 'He told you he won't. You guys are friends!'

'He always says that to his friends before he pops 'em'.

Miles Benowitz had heard enough. 'You got five seconds,' was all he said. In the silence Hardy took a hard swallow and blinked twice. His lips moved as he counted quietly to himself. At four he slowly removed his gun from my chin and left behind a stinging red ring of flesh. With my eyes locked to his I took the grenades from his jacket, put them in my own. Then he pulled out his crucifix, gave it a kiss and let it fall to his chest.

'Let's go,' I said, and we crept in like rodents through the back door.

14

I knew immediately it wasn't her, but I wasn't expecting to hear another voice and it threw me a bit.

'Hello, Monica?'

'*Nein, Sie ist nicht da!*'

'Uh, I'm sorry, I don't speak . . .'

'*Ich spreche nicht English!*' Click.

Shit. Who the fuck was that? Fucking rude bitch. At least it was a woman. Maybe a roommate. I should have asked the other night.

Riccardo Montefiore's building looked like an armed fortress. Franchise soldiers stood in the front yard, loitered in the doorway, several others hung out on the sidewalk; anyone walking within a hundred feet of the place was scoped out for possible execution. So far Hans Kopp and Victor Rudiyov hadn't tried to hit us back, and yesterday I heard that Riccardo Montefiore made a recent investment in the construction company next to Yossario's site. Gradually Yossario and Vita were being frozen out. There were squabbles amongst the workers and supplies began to dry up and most times guys were sitting around waiting for some piece of equipment to arrive that wasn't coming. Then, when they had their pay cut and their benefits slashed, they lost all respect for Yossario and his son. This morning I saw Vita with his head in a bandage and I couldn't help knowing we were responsible for that.

'So, how'd it go?'

Riccardo leaned back in his tall leather chair while Manny sat up on the edge of the desk; Manny got a real charge out of the details and sometimes had a question or two about minor nuances like brain matter or viscera.

Leaving out the part about Hardy jamming his gun in my chin, I told them what happened.

Adam Gottlieb was the first one through the door and he immediately blasted some old guy in the face; there was a dull splat and the body fell like cotton to the floor. We froze, listening to hear if anyone was coming. Nothing. Adam looked down at the old guy, maybe seventy or eighty years old, it was hard to tell with his lower jaw missing.

'Don't shoot anybody in the fucking face!' I whispered.

'I'm sorry, it was an accident.'

We crept through a wood-paneled hall lit by a light bulb hanging from the ceiling, towards the front of the club where four men sat at a table playing a strange board game with triangular dice. There was a flag on the wall, like at a lodge meeting: an eagle with a soccer ball. By the time the first one saw us it was too late. We tore them apart as if they were clay pigeons. Two jumped up and tried to flee but I popped them with clean heart shots while my colleagues fired at their legs and arms. One fat old guy in a wrinkled white shirt and black tie crashed onto the table sending it in pieces to the floor. Hardy pumped four shots into his ass and laughed each time his body jerked. Miles Benowitz changed clips, Hardy reloaded his .44, then they started cracking bullets through the walls; it sounded like raindrops pounding on a tin roof. I raised my hand and the firing stopped. We listened. The room was eerily silent. A lake of smoke hovered up near the ceiling. Then something slid to the floor in a side room and I took off with my gun.

An old lady with stiff gray hair and wearing a waitress's uniform was flat on her back oozing blood from her neck, chest and stomach. She was dead and must have been standing behind the wall when we came in and thought she'd be safe by staying there. The floor was covered with bleeding dead old men; no one here was younger than seventy. Miles Benowitz stepped over the bodies with incredulity and asked, 'Are we at the right place?'

'There's no mistake.'

Hardy started lining the bodies up on the floor then told me to bring out the waitress.

'The waitress stays where she is,' I told him.

'We're supposed to do everyone, right?'

'The waitress stays where she is.'

'But what about our orders? You're the one that loves orders so much. We have to follow orders, remember?!'

'Shut the fuck up.'

'Fuckin' hypocrite, Tony. I always knew it.'

Adam Gottlieb came out of the bathroom wearing gray coveralls and a cap with flaps over his ears.

Hardy grinned, 'Who the fuck are you? The Easter bunny?'

Chuckles as Adam said, 'Fuck you. And gimme the saw.'

I plopped the bag on the desk and Manny leaned over and checked the contents, gave a quick count and looked at me.

'So, where's the waitress?'

'What?'

'The waitress. Where is she?'

'I left her there.'

'Where?'

'Back in the club.'

'What?'

'She wasn't part of the tableau.'

Manny's eyes ignited. 'Part of the . . . Are you fucking with me?'

'No.'

'Then why ain't she here?'

'Because she was an old lady, Manny. Somebody's grandmother. These were old men! They were all civilians. We slaughtered harmless old men. For what? What did we gain for the Franchise tonight?'

Riccardo swiveled around on his chair and took a hit on his asthma inhaler. I knew he would back me up on this.

'You know, you have a very bad attitude for somebody who did the wrong fucking thing!' he snapped, pissed as shit. 'I don't care if she was the fucking queen of England or your mother. You were told everyone and you didn't do everyone. What the fuck's wrong with you? Are you giving orders now or following orders?'

I answered with a chill, 'Following orders.'

'Then you better start fucking doing it! You're not given all the facts, Tony. You're here on a "needs to know" basis. So just do what the fuck you're told, and don't make judgment calls you have no right to make. If that gets to be too much for you, let me know and we can make other arrangements.'

He never spoke like that to me before, or made any kind of threat, and when his eyes glazed over like unpolished glass, impenetrable, otherworldly, I realized how precarious my position had become, how unimportant I was to the whole operation. Manny spoke up, his tone was sympathetic, more explanatory than threatening.

'You gotta understand something, kid. Pranks like that little stunt with the kraut's son ain't gonna work no more. That was a good thing. That was using your heart. But now you gotta start using your head. It's a whole new ball game, and we're in the World Series.'

I was tempted to ask for a bag of peanuts and Cracker Jack, but I was close enough to death without it. It seemed with every new assignment I was sinking deeper into damnation, no longer taking out thieves and traitors and people trying to fuck with us; now I was a butcher and an animal. A killer of children. And what bothered me more than anything else, was that it didn't horrify me as much as I wanted it to.

There was a tap on the door and Henry Pembleton stepped in behind it. Carrying a bulky leather satchel with the latch broken partially off and wearing Coke-bottle eyeglasses, Henry Pembleton was Lawrence Talbot's assistant. A brilliant yet disgraced former tax attorney with American Express – though, to be fair, the charges of mail fraud, perjury and impersonating the food critic of the *Newark Star Ledger* were eventually dropped – he had been groomed to succeed Lawrence Talbot in case what had happened ever happened. Henry Pembleton was also the guy who brought us into the 21st century by computerizing the books and electronically tracking the various businesses and holdings. Lawrence Talbot preferred pen and paper and his own brilliant mind – 'Less clues, tighter control!' – but the fact of the matter is, I've made more money ever since Henry Pembleton put it all in the computers.

Back in the apartment Hardy was sitting on the couch watching TV. He wore jeans, a button-down shirt and a Nazi armband. 'Hey Tony, check it out, look, they show tits on German MTV! Look at that!'

'Hey Goebbels, you can't wear that out on the street. It's illegal.'

'What's wrong with this shirt?'

'Not the shirt, Fuck. The armband.'

'Let me ask you something. Does it look like I'm goin' out, or does it look like I'm watchin' TV in the privacy of my own fuckin' home, thank you?'

'One doesn't exclude the other.'

'What the fuck does that mean?!'

'It means if you get picked up by the police you'll be in real fucking trouble.'

Hardy sat up, 'And who's gonna put me there?'

'Hey, don't make something out of nothing. I'm not threatening you, and I'm not disrespecting you. I'm just telling you something, that's all. So chill the fuck out.'

'I *am* chilled the fuck out! You should chill the fuck out.' Hardy followed me into my room. He was on a mission. 'I wanna know somethin'.'

'What?'

'Why did Riccardo want those heads so bad?'

'You know I'm not supposed to talk about that.'

'But I'm askin' you anyway.' Hardy stood in the doorway, needy, lanky, like a cartoon dog. In his own misguided way he needed to know that we were friends again.

'He's gonna sell them back to the families,' I said.

'Sell them?'

'Yeah, he figures the Russians won't want to bury headless relatives, so he's gonna sell the heads back to the family members.'

Hardy chuckled darkly. 'You gotta be fuckin' kiddin' me.'

'No, I'm afraid not. Henry Pembleton drew up an invoice, including all the expenses, the supplies, labor, plus a thirty-five per cent mark up.'

'That's fuckin' beautiful; that's fuckin' brilliant! That's why he's the boss. You see, Tony? He's a fuckin' genius. I could never think up something so twisted.'

'Don't sell yourself short.'

'Hey, you wanna grab a bite to eat?'

'Sure. Take off the armband.'

We sat at a side table where we could keep our backs to the wall. Hardy bit into his Big Mac like he hadn't eaten ever; I sipped my vanilla shake and watched a tall prostitute in white leather shorts and thigh-high boots strut past the window.

'There's something I want to talk to you about.'

'Shoot.'

Hardy pulled onto *Oranienburgerstrasse*. Caught behind a tram, he beeped his horn twice and sped around the slow-moving wagon. Stuffing the last few French fries into his mouth, he said, 'I don't get it. What's the catch?'

'There's no catch. I just want you to leave her alone.'

'Maybe I'm missin' somethin' here, but who the fuck are you . . . her father?'

'No, I'm not her father.'

'Then what?! I don't get it. The krauts don't believe in age discrimination, why should I?'

'Come on, this has nothing to do with age discrimination. Heinrich is a fucking lowlife; that doesn't mean you have to be one too.'

'Tony, why you gettin' so moral on me all of a sudden?'

'I'm as immoral as anyone, you know that.'

'Then what do you care about some cheap gooky little slope who can't even speak English?'

'I don't know. Whatever my reasons are, maybe I don't know myself. Look, Hardy, it's just obvious. Why can't you just leave her alone?'

'Why? Because we have a special relationship now, chief. I mean, it's the most natural thing in the world, ain't it? A guy and his first slope pussy? That's a very close bond. Ask any Vietnam veteran – nine out of ten times he can tell you the name, date and place of his first gook pussy. Besides, she's in love with me; it would break her heart if I just ended it like that, and I can't do that to her. I'm sorry, Tony, but I can't do what you're askin' me to do.'

Hardy looked out the windshield. For him the conversation was over, his stubborn brow blocked any further reason from entering his skull.

'I would like you to reconsider.'

That got his attention. I told him, 'You know I'm not

179

telling you what to do, you know that, right? You can do whatever the fuck you want. You're a free man. I'm just asking you for a favor. As a friend.'

He was intrigued by this approach. It was something he hadn't considered. I raised the offer.

'It would square us with last night. The .44 in the chin thing, remember? I would forget that completely. You would never have to spend a sleepless night wondering when I'm gonna appear out of nowhere to take revenge.'

'I knew you were gonna want revenge.'

'Nobody pulls a .44 on me and gets away with it.'

'You fuckin' liar. You promised.'

'I promised not to pop you. I didn't promise not to take revenge.'

'Fuck. That's semantics.'

'Then pick the alternative. A way that makes us both relatively happy. After all, it's the "Christian" thing to do.'

If disappointment had a face it would be the one Hardy wore right now. 'So that's the deal, huh? You're tellin' me we're square if I do you this favor? Stay away from . . . What's her name? Ba Fongool?' He grinned crudely at his own joke.

'La Fontaine. That's what Heinrich called her. We'd be completely square.'

He thought about it for all of two seconds, then announced, 'Okay. She's gonna be heartbroken, but for you, my friend, it's a deal. We're even now, right?'

'I have your word? You'll leave her alone?'

'I just said so, didn't I? I keep my promises.'

'Then we're even. Thanks. I appreciate it.'

He stopped at a red light next to a Turkish *Imbiss* with a thick pole of meat revolving in the window. I got out and leaned back in the window.

'I'm gonna take off; walk around for a bit.'

'You're kind of a lone wolf lately, huh?'

'Just wanna do some thinking.'

'Well, don't think too much. It's not good for the brain.'

'Thanks for the advice.'

'*Sieg Heil, Herr Commandant!*'

I dialed with trepidation, hoping I didn't get that rude chick again.

'Hello Monica, it's me. Tony.'

There was a pause. It took a second for her to answer.

'*Hallo*, Tony.'

'How are you?'

'*Gut. Und* you?'

'I'm okay, I think.'

Silence.

'Are you there?' she asked.

'I want to see you again.'

'When?'

'Now.'

'Oh . . . I can not. I have friends here for dinner.'

I felt holes open up inside me in places I didn't know existed. There was a long silence, this one longer than the last, until she said, '*Hallo*?'

'Yeah, I'm still here.'

I rang the bell and a buzzer sounded. The wooden stairs were warped and the banister was loose and wobbled under my touch. The hallway was dark, the only illumination came from a single streetlight outside. I cautiously went up to the second flight and saw a dim red square glowing on the wall. I pressed it and the hallway instantly lit up.

Monica waited outside her door on the fourth landing, gave me a smile and a peck on each cheek, then led me inside her apartment. In the kitchen three people sat at a square table, two men and a woman. The table was set for five places with a tall steaming pot in the middle and bowls of potatoes and salad set around it. Monica introduced me to Marcus and Volkmar, and her friend Anneke; I could tell from the smirk on Anneke's tight citrus face that she was the one who answered the phone yesterday afternoon. Marcus and Volkmar spoke English fairly well and asked me 'where in America' was I from. They'd both been to the US and were now in medical school with Monica. I sat down at the table and Marcus scooped out globs of soggy mushrooms he and Volkmar had picked that afternoon in a field. The meal consisted of handpicked mushrooms, boiled potatoes and green leafy salad. Monica filled everyone's glasses with red wine, then refilled her own glass and drank. For the rest of the evening they spoke in German. Occasionally an English phrase or sentence would jump out and grab my attention, then just as quickly sink back into the porridge of sound leaving me alone and isolated again. Occasionally Monica would try to translate some of the subjects for me, would look to Marcus for certain words she couldn't translate, but most of the time they talked as if I wasn't even there. I picked at my food and wondered why she invited me over tonight. Maybe she wanted to prove a point, to show how crazy it was to think that anything could happen between us, that the vast differences between our lives and our upbringing made any kind of deeper connection impossible. I began to wonder if one of these guys was her boyfriend. So far neither one had shown her the slightest preference over Anneke.

Anneke got up and left the room, then came back with her jacket; Volkmar got up with his jacket and a familiarity that told me they were a couple. Marcus sat there not getting up or putting on his jacket. Anneke spoke to Monica in the doorway while Marcus and Volkmar mumbled back and forth at the table. Then when Anneke called Volkmar to the door Marcus got up and grabbed his jacket; my stomach unraveled like a cheap rubber snake. Marcus shook my hand and left with the others. When Monica and I were alone she said, 'I am sorry, I speak with friends most German.'

'It's okay, it's easier for you. I wish I could speak another language. In school I never paid attention to what was going on.'

'*Warum*?'

'It didn't seem important at the time. The teachers didn't really give a shit. They had enough problems just keeping us from killing each other. I know a little bit of Spanish from the street, I can curse in Italian, but that's about it.'

She grinned. 'In the school I learn French and Russian.'

Manny Simone flashed before my eyes. 'Why Russian?' I asked.

'In GDR we learn not English. Many Russian people live here. So . . . we learn Russian.'

'Must be a hard language. Do you still speak it?'

'*Nein!*' she said with a laugh; how preposterous to ask.

'Where did you learn to speak English?'

'In the *Universität und von* movies.'

'The only German I ever learned from movies was "*Achtung! Sieg heil!*" You know, *The Dirty Dozen*. Movies like that.' Monica didn't seem impressed by my German vocabulary. She refilled both our glasses with wine and we sipped. Ten minutes later the bottle was empty and we were drunk. Monica asked if I wanted to go out for a walk. The streets were wet and dark, a dense mist hung like gray silk in the air. Every block was under reconstruction of some sort, scaffolding covered long stretches of sidewalk and huge green dumpsters sat in the gutter. The older buildings and storefronts were being torn down and replaced with clothing boutiques and fancy restaurants. The contrast of old and new was not a harmonious one. Monica told me it was all happening too fast, that every week some familiar, cherished place from her childhood was replaced by something new and strange. It was unsettling to her. Building by building the whole neighborhood was being lobotomized.

Monica let out a sigh and stopped on the corner, until a friendly green figure like a leprechaun appeared in the traffic light. Frozen in mid-stride he told us to walk and we started across the tram tracks. A tall, lanky old geezer with white hair stumbled out of a sidestreet. He held a bottle of booze in one hand and a trumpet in the other. He staggered off in the opposite direction and the murky starless night swallowed him up until he was gone, leaving behind a melancholy jazz standard I recognized but couldn't name. Monica threw me a look and grinned.

We reached an ancient Gothic church sitting in the middle of a square. Nearly covered over by twisting vines, it had blackened spires and a broken cross on top; the only thing missing was a hunchback lurking on the roof. Monica asked if I was sick.

'It's okay, Anthony, just close your eyes and let go.'

'Daddy, I wanna go down now. Mommy's gonna be mad!'

'Nonsense, we can do it. I'll hold your hand; we'll go together. Like the angels. Have faith, son, and nothing bad will happen to you. Just concentrate, and trust me.'

I was never more terrified in my life. The ground below looked a million miles away. My father took another step toward the edge, his shoes scraped on the coarse tarpaper shingles like a rake scraping against a sidewalk. I pressed my sneakers as hard against the surface as I could, trying to get a firm grip underneath me. My father clutched my hand tightly and gave me a gentle tug forward. His shoes began to slide towards the rain gutter that lined the church roof, regaining traction and stopping just short of the edge. Throughout he beseeched me to have faith, to pray; and I *was* praying, praying not to throw up, because any forward thrust would have thrown me over the edge. I felt my legs grow warm, then cold as I had peed my pants.

'No, I'm fine. Just felt a slight cramp.'

Monica told me she didn't know if the church was still used, then added that she'd never been inside a church.

That peeked my interest.

She creased her brow and pursed her lips; it was obviously a question that required serious thought. A moment later she replied, 'I see no proof of him, nothing to show of God.'

So simple and to the point.

'What about faith?' I asked. 'Anybody can believe in God when there's proof. That's easy. What about when there isn't any proof? That's the true test of faith, isn't it?'

'People believe *on* God because they have *Angst*. They have . . . fear of Hell.'

'Aren't you afraid of Hell?'

'*Das gibt's nicht,*' then she started speaking to me in German as if I understood the language. From what I could gather she didn't believe in Heaven or Hell but she liked Jack Nicholson.

We turned onto a narrow cobblestone street with concave dips in the middle. The sidewalk was made out of planks of wood and old shuttered shops sat abandoned and leaning to one side. A billboard for West cigarettes was the only hint of 21st-century life. Through the mist it began to drizzle and Monica glanced up at the sky. I reached over and wiped her glasses with my thumb, smearing them worse than they were, but she grinned and said, '*Danke.*'

She took off her glasses and put them in her pocket. Her cheeks were swollen red and her chapped lips parted slightly revealing the gap between her teeth. When she glanced down the street and squinted at something in the distance, my sides collapsed. I couldn't quite figure it out; she was not a stunning beauty; I'd certainly been with far more physically attractive women, some of the most beautiful hookers in New York City, in fact. Yet, Monica moved me in ways that no woman had ever moved me before. In her presence I wanted to be someone better; I saw possibilities for myself that I never knew existed; it was inspiration that both excited and scared the shit out of me. She furrowed her brow and pondered the words; I don't think she fully understood them.

'I want to kiss you,' I repeated. 'I've been thinking about it all night long, and I don't think I can stop myself. If you don't want to kiss me, that's all right, but I'm gonna kiss you.'

She looked at me with a hint of fear, a drop of discomfort. I leaned in and kissed her on the lips and she didn't react at first, then her tongue met my own in a whisper of warm submission; we held each other tight as several people came by and separated around us, chuckling as they passed. Desperately lost in one another's arms on a quiet crumbling street in East Berlin, I made sure to keep my left side away from her body so she wouldn't feel my gun.

I don't remember walking to her building but we kissed in the doorway for a long time. When she stepped back her hair was matted with rain and her eyes were tired bags; she wore a drunken grin and stood a little unsteady. She looked like a train wreck. I told her I wanted to see her again. She nodded her head and told me she 'must now go', then she kissed me on the lips and went inside. I watched her in the hallway until she started up the stairs and was gone. On the cab ride home I shook with fear, the fear of realizing you needed someone, of falling in love. I hadn't felt that vulnerability in many years.

Becky cried in my arms, her face was white with worry and her eyes had dark bags and lines under them. I told her it would be all right, that Barry would show up, that he probably went to Atlantic City without telling anybody. Clarissa was already in bed but had seen her mother weeping on the phone and after she asked me why, I told her Mommy was sad. With eyes mature beyond her years Clarissa asked if I was in trouble again.

'No. This has nothing to do with Daddy. Get under the covers and I'll tell you a bedtime story.'

At its conclusion, Clarissa rolled her eyes and scolded, 'Daddy, that's ridiculous! Animals can't talk or dance, and rain has nothing to do with happiness or sadness. It's only condensation in the clouds.'

'Oh.' I tucked the blankets tight around her sides and told her Mommy was crying because Uncle Barry had disappeared, and that tomorrow would be a better day. Then I sat with her until she fell asleep.

Becky was dialing the phone when I came in, said she was going to call up Manny Simone and Marty Oppenheimer and Bottle Rocket Al and any-and-everyone her brother ever worked for or hung out with. I took the phone and hung it up, saving her the embarrassment of their lies and promises only to become next week's funny story. I poured her a half jelly jar of vodka and sat with her on the couch, held her close and rocked her in my arms until hopefully, like Clarissa, she might fall off to sleep and tomorrow would be a better day.

Barry ordered the shrimp scampi with linguini and I had

the lasagna with meat sauce. He looked at me with worry and I assured him it would be all right, that all he had to do was hide out for a week or two and it would pass. I told him to call Billy Baccarat in Arizona and crash at his ranch until it was safe to come home.

'I'll square it with Manny,' I promised. 'I'll convince him you didn't say anything.'

'That's the truth!' he insisted. 'I didn't tell them a Goddamn thing! They tried to get me to talk, tried to make all kinds of deals with me, but I told them to go fuck their mothers. I ain't no snitch!'

That's when I knew for certain he ratted his guts out. Fuck, Manny was right.

'Manny, he's my wife's brother.'

'He knows you, he trusts you; he'll never expect it from you. The fucking guy's a junkie and a rat and a threat to all of us. He's gonna fuck us up the ass, and *you* most of all. Don't you think your name came up on those tapes?!'

'He doesn't know anything about what I've done.'

'He's shining light where darkness reigns, kid. Once they start looking for things they find them. Think of your family, because he's gonna take that away from you. When you're doing time upstate, you think he's gonna give a shit? You think he's gonna help them? The Government is paying him up the wazoo to fuck us.'

Becky paced the room, clutching a tissue to her nose and sick with despair. 'Something happened to him, I can feel it. Those bastards you work for, they never liked him. They blamed him for everything that ever went wrong.'

'Becky, nobody blames him for anything. Why do you always jump to the worst possible conclusion? Please, come here, sit down and relax.'

'I can't relax. I'm worried to death over him.'

'Maybe he just got sick of it here and went somewhere to

clean himself out. Would that be such a bad thing?'

'Oh God, Tony, if you know something you better tell me. I swear you better tell me.'

'I don't know anything because there's nothing to know. I promise!'

Becky dismissed me with a sigh and continued pacing the room.

'This is going to kill my mother. This will destroy her.'

'Nobody's going to be destroyed.'

'And what happens next? Do they come after me? What about Clarissa?'

'Now you're talking crazy! Nobody's coming after you or Clarissa. It doesn't work that way! Don't you understand?'

She didn't, and just kept pacing with worry and distraction.

'I want you to stop moving for a minute. Please.' Becky stopped and looked at me. 'Nothing's ever gonna happen to you or Clarissa. I want you to know that. I don't know where you get these crazy ideas, but they're never gonna happen. Never. I promise you.'

Becky fell on my shoulder, moaned in my ear, 'Talk to Manny, tell him Barry didn't do anything, tell him it's all a mistake. Everybody gets arrested at the club. It wasn't his fault.'

'All right, I'll tell him that, but he's gonna say I'm crazy, that Barry's probably shacked up with some broad somewhere. And you know what, Becky, it wouldn't be the first time Barry's done that.'

'Just talk to Manny, Tony. He'll listen to you.'

'I will, but you'll see, Barry's gonna come marching through that door one day clean and sober, and then we'll all feel like fools for worrying so much. And I want you to give him shit for putting us through all this hell, okay?'

Becky forced a grin, wiped the tears from her cheeks and

sniffled, kissed me softly on the lips. 'Thank you . . . I love you.'

'I love you too.'

Manny wanted a Columbian necktie; ever since he'd read that article in *National Geographic* on the Columbian drug gangs. I'd done it only one time before and found it to be difficult and dangerous, as the amount of blood splashing all over the place left a river of clues. Pulling the tongue out through a slice in the neck was no easy task either.

Barry swallowed the last of his cappuccino, I asked for the check and we got up to leave. Out in the parking lot he kept glancing over his shoulder, he was spooked and I tried to reassure him he was safe. I gave him a few thousand dollars in cash and told him to drive out of the city tonight, and to call his sister once he arrived in Arizona. When he turned to get in his car I wrapped the wire around his neck and took him down to the gravel. It crunched and cracked under our weight and he thrashed and flailed like a clubbed seal but I knelt on his back and lifted him up from behind; I didn't want to see his face, couldn't bring myself to see it; I knew his eyes would be big and dancing with terror, his tongue would swell up and try to jump out of his mouth, his entire face would inflate like a red rubber balloon and blood would pour out of his ears. Instead I had the sloppy sound of his choking and gasping, the sound of life being cruelly squeezed out of someone, the music of brutality playing in my head.

When he stopped moving I released the wire and pulled a pair of rubber gloves out of my pocket. Bitter wind rustled under my clothes and I felt someone watching me from an alley next to the restaurant, invisible eyes hiding in the darkness, a presence that stirred in me profound dread. I lifted the body, already soiled with piss and feces, into the back seat of the car and drove off into the night to finish the job.

I drove around for an hour, enough time to convince her I'd talked to Manny and that everything was all right, but once I stepped through the door I knew she had found out the truth. How she found out I wouldn't learn for another two weeks. Her voice shook with rage and she came at me with her fists beating my face and chest, collapsing to the floor at my feet. Calling me an animal, a monster, other things I couldn't understand through the halting, anguished sobs.

'Becky, you're wrong! You don't understand . . .' But she wasn't wrong, she did understand. And I couldn't deny it strongly enough, some sick part of me didn't want to. Instead I wanted to tell her that her brother betrayed us all, that he was a sick fucked-up junkie willing to send me and everyone else to prison, in the process destroying a dozen lives to save his own neck. I ran into Clarissa's room but she was already gone, her things had been packed in bags on the bed. Becky's voice was scratched and raw as she told me Clarissa was gone forever and that I would never see her again. That was a promise she kept.

The last time I saw Becky was through binoculars as she was rushed into a grand jury room to testify. I was sent into hiding in a basement apartment in South Orange, not seeing the light of day for three solid months, while Manny Simone and Riccardo Montefiore settled matters on my behalf – indirectly threatening Becky's parents with brutal death and then not so indirectly threatening to go after her aunts and uncles and cousins one by one until there'd be no one left. A family completely wiped from the face of the earth. Shortly after that Becky just vanished one day. Manny told me she was in the Witness Protection Program and living out west somewhere. I believed him because I needed to.

I heard a sound in the flat. A group of people were talking loudly in stilted English and I crept in with my hand inside my jacket. A thick cloud of cigarette smoke hovered near the ceiling and seven kids with shaved heads and tattoos sat on the living-room floor watching *Pulp Fiction* in German – it was Hardy's favorite movie. They wore ripped leather jackets and army boots and had chains and pipes hanging from their waists. Hardy sat in the middle chugging from a bottle of Jack Daniels as all eyes landed on me.

'Who are these creeps?'

'These are my friends,' Hardy said with an indignant grin. Two kids slid against the wall so they could keep me better in sight.

'Where did you find them?'

'In the East. Invited them back for a little drink.'

'Get rid of them.'

A huge strapping kid six-feet tall and no older than fifteen years old, flicked his cigarette against the wall and got up, spoke in a thick, awkward tenor, 'It is okay, we are friends. We like Americans,' then he held out his hand.

I noticed strands of long black hair scattered on the carpet; chopped unevenly, some of the ends had thick wet blood on them.

'What's that from?' I asked.

Hardy giggled, took another gulp of Jack. 'We ran into some gooks, can you believe it? They got their own gook mafia out here, fucking interlopers. They sell smuggled cigarettes. I'm gonna talk to Riccardo about it; see if we can get a piece of that action. Here, you want one?' he held out a carton of Marlboros.

'No. What about the hair?'

'Oh,' he snickered, 'the wife was pretty. We made her less pretty.' The others roared with laughter; the two against the wall didn't understand and only laughed after everyone else did.

'Did you kill a civilian?'

'No, we just had a little fun. They're fine. Probably won't remember a thing tomorrow.'

They all laughed as John Travolta crashed through the glass shower door and died.

15

The next morning Hardy and I arrived at the construction site to find four police cars parked around the trailer. Eight cops in dark green uniforms and carrying machine guns stood at attention along the perimeter. Two dozen workers sat idly at the dug-out foundation smoking and mumbling in Turkish. Adam Gottlieb and the cousins leaned against a white BMW eyeing the cops with boredom.

Adam said it matter-of-factly, then added, 'I'm surprised it took them this long.'

'Shakedown?!' Hardy exclaimed. 'From them?! They look like fuckin' valets! I was gonna ask one to park my car.'

'They're carrying Uzis,' I advised.

'I'm cool,' he said, then started for the trailer when a cop barked something in German and motioned with his weapon.

'I'm goin' inside!' Hardy snapped. 'I work here!'

The cop went after him but I ran up and opened my wallet, showed him a picture of Clarissa as if it were an official badge.

'*Alles Klar*,' I told him, then went inside behind Hardy as the cop yelled after us.

Everyone turned as we entered. Riccardo Montefiore and Manny Simone sat on chairs across from the couch where an angry-looking bastard wearing a decorous green uniform and matching felt beret sank deep into the cushions. Beside him was a drab gray suit, the man inside it looked like compacted sand, brittle, yet coarse, dull; an attaché case rested on his lap and both men held smoldering hand-rolled cigarettes between tobacco-stained fingers. Yossario stood by the filing cabinet, Vita and

Heinrich sat stupefied on a desktop while Henry Pembleton worked at his computer screen, oblivious to the business going on just four feet away, but coughing regularly to let everyone know the smoke in the room was causing him discomfort. Riccardo introduced us to Captain Schaffner, who barely gave us a glance, then Yossario shifted his weight and his soft leather shoes squeaked like mice, the look on his face told me things were going not so well.

Schaffner spoke in rapid bursts, his voice was abrasive, condescending; words came out of his mouth like fists.

'Your permits are not in order. This company is fake. I will close your workplace.'

'You have no right to close our workplace,' Manny announced, while Riccardo fingered a stack of five-Mark coins in his hand.

Schaffner insisted, 'This is a *türkische* workplace.'

'We're a legal German company. Henry, over there, is the owner. He's German.'

'Heinrich,' Heinrich corrected.

Manny added, 'And we have all the paperwork to prove it.'

'We know the lies,' Schaffner muttered.

Riccardo put the stack of coins on the coffee table in front of him, then leaned forward and spoke to Schaffner in German. Schaffner grinned and his teeth were a mass of decaying pebbles, he whispered to the gray suit who wrote something on a slip of paper and slipped it back to him. Schaffner held it out for Riccardo to read before crumbling it in his fist. I laughed to myself; Hardy had been right, different things are the same all over. Manny got up and went behind his desk. Seven seconds later he came back with a thick yellow envelope which Riccardo placed on the table in front of Schaffner, who looked at it as if it contained naked pictures of his mother. He spoke directly to Yossario.

'Tell your friends this is not America. They have much to learn. I send a colleague to see you each Friday. And the permits must be made good each week.'

Riccardo looked up, 'Each week?'

'Each week.'

'That's a lot of money.'

'Just pay it.'

Schaffner and the suit got up from the couch leaving craters in the cushions. When Riccardo held out his hand, Schaffner looked at it with amusement, then shook it weakly.

'It seems the Americans bring more than hamburgers and Coca Cola this time,' he remarked, and there was sadness in his voice, a weary resignation that struck me as profound.

Outside Schaffner barked at the cops and they all got in their cars and drove off.

Yossario was the first one to speak, his whining voice scratched inside my ears like a bent coat hanger. 'I do not undersssstand. What was he talking about? Heads! What heads?'

Manny snapped, 'He was talking figuratively.'

Yossario continued, 'We can not pay them bribesss each week! We jussst can not do that!'

Riccardo whirled around, found Yossario in his sights but spoke in a reasonable, non-threatening way. 'I have no intention of paying them another *Pfennig*.'

'But didn't you hear him? He will ssshut usss down! He can remove our permitsss!'

Riccardo burst like a ruptured spleen. 'HE WILL DO NOTHING TO STOP THIS OPERATION! DO YOU UNDERSTAND THAT!? NOTHING!' His voice shook the walls and the room grew silent. Nobody moved, until a second later blood trickled onto Yossario's lip and Vita pulled out a handkerchief and held it to his father's spout.

'What's wrong with him?' Riccardo said.

Vita answered, 'He has weak *Nase*. It bloods.'

'I'm okay,' Yossario said.

'Take him to a doctor, get him checked out,' Riccardo said.

'I am fine, it happens all the time. It'sss nothing.'

'You're getting blood on the floor!' Manny scolded. He truly hated a mess. Then he ordered everyone out of the trailer, including Henry Pembleton who didn't utter a sound, just filed out with everyone else. Hardy went toward the door and Manny called out, 'You stay.'

Once we were alone Manny was on it. 'This is because of the Russians, you know that, right? How else would he know so much about us?! Or the fucking heads?!'

'It's moot how he knows. The fact is . . . he knows. We have to deal with it. Any ideas?'

Manny folded his arms, rubbed his chin. I could tell he'd been waiting for this moment, his moment to shine. Before he could begin, Hardy leaned forward, 'Hey, we can always –'

'We can't pop a German police captain!' Manny shot back and Hardy deflated like a punctured tire. Manny continued, 'But we can create a diversion. Something to keep him busy.'

'Let's hear it.'

'Let's say a major shitload of heroin comes pouring into the city, some of it bad. Junkies start dropping like flies on the sidewalk; we could even plant bodies in nice neighborhoods. Soon the good people of Berlin rise up in anger, and the cops step in. As it turns out, someone very high up on the force is involved. Maybe a kilo and lots of cash are found in his home. We buy a friend at a daily newspaper, some lowly underpaid reporter with a gambling problem; he might find that to be a newsworthy story.'

'It's not a very easy thing to pull off,' Riccardo said. 'We need to bring in a large quantity of heroin and a secure way to plant it.'

Hardy mentioned his new friends.

'Skinheads,' I said. 'Fucking Nazis.'

Manny was pissed. 'I thought I told you not to fraternize with the locals.'

'I wasn't fraternizin', we were just hangin' out.'

'That's what fraternizing means!'

'Oh.'

Riccardo asked with genuine curiosity, 'How did you meet up with skinheads? I thought they hate foreigners.'

'They hate the Russians more than we do,' Hardy said. 'They ain't so bad, Riccardo. They're cool guys, and they'd be happy to help us out. We could pay them in guns and ammo.'

I pictured Hardy's skinheads with guns and ammo let loose on the streets of Berlin. Manny wrinkled his brow; apparently he saw the same picture.

'I don't like this skinhead thing,' he said. 'It's a fucking cesspool of uncertainty, and it's downright un-American. Besides, we got a fucking rat somewhere on the inside. I want the circle to get smaller, not bigger. You got that, Hardy?'

'Uh, yeah.'

Riccardo Montefiore stood up, pinched the crease of his pants and said, 'Look, let's not give ourselves a tumor over this. It's really quite simple. Schaffner's married.'

Those two words silenced the room. We looked at each other. This was the part of business I hated; it never used to be this way.

'I didn't see a wedding ring,' said Manny. 'I checked.'

'They wear their wedding rings on the right hand. Believe me, he's got a wife. I'm sure he's got kids too.'

'Well, that certainly cuts to the chase.' Riccardo and Manny turned to Hardy simultaneously. Hardy didn't get it at first, then his grin curdled like sour milk. 'Get me a name and an address,' he said.

She folded her hands on her lap and wore a crooked, uncomfortable smile. She was trying to prepare me for something difficult, and I went along with the ritual, struggling to hide my glee and excitement. I knew this was it, the news I'd been praying for. This time he finally did it, successfully. Gone from our lives forever. Only the method was in question. Was it too many sleeping pills or did he slice open his wrists until his veins were empty; maybe his body was found frozen to death in an abandoned field.

'A terrible thing has happened,' she began and I almost let out a trill of laughter. My stomach was dancing; it was the happiest I'd felt in several years. Not since he disappeared for three months two winters ago.

By the time my mother finished I felt like I'd been struck with a lead pipe.

I had never traveled in a plane before; had never been more than an hour outside of New Jersey. Washington was something I'd only heard about on the news because of the president. I never knew that there were two of them, one a separate state. When my ears popped during takeoff I thought something snapped inside my brain, a consequence of too much grief and anxiety in too short a life span. A stewardess appeared over me; she was unnaturally tall. 'Are you all right?' she asked. 'Is there anything I can get you?'

I noticed other passengers looking at me strangely. I answered that I was fine, that I'd never flown before. The

200

stewardess smiled and told me there was nothing to be afraid of and that if I wanted anything at all to just press the call button.

I was picked up at the airport by an obese jolly aunt I'd never met before and taken to a hotel room where I would meet up with my mother and father later that night. In the meantime I lay on the hard, tightly made bed and stared up at the ridged stucco patterns in the ceiling, saw outlines of naked European women staring back at me. I masturbated without joy or pleasure, feeling barely anything at all, hoping the sudden release of anxiety would somehow snap me out of this abstract dream gone south.

Carrie looked like she was sleeping, lying with her hands folded on her chest and wearing a dark blue skirt and white turtleneck sweater; the sweater was to cover the rope burns. Her face was relaxed, serene, happy in a way I'd never seen her look before, as if she had found something that no one else had ever found, no one who hadn't taken the plunge. I spoke to her with my mind, asked if she could hear me, what it was like, was it better? I asked her about God and the Devil and Dennis McColluck's father who died when we were in fourth grade. The vague mumbling of my own father answered me back. He sat in the first row beside my mother, gripping a cane tightly in his trembling fist with his gaze in some far-off other dimension, his voice a vibrating mantra of delirium; no one could tell if he was aware of his daughter's suicide or not.

'Oh my God! What happened?!'

I was crying and holding my head; blood poured down into my eyes and my hair was dripping wet. She grabbed a rag from the sink and pressed it against the wound; I cried out.

'Hush up!' she scolded with authority. 'I have to see where it is! Move your hand! What happened?'

'I got hit with a can.'

'What?!'

'We were playing in the woods and Benny Deakins threw a can at me.'

'What kind of can?'

'I don't know, a soda can.'

'Sit back. Lift your head. You got a nasty cut; it may need stitches.'

'I don't want stitches.'

'Then you better hope it stops bleeding soon.'

'Can't you do something?'

'I don't know. Sit here.'

'Where's Mommy?'

'She went to pick up Daddy.'

She came back with the blue-plastic first-aid kit she'd gotten recently from her Girl Scout troupe, opened it and took out some gauze, adhesive tape and a small bottle of hydrogen peroxide. I cried out as she dumped the whole bottle of peroxide on my scalp, sizzling foam bubbled up out of the slit and it got very cold, airy; seconds later the pain went away. Carrie wrapped sterile white gauze around my head until I looked like The Invisible Man, then taped it snuggly in place. When my mother came home she shrieked at the sight of me and rushed me to the emergency room. The doctor was quite impressed with the job my sister had done. He said no stitches were needed, then he gave us both lollipops and told my sister she would make a fine nurse.

The next day I took four milk crates from Matty's candy store on the corner and nailed a plank of wood across the top. Carrie stood behind the counter in her beige Girl Scout uniform and white nurse's cap, laying out her first-aid kit. I hung a sign in crayon announcing First Aid Stand on the front and for the next six days every boy in the neighborhood came by with minor aches and bruises, scraped elbows and scabbed knees which Carrie tended with the care and concern of a surgeon. Daddy came by and Carrie put some antiseptic on his bleeding lips and gums, covered them with salve. By Saturday the first-aid stand was shut down when Mrs Henry complained to the police that Carrie was operating an unlicensed medical center; this in retaliation for Daddy eating her roses.

After the funeral I sat with my father in my aunt's living room while everyone else was in the dining room eating cold pasta salad and sandwiches. My father stared at the blank TV, his dirty unshaved face covered with yellow-gray stubble. He smelled of urine and cheap cologne. I waited till we were completely alone, then I told him, quietly, 'This is because of you. Do you understand that? Can you hear me in there? This is because of you. You killed her. You've been killing all of us for years. Are you happy now?'

Something stirred inside him, his eyes narrowed, focusing across the room on a metal ashtray with a silver propeller airplane attached. He began to moan softly, agitatedly. I took out my pocket knife, leaned down and lifted the cuff of his pants, pulled down his brown polyester sock and began to carve a 'C' into his ankle. He stopped moaning at the first slice of the blade. I made sure the cuts were deep and clean, then pulled up his sock. He hadn't moved an inch, his face still locked into a frozen mask of bewilderment. I put the knife away just as my mother came into the room.

'Aren't you hungry? There's a lot of food out there.'

'I don't feel like eating.'

'Are you okay?'

'Yeah.'

'You've been so quiet, you haven't said a word since you've arrived. It's all right to cry, you know. You should-

203

n't feel ashamed. It's natural.'

'I don't feel like crying.'

'If you do – when you do – you just go right ahead. It's not good to keep everything bottled in. Has your father said anything to you?'

'No, nothing.'

She looked at him, let out a tired sigh, then took him by the hand and led him into the dining room to eat. I saw a line of blood on his shoe as he left.

16

'**W**hy don't you come with me?'

'You don't need me hanging around. I'd only be in the way.'

'You can be lookout, watch my back.'

'It's better than watching your front, that's for sure.'

Hardy let out a laugh and turned left past the outdoor vegetable market. 'That's what I miss about you,' he said. 'That's the old Tony. The fuckin' funny Tony. Where's that guy been lately?'

'He must'a been outta town.'

'Well, I'm glad to see him back. I sure missed him. Maybe now we can hang out more, like we used to do.'

'We spend most of the day together.'

'Yeah, but that's work; it ain't the same.'

'No, I guess it ain't.'

'I just want things to go back to the way they was. Before all this bad blood came up. Like the good old days. Remember? We were a great team, you and me. We kicked ass.'

I stared out the windshield until he finally broke his gaze and glanced back at the road in front of him.

'You're only going to scare her tonight, right?'

'I don't know,' he said. 'I thought I'd play it by ear, see what comes up. I'm like an artist, Tony, I need room to improvise; can't be locked in to the method of my art.'

'Just don't get carried away.'

The old Hardy came back fast. 'I been doin' this how fuckin' long!?'

'If you kill her, no bonus this year. That's all I'm trying to say.'

'I'm just gonna have a little fun, rough her up a bit. Just like with Alphonse Lettieri's wife?'

'That's what I mean. You were lucky her body never turned up.'

'What are you talkin' about?!'

'You drove off with her. She was never seen again.'

Hardy laughed easily, the thought gave him genuine pleasure. 'Remember Jamey Love? Nigger pimp in Trenton? Wears a bone through his nose like he's some kind'a African motherfuckin' prince?'

'What about him?'

'Well, after I fucked Al Lettieri's dirty-rag-of-a-wife, I took her up to Jamey's house, alive! Sold her for a grand. Nigger put her to work in the upstairs lounge. She's been whorin' ever since.'

'She was in her fifties.'

'Hey, I ain't responsible for what some guys'll fuck, but she had a real tight snatch for an old bitch. Guess I owe you five bills on that one, sorry . . . But the fact is, she's alive and doin' fine. She still thanks me for settin' her up. I saved her from a dreadful life of Al Lettieri's hairy fuckin' back! Remember that thing? It was like a dead beaver. Now she's livin' the excitin' life of a prostitute and she couldn't be happier.'

'You should get an award.'

'Maybe I'll take the cop's wife to Heinrich's club. Put her to work for the good guys for a change.'

'You can let me out over here.'

Hardy pulled over at *Eberswalderstrasse* and *Danziger* and I got out. Then I leaned back in the car. 'Remember your promise to me. About La Fontaine.'

'Hey, what am I, a fuckin' idiot?! I remember my promise. I gave you my word, now fuck off!'

I slammed the door and went to the tram stop around the corner.

206

Monica stood in the doorway wearing a long sarong-like skirt, white wool sweater and army boots. Her hair was tied in a bushy ponytail. She wrapped her arms around me and we kissed for a long time. When we parted she led me into her apartment, into a small back bedroom where a mattress lay on the floor and boxes of clothing lined the floorboards. A small wooden desk stood under the only window. There were thick black textbooks on a shelf next to the desk, also a huge yellow dictionary for English/Deutsch translations. On the left corner sat a framed picture of a skinny guy with long hair and holding a guitar. I'd seen him before but couldn't place where, until a second later his ridiculous laugh bounced like a spent shell-casing around the inside of my skull, he was the strung-out junkie guy in the nightclub who dropped dead on the dance floor, the one she saved. She told me he was her brother, the musician.

'Are you close to him?'

'*Wie bitte*?' She didn't understand. I let it drop, the similarities were too bizarre to contemplate.

She asked me what I wanted to do and I told her whatever she wanted to do, but I hoped she wanted to stay home.

The movie was in English but had German subtitles. We sat in the third row, holding hands and crouching deep in our seats. It seems the Germans don't have very many curse words in their language, for every profanity uttered in English, the screen read simply, '*Scheisse!*' Monica told me that meant 'shit'. We left through the planetarium section of the theater and walked onto an unlit desolate street, winding up at the Titanic for drinks. We sat at a round table near the back. I took her hand in mine and kissed it. Monica's cheeks glowed red in the candleflame and her glasses shimmered yellow. On the jukebox Dylan knocked on Heaven's door.

'Hey, Tony!'

He startled me for an instant. Had my reflexes been sharper, Jonathan might have gotten seriously hurt. Instead I introduced him to Monica. He gave me a knowing smile, then spoke to her in German; I could see her surprise at how well he spoke it. I noticed the shoebox under his arm and tried to buy two space cakes, but Jonathan refused my money. Then he told me to call him soon and disappeared into the herd at the bar. I slid a space cake over to Monica and she grinned and when the gap between her teeth showed through I wanted to confess my lifelong love to her.

Instead I ate a space cake.

Someone came through the door and I wondered if this were the only bar in Berlin.

Except for the cane at his side and a slight limp beside it, he seemed to be in good shape; I was glad for that. He squeezed left through the crowd and came towards the bathroom in the back, plodding closer to where we were sitting, winding his way around chairs in his path. I scratched my head to cover my face when I noticed Monica watching me curiously, chewing slowly on her space cake. What happened next is something I still can't explain. Maybe it was the hash creeping up on me like a pair of women's hands, or maybe I simply forgot who I was for a second, because as he reached the table I looked up and said, as if we were the best of friends, 'Hey, Ulf! *Wie geht's*?'

He stared at me, his mouth in a confused half-grin, until the recognition set in. I keyed on his hands, any sudden reach into his jacket or waistband and I'd be on him like a pit bull, but he just stood there gaping. I think his life was flashing before his eyes. He seemed much braver back on the night he'd been shot, but sometimes shock, loss of blood and a bullet to the gut can do that to a person. He pivoted around on his good foot and hobbled quickly out the door. I told Monica we had to go. The urgency in my voice told her it wasn't a question. She waved the waitress over and reached into her bag but I held it closed.

'Twenty-four Marks,' Monica said, after reading the receipt. I gave the waitress forty Marks and after she returned my change I left five Marks on the table. Monica told me, 'In Berlin is *besser* you give tip when you pay.'

I glanced over my shoulder and nothing was out of the ordinary, until we reached the corner. Four men in long dark coats were following us, horseless men of the apocalypse, seemingly moving in slow motion. A magnificent effect, except that here, and now, where people strolled on the sidewalk and potential witnesses lurked in every doorway, a shoot-out in the street didn't seem the best way to keep my anonymity. Monica turned to see what had caught my interest and the men stopped short – all cards face up. They stood there; nobody moved for a long moment. Monica sighed audibly and asked, 'Know you them?'

'Yeah, they're old pals.'

But they were young, well dressed and physically fit; they could have been the German satellite for the Franchise. The tallest one in the middle was talking to his partners, deciding what their next move should be. I didn't need to decide mine.

'Are you wearing comfortable shoes?'

'*Was?*'

Before I could explain, two of the men reached into their jackets and I grabbed Monica by the hand and we took off down the street. She needed no prodding. A riot of footsteps broke after us, heavy leather shoes clomping clumsily on cement, shoes not fit for running or catching someone; I was grateful for that. We ripped around the corner and ran under a tall skeletal scaffolding. I stopped short and tried to kick out a support beam; after two attempts the middle caved in and dust and debris crashed onto the sidewalk. I grabbed Monica and turned into a winding driveway made of stone. I didn't know where to go or how to get there. I only knew we had to get off the street. Monica's palm was slippery with sweat, fear and the adrenal rush of being chased for her life, but she stayed with me step for step, taking long strides and sucking air into her mouth like a long-distance runner.

At the end of the driveway a tall passageway led to a dirt courtyard where a cement wall blocked us from going any further. To the left was a wooden garage with two junked cars up on blocks, to the right was a chicken-wire fence with a small hole in the middle, fit for a child but not for an adult like Monica, or myself. The men were closing fast, their shoes thudding like dropped potatoes on cobblestone brick. I took out my gun and Monica's eyes grew wide at the sight of it but she didn't say a word. All at once my head began to throb, the buildings melted to one side and I tingled with electricity; it felt like a million crawling insects had emptied from my stomach. When I looked into Monica's face her cheeks were burning and her eyes dripped like warm caramel; we were both completely stoned.

I pulled her aside and cocked my weapon, leaned against the building to hold myself steady, tried to focus at the mouth of the driveway. The first bastard through that mouth bites eternity, I laughed to myself. Monica put her lips in my ear and whispered, '*Komm*!' then she pulled me to the end of the chicken-wire fence where a dirt path appeared out of nowhere, leading into darkness. The earth was moist under my feet and tall weeds brushed my face; the balmy tang of overripe foliage burned like ammonia in my nostrils. We stumbled through two back courtyards past old cars, climbed over a broken picket fence until we came to a paved patio closed in by apartment buildings all around; the only way out was the way we came. A few yards over, shoes thumped dully on grass and soil, but only two men were following now. The other two, I imagined, went around to try to cut us off. Facing me were three metal doors similar in type to the door at the old-man's social club. All were locked. In the adjacent courtyard a metal trash bin tumbled over and someone cursed in anger. I hurriedly screwed a silencer onto the end of my gun. It now felt like a block of iron but I managed to lift it up and take unsteady aim as Monica softly called me over to the corner of a brick building where another dirt pathway opened into more blackness. Taking me by the hand she led me past stacks of bricks and sacks of cement into an alley so narrow I had to turn sideways to fit through. A sharp metal bar sticking out of the wall ripped my jacket and nearly removed my spleen, but I figured she knew where she was going, we were, after all, in her neighborhood. But when she pulled me down a deep alley in between two brick buildings with only one way out in each direction, I realized my mistake: Monica didn't know this place any better than I did. We were trapped if we stayed here, so I stopped at a broken window about three feet off the ground and ordered her to climb inside. Her face collapsed.

'Let's go! This ain't a fucking game!'

I helped her over the shards of glass and climbed in behind her, took her hand as we crept slowly into the icy black void. Four steps later I buckled and nearly snapped my ankle. The hard cement floor was pocked with wide craters, coils of thick chain sat like sleeping snakes beside them.

Outside a dog barked in the distance and the wind blew in whistling swirls until the mechanical rumblings of a tram snuffed them out. There was no other sound, maybe we'd lost them.

Still tingling with dizziness, I tried to will myself sober but the insects kept their exodus under my clothing. We moved deeper into the room and Monica didn't utter a sound, her profile glided smoothly through the darkness like a dim beam of light, a fragile determination on her mouth, seemingly unaware of the true danger she was in. When she looked at me I avoided her gaze.

At the rear of the building was a steep cement staircase that ended in darkness. Looking up into the murky abyss Monica pulled her hand free and took a stubborn step back; she wasn't going up there unless her life depended on it. Sparks shot from the banister and I whirled around and fired two quick puffs at the dark figure climbing through the window. Bullets punched through his chest and cracked into the brick wall behind him. He cried out as he flew back into the alley, dead before he hit the ground. Monica gasped as reality slapped her with a blunt rubber hose; I thought she might puke. Instead she took off up the stairs as two more men appeared in the window frame. I turned the corner of the first flight as the room erupted with bolts of light and exploding brick. They fired blindly into the dark and I nearly laughed with relief as I was sure they'd never come in after us, not now, after making so much noise. My next problem would be the police. Monica kept moving ahead of me, turning the banister for the next flight and the next until she disappeared abruptly from view. I took off up the stairs to find her fallen through a hole in the cement, dropped to her thighs and struggling to lift herself out.

'Are you all right?' I asked.

'*Ich weiss nicht.*'

'What does that mean?'

'I don't know,' and the annoyance in her voice told me she was okay, at least not seriously hurt.

'Relax, quit squirming. You're gonna jam yourself in worse.'

She spit out a sequence of words that needed no translation.

I took her by the hands and tried to pull her out when a chain rattled on the ground floor. The fear on Monica's face told me she heard it too. They were in the building and moving toward the stairs!

Monica tried frantically to lift herself free but I told her to stop, to be quiet. We froze, listening carefully. At the bottom of the stairs footsteps started their ascent. I turned to meet them halfway, pictured my bullets ripping through flesh and bone, shattering ribs, a Rorschach test of gore, vivid pictures that gave me pleasure and motivation, until Monica called my name. The men were rushing up the first landing and turning for the second. Gripping Monica under the arms I tried to lift her out; her breath hummed of wine and menthol cigarettes. Little by little she came wriggling free and I placed her down on the floor just as the men came into view through the hole in the cement. I fired three quick pops and the first guy flew back onto the others, his chest perforated and bleeding smoke. I jumped back just as seven shots answered me. They stayed down on the stairs below, whispering between themselves.

'Can you run?' I whispered to Monica.

'Yes.'

'Then go, and be careful.'

She started up the next flight of stairs while I planted my back against the wall, feeling it press into me, trying to stop it from swaying. Something swirled in the soup below and I fired five rapid puffs from my gun, brass shells sizzled off the wall and shot past my eyes, spent sulfur seared my nostrils, then a voice groaned and a body tumbled clumsily down the stairs stopping with a wet snap. At the top of the landing Monica stood at a rusted metal door that was chained shut by a padlock. She tugged on the chain and kicked at the door, threw me a look of genuine despair. I told her to step back, steadied my gun against the padlock and blew it apart. As she unwound the chain from the door I ran quietly down the stairs and emptied my clip at the footsteps coming up. I didn't wait to see if I'd hit anything. On the roof I changed clips, pocketing the old one, and looked around for Monica, who stood at the far ledge overlooking the buildings that surrounded us. One appeared close enough to reach by jumping. But coming up beside her, I could see there was at least a six-foot gap to bridge; I didn't think I could make it. Looking down I was punched by a fist of vertigo, so I started back to the door when Monica took my arm and spoke into my mouth, softly, with conviction, '*Nein*. No more kill. *Wir springen zusammen.*' Then she gripped my hand and pulled me forward.

'Wait. You don't understand!' My words fell out of the air like dead pigeons as we took a running leap and soared barely over the ledge, landing on the other side in a heap. Monica came up immediately, wiping her hands on her skirt, my palms were scraped and my knee throbbed in pain. I saw a small metal shack at the far corner, some kind of electrical housing unit, which appeared to be the only way down, and as we crept over a shot cracked the night and Monica dropped to the ground. I dove on top of her, covered her with my body.

'Are you okay?! Monica! Are you shot?!'

'*Ich bin* okay.'

I dragged her over behind the shack and went back to the ledge. He crouched low keeping out of sight, his shoes scraped harshly on the tarpaper surface. I recognized the faint click of a metal gear as he reloaded his revolver. It seemed crazy to me that he would risk a shoot-out with the police, whose sirens wailed in the distance, but like his colleagues, like the entire clan it seemed, he was relentless, homicidally driven, and for that he had my respect, as well as my complete concentration, because now he would die. I laid low, waiting for him to appear, groaned out, 'Steffi, help me, I'm shot!'

His head bobbed up above the ledge, then disappeared. I groaned out again, hoping Monica wouldn't take the bait. His head appeared once more, this time lingering a bit longer, searching for me along the perimeter of the rooftop. He stood up into a crouch and studied the drop between buildings, then took a step back and began his leap. I jumped up and caught him in mid-air, his head snapped back as if on a hinge, a tube burst from his neck wildly gushing ink and a soggy sound gurgled from his mouth. He seemed to float there for a moment, suspended in motion, until he sank from sight clutching the air as if he could hang from a cloud, followed by a dull thud. I raced back to Monica who was kneeling behind the metal shack and had witnessed the whole thing. As I helped her to her feet she seemed stunned, in a trance, unable or unwilling to break her gaze from the space where number 4 had bitten eternity. I realized then the true dilemma I faced; she'd seen things tonight that no one who wasn't intimately part of the Franchise had ever seen before. But worse than that, much worse, she could place me at the site of a multiple murder and had seen me commit the acts.

Police sirens turned the corner and the good citizens of Berlin yelled in the streets and Monica still hadn't moved an inch.

'We have to go,' I ordered. 'Now!' Avoiding her gaze I moved her toward the door in front of me. She walked heavily, her feet plodding like blocks of wood, and for a second, less than a second, in the blink of an eye or the time it takes to snuff out a candle, I thought of eliminating the witness.

17

I pulled her by the hand through unlit backstreets, keeping close to the buildings and ducking into alleys at every passing car. Her feet slapped the pavement as though she were a stubborn child on her way to the dentist. She gave me one-word directions when I asked where the hell we were, until finally, we arrived at her doorway. If Riccardo Montefiore or Manny Simone or any one of my colleagues could see what I was about to do, I'd be finished.

My heart ached as I grabbed her by the shoulders and told her, 'Go inside now, forget what happened tonight. Do you understand? You never saw me, I don't exist. If you tell anyone what you saw tonight you'll be killed. Do you understand what I'm saying to you? Tell me you understand!'

I shook her angrily and it startled her, but she answered yes, that she understood. I was glad for the shadow on her eyes.

'Now go inside. You're safe as long as you keep your mouth shut.'

She hesitated, then reached into her bag and started to turn toward the door.

Blue light streaked the doorway and before Monica could turn I pinned her into the corner with my body, covered her mouth with my palm. With my other hand I gripped her throat; whispered in her ear not to make a sound or I'd snap her neck. The police were shining hood-mounted searchlights into the alleys on both sides of the street. They stopped about ten feet away from us. I pressed Monica harder into the corner, felt her body trembling against mine, fragrant sweat rose up from her clothing. A cop got out of the passenger side and took a step around the front of his car, peering into the alley directly across the way; if he turned around he'd probably see us. I pulled out my weapon and Monica shook her head 'no', but didn't try to speak out or make a sound. The cop shined his flashlight into the alley, took another few steps forward, then his partner called him back and he got into his car and they slowly drove past Monica and I without a glance. I released her and stepped back. She looked at me with relief until I told her, 'Now get the fuck inside and don't say a word to anyone!'

She searched for her keys on the ground, then stopped and looked up at me.

'What!?'

'*Bitte. Sieh doch mal,*' she said, then pointed to a small circle of blood on the ground, showed me the red on her palm; my jacket sleeve was dripping onto the pavement. She took my arm but I pulled it away. Angry; paranoid. Why wasn't she afraid of me? Was Manny Simone right? Are the Russians so clever they can plant a person anywhere and under any circumstances? Part of me wanted to pop her right then and there, just to play it safe, but the other part scraped away the patch of blood on the sidewalk and followed her into her building, up into her apartment.

At the table she pulled off my jacket one sleeve at a time. My shirt clung to me like an extra layer of skin. At the top of my biceps were granules of gray cement flaked around a half-inch gash; not a bullet wound, a piece of concrete must have ricocheted off during the fire-fight – a friend of mine once got hit behind the ear by a ricocheted piece of brick; killed her dead, sure as any bullet.

Monica got a small kit from another room and began cleaning the wound with professional detachment. Then she bandaged it tightly with gauze. It was only then that she inspected her legs, pale slender limbs with scratch marks running down the shins. As she dabbed them with antiseptic I washed my hands in the kitchen sink, black soot and the stench of cordite came off reluctantly. After several scrubbings I turned around and Monica was smoking a cigarette. Two glasses of wine stood on the table in front of her, I hadn't heard her pour them. I sat beside her and downed my wine in one swift gulp, poured another glass and downed it the same way. She watched me with a strange analytical gaze, like studying a germ under glass; the fact that she hadn't said a word about what happened tonight gave me some comfort, yet, my instinct told me I couldn't trust her. Something about that excited me.

Barry led me through the hallway, past the mailboxes and main staircase, past several old bicycles locked to a water pipe and five crates of empty milk bottles. Muted daylight from the alley spilled in through wire-mesh windows as we came to an apartment in the back of the building.

'Hey Tony, this is my sister, Becky. Becky, this is Tony.'

'Hey,' I said.

'Yeah, hey,' she said without a glance in my direction, then turned to a row of albums next to the stereo. The first thing I noticed was her legs, pale and muscular, the shapely legs of a dancer. She wore a short blue dress and white socks with red sneakers. A perfectly round ass peeked just underneath her hem. Her hair was a reddish hue and curly, hanging to her shoulders, which had the same milky pallor as her legs. If Barry was aware of me checking out his sister, he didn't show it; he must have been used to it, having a sister with a body like that. When he went to his room to retrieve the ten hits of mescaline I was buying, Becky turned around to the opening strums of *All The Young Dudes.* She looked at me with boredom, possibly contempt, her eyes were large and green, unnaturally round, and there was genuine animosity in them.

'So, who are you?' she said, as if she were talking to a servant, or a pet. 'How do you know my brother?'

I wasn't used to having people address me that way. But without missing a beat I replied, 'I work at the club. How do you know him?'

'I'm his . . .' She stopped short, annoyed for a second. Then looked to see if I were being serious or not. I didn't blink.

Two weeks later Becky and I moved in together. I took a large apartment over the Forsythe Room and we set up house.

'I don't hate you anymore,' she announced proudly, as if it were a major accomplishment.

'Good, because you shouldn't.'

'But I did and you're lucky I don't now.'

'You're lucky I don't hate you for hating me.'

'Why should you hate me!? You're the criminal!'

'But a nice one.'

She let out a hard breath, her way of chuckling without chuckling.

'Come here,' I prodded. 'I want to make love to you over the couch.'

'I'm not your love toy.'

'I was thinking "fuck doll".'

Becky let out a grin, then just as quickly withdrew it; I wasn't getting off the hook that easily. For six months we'd been trying to make this work, this volatile cocktail of anger, irritation and incredibly intense sex.

'I want to know what you're gonna do,' she said seriously.

'I've already told you, there's nothing I can do.'

'Speak to those creeps you work for!'

'I can't do that. Come on, come here. I want you. You're killing me with those legs.'

Becky playfully swung her skirt up off her thighs, luscious thighs with a small patch of nicely trimmed bush in between.

'Will you please come here and sit on my face! We can discuss the problem like adults.'

'There's only one adult here.'

'We can discuss that too, little girl. Now get the fuck over here before my cock explodes. Then you'll have to clean it up.'

'Are you going to return them?'

'No.'

'They don't belong to you.'

'They were stolen before I got them.'

'His family's in trouble. He needs the money. That's why he was doing it!'

'Look, it's too late. The fucking guy was warned not to sell them on Franchise territory. I'd say he got off pretty easy.'

'Franchise territory! You make it sound like a McDonald's!'

'We actually own a few McDonald's.'

Becky whirled around with fire in her eyes, 'Listen, you! I ain't one of your fucking mooks,' jabbing her finger in my direction. 'Don't talk to me that way or you'll be sorry.'

'I'm sorry now.'

'I mean it, Tony! I'm getting really fucking pissed!'

'What are you so fucking pissed about?'

'He's a good friend of mine!'

'Then get better friends.'

'I'm not fucking kidding. I'm asking you to do me a favor.'

'I can't.'

'You don't want to.'

'I'm telling you I can't! What the fuck do you want me to

221

do?! It's history, it's over! Now drop it before you get *ME* fucking pissed.'

Becky threw me a wretched look, but kept her mouth shut; she knew better than to push me too far. She took a deep breath and leaned against the wall, tried a different approach. Reason.

'I don't know how you can say you love me if you won't do me this little favor.'

'Becky, I'm sorry, but it's too late. They're gone, and I can't get them back.'

'I see. If you can't do something for me, maybe there are a few things I can't do for you either.'

'What the fuck are you talking about?'

'Oh, little things like . . . say . . . blow jobs. Intercourse.'

'Are you threatening me?'

'No, of course not. I'd never threaten you. Consider it more . . . a promise.'

'If you don't want to give me blow jobs anymore, you could just tell me. You don't have to make up an excuse.'

'Who said I wasn't gonna give blow jobs?! I'm just not gonna give them to you.'

That was my trigger; the thought of her with anyone else made me blind with murder. 'Let me catch you . . . I swear, I'll kill *you*, *him*, and *myself*.'

'And probably not in that order, Einstein.'

She leaned against the desk and folded her arms, her lips in a determined pout that I found irresistible. Her natural expression was a pout, but this one was more extreme than usual.

'Listen, you don't understand, the sets are cable ready! Nobody's gonna wanna give them back.'

'Tell them you made a mistake. You have ways of convincing people,' then she bent over, easily touching her toes with her fingertips, a dancing exercise she'd adopted recently to drive me nuts. 'Think it over, because I'm serious.'

'Please, give me a fucking break!'

She started pressing her toes with her fingertips, stretching the back muscles of her thighs, then when her breasts fell out of their nest like two overgrown Dodo eggs, I caved in completely. But she wanted a guarantee.

'My word is my guarantee! I told you I'll get the fucking things back, probably pay twice what I sold them for, but I'll get them and give them to your fucking asshole friend, Anthony Marangano, who's lucky he doesn't have a broken neck for fucking with people he should know better than to fuck with. All for you, okay? Would that make you happy?'

'Yes, it would.'

'Okay, good. Now please get over here right now and fuck me like you mean it, or I'm gonna rip my heart out and throw it against the wall.'

'Do you promise about the TV sets?'

'I gave my word. I always keep my word.'

'And you're not going to beat up Anthony?'

'Of course not! What do you think I am?!'

'Well, in that case . . .' Becky slid the dress from her shoulders and it splashed at her feet. She unwound the bra from her arms and slipped off her panties. Wearing only shiny black shoes with buckles on the side and white socks underneath, she came over to the couch.

I kissed her gently with my hand on her throat, feeling her blood pump against my thumb. She moaned and her tongue entered my mouth with the tart taste of cheap Merlot. A fire ignited in my gut and I pulled her down on the floor and she tumbled clumsily as her raw legs slapped the polished wood. She put her hands on my chest and tried to push me off but I held her so she couldn't move and then

223

she began to struggle; I wanted her to. I was burning with rage and fury and I needed to hurt her somehow, to show her that the world isn't fair and good people get fucked over and there's no reason or logic to any of it, that whatever the fuck makes her so high and mighty with her compassion and understanding in the face of so much pain and senseless suffering was nothing but a Goddamn fairytale. I threw my forearm across her throat, pried apart her legs, sank down onto her and started thrusting through her clothing and grunting in her face like the monster Becky knew me to be. Tears fell out of her eyes and she sniffled and shivered and tried to toss me off but I pulled up her skirt and ripped at her panties. She lunged at my face and chomped into my tongue; I let my blood pour into her mouth until she let go. I whispered into chapped, trembling lips, 'How do you like it, Monica? This is what it's like; this is how it is. Do you still want to help people and make the world a better place? How can you help anyone? You can't even help yourself!'

She shook her head from side to side, crying with angry red teeth. I reached down and undid my pants and felt her flesh tighten with resistance and hostility. I threw my weight down and sank deeper in between her legs, trembling with satisfaction as ravaging her this way would make her remember me for the rest of her life, and now all her dreams would be nightmares and maybe – JUST MAYBE! – she'd drop in despair and disgrace from the closet door with rope she'd buy at Sears and Roebuck so her brother could come to her wake and not once cry out or shed a tear. But when Monica stopped moving and the life-force drained from her eyes, when her arms fell limp to her sides and she lay as still as a newly made corpse, I found myself alone, as alone as a person can be. The fact that Monica would look on that as victory, transcendence, made my stomach retch.

I rolled off her, feeling like something made solid, with no moving parts or purpose. Like a blunt object. She wept silently with her head nestled in the corner. I lay at her side, kissing the cool hardwood floor smelling of old food and cooking oil, and laughed darkly to myself . . . When do I pay for my sins?

When I got back to the park there was a crowd of men standing around the entrance to the flat. A voice called me by name from the bushes. He was hiding behind a tall patch of thorn hedge, the panic in his voice made my skin crawl.

'What kind of trouble?' I asked.

A group of armed Turks and Franchise soldiers huddled at the steps to the entrance. Premig stood on the top step with his arms folded and a squint on his face. No one said a word as I walked up and brushed past. Adam Gottlieb and the cousins were waiting in the outer hallway.

'Have you heard?' the cousins asked me simultaneously.

'Heard what?'

Adam Gottlieb said, 'You better get your ass inside quick. Manny and Riccardo are in there and they're fucking pissed.'

Manny Simone nearly jumped down my throat. 'Where the fuck were you tonight?'

'With a hooker!'

'Why didn't you go with Hardy?'

'He told me not to. Said I would be in the way.'

'Who's this hooker you were with?!'

'I don't know. A hooker! I didn't ask her name.'

'Was she Russian?'

'Of course not! What the fuck's going on?'

Riccardo Montefiore stayed seated on the couch, took a long pull on his asthma inhaler and nodded to Manny who began to tell me a story that was even stranger than the one Hardy just told me.

I noticed for the first time the scratches on his face; he had real fear in his eyes. When he spoke saliva spewed from his lips; he couldn't get the words out fast enough. 'She came at me with a meat cleaver! Somehow she knew. She opened the door and chopped into my shoulder – look at this!'

He showed me the four-inch gash under his neck, the slit was deep and oozing red puss. Too bad, I thought, two inches to the left and she would have chopped his jugular.

'I grabbed her,' he continued, lightly bouncing on his toes. 'But she was built like a fuckin' linebacker, the strongest bitch I ever met! I was clockin' her clean shots in the face – Tony! I knocked out her teeth. Look at my hand!' His knuckles were badly cut up. 'She wouldn't let go. I pushed her through a glass table. She was cut to fuckin' ribbons and she still wouldn't give up. I finally had to get on top of her and get my hands around her throat. She tried to claw out my fuckin' eyes with a piece of glass. I started slammin' her head against the floor until her neck caved in. Ten minutes after she was dead I was still squeezin' her fuckin' neck. I just cracked, but it was self defense! I had to do it! The bitch was fuckin' crazy!'

'What are you gonna do? Stay out here all night?'

'I can't go inside. They're gonna fuckin' pop me. Tony, you gotta help me! Talk to them. Explain it was an accident. Things just got outta hand. Tell them that.'

'Maybe it's better if you explain it yourself.'

'Nobody kills a fuckin' police captain's wife and goes un-popped in the Franchise!'

And looking up at the windows silhouetted against the plum-black sky, sinister yellow cat's eyes formed by the slits in the curtains, I was certain he was right.

Manny Simone stomped around the living room as if his feet were on fire. 'All he had to do was scare an old lady, that's all he had to do . . . How the fuck did he get into a shootout with four German detectives?!'

I was a little shaken by that last bit. Hoping to change the subject I said, 'What happened with the captain's wife?'

'I don't know if he even got that far. Schaffner must have had people following him tonight. They were running through the streets, jumping over roofs, witnesses all over the fucking place, right out in the open, four dead cops. Now the whole city knows we're here!'

'Are you sure it was Hardy?'

'Who else could it have been?'

The flame in my arm reminded me not to show any pain or tender movement. Manny grabbed two books from the coffee table and waved them in my face. 'What do you know about this?!'

'I've never seen them before.'

'The fucking guy is reading *Mein Kampf* and the Bible! What the fuck is going on around here? Is he turning into a religious Nazi?!'

'At least he's reading.'

Manny whirled around with a glare that had all the homicide in the world wrapped into it; it was probably the same look he gave Carlos Castenata before he ripped off his fiberglass arm and beat him to death with it.

Riccardo Montefiore remained still-water calm, not a ripple on the surface. But his colorless, lifeless eyes had been studying me, the bleary gaze of an eel. There are times when he can almost read minds. This was one of those times.

'Where is he?' he asked.

'Outside, in the bushes.'

Manny choked, 'What?!'

'He's scared shitless! And you both know how dangerous he can be when he's spooked.'

Riccardo spoke barely above a whisper, like melting ice in a glass, 'Can you unspook him?'

'Maybe. If I can talk to him alone.'

Manny stepped up, excitedly told me, 'Tell him he's not gonna be popped. Explain that we understand things got out of hand. He felt trapped and he had to protect himself. Tell him we just want to bring him in for safekeeping. You gotta get him in here.'

Riccardo added from the couch, 'Alive.'

'I'll do my best.'

But nobody kills four detectives and goes unpopped in the Franchise. So on the stairs I played out the story I would use: Hardy resisted my attempts to bring him in, then in self-defense I had to shoot him in the face with a modified .32 Kruger – I'd better catch him from the front to make it believable.

I crept up to the foot of the hedges, 'Hardy, it's me, Tony. Don't freak out.'

There was a rustling and someone moved forward out of the black foliage. I kept my gun ready at my side. Then Adam Gottlieb appeared, 'What are you doing here?'

'The same thing as you.'

Robert Herrencamp and Miles Benowitz came out behind him with their guns drawn and their teeth clenched and for a second I thought it was my time. Until Robert Herrencamp asked me, 'What did they tell you?'

'That Hardy popped four detectives tonight.'

He turned to his cousin, 'Fuck, it's true.'

18

Hunched over the aluminum basin, I threw up into the sink; strings of bile hung from my mouth like thick silver wires. I sunk to the floor with my stomach squeezed tight into a fist. Monica sat up slowly, feeling around for her glasses and winding them behind her ears, glaring at me with what I hoped was permanent revulsion.

We sat there in silence, except for the hum of the refrigerator and the flush of water through upstairs plumbing. Her shoulders rose and fell with every breath of air into her lungs. My arm burned in pain but every other part of me was numb, the hysteric, trembling sensation of having novocaine for blood. I wondered if Monica was replaying tonight in her mind the same way I replayed it in mine, from a distance, like something seen in a movie, unreal, fictitious, as a third-person narrative. The only hard evidence of it all, at least to me, was Monica herself, and the four dead bodies the police were by now pondering over, taking descriptions from witnesses, notifying wives and parents and calling them into the morgue to identify and weep over the remains of their tragic husbands and sons. I wondered if Monica had anything to do with the fact that I cared about any of that.

I rested my head against the wall, gazing into the battered white cabinets below the sink; schoolmates from my childhood stood frozen in the swirls of dried paintbrush strokes, playing Koko-ringa-leerio in the teacher's gravel parking lot.

'The whole family's crazy! They eat worms for dinner.'

David Patterson was the tallest kid in sixth grade, he stood over me poking his finger into my forehead, the tip of his fingernail jabbing like the blunt edge of a screwdriver.

Nobody spoke back to David Patterson and I wasn't going to be the first. By way of introduction he grabbed me by the shirt and tried to lift me off the ground, turned to the crowd around us and said, 'All right now, everybody pay attention.' Then he slapped me sharply across the face and threw me down. Tears formed in my eyes but I wouldn't let myself crack; this made him even more determined. He grabbed me in a headlock and dug his knuckles into my skull, gouging out bits of hair. Through clear liquid I saw the blurry faces of the girls from assembly, watching wide-eyed with excitement and wonder as David Patterson gave me one last punch on the head and threw me again to the ground. I immediately rolled over and sat up, still wouldn't cry out or utter a sound, though I could feel bitter tears stinging my cheeks.

Somebody yelled out, 'Look! He's crying!'

'No, he ain't, not yet!'

'Yes he is! Look at him.'

While they debated this, David Patterson towered over me; he looked seven-feet tall. 'Go ahead, little baby! Go ahead, cry! Little girlie girl! Boo hoo hoo!'

Somehow, somewhere, I got up the nerve to snap back, 'I'm not gonna cry! I didn't do anything to you, Davi . . .!'

Before I could finish he kicked me flush in the mouth, the warm taste of blood poured instantly from a deep gash on the inside of my lip.

'Now you got something to cry about!'

Ever more defiant I remarked, 'Hmmm, tastes pretty good, thanks David,' then sucked on the wound.

Several of his friends prodded him to really kick my ass now. I slid back along the ground, waiting for an opportunity to jump up and run, but David smashed me in the ear with his heel and the world went black for a second. When I could see clearly again, David was gone; the faces of my classmates appeared in front of me, their eyes focused on something just above my head. A freezing blast exploded over me and a blue curtain covered my eyes, I was soaking wet with filthy sewage dripping onto my lap. I nearly puked from the stench. I pulled the bucket free and the remaining sludge poured down my face. David had taken a pail of filth from the 'Poo Pond' and doused me with it. The crowd roared with laughter and I sat there freezing and ashamed and beaten into bewilderment; lastly I began to cry.

As I walked home David and his friends trailed after me, taunting me and calling me the 'Toilet Boy'; David was the loudest one, imitating my crying and pinching his nose because of the smell wafting off my clothing. My ears rang with tinnitus and I shivered from the filth freezing in my hair; David's laughter fell on my shoulders like feathers after tar, and I knew from that moment on, I would never be the same. The person that I was twelve minutes ago would never again exist. And with that realization, something just snapped inside. Like a cord had been cut, or a nerve severed, I was suddenly beyond it all; lifted up by a higher force. Disconnected to everything alive or living. A nothingness so profound and encompassing that watching David and his friends was no more consequential to me than finding a cluster of maggots under a rock; if I could I would have crushed them under my foot. That was a turning point for me, a discovery that would carry me through the rest of my life: The gift of non-existence. And I had nobody but David Patterson to thank for it.

'Are you keeping your grades up in school?' he asked, the smell of cherry-flavored tonic on his breath. He was lucid and meek, seemed to have his reason with him now; it didn't seem possible this was the same man who days earlier tried to smash his way into the television set, flailing around the room until he had to be restrained by two policemen and a medical technician. But my mother still sported the swollen black eye, nearly closed now, from that such episode.

'They're okay,' I answered. 'I still don't understand the times tables.'

'Well, it's just a matter of memorizing the patterns. It's not as hard as it may seem. One day you'll find that it all just falls into place. That's how it is with math.'

'I guess.'

'When I was a young boy not much older than yourself, my father used to help me with my homework. Grandpa was a smart man; he knew an awful lot about history, but he wasn't much help with math. You don't remember Grandpa. You were too young. He was already very sick by the time you were born.'

'Was he sick like you?'

'No, he had cancer. He died very quickly. I don't think I'll be so blessed.'

'Mommy says if you just take your medicine you'll be better.'

'I do take it.'

'Mommy says you don't.'

'Anthony, imagine if everyday you wake up and you're too tired to get out of bed. You want to go out and play with your friends. But you can't move. The blanket on the bed is too heavy to lift, air feels too thick to breathe; everything moves in slow motion. That's what the medicine does to me. And I don't want to live in slow motion. Do you understand?'

I wasn't sure whether I did or didn't understand. He gave me a sad smile and patted my head, gazed absently at the television set across the room, then snapped back and said, 'Come on, let's practice those times tables.'

It was dark when I pulled up; pockets of light fell from streetlights spaced ten-feet apart. David Patterson came out from inside the office, stepped into the first circle of yellow light. He wore gray-striped grease-stained overalls and his hands were black with grime. He looked dirty, had the ragged look of someone working long and hard in a thankless job of manual labor. I got out and stood by the driver's door, told him to fill it up and he went to the rear of the car and found the gas cap. His face had aged poorly, he had premature lines under his eyes and the angular features that in his youth made him look strong and masculine now seemed grotesque and out of proportion. He didn't give me a second glance and that disappointed me; I thought for sure he'd recognize my face, it hadn't changed that much, and I stood directly in the light so he could see my features. As the gas gurgled into my tank David Patterson gazed at the construction site directly across the street from the pumps, a new shopping mall the Franchise was building for Percy Dinunzio's brother-in-law.

I wanted to engage him, didn't want this one to be anonymous; I wanted him to know who it was and why it was happening.

'Something, the way it's all changing, ain't it? The neighborhood.'

He looked back curiously, beyond the new suit and expensive shoes. I asked, 'Do you remember when that was a ball field?'

'I sure do,' he replied. 'Used to play stickball against that brick wall in the summer. An old broom handle and new Spaulding, play all day long. Those were the days.' His eyes had the same luminous blue light that all the girls found so adorable back when he still had the world by the balls.

'That's right,' I said. 'Out back was a pond with frogs and

tadpoles; in the winter it would freeze up and kids would play ice hockey. Then they turned it into a sewer.'

'Yeah, I remember that; used to be called the Poo Pond.'

The nozzle on the gas tank clicked and he went to lift it out, topping off the meter so it read an even number, 14 dollars.

I scoped out the surroundings. We were alone. It was perfect, I could blast out his kneecaps and douse him with gasoline, set him ablaze and be gone in seconds. David put the nozzle back in its cradle and stood upright, about three feet away from me. He was looking at me sideways, nervous, tentative; I thought he might've guessed my intentions.

'We know each other,' he began and I looked up intrigued.

'Do we?' but David dismissed that with a sad smile.

'There's something I've been wanting to say to you for a long time, and I really don't know how to begin.' He glanced off down the road, then again met my eyes. 'I was a mean bastard when I was younger, a real fuck. I don't know why either. I mean, I didn't have a bad childhood; my folks were good people and they didn't raise me to be that way. I think back on some of the things I did . . . to people who did me no bit of harm, and I'm really at a loss to explain it. I want you to know . . . I'm really truly sorry. If there was any way to change the past I would. You never did nothing to me and you deserved a lot better. As I recall you were a pretty good guy. And well . . . I . . . I hope you can forgive me.'

I didn't say anything for a moment. Finally I told him, barely audibly, it was okay, that I'd forgotten all about it until he just mentioned it. I gave him a fifty-dollar bill and told him to keep the change; he seemed to appreciate the gesture. Then I shook his hand, told him no hard feelings and got in my car. Watching in the rear-view mirror as his shrinking figure dissolved into shadow, I was shaking with rage. That I could be so disarmed by an act of genuine compassion made me feel weak and helpless. I was ten years old again and walking home with tears and sewage on my face.

I lost track of how long I'd been driving, but as the chilled air of the turnpike swirled in my ears and the road in front of me grew endless in a hypnotic visual drone, the sour shame in my gut melted into something not so malevolent anymore, and I began to see things in a slightly different light. I had to admit, I was rather impressed with David Patterson. It took a certain kind of strength to expose himself to me like that, to seek forgiveness without excuse or rationalization, to be truly sorry; it was a strength I surely didn't possess. David Patterson was at one time the person I hated more than anyone else in the entire world. I spent days of my childhood masturbating to the violent fantasies of his horrific death, and now to find that the monster of my youth was but a sorry, simple man surprised and invigorated me. The fact that people can change, for the better – *that change was possible!* – was something I'd lost sight of, or just plain stopped believing in. Until seeing David tonight. I was tempted to drive back and tell him how close he'd come to getting popped. Instead, two weeks later I sent over Billy Becker from Brunswick to beat him within an inch of his life, just in case I was wrong.

My gun was lying under the table. It had fallen out of my jacket during the struggle. I took it and unscrewed the silencer, wished I'd taken the revolver, we could have played Russian roulette. I slid it across the floor to Monica's feet, told her, 'Go ahead, take it.'

She didn't move, just stared at it with a cross of fear and fascination. Someone knocked on the door, jiggled the knob back and forth, then knocked again. Metal scraped inside the keyhole as the lock was picked. Monica and I both looked at my gun on the floor, then the door swung open and Monica's brother stepped in. He was greasy and unwashed, his hair hung in clumps to his shoulders; a skin-and-bones specimen of hard addiction strung out on smack, big time. The sight of us sitting on the floor, disheveled and beaten as if we'd just made love, brought a sickening grin to his desiccated lips, until his eyes found the gun by his sister's feet. He looked at Monica with a twist of amusement, shook his head and stepped toward her room. She bolted up and shrieked with a fire I didn't think she had in her; the unexpected burst landed in my gut like a quivering rat. Her brother stopped in his tracks and stood there, unmoving, his back to us. His legs were matchsticks in stiff moldy blue jeans; a red plaid handker-chief hung over his back pocket. Monica was out of breath, throbbing with heat and fury; I thought I was the only one who could bring a woman to that peak of hatred. The brother continued on into her room and slammed the door, started trashing her furniture behind it; a scene I'd wit-nessed many times before between Becky and her brother. The door opened and he stepped into the hall crumpling a few bills into his pocket, stopped in the kitchen doorway. Brother and sister snapped back and forth like bickering wolves until he swooped down and reached for the gun on the floor. I snatched his throat in my palm like it was a rat-tlesnake. He gasped and tried to wriggle free but I held him fast.

'You can keep the gun,' I said, 'but I'm taking this.' Then I slid out the clip. When I shoved the gun back in his jack-et Monica cried, '*Nein!*'

'Shut the fuck up!'

I tossed her brother back on the floor and he clutched at

his throat and puked. Monica crawled over to help him, reached into his jacket and he shoved her away. He jumped up screaming in her face; her hair moved from the force; then he ripped the gun from his jacket and pointed it at me twice, once at Monica – the chamber still held a bullet (automatics always lock hot) – then he clutched his sides as if a giant invisible fist had punched him square in the gut. He swept the dish rack filled with dishes crashing to the floor, shoved the gun back in his jacket and stormed out of the apartment in tears. My prints were now permanently off the weapon, replaced by his. Monica fell back against the wall and seemed to shrink in size as the heat cooled inside her body. The lace of her left boot formed a question mark on the floor; her shin was scratched with long red lines and the flesh around them was a pasty, oatmeal color. Now when I looked at her she seemed old and dirty, like a used syringe, and there was something pleasing about that. She buried her face in her hands and began sobbing, every part of her shook with despair; it had been a while since I'd seen anyone cry so purely, so wretchedly. I envied her.

I got up and got her a glass of water. She took it reluctantly, then sipped over the rim; her cheeks were red and raw, a last teardrop fell onto her lap, grew twice its size then died slowly in the ragged fabric of her dress. I stood in the kitchen doorway, chuckled lightly to myself.

'*Was ist so komisch*?' she said.

'You are.'

'*Warum?*'

'Looks like life ain't so happy and carefree anymore, is it?'

Monica put the glass on the floor and looked up with anger and shame, pursed her lips and began to speak . . .

Hardy had been missing for more than ten hours. Riccardo Montefiore wanted everyone off the street until he

237

could gauge the fallout from the night before, so we all stayed close. In the office Heinrich swore up and down that he hadn't seen Hardy and had no idea where he could be, but Manny kept on him like a virus until Riccardo nodded and Manny backed off. Everything else went on as usual, except for the painful sighs of frustration coming from Henry Pembleton whenever he found something new that didn't add up, which today was quite frequently. Manny finally told him he sounded like an old woman and if he heard any more sighs he was going to put him in a dress. Henry then confined his frustrations to masculine groans of displeasure.

After lunch a cement truck pulled onto the site and started pouring globs of mortar down into the main foundation until Vita's younger brother, Mustaph, grabbed a fistful of the gooey stuff and inspected it. His face twisted like a burnt pretzel and he stormed into the trailer, came out with his father who grabbed a fistful of mortar like his son had done, let out a whine and snapped at Mustaph who in turn snapped at another worker and soon a dozen Turkish construction workers were yelling at each other and pointing to the blob of cement spreading out in the dirt.

'What the fuck is going on?!' Manny Simone appeared at the edge of the hole.

'The sssement! It is no good! There is too much water! Thisss foundation will crumble!'

'What are you talking about?! This is the mixture we always use! We've never had a problem before.'

'Thisss is dangerous! We cannot lay a foundation with bad cement.'

Manny jabbed a finger in Yossario's chest. 'You're nuts! I've been constructing buildings for thirty-seven years and I'm telling you this is absolutely good cement!'

'The contract is very clear on the mixture of sssand . . .'

Yossario turned to the truck operator and barked something in Turkish and immediately the engine shut off.

'Hey! I'm the one that gives orders around here. Whatever you just told him to do, undo it.'

'I can't let the work be dangerous!'

'Listen you, I don't want to have this conversation out here! Come inside with me and we'll talk about it.'

'I'm not leaving until the truck is taken away.'

'Why you fucking punk . . .' Manny grabbed Yossario by the shirt and the other workers yelled and rushed up and there was a moment where I didn't know if they were going to attack us or not. I leaned forward.

'Let's think this through, Manny. We got forty guys here with tools!'

Manny scanned the situation and released Yossario, but by then blood was pouring out of his nose and Mustaph brushed Manny aside and tended to his father. Vita appeared with Premig and demanded to know what was going on.

I told him there was a disagreement over cement. Vita's eyes told me to go fuck myself, then he led his father to a stack of sandbags and sat him down. Premig growled at the Turks, motioning with his rubber hand, discolored with dirt and soot, the pinkie finger missing, and they all murmured darkly and stepped back. Yossario's handkerchief was soaked and dripping onto his lap and Mustaph yelled at his brother who yelled at Premig who ran to the street and sped back in his car right up onto the dusty gravel. Yossario was rushed into the backseat and driven away by Premig and Vita, Mustaph stayed on and came back to the site where Manny stood waiting.

'Pour the cement, kid.'

Mustaph mumbled something in Turkish and it didn't sound like something nice.

'I said pour the fucking cement, kid.'

Manny stepped in front of him, blocked his path. Mustaph just stood there. A quiet hush rose up from the workers and if Manny tried anything with the kid I knew there'd be a riot. But Manny stood his ground and wasn't going to let anybody fuck with him unless Riccardo Montefiore said they could. I hoped Mustaph was smart enough to read the situation because the longer he waited the harder it became to resolve; I scoped out the opposing weaponry – hammers and screwdrivers and shovels and picks – and a mild trembling sensation grew out from the base of my spine. I said under my breath, 'Mustaph, come on, pour the cement. Nobody wants to get hurt here.'

He looked at me, then to the others around him, proud, loyal men with wives and children and endless manual labor etched on their faces. All of them prepared to fight and risk their lives for the honor of this kid, maybe the final confrontation over control of the company. Taking stock of Miles Benowitz and Robert Herrencamp and several others standing nearby, I figured we could take out about ten, fifteen before being overpowered and chopped to pieces.

The cement truck operator called out to Mustaph, who looked over with uncertainty, inexperience, then nodded his head. The cement truck operator climbed up in his truck and continued pouring the cement. Manny stepped back and Mustaph brushed past him. The workers slowly backed off, grumbling amongst themselves and glancing over their shoulders with raw contempt. Believe it or not, at that moment I envied Hardy; he wasn't part of this anymore.

'I DON'T WANT TO KNOW ANY OF THIS!'

She was startled by my outburst, my head rattled as if it were filled with ball bearings.

'Why are you telling me this? Is it supposed to change

anything? It doesn't matter. Don't you see? You can never win this game! Do you think tonight was an isolated incident?! I've done things that would make your fucking skin crawl! So don't try to impress me with your pathetic personal history.'

I didn't know why I was so angry; I should have been pleased. It's what I had been waiting for; a crack in the glass, the not-so-hidden flaw. But now that she had revealed it, I took it as a betrayal, she'd shattered the fantasy. What was left to believe in if we're all just swimming around in the same murky soup of degeneracy? It was ridiculous to be so bent out of shape, and yet, I couldn't help it. When she pulled up her sleeve to show the vague, mapped-out lines where the elbow met the forearm, healed now but no denying the history, I wanted to hurt her again, then go after her brother whom I held responsible for it all. Instead I gripped her face in my hands, tenderly, imagined her dead and rotting on the floor. One quick snap and it would be over; nobody would ever know anything, other than a former junkie died one day in East Berlin leaving behind a junkie brother with a gun responsible for four gangland slayings.

There was blood on her lip and I kissed it away. She wouldn't meet my eyes so I pulled her to the floor and now she fell soft and submissive with her flesh burning up from guilt and corruption and I could take her now that she was corrupt and impure. I ripped off her clothes and scratched at her thighs and she bit into my shoulder as we crawled into the bedroom where I shoved her down on the mattress half off the floor, spread her willing legs and sank deep inside her as we made cruel desperate love until our bodies ached.

Afterwards we sat in the kitchen drinking wine and eating canned peach slices. She asked me finally about the men chasing us tonight. I told her they were business associates from a competing firm.

'*Was* about the *Polizei*?'

'Just keep quiet. It should all calm down in a few days. Stay inside if you can. Don't go out.'

'I *muss* work.'

'Then be careful. I don't think I can see you right away. Maybe not for a few days or so.'

She let out a quiet chuckle, might have rolled her eyes in disbelief.

'What's so funny?'

'You.'

'Why?'

'We see us not again. Never. You come never back. *Verstehst du?*'

'Yeah, I think so.'

'You go now,' she added, and it was my turn to chuckle. I got up and went to the door while she stared at the clear splash of vomit her brother had left behind on the floor, her face partially hidden behind the veil of smoke she blew across the table. Her dark and dangerous adventure had come to its inevitable conclusion, as it was meant to, and for her, at least, tomorrow would be a better day. I closed the door and disappeared into the night.

19

The Countess was coming!

It seemed impossible, but once I saw Manny Simone fixing up the office in a fit of agitation and after Adam Gottlieb and five other soldiers were sent over to Riccardo Montefiore's building to provide security, it seemed less impossible. Why Riccardo would ever bring his wife over here with all the impending shit coming down was a mystery to me, but I didn't care what the reasons were; the Countess had a soothing effect on people. Everybody tended to behave a little more humanely when she was around, up to and including her husband. When Frankie Clark blew up Teddy Millstein's car without approval and accidentally killed Teddy's ten-year-old daughter in the process, Riccardo wanted to send a message to any other independent thinkers. Two hours later Frankie found himself chained naked to a chair in the basement of Riccardo's summer home.

'What is burning down here?' The Countess said coming down the stairs and waving her hand in front of her face. She'd been out shopping. 'You can smell it upstairs, the smoke alarms are going to go off.'

She stopped halfway down the stairs at the sight of Frankie's shivering body, his upper torso had been charred by an industrial welding torch. Her voice cracked like a whip. 'This is my home, Riccardo, not a medieval dungeon. He's not even conscious. If you're going to do something, at least do it right. I want this ended immediately. Do you hear me? You should be ashamed of yourselves, all of you.'

She scanned the room and none of us could meet her eyes; it was like being back in grade school. Finally Riccardo turned to Donnie Delapido, a med-school dropout now working as a pain specialist, who gave Frankie an injection of something that brought him around. Frankie's head lifted in a dizzy sour haze and Riccardo leaned into his ear, 'Now, are you giving orders or following orders?'

Frankie sobbed in a hoarse whisper that he was following orders.

'Then I order you to die.'

Riccardo looked to Manny who put a bullet in Frankie's left ear. The Countess didn't flinch as Frankie's head jerked, then slowly tipped over and emptied onto his shoulder. Riccardo Montefiore turned to her, his eyes triumphant, like fire in the snow. 'Is that better?'

'We'll be eating in twenty minutes,' she replied. 'Make sure you air out this room,' then she went upstairs to finish supervising dinner.

A caravan of conspicuous dark sedans pulled up and six soldiers hopped out scoping the street. The back door of the middle limousine opened from inside and bejeweled fingers reached out to a callused thuggish palm for support. Lucretia Montefiore stepped out and the world turned a shade brighter. She started for the house when she caught my eyes and stopped.

'Hello Tony. You look like you've lost weight. Isn't my husband feeding you?'

'He's feeding me fine, Countess. Just the other day I ate an olive.'

Lucretia burst out laughing and the soldiers looked up startled, as if they'd never heard her laugh before. More startling to me was the sight of Emily Talbot stepping out of the same back seat as Lucretia. Much like their husbands, Lucretia Montefiore and Emily Talbot never did anything together, let alone ride in the same car. Nobody had told her about Lawrence yet, because she wasn't crying or wrinkled with devastation the way the other widows always looked after the death of a husband. Instead she pulled the ends of her tattered wool sweater around her like an old school marm at the turn of the century and wore the same nervous look of discomfort that her husband always wore; she seemed out of place in any room that wasn't her own kitchen.

Lucretia looked back with a pinch of contempt, then strolled toward the house where six-foot Roger Wingtips, a neckless brute with the mind of a tadpole, waited with his hands clasped in front of him and his eyes focused on the ground, lips silently counting every step Lucretia took as she approached the door so he could open it in stride and she could make a stately entrance. I often found myself waiting for Roger to open the door just slow enough to smash her face with it, but today was not that day as she glided confidently past with no acknowledgement of poor Roger or the effort it took for him to accomplish this spectacular challenge.

The table had been set for a banquet, a celebration dinner for friends coming together. Arnie Imperiole was the center of attention and unofficial guest of honor, sitting beside Riccardo Montefiore and across from Lawrence Talbot, filling the room with his robust laugh and tales of financial conquest. His elegant wife sat beside him quietly sipping her champagne and shrinking in embarrassment. Arnie Imperiole owned several lumber yards and controlled the carpenters' union and was a respected friend and associate of the Franchise. Until he married Lucretia Tigrit, a mysterious beauty who one day just appeared in all our lives as if by magic. Seven years ago, to be exact, at the annual Fourth of July barbecue Arnie threw at his estate in Staten Island. Our wives and girlfriends were local girls with big hair and simple tastes; no one came from farther away than Pittsburgh. Our idea of exotic was when Bobby Cuomo went steady with some goth chick he met on the Lower East Side – what the fuck. But when Arnie introduced his new wife to us, a creature so completely alien to anything we'd ever seen before, we were thunderstruck. Nearly six-feet tall, her skin was the color of cappuccino and her hair was so black it was nearly blue; slender and statuesque, standing poolside in a blue silk robe, her legs seemed to go on forever; dark green sunglasses protected the mystery of her eyes and her lips maintained a tolerant, condescending smile whenever Arnie introduced her to another criminal bigwig, showing her off like a pair of brand new diamond cuff links. We didn't know how to address her because she didn't seem real to us, as if made of ice or stone, so we stood off near the bar debating her ethnicity. Tommy Farrell swore she was northern Italian because of her black hair and high cheekbones but Arthur Sanders thought she was Israeli because of her prominent nose and cool demeanor

'Get the fuck . . . Arnie would never marry a Jew!'

Turkish was the farthest thing from any of our minds. Riccardo Montefiore was unusually quiet that day. He seemed, if at all possible, humble. But I recognized the hungry glint in his eyes, and when he stared with that very look at Arnie's wife that afternoon I knew it was only a matter of time.

'Hey Tony, I want you to drive Arnie's wife home, make sure she gets in safe. Then come right back. We're gonna be here for a while.'

It was an unusual request; I was not a driver and hadn't been for seven months, but I didn't question it, and actually looked forward to spending some time alone with her; it would make for an interesting story later with Adam Gottlieb and the guys, who snickered as I walked past their table.

Before getting in the car she stood at the back door waiting impatiently for me to open it. Without so much as a glance in my direction she slid gracefully into the black leather interior and we started off for the thirty-minute ride. On the way she didn't make a sound, it was like driving with a corpse. I heard the leather seat groan and a purse click open; a scarf of cigarette smoke floated past my eyes.

'Do you mind if I smoke?' she asked, her voice crisp, clear, no hint of a question in the tone. It was the first time I'd heard her speak.

'No, not at all,' I replied.

We drove for another ten minutes in silence, punctuated by the nervous clicking of the turn signal on left-hand turns and the forced dismissal of smoke from her lips.

'Do you think they'll be very long tonight?'

'I don't know.'

'I hate these parties.'

'Yeah, I do too.'

The seat rustled as she shifted her legs.

'How long have you worked for my husband?'

'I don't work for your husband. I work for the Franchise.'

'I see,' she said, as if surprised by the fact. 'How long have you worked for . . . "the Franchise"?'

'A couple years.'

'You look like you should still be in school.'

I sped up a little, twenty miles over the speed limit.

'Tell me something.'

'Yes, Ma'am?'

'What exactly does the Franchise franchise?'

'Well . . . a lot of things. We help things get made.'

That elicited a cold, cruel chuckle. I sped through a red light but she hadn't noticed, staring instead out the side window at the bulldozers and cranes sleeping on the Weissglass lot, the site for the new youth detention center across from the little league baseball field; whoever planned that one was my hero.

'I've seen you before.'

'Yes, I've been to your home several times. In the back yard.'

'Yes, that's right. I remember. You work for the tall man.'

'I'm actually employed by . . .'

'Yes, I know. The Franchise. But it's all run by the tall man, isn't it?'

'It's a big company.'

'What exactly do you do for the "Franchise"?'

'I help out.'

'Is that what it's called?'

Her eyes found mine in the rear-view mirror; they were angry, hostile. I made another turn and wished I were closer to her home.

'How old are you?' she asked. I didn't answer, kept my eyes on the road. 'Did you hear me?'

'I'm twenty-one.'

'You're rather young to be a gangster.'

I didn't know how to respond to that, so I didn't. I wondered if maybe she was drunk, though she wasn't slurring her words.

'You seem pretty shy for a gangster.'

No comment.

'What are you so shy about?'

'I'm not shy.'

'Then what are you afraid of?'

'I'm not afraid.'

'Aren't you afraid of Mr Montefiore?'

'I have no reason to be.'

'That's good; fearlessness is good. Because I'm not afraid of him either.'

It was getting too strange now, and when things got too strange someone's life took a turn for the worse.

'Do you know why I'm not afraid of him?'

'No, Ma'am, I'd rather not know.'

'Aren't you curious?'

'I can't say that I am.'

'Because he's nothing but an animal.'

'Sometimes animals bite.' The second it left my lips I wanted to take it back.

'You think you're pretty smart, don't you?'

'No, I don't, Mrs Imperiole. I apologize for that. I meant no offense. I should probably just keep my mouth shut from now on. If you don't mind.'

I drove past the Shalimar lit up in gold with the gaudy marble fountain spraying colored water in the air. A wedding reception had just let out and two Mexican valets in short red vests were running out to retrieve the guests' Cadillacs in the parking lot.

'What kind of man is Mr Montefiore to work for?'

'Excuse me?'

'Do you like him?'

'Yes. I do.'

'How tall would you say he is?'

'I really couldn't say.'

'Would you say he's six feet two inches, or taller?'

'I really couldn't say.'

'He's a tall, cheap murderer.'

I kept my mouth shut.

'Don't you have anything to say to that?'

'I would have to respectfully disagree.'

'About what? That he's tall and cheap, or a murderer?'

'We're here, Mrs Imperiole, home.'

'Pull up the drive; stop at the door.'

I drove onto the circular driveway, past the wrought-iron gates and a tall trimmed hedge, around to the main pillared entrance lit overhead with orange spotlights. I put the car in park and waited for her to exit. I wanted to get away from her as fast as I could. She just sat there without a sound until I ran around and opened the door for her. When she got out she walked past me without a glance.

'I want you to come in with me. I don't like to enter a house alone.'

'Yes, Mrs Imperiole.'

'I'd rather you didn't call me that; coming from you it makes me feel old.'

'Yes, Ma'am.'

'That's even worse.'

I followed her into the front foyer where a cascading waterfall with a small statuette stood in all its tasteless glory; there was a permanent fake flower garden taking up another corner of the room. The living room was huge, plush white carpeting covered the entire floor, and the off-white couches and lounge chairs were wrapped in plastic; I couldn't believe my eyes. Mrs Imperiole saw my face and remarked, 'My husband fancies himself an interior designer. There's no stopping him.'

'You're kidding me.'

'Do you think I would furnish the place this way?'

Her eyes told me I'd better agree in a real hurry.

'You have my sincerest sympathy. No one should have to live like this.'

A small line of humor cracked her face, immediately replaced by apprehension. We stood there looking at each other. She was about to do something that once done couldn't be undone; the uncertainty of crossing a border; she was deciding if she could trust me or not.

'Is there anything I can help you with?' I asked.

'I have something I want you to bring back. It's really, really important that it gets to Mr Montefiore. No one else, but him. Can I trust you to do that?'

She went upstairs and left me alone with the waterfall. The constant splash of water made me realize how badly I had to pee, but I wasn't going to ask for the bathroom. She came down with a thick black leather valise.

'Mr Montefiore is expecting this; make sure only he receives it. You're not to open this or look inside, is that understood?'

'Completely. Anything else?'

'That's all. You do that and you'll have done a good deed for the day.'

'I always wanted to be a Boy Scout.'

'You better leave now,' she said, already bored with me. I stepped to the door and turned around.

'How about "Countess"?' I asked.

'Excuse me?'

'The Countess. Instead of Mrs Imperiole?'

'The Countess?' she looked up intrigued. 'Why Countess?'

'I don't know. It just seems to fit.'

'I'll think about it.'

I turned to go and she called after me, 'Make sure . . . Mr Montefiore. No side trips.'

Seeing her in the doorway next to the waterfall, her rigid posture and proud eyes, arms folded tightly in front of her, I thought of an exotic bird in a gold-plated rhinestone cage.

I clutched the valise under my arm with a burning curiosity, but not enough curiosity to risk my life. The party had moved to the back room and I entered to see Arnie Imperiole lying in a beaten heap on the dirty wood floor. His clothes had been ripped to shreds and his face had been battered and there were small puddles of blood scattered about; I accidentally crunched a broken tooth under my shoe. Riccardo looked up and immediately grabbed the valise and handed it to Lawrence Talbot who sat waiting at a table with his calculator and notebook. He scraped up a fist of phlegm, spit it into his soiled handkerchief, then proceeded to open the valise and take out thick leather-bound books. Occasionally Arnie let out a groan but for the most part he remained unconscious for the several hours it took for Lawrence to audit his books.

When I went back to pick up the Countess she was waiting in the foyer. The waterfall had been turned off. She had four suitcases and a shopping bag. I loaded them into the trunk and she again waited by the rear door until I opened it for her. This time she didn't utter a sound, pensively smoking a cigarette with her mind a thousand miles away, as if we'd never spoken a word to each other; I preferred the silence. I was to find out two months later, quite by accident – overhearing a phone conversation between Riccardo Montefiore and Bottle Rocket Al – that the Countess studied accounting in school and was a licensed CPA.

'Join me for a coffee.'

I followed her out the door trailed by Roger Wingtips and two other neck-deprived bodyguards I'd never met before and didn't care to meet now.

Lucretia walked along *Adalbertstrasse* toward *Oranienstrasse*, studying the surroundings with familiarity, stopping occasionally to gaze into a storefront of electronics or second-hand jewelry. I walked beside her and let her reminisce.

'See that street down there? The wall came right across there, cut the block in half.'

'No shit.'

'I used to write my name on it in chalk when I was a little girl. It was a dead-end street. You couldn't even drive down it. It's amazing to see it all opened up. What are the nights like? Are they cold?'

'No, not compared to back home.'

'Is a sweater enough to wear?'

'Sure. A sweater, or a light jacket. How long are you planning to stay?'

'I'm not sure.'

Lucretia got silent and I waited patiently for her to get to the point; she never discussed things like the weather or what clothes to wear.

We reached a quaint café on the corner of *Oranienstrasse* and *Heinrichplatz* and Lucretia took a seat at a table near the huge plate-glass window. The tables and chairs were simple wooden artifacts and the walls had hand-painted posters of upcoming local events; there was a dusty piano against one wall and some kind of whaling spear mounted over the cellar stairs. Roger and the bodyguards waited outside by the curb while Lucretia stirred her coffee though she didn't add anything to it, then tapped the spoon on the edge of her cup and placed it softly on the table. Sipping her drink she looked at me over the rim of the cup.

'You seem different somehow,' she said. 'You look better. Europe has had a good effect on you.'

'If you say so.'

'Don't you like it here?'

'It's okay. I'll be happy when this whole business is over with.'

'What do you know about Hardy?'

'What everybody else knows. He's gone. Nobody's heard from him.'

'Where do you think he might be?'

'I don't know.'

'You two lived together; did he ever say anything?'

'What? They sent you to pump me for information?'

'Relax. I'm just talking with you. It's a mystery, is all.'

'He made friends with some skinheads; he might be with them.'

'That's highly unlikely.'

'Why is that?'

The Countess leaned forward and lowered her voice, told me the ever-increasing bizarre story of Hardy and Captain Schaffner's wife. 'That's why I doubt very much he's hanging out with skinheads,' she concluded.

'He's more enterprising than I thought. It's kind of lucky for us.'

'How do you figure that?'

'It doesn't point to us directly.'

'What about the four detectives? Who does that point to?'

It was a Lawrence Talbot sort of question, and as usual I didn't have an answer for it. I was myself curious as to why we hadn't been shut down or arrested by the police yet.

'They forgot to put lemon in your beer.'

'What do you mean?'

'I ordered you a *Krystal Weizen*. That's a Bavarian beer and it's served with a slice of lemon.'

Lucretia looked over for the waitress, a punked-out chick with neon yellow hair and faded ripped jeans.

'The beer is fine,' I said.

'If you're going to drink German beer you have to drink it properly,' she scolded. Then proceeded to scold the punked-out chick, who brought me a slice of lemon which I plopped in the glass. Lucretia waited until I sipped and made the necessary acknowledgements.

'When are you going to tell Emily?'

'Tonight.'

'Why bring her all the way out here to do that?'

'How should we do it, over the phone? We're all here now. She'd be alone back home.'

A short hunched-over hag hobbled into the café wearing

a black shawl and dirty robe and holding a straw basket in her hand. A skinny little girl maybe six years old stood at her side gripping her hand and together they went to each table begging for change and when people wouldn't pay the hag held the basket under their faces and pulled her little girl forward to argue the point. I reached into my pocket for some change but Lucretia took my arm.

'That's a disgrace, to use her daughter that way.'

'Maybe they're really poor.'

'I was really poor; my family had nothing. I grew up in a squat house. My mother never used me to beg. This is a scam.'

'How do you know?'

The hag came over to our table and Lucretia scolded her in Turkish and the hag argued back and the young girl stood there trying to shrink behind her mother's hip. A tall guy with long wavy hair and an amused smile came by and escorted the hag out of the café, then turned to Lucretia and apologized and everything went back to normal.

'Wouldn't it have been easier just to give her a couple Marks?'

'Probably,' she replied with a cruel, girlish smile, then sipped her coffee. I had to laugh, she reminded me so much of Carrie when she smiled that way. I took the lemon slice out of my beer and put it on the table.

20

Emily had been told that Lawrence was sent out on a secret job under Riccardo's direction and was coming back the next day; that's why she hadn't heard from him for so long. Over dinner she barely touched her food and teetered on the verge of crumbling; whether she suspected the true nature of her husband's absence I couldn't tell for sure, she was always pretty bugged out.

After dinner I went through the park and sat at a café drinking coffee and watching small Turkish kids play soccer in the street; their ball bounced twice then stopped dead against the curb, it was punctured. One little girl with black stringy hair and smudged cheeks walked past on bare feet wearing a tattered blue dress; she held a dirty rag doll and laughed a simple child's laugh and I tried to remember if I had ever felt that young and carefree. I imagined them all grown up and living their lives under stress and poverty. Then someone flashed like wildfire through my mind. I wondered what she was doing, if she were hanging out in her apartment with friends eating hand-picked vegetables and drinking two bottles of wine; then I imagined myself as someone else across the square watching me sit here drinking coffee and would I look as truly lost as I felt. A small green police sedan drove by and slowed near the corner and I reached into my jacket until the cops turned down the block and disappeared from sight. I thought of Hardy and Captain Schaffner's wife, how out of control the whole thing had gotten, the fact that Hardy went to her house not alone but with his new skinhead friends whom he probably thought would add to the fun, and that once inside the skinheads beat her senseless and ripped off her clothes and spray-painted swastikas on her body and burned her with cigarettes and forced her to drink ammonia – the Countess told me her eyes had been plucked out and were still missing. When Hardy tried to stop them he got chopped in the neck with a machete, then they smashed a chair over his head and kicked him until he was unconscious. Hardy woke up to find himself alone in the house with the cold body of Schaffner's wife ludicrously wrapped in his arms.

Adam Gottlieb took the seat directly across from me. Wearing a grin of victory he announced, 'We're roommates.'

'What do you mean, roommates?'

'Manny wants me to bunk down with you. He don't want nobody livin' alone. He said it's for everybody's protection. I'm gonna take Hardy's room.'

They didn't trust me anymore.

When I got back to the apartment there was a car waiting to take me to Riccardo's building. I got in without any questions and was silently driven the five-minute ride. The streets were wet and grayer than usual; there was a muted, somber melody in the air, like an old blues tune played on a scratchy record; a train rumbled by on elevated tracks twelve feet above the car; somewhere in the distance a church bell rang; droplets of rain clung to the windshield until the wipers sliced them into oblivion. We drove past the block that Lawrence Talbot used to live on, though we didn't drive down it.

I followed a carpeted corridor to the back staircase made of cracked cement; the staircase led down below street level where a muddy puddle clogged a rusted drain in the middle of the hall. A woman was sobbing softly behind the last door at the end. I knew then that Emily Talbot had been told of her husband's impressive plunge into the next dimension. Until she lifted her head revealing the bruises on her eyes and the blood on her lips; she'd been beaten badly, at least for a woman. The Countess turned sharply from the window and the blackjack flapped idly in her liver-spotted hand; Riccardo Montefiore eyed me with something close to disdain; Manny Simone wore the usual scowl of contempt and a charcoal tie. Emily Talbot caught my eyes and shuddered, as if she were hooked up to an electrical outlet and zapped with juice; I checked to make sure she wasn't.

The Countess snarled into her face, 'As you can see, Emily, we're prepared to do whatever it takes to get to the bottom of this. So you can tell us yourself, peacefully, while you still have lips. Or we can find another way.'

'There's nothing to tell,' she said, then flexed her wrists tied by straps to the arms of the chair. The scenario was familiar enough, this was the Montefiore courtroom and the Talbot family was in serious trouble. Henry Pembleton had discovered two million dollars missing and unaccounted for in the books and nobody could believe that Lawrence Talbot could, or would, make that kind of mistake, which left only one other conclusion.

The Countess took a step forward. 'My husband taught me a good cure for "nothing to tell".' She cracked Emily's face with the blackjack so hard half a tooth went flying across the floor.

'Is there something to tell now, Emily?'

Emily spit out a mouthful of blood, then looked up at the Countess with a toughness I didn't think she had in her. 'You were always a filthy tramp, Lucy. You still are.'

'What did you say to me, Grandma?'

'Why don't you tell everyone about your time in Detroit? . . .Walking the streets as a tart. Tell them about your kids. Your oldest son. Tell them what happened in San Diego.

With that lieutenant. See, you can polish a turd, Lucy, but it's still just a turd.'

That was the only time I'd ever seen the Countess lose her temper. After the attack Emily's head slumped over on her shoulder and her milky-blue breasts sagged flat on her stomach, pieces of a broken lamp still clung to her hair. She looked dead, except for the wheezing sounds coming from deep in her lungs. The Countess turned toward the back wall, shaking with rage. Riccardo put his arm on her shoulder but she brushed it away. She said with a small crack in her voice, 'Did you hear what she said about me?'

'Nobody listens to her.'

Manny Simone motioned me to follow him outside.

'She ain't gonna break,' he began. 'She'll die before she betrays that bastard, even in death.'

'Maybe she's telling the truth, maybe she doesn't know about it.'

'What are you . . . her attorney?! She knows everything he knows.'

He was right. 'So, what do you want me to do?'

Within two minutes of pulling out I saw him in the rear-view mirror. He wasn't very good at tailing people, but then, it occurred to me, that was the idea, they wanted me to know. I was slightly hurt that they would give Roger Wingtips the job, an incompetent driver to say the least. I downshifted into second and floored the pedal, took off screeching around the corner, heard Roger behind me try to do the same but the engine over-revved and the tires squealed in place and by the time he hit the intersection I was through an alley and racing to the next corner. I skidded left then made the first right onto *Manteufelstrasse*; Emily's head thumped against the passenger window and she let out a moan. I drove along *Pücklerstrasse*, a colorful street of taverns and Turkish storefronts onto *Naunyn-*

strasse, which got me onto *Mariannenplatz*, a cobblestone circle with chunks missing from the road and children riding bikes around a fountain of black statues holding fire hoses. On *Köpenickerstrasse*, a busy street of billboards and trees that cut across a large part of *Kreuzberg*, I drove east, toward *Treptow*. Roger Wingtips was long lost by now and would shortly go back to report how he fucked up.

Emily made a hoarse gurgling sound and I wondered if there were any internal injuries that I didn't know about. I continued east until the buildings became grime-stained boxes with windows. Drove alongside a riverbank searching for the side street that would take me to the water's edge. I'd seen this street on the map, knew if I just went with the water it would lead me eventually to this unpronounceable Polish-sounding road. Emily sat up, watching the river appear in front of her, calmly, impassively. She didn't say a word when I put the car in neutral and shut the engine. She wouldn't look at me, just stared straight out the window. Her lower lip quivered for an instant, then held still. She wasn't gonna let me terrify her. Not this woman who had me in her home on holidays. Emily Talbot, everyone's grandmother, Lawrence's wife. When I looked at her now, blackened eyes and swollen lips, all I saw was a panda bear.

'I think we should get out of the car.'

Emily opened the door and stepped out. I got out behind her. She glanced at the tall weeds bending in the wind and a huge metal crane towering above them. The water lapped softly on slimy mud and it made me feel light, a little stoned. I screwed the silencer onto my gun and followed Emily out towards the water's edge. I was actually looking forward to this one.

*

When I got back, Manny Simone was pacing the floor like an expectant father. The Countess turned with gasoline and lit matches in her eyes. Riccardo Montefiore sat behind his desk fondling his stack of poker chips, then he put his forearms straight out on the desktop and leaned forward, the room grew silent for this gesture. When the big moment arrived it was with a whisper.

'Where have you been?'

'Out doing a job.'

'Was it your job to disappear like that?'

'Like what?'

Manny's voice cracked in the room like thrown glass. 'Like a fucking rat! A traitor!'

'I ain't a rat, Manny. And you know that.'

'Then answer the fucking question,' he said.

The Countess asked, 'Why did you take off?'

'Because I ain't a fucking mook either.' The Countess lifted her eyebrows. 'It's one thing to find out your people don't trust you anymore, that's bad enough, but then to put Roger Wingtips on my tail, that was the final kick. You don't trust me? You want me followed? You better put someone better than Roger on the job. No offense to Roger.'

Manny shot back, 'What did you do with the body?'

'I dumped it in the river.'

'Do you remember where you dumped it?'

'Pretty much.'

'Let's do some fishing.'

'Good luck. I cut it open, filled it with rocks and watched it sink. You'll never find it.'

'Yeah, I thought you'd say that,' he said, jabbing his finger in my chest. 'Pretty fucking convenient though, ain't it? That you popped her without any witnesses!'

'Manny, listen to yourself.'

'Without any proof or corroboration.'

'Who said there isn't any proof.'

Manny stopped in his tracks, looked at me, they all looked at me. Until I reached into my pocket and casually tossed Emily Talbot's left ear on the desk. It sat there facing up, the dried blood crusting along the serrated slice, her pink freshwater pearl earring acting as a toe tag. The Countess leaned forward, her gray eyes as big as quarters. 'That's her ear!' she exclaimed, and looked at me with new-found admiration. Her husband nodded in agreement. Manny took a step back and gave me a cold, dark grin, he liked when I pulled shit like this.

'Emily, I'm supposed to shoot you in the back of the head.'

'Yes, I suspected as much.'

'Do you have anything you want to say?'

'I can't think of anything appropriate.'

'I have something I'd like to say.'

'What is it?'

'Why did he do it?'

Emily took a slow breath, looked out over the water behind her, then turned back to me. 'Tony, you should know better than that. They got rid of him and now they're trying to take his share. Do you really think Lawrence was an embezzler? He gave his entire professional life to the Franchise. He'd been offered other jobs, executive positions in big corporations, for higher pay; he could have taken them. But he was loyal to you all.'

'That's what makes him look so guilty.'

'Yeah, well, don't forget something . . . Riccardo has a history of fixing the books when he wants something for himself.'

Emily was hard to reason with when she had ammunition like that. 'Turn around,' I said. She gave me one last look, then slowly turned around, crossed her arms as if she were cold; I could picture her lips sealed tight, a little annoyed by the inconvenience of it all. I tingled with the thrill of violence, curious to see how her head would splat; bullets and bone are unpredictable that way, the colorful art of death.

Emily maintained her righteous stance. I thought of the stolen money, the betrayal, the lies she and Lawrence had been deceiving us with, playing us for fools. I pictured them doing horrible things to people I knew – the same psyche job I used for all the hits – but here, and now, for the life of me . . . for the lives of Emily and me, it wasn't working. I just couldn't seem to give a shit. It didn't matter to me one way or the other. The money, the Franchise, my life, nothing seemed worth the price anymore.

Emily heard my footsteps and turned around, a puddle of mud fizzled around her shoes where she had peed herself. She walked to the car and got in, sat in silence as I started the engine. By now Manny would have half a dozen cars out searching for me so I had to keep off the main streets.

An hour later I pulled up to the rear entrance where the buses made their U-turn and parked. She looked at me with the face of a beaten middleweight.

'What happened to Lawrence,' she blurted out. Her swollen lips stumbled on the words.

'It's not important.'

'To me it's important. I've a right to know.'

'Yes, you do. But I'm not gonna tell you.'

'Why are you doing this?' she asked, and I knew she meant us being there.

'I don't really know. None of it makes any sense. I guess I've lost my nerve. Your husband would be ashamed of me.'

That brought a grin of missing teeth and bleeding gums.

'I think Lawrence would understand in this case.'

'I don't know. He was pretty hard, your old man.'

'Only on the outside,' she said, and the image that popped into my mind put a chuckle in my gut.

'Damn, we had some good times, though, didn't we? Sitting in your kitchen Sunday mornings, waiting for him to come down with some business. You'd try to marry me off with girls in the neighborhood. Remember you tried to fix me up once with your niece, from Pelham.'

She nodded.

'Lawrence went ballistic! Threatened to have me popped if I ever went near her. I'd never seem him so furious.'

'He was just letting off steam.'

'He was right. I would have given her nothing but grief.'

'You don't know that.'

'Well, anyway, I really felt like we belonged to something back then, you know. It felt like . . . family. It was a real family. All together, fighting for a common goal. Now it's so . . . different.'

'Things change. People change. It was never really the way you describe it.'

The question surprised her, coming out of nowhere like that; it took her a few seconds to respond. 'I've already told you.'

'That was before, when I was gonna pop you. Now I'm asking you again, person to person, in the relative safety of a public place.'

She gazed stubbornly out the window, at the entrance of the *Zoologischer Garten*, the main train station in Berlin. 'I'm sure they're watching the airport,' I said. 'They might even be here for all I know. We have to get you some kind of disguise.'

'One point six million,' she said.

'Manny says two million is missing.'

265

'I don't care what Manny says. We took exactly one point six million.'

'So you knew about it.'

'Of course. I supported him completely, encouraged him, in fact. We did everything that way.'

'You guys had a terrific marriage. Where is the money now?'

'You know Lawrence, it's hidden in different accounts all over the world. You'll never find it.'

'I was hoping you'd say that. Here's how we play it.' When I finished she said, 'Do you think they'll believe that?'

'No, I don't. But we'll have to convince them.'

When I dropped her back at the station, she hurried out of the car with the floppy hat pulled deep onto her head and the beige scarf growing red on the side of her face, dark sunglasses hiding her purple eyes; she blended in with the other homeless misfits as a sort of a den-mother from Hell. I watched her skitter past the glass doors and disappear into the crowd as it just opened up and swallowed her whole.

I put the car in drive and went to face the orchestra.

21

Vita sat on a hard wooden bench in the middle of the hall. He looked up startled as I stepped over; I still had the walk of a killer. I sat beside him, neither one of us said anything by way of greeting. Premig watched us from the end of the hall, squinting into the sunlight coming through the grated windows on the right side. The floor was green linoleum tile covered by a checkerboard of shadow, cinder block walls a faded yellow burn, a cork bulletin board mounted on the far wall leaked papers to the stairs; the overall scheme reminded me of summer school in sixth grade, of captivity and helplessness.

'He seems to be in good spirits.'

'He is dying,' Vita said curtly.

'I know. I'm sorry.'

Vita held me with a puzzled look. 'Why come you here?'

'To pay my respects,' I answered. 'I like your father.'

Vita looked down at the floor; he seemed to accept that. 'No one comes to see him. *Nicht* his *Freunde oder Mitarbeiter*. No one.'

'I'm sorry.'

'He has lost honor.' Vita wrung his hands together, pressing brown flesh into a mushy clay ball.

A woman stepped out of a side room wearing an orange robe and a veil over her face. She carried a tray of multi-colored paper cups and her shoes were scuffed and ripped at the back seams. Vita sat back and the old bench creaked.

'Without your father to slow things down, Riccardo Montefiore will take over the whole business for himself.'

'And you will help him,' Vita said. 'You will take from us what we worked with our blood and sweat to build. You have dishonor my father, and leave us now with nothing.'

'I don't want to take anything from you.'

Vita scoffed; his reaction to nearly everything I said was to scoff. Then he mumbled something in Turkish under his breath.

'You got a family? Wife and kids?'

Vita fixed me with dark, contemptuous eyes. It was the first glimpse I'd seen that he was capable of violence. 'You will never find them,' he snapped.

'That's good. That's real good. Why don't you take them and go on a vacation for a little while. Disappear till things here blow over.'

'I will run not from criminals.'

'Listen, Vita, don't be a fucking mook. This is a waiting game. And we can't win. I know it, you know it, and they know it. We're dead here. We should have never come out.'

'*Das stimmt!*'

'But the fact is, we're here, and until we're gone anybody associated with us is gonna get hurt. When it's over there's gonna be a small window of opportunity . . . when everything is in chaos. You know the business, it's your family . . . you be the guy to come in and restore order.'

'*Scheisse!*' he spat in disgust.

I sat in silence for a long minute. Vita's gold watch ticked faintly underneath his starched oak sleeve, his strong musk cologne rose through the ghost of alcohol floating through the hall. Becky had just finished rubbing down Clarissa with alcohol and cotton swabs, her fever was up to nearly 104. I was scared. Becky rubbed Clarissa's chest and neck, down her arms and legs; Clarissa just lay there burning up inside, a look of bewilderment on her swollen cherub face. I was glad to have the diversion of a phone call until I heard the panic in Manny Simone's voice. I drove out near the Goethals Bridge and made a right onto tree-lined Kennedy Boulevard and three blocks south on Kennedy saw who I was looking for. Hardy stood off to the side of the road watching cars fly down Kennedy Boulevard in a dizzying blur. He crouched like he was in a footrace, then darted out in front of a blue Mazda. The Mazda swerved out of the way and Hardy slammed into the side door and spun to the ground cursing the driver before his head cracked hard against the pavement; he lay there stunned for a moment.

'What the fuck are you trying to do?'

Hardy looked up with tears in his eyes, his face as pink as I'd ever seen it. Blood dripped from a cut on his forehead.

'She left me! She fuckin' left me, chief!' He sobbed on the last two words, then flung himself back into the lane of traffic. Horns blared and a green Pontiac skidded short and Hardy slammed his fist on the front hood and screamed at the poor woman for stopping. I pulled him out of the street and over to my car; he seemed to melt under my touch, until he darted off at a speeding van. The van beeped its horn and swerved out of the way. I grabbed Hardy and threw him onto the front seat of my car. He clutched at his hair and cried out, 'Oh God . . . I feel . . . so horrible! I wish I could put this feelin' in a pill, I'd give it to my worst enemy. I don't know if I can live without her, Tony. I don't know if I can go on. What am I gonna do?!'

'You're gonna celebrate your new-found freedom, chief. I mean . . . what the fuck . . . she's not worth killing yourself over, is she?'

'I wanted to marry her.'

'Oh. I'm sorry. Come on, let's go get a drink.'

On the ride back to Newark Hardy cried like a rainy day. I'd never seen him cry before, or show any emotion that would prove he was human, but then, neither had I.

*

When I came in, the Countess was yelling in German at Heinrich while Riccardo stood off to the side bouncing poker chips in his left hand, his asthma inhaler gripped in his right. He looked dull, tired; for the first time since I'd known him he looked old. The Countess stabbed her finger in the air and barked at Heinrich and he stammered and stuttered and was completely spooked by it all; I knew it was only a short time before he just disappeared into thin air. Henry Pembleton sat in the corner reading from a computer screen, typing numbers into his calculator and sighing painfully at the discrepancies. Manny stepped in from outside and told me to follow him and we went around to the back of the office where dozens of men in hard hats worked under the supervision of Franchise soldiers in hard hats who stood out by their doing nothing. Manny stopped at a corner where cinder blocks held up the trailer two feet off the ground.

'Take a look under there,' he said. 'And do it discreetly.'

I pretended to drop something at my foot and crouched down to pick it up. I felt the sting immediately, like acid burning through my nostrils. Underneath the trailer were intertwined roots, as though from a great tree; until my eyes adjusted to the dark. Then I saw the arms and legs of human bodies, about a dozen in all.

'Two days ago we brought over Donnie Smokestack's crew, from Fort Lee,' Manny said gravely. 'Very secret, put them up in a safe house nearby. Now it's completely abandoned, nobody's heard from Donnie since yesterday. There's no sign of a struggle or resistance, nothing; they disappeared without a trace. Until today.'

'You think this is them?'

'What do you think?!' he snapped, a wrecking crane knocked down an old building to our right. 'Three people knew they were here. Me, Riccardo and the Countess.'

'Plus Donnie's guys. Somebody could have blurted something out. We don't necessarily blend in with the surroundings here. Kopp and Rudiyov could also have people working customs at the airport.'

'Well that doesn't explain how the fuck they got these bodies under the office! We have soldiers here at night, nobody saw or heard a thing. It's like . . . fucking supernatural! Now we gotta hit 'em so hard and so dirty . . . they'll be lucky to have any kids left when we get through. And it don't give me any pride to say that. But, that's the way they want to play it, fuck 'em.'

Manny strolled toward a huge square pit lined with steel girders and turned to me. 'Those things can't stay under there another day, they're beginning to rot.'

I scoped out the hole, about ten feet deep, and the piles of sand standing around it. Manny added, 'This hole gets filled in with cement first thing tomorrow morning.'

I did the math. 'With three or four guys, I wouldn't give it another thought, Manny.'

Manny looked at me with gratitude. 'Let me tell you, kid. When the clam turns bad it gets pretty fucking ugly.'

Later that night, after midnight, I was somewhat sad to see an old friend come out from under the office. I was an usher at Jesse Smith's wedding. After his cousin canceled out on the bridal party two days before the special day, Jesse asked me to fill in as a favor and we became friends, though we never worked together. Jesse's wife was a pretty Irish girl named Eileen with green eyes and long red hair, but natural red hair, not dyed. I wondered if I missed anything by never having had a natural. Jesse had been shot in the back of the skull, as were all the others, except for two whose heads were nearly severed by bullets fired into their necks. Cold, brutal, this was an awesome job; these killings could have been done by robots.

Bobby De Cicco and three of his crew wore plaid bandanas and welding goggles on their faces, thick rubber gloves on their hands and coveralls with boots, but it wasn't enough to keep them from getting coated with death oil. Several times they had to stop to empty their guts in the dirt. Bobby crawled out from under the trailer and growled, 'Why don't you give us a fucking hand with this?'

'Because I'm supervising.'

'Well get off your ass and do something!'

'Be patient, Bobby, the day will come when you're the supervisor. Until then just do your job.'

'I ain't a fucking grave digger, man, that ain't my job. We're fucking sick to our stomachs down here while you're up there with your thumb up your ass!'

'You better shut the fuck up, Bobby. Or we'll be pulling your body out from under there.'

Bobby looked up with panic, it was good to see I hadn't lost my bluff. 'I'm sorry, Tony, I didn't mean anything . . .'

'Let's just forget it, and get this over with, okay?'

Bobby reached back under the trailer and dragged out Donnie Smokestack's naked body. Bobby stood up in disgust, then nearly jumped out of his skin.

'He's alive!'

'Keep your voice down! No, he's not.'

Bobby's crew appeared around him as three fist-sized lumps wriggled around inside Donnie Smokestack's stomach. 'Look, he's moving! He's still fucking alive!'

'Those are rats,' I said.

'What?!'

'They climb in through the orifices, they're looking for food.'

'You gotta be fucking kidding me!'

'No, I've seen it before.'

I silenced my gun and aimed it over the largest lump,

pumped a round and it squealed and stopped moving.

'See? Nothing to worry about. Okay, let's get back to work.'

Bobby and his crew looked at me with a cross of disgust, hatred, and awe.

At four in the morning Roger Wingtips came onto the site and told me Manny wanted to see me. I figured it was to get the list of names and to hear that the bodies were buried under two feet of sand for tomorrow morning's cement pouring. Roger pulled out a map and scanned the streets from the front seat while I sat in back with the Countess.

'You smell horrible,' she said, scrunching up her nose and opening the window.

'Do you know where I've been?'

'Yes, I do.'

'Then give me a fucking break.'

Her eyes turned to stone, anger flattened her lips; I'd never spoken to her that way before. 'Don't get too familiar with me,' she warned. 'You'll be very sorry.'

I looked out the side window at a restaurant still open with people inside it. The Countess let out a soft breath.

'What's come over you all of a sudden?' she asked.

'I saw an old friend back there. It wasn't very pretty.'

'I'm sorry.'

'Jesse Smith. He used to work in your ex-husband's union. He was at your house a few times – big kid, dirty blond hair. Had a tattoo of the Virgin Mary on his arm.'

'I'm sorry, I don't recall.'

'He used to make her dance by flexing his muscles.'

'I'm sure I would have remembered that.'

'I didn't know he became a soldier.'

'Close friend?'

'No, I just wasn't expecting to see him here.'

'You look exhausted, you should get some sleep.'

'I will, once I report in.'

'You were right about the police,' she said, as if that were a natural segue. 'We heard from the captain. He sent someone over for his weekly payment. Business as usual. He thinks the skinheads did it.'

'Great. Let him look for skinheads.'

'No, I'm afraid that's not so great.' Her eyes flashed novels that took me deep into East Berlin to look for a gang of homicidal Nazi skinheads.

'These skinheads were in your flat,' she said, like cool running water. 'Could you remember them if you saw them again?'

'I don't know. They all look the same to me.'

'We have to find them before the police do. It's more important than getting revenge for what happened back there,' throwing her head back towards *Potsdamer Platz*.

'Do you want the list of the dead?'

'No, give it to Manny.'

Roger Wingtips made a sharp right-hand turn with the map pulled taut over the steering wheel and I could tell from the two festering pimples on the back of his neck that he didn't know where the fuck he was going. The Countess leaned forward, 'Roger, make the next left then the next two rights.'

'Yes, Mrs Montefiore.'

She sat back and asked me, 'Do you like museums?'

'Yeah, they're okay.'

'Riccardo hates them. Hates to be on his feet for so long.'

'You got anything here to drink? I need a drink.'

'Roger, get the bottle in the glove compartment.'

I gulped down five swallows before the stench of rotting meat oozed reluctantly out of my sinuses. After two more I was pretty well buzzed. The Countess poured herself a capful of tequila and flung it down like a professional; I had to smile. She wiped her mouth with her fingertips and said, 'So, tell me about Emily.'

'What about her?'

'How did she take it?

'Take what?'

The Countess gave me a condescending smile; it always made me feel small.

'Why the sudden interest? We never discussed things like that before.'

'Because I want to know what she said. Did she say anything? About other topics?'

'I don't remember. I wasn't listening.'

'She must have said something.'

'Yeah, she was talking.'

'And you must have been listening to know that she was talking.'

'Well, yes, in a manner of speaking.'

'What did she say? I'd like an answer.' There was no getting around it, she wanted an answer.

'Well . . . she started crying and begging for her life, saying she can't believe it's happening; pleaded with me to spare her for old times' sake. Swore to God she was innocent.'

'Was she on her knees?'

'At one point, yes.'

'Did she say anything else? About me? Anything at all?'

'The only thing she said was that you were a liar and a tramp, and that you and Riccardo framed her and Lawrence.'

'A liar and a tramp.'

'Well, I'm paraphrasing.'

'Then you popped her and cut off her ear.'

'Well . . . not necessarily in that order.'

The Countess looked at me, then cackled loudly, cruelly,

her laugh was shrill and filled with malevolence; it was hard to believe I once admired this woman.

On *Köpenickerstrasse* Roger pulled into a long driveway that led to a formidable wrought-iron gate and I wondered what we were doing here, more so after two Turks stepped out accompanied by a soldier I didn't recognize who motioned to the Turks to let us in. Roger drove into an old factory complex with a tall circular tower made of bricks and a loading dock beside it; to the left were warehouses and the rusted skeletons of trucks sitting on planks of wood. Around the back a red-brick building faced out to a muddy stream. Roger Wingtips pulled up to the door and let the car idle. The Countess turned to me. 'I have an extra ticket for the Cy Twombley exhibit at the *Neue* National Gallery this Saturday,' she said. 'Would you like to accompany me?'

'Sure, if I'm still alive.'

She took my hand and gave it a squeeze, 'I'm worried about you. You seem morbid.'

'No, I'm okay. Just a little overtired, that's all.'

'Get some rest. Don't worry so much, everything's going to be all right.'

'I know.'

'But do you really know that, or are you just saying it?'

'No. I have full confidence in you and Riccardo. We'll come out of this okay.'

'That's right. If we all stick together . . . just like always. Now go inside, Manny's waiting. Don't forget, we have a date for Saturday.' With those words the chill of betrayal jolted through my limbs, because that's how it happens, with a reassuring pat on the back and plans for a future meeting. Monica ached inside of me. I wanted to see her one last time.

A jackhammer drilled nearby sporadically, on and off, on

and off, every few seconds. Manny sat at a desk in the first room. He glanced up with wire-framed glasses halfway down his nose. He looked a hundred years old with his glasses on.

'Well?' he barked.

'It's done. Here's the list. When did Jesse Smith become a soldier?'

'When I made him one. Why, you got a problem with that?'

'No, his wife might have a problem though, being that he's dead.'

'Count yourself lucky you ain't with him,' he quipped. When he didn't follow it with a friendly smile I knew it wasn't my time yet. The jackhammer started up again and I realized it was somewhere in the building. Manny didn't seem to hear it, so neither did I.

'The Countess tell you what we gotta do?' he asked.

'Yeah. Shouldn't be too hard. *Marzahn*'s a friendly place, I hear. People should be real helpful.'

'What do you want me to say, kid? We just let them run around and implicate Hardy. We might as well shoot ourselves in the fucking head right now and get it over with. No. We gotta find them before the cops do. That's all there is to it. I know you been up all night, but you can sleep when we get back. Two hours, tops.'

'We bringing Heinrich?'

'He's working on something else right now.'

'We might need help with the language.'

'I got that covered!' Manny snapped; on and off like a light switch. 'Any more fucking suggestions before I lose my temper?'

'No, that's it.'

'Good. Stay close. We leave in fifteen minutes.'

Manny started scanning the list of names and I strolled

along the corridor toward the back of the building, in the direction of the jackhammer, which had stopped abruptly.

A thick red sack hung from the ceiling, two feet off the floor; it looked like a heavy bag for boxing. As it swung lazily on the chain, rotating 180 degrees, Heinrich's naked body faced me, upside down, completely covered in red paint. His torso and limbs were marked by dozens of thin black lines about two inches long. Adam Gottlieb turned to me wearing a blood spattered doctor's smock and holding a straight-edge razor in his hand. He wore rubber latex gloves and a surgical mask over his face. He removed the mask and grinned with a hint of shame. 'I been promoted,' he said.

'Promoted? To what? Does Manny know what you're doing?' I said.

'Who do you think told me to do it?'

'He told you to cut him up like this?!'

'He told me to find out where Hardy is.' Adam then turned to a long-haired rock-and-roller kid in black jeans and a Pantera tee shirt wearing work gloves and holding the jackhammer standing up to his knees in a big hole in the floor. 'Bring him back,' Adam said.

The kid rested the jackhammer on its side, threw off his gloves and jumped out of the hole and filled a plastic bucket with dirty water from a rusted pipe, emptied a half bottle of some green cleaning liquid in it, then doused the whole thing on Heinrich who jolted awake but could only let out a gurgling moan as red foam bubbled from his mouth. Blood rained from his hair and there was a five-foot-wide puddle underneath him. Adam wore rain galoshes over his shoes, but as blood began to congeal, the rubber began to stick to the floor.

'It's the death of a thousand cuts,' Adam explained. 'An ancient Chinese tradition. They used it during the Cultural

Revolution. I read about it in a magazine. Check it out,' he pointed to the foam frothing out of Heinrich's face. 'His blood drips into his nose and mouth, eventually he's too weak to spit it out and he slowly drowns to death. On his own blood. Unless he TALKS!'

'You're a fucking amateur, Adam.'

'What's your Goddamn problem, chief?!'

'You're not going to get anything out of him this way.'

'Hey, how about giving me a little fucking support over here?!'

'This ain't a fucking therapy session! Did you offer him a choice? The possibility of life? Where's the carrot?'

'What the fuck are you talking about . . . carrots?!'

'You probably just strung him up and went to work.'

'Well . . . yeah. What's wrong with that?'

'What did you offer him in return for information?'

'Plenty! His family's on the way over. You hear that, Heinrich? Your wife and kids should be here any minute. They're gonna see their daddy chained up like a pig in Chinatown. Then while you're still alive to watch, I'm gonna cut off your wife's nipples and make your little boys eat them.'

Heinrich struck like a cobra, spewing blood into Adam's face and nearly knocking him over. Adam turned away, gagging and puking on his shoes, then he lunged up swinging the razor and screaming hysterically in unison with Heinrich's screams as the kid jumped down in the hole and let the jackhammer roar. Ribbons of blood hit the wall and also the kid beside it and the kid dropped his instrument and hopped up cursing that he was gonna get AIDS. Adam ordered him to dump another pail of water on Heinrich and after he did, Heinrich shook the blood out of his eyes and nose. 'Tell me where Hardy is and this stops. You can go home. Where is he?'

'I don't know,' he wept, sobbing weakly. His eyelids fluttered and thick red strings fell from his hair and his head was unnaturally swollen from being upside down and with every breath he let out another gasp of delirium.

'You're losing him.'

'He's still conscious!'

'He's nearly gone. Once his mind cracks for good, that's it. He'll never talk. I wonder what Manny will say then?'

Adam looked at me, concern gripped his face.

'Listen to me, Adam. I'm not attacking you, but I know a little bit about interrogation. You can't give someone a constant assault of pain, it loses all effect. You have to work on his mind, create an ebb and flow, a threshold to approach then withdraw from, otherwise there's nothing to compare the pain against. It's a very intimate relationship and you have to take it seriously.' The words flowed naturally from my lips, spoken from first-hand experience, and Adam scooped them up like coins in a slot machine. I told him, 'Give him a rest now or it's over. We lose. We learn nothing.'

'He ain't got much time left, Tony. Look at him.'

'Give him two minutes to think things over, then in two minutes you resume.'

Heinrich swung passively from the ceiling, his eyes locked open in bewilderment, ankles tightly wrapped by chain, the joints stretched like rubber; they were both broken. The kid started checking his hands and clothes and getting agitated.

'Fuck, I gotta get cleaned up. I need to be sterilized!'

Adam touched his forehead where a splotch of red got smeared by his fingertips. 'Go ahead,' I offered. 'You both get cleaned up. He ain't going anywhere. Tell Manny I'm back here waiting for him.'

Adam turned to the kid and said, 'All right, let's take a break.'

Adam took off the smock and threw it over a chair and as he turned to leave he took the kid by the arm. 'Hey, Tony, this is my nephew, Jake. He just came in this morning. He's working with us now.'

'Congratulaions. Sort of.'

Adam and Jake chuckled, then Jake made a pistol with his fingers and clicked his tongue, his idea of a farewell gesture. I waited till they were both down the hall, then I crept to the door and silently closed it, went straight to Heinrich who tried to shake the blood out of his eyes; when he opened them they were the only part of him not red; he looked like a mime in a Satanic minstrel show. He tried to tell me something, but only a breathy wheeze came out of his lungs. I crouched down and put my ear to his mouth.

I told him, 'No, it's only a bluff. But even if they do pick them up, they won't hurt them once you're dead. There's no reason to. Manny won't do that, it's too risky. They're safe . . . once you're dead. Do you understand?'

Heinrich got very still, silent, except for the gulping and snorting sounds as blood continued to leak into his nose. I screwed the silencer onto my gun, told him what I was going to do and how I was going to do it.

I spotted a cut just below his ribs and gently worked the barrel into the slit, aimed toward the floor; the bullet would get lost in his body and nobody would ever know what happened. The hall outside was quiet, too quiet; I was afraid the shot, even silenced, might be heard. I let out a loud cough as I pulled the trigger, the barrel puffed inside his chest and the top of his head popped off; the bullet took a chunk out of the cement floor. I turned toward the door and heard nothing behind it, so I crouched down to see if I could put his scalp back on, when his brain splashed to the floor in pieces.

Naturally the door opened then and Adam Gottlieb came in with his nephew Jake, followed by Robert Herrencamp and Miles Benowitz. They all together looked at the mess on the floor and at me standing there with my gun in hand. A wisp of smoke seeped out of Heinrich's side to eliminate any question of what I'd done.

'What the fuck did you do?!'

'Don't move, don't fucking take a step!' I screamed, louder than what was called for, pointing my gun.

'Tony, what the fuck's going on?' Robert Herrencamp pleaded.

'Where's Manny?' I demanded.

Miles Benowitz pleaded next. 'What the fuck . . . Tony, what are you doing? We're your friends.'

'Where's Manny?' again.

'He went out for a pizza,' Adam sneered, then grinned darkly.

I backed toward the side wall in case anyone lurked in the back rooms. I called out for Manny. He was the one I feared most in this kind of situation. Jake, the kid, glared at me with risk rolling around in his eyes like dice; I was sure I'd have to kill him.

'Adam, tell your nephew to chill out. He's got nothing to prove.'

'Chill out, Jake. You got nothing to prove.'

'Okay, Uncle Adam.'

Miles Benowitz chimed in, 'Tony man, we're all in this together. If there's a problem, chief, put down the fucking gun and let's work it out.'

'I'm afraid I can't do that, chief. Now I need you to put your guns down on the floor, one at a time, carefully. You first, Adam.'

'It's in my jacket; I didn't expect to be betrayed by one of my best friends.'

'Robert, put your gun on the floor. Miles, don't you make a move. I don't want to hurt anybody, so don't make me do it.'

Robert Herrencamp slowly reached into his jacket and with his thumb and index finger gently placed his gun on the floor.

'Now kick it over here, toward me.' He did. 'Come on, Miles, same thing.'

'Tony, what the fuck, have you lost your fucking mind?'

'Yes, I have. Now put your fucking gun on the floor, or Heinrich's brain is gonna have company.'

Miles reached in his jacket for his gun and when Jake's forearm twitched I blasted him in the chest before he could swing his blade. I whirled and shot Miles Benowitz in the shin and Robert Herrencamp in the thigh. Both fell screaming to the cement with a wet slap as Adam reached behind him but found my gun in his face.

'Release your hand slowly. Put it up where I can see it.'

Robert Herrencamp clutched at his leg and looked up crying.

'Why the fuck did you do that?'

Miles' shin was shattered, shredded bone stuck out like a celery stalk and he gaped at it in astonishment. I kicked his gun away into the back of the factory.

'Sorry, guys. But I need some time. This gives me that.'

'Time for what?!' Robert cried.

Adam answered, 'To go back to his Russian friends, give them a report. You're working for them now, ain't you?'

'I'm not working for nobody. Not even myself. Guess you guys have noticed . . . I've been going through a hard time lately. I really wish I could explain it to you. But it's pretty confusing. It's like . . . the world's been turned upside down or something. I feel kind of lost, and the only thing I know for sure is that I have to get away from all this. I can't do it anymore.'

Adam glanced around at his feet. 'You have a unique way of quitting.'

'Turn around, Adam.'

'No fucking way.'

I put the barrel up to his cheek, aimed up into his skull, told him, 'If I was going to shoot you in the head I would have done it already. So turn around so I don't have to do it. Because you know that I will, right?'

'Yeah, I do.'

'Then turn the fuck around.'

Slowly Adam turned his back on me. I took the gun from his waistband and tossed it into the corner. Adam looked down at his dead nephew. 'That was my sister's kid, Tony. What am I gonna tell her?'

'Tell her the same thing you told Jeffrey Campbell's mother, after you raped his wife and then beat him to death for complaining.'

'Ancient history, Tony. You're boring me.'

I cracked him suddenly on the crown of his head and he splashed face first into the pool of Heinrich's blood which now covered nearly half the floor.

Robert looked up. 'What the fuck! Why didn't you hit me in the head?! Fucking bastard! I'm gonna bleed to death unless I get to a hospital!'

'You think Manny's gonna let you go to a hospital with a gunshot wound?'

'Fuck!' Robert cried as his leg continued leaking between his fingers. A couple of cars pulled up outside; tires cracked the loose pebbles in the yard before skidding to a stop. Several car doors opened and closed and Manny ordered people inside. I bolted toward the back of the factory as Robert cried out for help. I peeked out a side window and saw the cars parked near the rear entrance. I hopped out and took off toward the street, kicking up dust from the dirt. On *Köpenickerstrasse* I ran east and screeching tires followed. I took off down a narrow cobblestone street and ducked into the first alley I came to. A gray sedan darted past and footsteps clomped awkwardly on the cracked sidewalk and I went deeper into the alley which took me along the river's edge where a fence kept me from getting near the water. I followed the fence which led into some woods and climbed through a hole the size of a manhole cover. On the other side I came to a dirt path on each side of which were wooden wagons, like trailers only smaller, the kind used in the circus to transport animals. They were all boarded up with wooden steps in front of the door and heating exhaust pipes sticking out from the roofs and there were large drums filled with water and campfire sites with burnt ashes and I'd apparently stumbled onto some kind of squatters' camp. I crept softly along the path, the glistening ball of the TV tower and the smokestacks of surrounding factories the only signs of city life beyond this compound. I came to the last trailer and sitting on the steps was a guy about thirty years old wearing ripped jeans, no shirt or shoes and smoking a hand-rolled cigarette; his arms were covered every inch with faded green tattoos. He watched me with the same curious squint that I surely watched him with. I kept my hand near my jacket, just in case. I could barely keep my feet moving, my whole body ached, even my hair, and after I stumbled twice and nearly fell over the guy jumped up and ran to help me. I fell into his arms as exhaustion hit me over the head with a wooden chair. He dragged me over to his steps and eased me down. Said something in German and when he saw that I didn't understand added, 'I speak English,' with a heavy accent.

'I need to hide; do you understand? Hide?'

He looked back over his shoulder where the sounds of skidding tires and men yelling were heard, looked back at me. 'You run from *Polizei*?'

'Yeah, *genau*,' I answered. '*Polizei*.'

He glanced back over his shoulder, then led me inside his trailer.

22

'Sometimes bad things happen for good reasons.'
Hardy lifted his head from the bar, took a deep breath and let it out slow, turned to me with his face still red and puffy.

'What the fuck are you talking about?' he sniffled.

'Can I be perfectly honest with you?'

'I don't know. That depends.'

'On what?'

'On whether I like what you're gonna say or not.'

'Then I can't be perfectly honest, can I?!'

'I don't know. I'm confused.'

'Well listen to me.'

'I gotta pee first.'

'Again?'

Hardy went around the bar to the men's room in back. Chuckie Darabont sat in front of the TV sipping his beer. He scooped out the last few peanuts in the bowl and asked Jimmy the bartender for another refill.

'Hey Chuckie, that's the second bowl of nuts you went through today; this ain't your fuckin' private cafeteria.'

'What are you talkin' 'bout, Jimmy? As long as I'm eatin' the nuts they make me thirsty, then I drink beer; that's the psychology of it. You should be happy.'

'Yeah, except you sit there all fuckin' day and only buy two beers.'

'Okay, pour me another.' Chuckie counted his change on the bar and looked up. 'Hey Jimmy, I'm twenty cents light; can you float me the difference?'

'You gotta be fuckin' kiddin' me!'

I called out, 'Hey Jimmy, I'll take care of it.'

Chuckie's face lit up, 'Gee, thanks Tony, that's sweet, man.'

Jimmy filled a glass from the tap and grumbled under his breath, 'You only encourage him, Tony.'

Chuckie yelled back, 'If the guy wants to buy me a beer, Jimmy . . . This is still America.'

'Shut the fuck up!'

Chuckie got his drink and smiled at the foam on top like a kid with an ice-cream cone. Hardy came back, his face dripping with water. He sat down and gulped the baby white onion in his Martini, then glanced around, caught Chuckie raising his glass at me in toast.

'What the fuck you lookin' at, asshole?!'

Chuckie shifted his gaze and I took Hardy by the arm. 'He's okay; come on, let me talk to you for a minute.'

I led him over to a side booth where we were alone, sat him down on the plush metal-flake red cushion and tried to explain why he had to get a fucking grip on himself, but his eyes looked in every direction except mine. 'What the fuck are you looking at? You expecting someone?'

'No, I'm just checkin' the place out.'

'Well pay attention. I'm trying to save you some heart-break.'

Jimmy brought over two more drinks and placed them on the table. Hardy gulped his drink in one shot and got up.

'Where you going?'

'I gotta pee again.'

'This is like . . . five times already!'

'Well, I gotta go again.'

I sipped my Crown Royal, finished it, and by the time Hardy came back I had to go. 'Sit here and don't go anywhere; I'm not finished, okay?'

'What are you, my fuckin' guardian?'

'You should be so lucky.'

The bathroom reeked like a zoo. There were four urinals

against one wall; on the opposite wall were the toilet stalls. The third stall was the one where Louie Ryco bought it in the throat last year. During the awkward ballet of his murder his shoe fell off and got left behind. Jimmy found it and nailed it up over the bar; for three months it stayed there as a memorial to the posthumously named Louie 'Floorsheim' Ryco.

I noticed several quarters lying on the plastic net of the first urinal. Quarters sat in each and every urinal. Glistening with piss and water. Chuckie Darabont stepped in and went to the last urinal. 'Fuckin' beer, you never own it, you only borrow it. You know what I mean.'

Hardy had finished another Martini by the time I came back.

'Your theory is flawed,' he said with a slur. 'Besides, I was the one who got her into strippin' in the first place. She wanted to be a teacher, if you remember. She owes her career to me! God . . . Tony, what am I gonna do? I love her so fuckin' much!'

Chuckie Darabont came back to the bar and Hardy got up, wiped his eyes. 'I'll be right back.'

'You gotta be fucking kidding me.'

'Hey, I ain't feelin' too good, okay?'

'Go ahead, piss your heart out.'

Hardy lumbered to the end of the bar and disappeared around it. A moment later he came charging out like a man in flames, ran straight to Chuckie Darabont and ripped him from his stool. Chuckie let out a squeal as Hardy tore through his pockets, threw a handful of quarters to the floor, then held Chuckie at arm's length. Two maintenance guys from the paint factory stopped playing pool to watch Hardy announce that Chuckie was a fucking pervert, that he had plucked quarters from the urinals and only a fucked-up pervert would stick his hands in a urinal for a couple of piss-stained quarters. Chuckie could only stammer back as the quarters at his feet signed his confession. Before I could intervene Hardy cracked him in the face with a glass of beer and Chuckie collapsed to the floor bleeding before he knew what hit him. Jimmy stayed behind the bar, a towel in his hands, watching with satisfaction as Hardy began stomping furiously on Chuckie's head, grinding his face into the broken glass on the floor. Chuckie lay curled up in a ball screaming for help as Hardy smashed his heel into his ear. I grabbed Hardy's arm but he threw me back like a madman, threatened to kill anyone who came near him, waved his .380 around the room and everyone jumped to the floor. Hardy cocked his weapon, stood over Chuckie, bouncing on the balls of his feet, back and forth; his eyes were the color of tin. I could see the idea spinning around in his twisted little mind; that quickly, in an instant, it's done and can't be undone. I spoke softy from the floor, 'Don't do it, Hardy. Manny knows his family.'

The mention of Manny gave Hardy pause; it was possibly the only word in any language that could stop him from doing something. His shoulders heaved with air and he let out a sigh. Once he lowered his gun I tackled him from behind, knocked him to the floor and tried to pin him down. Hardy didn't resist, just lay there underneath me laughing like an idiot.

'What the fuck was that about?!' I demanded, furious.

Hardy roared and told me, 'I set a trap and caught a rat!'

'All you caught was a poor desperate guy with no money!'

'Fucking pervert!' Hardy screamed at Chuckie's inert body on the floor.

'Come on, let's get out of here!' I took Hardy by the arm but he shoved me away. 'I'll come under my own power,' he barked, then started for the door. I turned to remind

Jimmy that nothing happened here but as Chuckie began to move Hardy grabbed a bar stool.

Chuckie was a broken heap by the time Hardy got finished. Jimmy made us drag him outside and leave him in the alley. I wondered what Chuckie's sister Melody would think if she saw her younger brother like this. Melody Darabont, an ex-girlfriend from the neighborhood, a sweet and kind girl who loved me dearly and whose heart I trampled on. I tried to imagine the pain and heartache she would feel. But I couldn't imagine it. I slipped three hundred bucks in Chuckie's pocket and hoped he wasn't robbed before he regained consciousness.

When I woke a young woman sat near the open doorway breast-feeding a baby. She wore a wool shawl over her shoulders and a long flowered skirt, but faded, nearly colorless. Her feet were crude, misshapen, her toes twisted and the nails were dense and gray, like granite. Unlike her feet, her face was pretty with simple features on a round milky pie. The cramped trailer had barely enough room for the single mattress and shelves that were opposite it; ragged carpet scraps covered the floor and yellowed newspaper clippings made up the wallpaper. At the back end stood a small iron stove for heat; a metal plate underneath it held a pile of ashes. A cardboard box kept forks and spoons, a ladle and a spatula; beside it stood a stack of chipped dinner plates. I heard a soft purring sound, like a large cat sleeping, but then realized it was coming from the woman, she was humming to her baby. I wasn't sure how long I'd slept but from the waning orange light outside, it must have been nearly twelve hours. I stirred and the woman looked over, lifted her baby a little higher onto her bosom, then called outside. The guy with the tattoos appeared.

'Are you okay? Sleep long time.'

'Yeah. Thank you.'

'Something eat?'

'What time is it?' I asked, though I was starving.

The guy looked at a wristwatch tied to his wrist with string. '*Halb Neun*,' he said. My face asked to see the watch and it read eight-thirty. I'd slept for nearly fourteen hours and I was still exhausted. 'Did anyone come looking for me?'

'*Nein. Keiner.*'

I asked him where *Köpenickerstrasse* was and he pointed to his right. I told him I had to go east when it got dark and he looked over his left shoulder. His wife took the baby and left the wagon and I felt my gun shift inside my jacket.

I sat in the doorway while Lars and Heike cooked vegetables over an open fire. Filthy chickens ran wild on the dirt; a lamb trilled nearby. Four heavy-duty squatter chicks with neon red hair and dirty clothes came by and stopped to talk to Lars and Heike, throwing suspicious looks in my direction. After they'd gone I asked Lars if there was a bathroom and he laughed and pointed to a brush of tall weeds. Dinner consisted of watery green stalks and rice. I sat in the trailer doorway while Lars and Heike sat on stumps of wood; Heike held her crying baby with one arm while she ate with the other. I noticed her staring at my shoes, still caked with dried blood around the seams. We ate in silence; not once did Lars ask me who I was or why I was running.

'How old is your kid?'

'*Bitte?*'

'How old? . . .Your son?'

'*Ach so*, he is ten month old.'

'Cute.'

Heike smiled and heaved him higher on her arm.

'How long before it gets dark?'

'*Wie bitte?*'

'The sky . . . Night?'

Lars looked up at the sky, still light and blue.

'*Eine halbe Stunde*,' he said. Then put up three fingers, '*Dreissig Minuten*.'

I finished my plate and put it aside. 'Have you been living here long?'

Lars considered this question before answering. 'Six *Jahre*,' he said. '*Vor der Wende*.'

Lars saw immediately I didn't understand, then he told me, in slow limited English, about the collapse of the Berlin Wall. When it was up it stood right in front of the trailers, he said; we were just on the west side. He used to throw packs of cigarettes over the top for the patrol guards, he thought it might make them less likely to shoot to kill at somebody trying to sneak over. He said in *Treptow* you could see people in their apartment windows in the East while they could look out at people in the West and some people would rent out their apartments so families could wave back and forth to each other; I couldn't imagine how strange that must have been. Heike interrupted and motioned to the darkening sky; Lars turned sharply and they bickered back and forth and then just as quickly settled down in silence. Something was up, I could tell by the nervous looks they tried not to throw at each other.

The next thing I knew he wanted me to sleep with his wife. She wanted to have another baby close in age to their son and Lars was sterile and when I asked how she got pregnant the first time he said from a friend and when I asked what happened to the friend he told me he was dead. Heike sat there looking kind of embarrassed while her boy slept in her arms. I was speechless for a moment, playing out different scenarios of motive and angle, trying to find the catch, until it seemed there wasn't any catch at all, it was simply a couple who wanted kids and didn't care who gave them to them.

The entrance was less threatening to me now; that's what gave me the courage to just walk in the front door. Wearing the ripped jeans and long-sleeved striped shirt that Lars gave me I stepped to the front desk to find it vacant, no guards or nurses, no one to stop me from creeping up the stairs. On the first floor someone walked softly with rubber soles squeaking on polished linoleum tile; I waited till the steps faded away then continued on. I came to a nurses' station where two nurses pored over a magazine, then I reversed direction and went up to the third floor. It had the distinct smell of old age, the sour blend of fermentation and decay. I walked along the corridor when someone stepped out behind me. I turned to see a stern-faced young nurse with short black hair staring at me; she was not amused. She said something curt and I told her I was looking for Monica. She didn't understand until I repeated the name. Then she eyed me up and down, turned and walked through the hall, stopped and looked back; her eyes told me to follow her, that she didn't have time for this non-sense. She led me up to the top floor and along a corridor where administrative offices sat behind frosted glass doors. The young nurse opened the second door from the end and Monica sat at a long marble counter eating a sandwich and studying out of a textbook. She didn't seem pleased to see me. She and the nurse spoke a few words. Then the nurse gave me a parting look before leaving. Once the door was closed Monica went back to her book as though I wasn't there. She wore a blue button-down shirt and gray slacks, a white smock that reminded me, chillingly, of Adam Gottlieb the night before. I strolled around the counter, littered with test tubes, medical encyclopedias and precision instruments; a hanging skeleton stood in the corner beside a long green chalkboard mounted on the front wall. A classroom of some sort, it was not unlike the biology labs in the annex buildings of the high school back home. Monica finished her sandwich and said without looking up, '*Was machst du hier?*'

'I wanted to see you again.'

'*Warum?*'

'Because I needed to.'

She threw me an angry glare. 'I said we see us never again.'

'I know.'

'You go now.'

'No. I go now not.'

She got up from the table and tried to move past me but I took her arm. 'Monica, listen to me.'

She looked up with even more anger.

'Please, two minutes of your time. Two minutes. Then if you want, I'll disappear. You'll never see me again.'

She didn't try to push past me; perhaps the desperation in my voice made her stand back and listen. So I poured out my guts, told her about my life in the Franchise and about coming to Berlin and about Victor Rudiyov's daughter and Ulf Kopp and everything that happened since then right up to and including Heinrich's unfortunate end and then running away and sleeping in the squatters' camp and now hiding from my friends who were surely out looking for me. I told her I wanted to change my life and that I wanted her to help me; that brought a mocking grin to her lips.

'I don't want to kill anymore,' I said. 'I don't want to hurt anybody. I want to change. Do you understand? I want you to help me. Before it's too late. I want to be with you, even if it's only a short time. Please.'

She didn't say a word at first; her breath hummed softly out of her nose. I smelled the fragrant spice of baby powder and perspiration. When she spoke she spoke quietly. She said 'No', then took a clipboard and pen and brushed past me to the door.

The bones of the skeleton were real; they had the dry powdery texture that old bones get. I checked the skull for cracks or holes; maybe this was a homicide, but the cranium was intact. I sat in the swivel chair behind the counter and rested my eyes. I dozed off because the next thing I remember was Monica standing in the doorway watching me, with suspicion, dislike. 'Why stay you here?'

'I have no place else to go.'

'Go to your *Freunde*.'

'They'll kill me. If I'm lucky.'

She folded her arms and leaned against the doorway. '*Was willst du*?'

'I need a place to stay for a few days. Till I figure out what to do.'

She pursed her lips; thought hard for a moment. Everything was a major equation. 'I work still four *Stunden*,' she said and I assumed she meant hours.

'Can I wait for you?'

'Okay.'

She returned after five in the morning and hung up her smock in the closet, then stood at the door waiting. '*Kommst du mit*?'

'*Genau*.'

She led me into the hall.

On the street I pulled her close to the buildings, keeping us both in the shadows. I told her to take the side streets home and realized with regret that she knew that already. Whenever passersby came towards us we stepped into the nearest doorway. Monica didn't speak until we arrived at her flat. She turned and stopped me from following her into the building, told me I had to wait outside. 'Perhaps my boyfriend *ist Zuhause*.'

'You have a boyfriend?'

'*Genau*.'

'How many people have keys to your apartment?' She thought about it, then said, '*Ich weiss nicht*.'

I backed into the corner and did what my instincts and experience told me not to do: I waited. Every shadow was scoped out and analyzed; I wouldn't underestimate Manny's reach to get me. Her face appeared as if from underwater in the pane of glass.

'Where's your boyfriend?'

'He is *nicht da*.'

The wooden banister had a carved lion's head at the bottom, I'd never noticed it before. I rubbed my finger against the polished fangs before Monica led me up the four flights to her apartment.

I sat at the kitchen table while she went into another room, separated from the kitchen by a small hallway. She came out with a couple blankets and a pillow, laid out the blankets on the floor and put the pillow at the end; I took that to be my accommodation. She turned and went back into the other room, her bedroom, I guessed, and closed the door. I took off my shoes and scrubbed the blood off the sides, then went to sleep.

The next afternoon Monica's feet walked past my face. She wore red socks up to her ankles, a large tee shirt down to her thighs. Standing at the kitchen sink she filled a pot with water and put it on the stove. Without looking at me she stepped into the bathroom to the side. I got up, folded the blankets and sat at the table, heard the toilet flush and the water run. Monica came out of the bathroom and walked past me into her bedroom, closed the

297

door. When she came out she wore tight blue jeans and a button-down shirt too small for her. She sat across from me at the table, watched the flame under the pot of water, got up and took it off the stove. Then she made two cups of tea. I put my gun on the table. Monica sat down without any reaction.

'I think I should stay low for a day or two. They'll be watching the airport and the main train stations. I'm not sure how many guys they got out looking for me. Can you help me get a car?'

'I have no car.'

'I want to buy one. I have about two thousand Marks on me.'

'I try.'

'I need to do it secretly.'

'We see.'

She sipped her tea, then lit a cigarette and laid it in the beanbag ashtray on the table. Smoke seemed to drift out of her cheeks; her complexion looked raw in the sunlight, a swollen, irritated red. I glanced down at the floor where I attacked her the first night here. When I looked over she was staring at it too. She pursed her lips and said, 'I go out today. I must in *Bibliothek* to study.'

'What time will you come back?'

'*Ich weiss es noch nicht.*'

'When do you have to work next?'

'*Samstag.*'

'When is that?'

'Two days.'

'Saturday. Don't worry, with a little luck I'll be long gone by then. What do you do at this hospital exactly?'

'I work heart machine. For heart test.'

'An EKG machine?'

'*Ja, genau.* EKG.'

'I haven't had an EKG since . . . well, I don't think I've ever had one.'

Monica showed not the slightest interest in my medical history. She finished her tea and went into her room, came out with her backpack and jacket, went to the door.

'*Bis später*,' she said.

'*Genau*,' I answered.

'*Du kannst das nicht sagen.*'

'*Danke*.'

While Monica was out I found a box of tools and started fixing things in her flat. Her cabinet doors were hanging off and one was upside down, several floorboards were loose and coming up, her platform bed had no screws or nails holding it together. The work kept me occupied and distracted, it was the most peaceful afternoon I'd spent in years. Later I pictured Manny Simone and Riccardo Montefiore and the Countess in their office, attempting to make sense out of it all. Three confused, outraged faces pondering why. I wondered if it wasn't too late to go back and plead temporary insanity. I watched TV until eleven o'clock. Monica still hadn't called – in fact, the phone hadn't rung once. I didn't know what to do, so I sat in the kitchen planning my next move. At two o'clock a key was put into the lock and I went for my gun but then sat back as Monica swept in wearing her backpack. She didn't say a word as she went to the sink for a glass of water. She noticed immediately the repaired cabinet doors, found the floorboards secured in place and level with the floor; she turned to me and her eyes were glassy, drunk; there might have been a smile in them. She said she had been out with friends for dinner and drinks.

'Were you with your boyfriend?'

'*Nein*. Girl friend.'

'Why didn't you tell me you had a boyfriend?'

'*Nicht wichtig*,' she said by way of brushing off the question. 'Have you eat food?'

'Yeah, I helped myself to some cheese and bread. Made a sandwich.'

'Is that *genug*?'

'I don't know what *genug* means.'

She didn't respond.

'When you came home did you notice anyone hanging out on the street? Anybody that looked like they didn't belong?'

'No.'

'I want you to keep an eye out for anyone that looks like they don't belong, okay?'

Her eyes landed on the psychedelic stripes running down my shirt sleeves.

'I know, I need to get some new clothes. I got these from the squatter guy I told you about. Maybe I can buy some clothes in the neighborhood.'

'*Ja, es gibt* second-hand *Markt* for *Kleider*.'

'Believe it or not, I actually understand what you're saying.'

'*Gut*.'

'Did you tell your boyfriend about me?'

'You?'

'About meeting me. You and me, together. The last time.'

'No. He knows not.'

'Why not?'

'*Nicht wichtig*.'

Monica stepped into the bedroom doorway; she was a tall woman. She turned back and told me she was going to watch TV.

We sat side by side watching the screen. I didn't understand any of it until she went past a local Berlin news program. Police action was universal. Several green cars with flashing blue lights sat in an open field. In the background were the tall white Lego apartment buildings topped by one of three primary colors. I knew who lived in that area.

'What is he saying?'

'He say six people are *tot*.'

'Who are they?'

'They know not.' Heaps of what appeared to be old clothing smoldered on the ground. She asked, 'Did you do that?'

'No. That's what I'm running away from. Some skinheads killed a police captain's wife. One of our guys was involved too. We were ordered to hunt down the skinheads and kill them so there'd be nobody left to connect us.'

Monica looked at me with surprise, let it sink in. 'How many people have you kill?'

I had to think. 'Counting Heinrich and Adam Gottlieb's nephew last night . . . twenty-two.'

'*Zweiundzwanzig*,' she said softly. Her forehead creased; the number disturbed her. 'How feel you *darüber*?'

'When I think about it, the things I've done, the suffering I've caused, I wish I were never born.'

Monica watched me with unblinking eyes, she was still thinking about twenty-two murders. I leaned back on my elbows and watched TV.

Church bells bellowed, deep, rock-solid bells louder than any I'd ever heard before, just outside the window. The sun pushed into my eyes and I sat up in bed next to Monica. We'd fallen asleep with our clothes on watching TV. Monica rustled awake and yawned, grabbed her pack of cigarettes next to the bed and lit one. Her third breath of the day was cigarette smoke. I stood up and my bones ached, I felt like a fifty-year-old man with arthritis. Monica got up and went into the bathroom, peed loudly in the toilet, then flushed it and reappeared after washing her hands in the sink.

'I call friends today, about you buy car.'

'Great. Tell 'em it's cash. And no paperwork.'

'I make tea now.'

At noon Monica went out and bought me some clothes at a second-hand store around the corner. Jeans and a pullover, a black shirt, a worn-out black leather blazer that she got for 35 Marks, a good price, she said. I heard her fumbling around in her room and saw planks of wood and steel brackets on her bed; she mentioned that she was going to put up book shelves. I offered to help. Monica sat on the bed while I tried to find beams underneath the plaster. The walls were dense, solid. Monica had nothing but simple tools so I drilled into the plaster with a screwdriver and hammered in screw anchors to hold the brackets. Once the brackets were up and secured in place, I asked Monica to help me hold the shelves for mounting. She stood close to me on the bed holding a plank of wood, her skin smelled of scented soap and lavender. As I fit the first shelf in place she said, 'You are good at this.'

'I think I could've been a really good carpenter, or handyman. I always loved making things with wood. In school we had wood-shop classes. Mr Cutler took an interest in me; said I had real talent. He would help me out, loan me tools when I needed them. Then, there were family problems and I had to help my mother, you know. Okay, that's the first one; it seems pretty secure. What do you think?'

She grinned, then when our eyes met she got embarrassed, nervous.

'I can do the rest,' I told her. 'Why don't you go make some calls and see if you can get me a car?'

Monica hopped down off the bed and went into the kitchen. Before I fit the last shelf into place she told me a friend of hers had a car to sell, it could happen as soon as tonight. At six o'clock she boiled a pot of water and heated a pan on the stove. I nearly freaked when she opened a jar of tomato sauce and emptied it into the pan.

'What are you doing? That's no way to cook gravy. You can't put a jar of sauce in a pan and heat it up. That's . . . that's just wrong.'

She looked at me puzzled, didn't understand. I searched the counter and found in a straw basket some tomatoes, onions and a clove of garlic, cut them into tiny bits and added them to the sauce. I sprinkled in oregano and salt, a splash of wine and a touch of sugar to sweeten it, all the tricks I learned in Emily Talbot's kitchen on Sunday mornings. Monica peered over my shoulder as I stirred the thick dark paste; I thought for a second of kissing her, her face so close to mine, but she backed off and went back to her glass of wine on the counter. After dinner I asked if she had a map and she took out a huge atlas and opened it on the table. Pointed out where we were, and other landmarks like the TV tower and the *Brandenburger* Gate. She asked where I wanted to go, once I got my car.

'I don't know, where would you suggest?'

She scanned through the pages. 'Prague is *schön*. Very old. Slovakia is *auch* good. I drive there for Christmas last year.'

'Do people speak English in these places?'

'Some. Not all. Like here.'

'Would I be able to blend in? Would I stick out?'

The very thought made her grin. A second later I found it.

'There it is! That's where I want to go!' I pointed to an orange splotch on the map. 'I think it'd be perfect.'

She thought about it for a second, then broke into a grin and nodded her head. '*Stimmt*. Perfect for you.'

Near eleven o'clock she told me we were going to meet

her friend with the car. As I went to the door she felt the pockets of my jacket.

'*Nein*. That stay here,' she said, meaning my gun and my nerves immediately plucked with betrayal. I thought of the angles, the different scenarios and treacheries; all of them oblique and starring Monica as Tokyo Rose.

'You kill no more,' she said. '*Richtig*? No more kill. That's what you say? No gun.' She threw me a look that told me it was over if I didn't agree.

I put my gun in the second drawer in between the aluminum foil and plastic wrap and we went down to the street. I felt naked and vulnerable, but tonight I was prepared to accept whatever fate, or Monica, threw my way.

23

The engine hummed steadily, choking occasionally but then spitting right back in rhythm. It was a 1984 Opel two-door sedan, off-white and nondescript. Bernhard stood by the engine. Tall and lanky wearing dirty blue jeans and a ripped tee shirt, he reeked of sweat and mildew. Monica stood beside him holding a cigarette and talking animatedly. I'd never seen her use her hands to speak before; I wondered if this were her boyfriend. After checking the interior, making sure the head- and brake-lights worked, the clutch and transmission engaged, I asked him how much he wanted. His English was much better than Monica's.

'Two thousand Marks,' he grinned.

I knew then that Monica had told him how much I had to spend; that minor betrayal poked at my side. I told him I couldn't do it for more than one thousand. He looked crushed, wasn't prepared for haggling, I guessed; he'd probably never been to Orchard Street on the Lower East Side. Bernhard started talking to Monica and waving his hands and she snapped back and soon they were arguing until Monica took a step away and looked at him with a steely gaze; Bernhard shrank under it, slapped his hands against his pockets and announced, 'All right! Give me fifteen hundred and it's yours.'

'I'll give you twelve.'

'Thirteen.'

'Done.' Maybe he'd been to Orchard Street after all.

I paid him with eight one-hundred-Mark bills and the rest in fifties, shook his hand and took the keys. I wanted to drive straight back to her flat but Monica told me she wanted a drink.

'*Kommst du mit*?' she asked, walking with Bernhard down a long narrow alley made of dirt and sand. I followed them into a pool of light from flood lamps bolted into a brick wall overhead. The windows had been painted over in black; underneath them a row of oil drums reminded me of Billy Corrigan and his brother Flaky still sealed tight and decaying in the Staten Island landfill.

A lighted window stood out of the void and as we got closer I heard music and people behind it. Bernhard opened a huge wooden door and inside was a candlelit pub filled with young people. About ten large wooden tables stood around the room and people sat with each other whether they were acquainted or not. I scoped out the surroundings and there didn't seem to be anybody who posed a threat, so I chilled and went to the bar with Monica.

'How do you know Monica?' Bernhard asked and I told him, 'We went to school together.'

He chuckled, then advised, 'When you start the car in the morning, when it's cold, give it a lot of gas. It'll take a little longer to get going, but it'll go.'

'You speak English really good.'

'I lived in South Dakota for a year. With a German family on a farm. Cows, sheep, chickens, horses. It was the smelliest place I'd ever been in my life.'

'Have you ever been to Bayonne?'

Some people got up from a table in the corner and we rushed over and sat down. In minutes the room filled up to where there wasn't any place to stand or move. People stood packed into place and talked to whoever they were facing. Bernhard was looking around the room, smiling at everyone who caught his eye.

'I can't stay long,' I spoke into Monica's ear.

'*Ich auch nicht*.'

There was a movement through the crowd and people

pushed up against tables and as they parted Jonathan appeared with a shoebox under his arm. He squeezed his way past when he caught sight of me and called out, 'Hey! What are you doing here?'

'Drinking. What are you doing here?'

'Working.'

'You seem to be everywhere.'

'What can I say? It's a small city and I'm always on the move. You know how it is.' He glanced at Monica sitting beside me, then gave me a wink. I wished he hadn't, I hated winking.

'What do you got tonight?' I asked him.

'The usual.'

'I'll take three.' I handed him a twenty-Mark bill and he gave me three space cakes plus a five-Mark coin. Bernhard's face lit up at the sight of the aluminum-foil disk; I gave the second to Monica and kept the last for myself. Jonathan slipped me one more under the table. 'Here, special offer for Americans.'

'That's very patriotic of you.'

'We gotta stick together, right? Hey, man, call me; let's meet for a drink, okay?'

'Okay, I'll call you next week.'

'I gotta get back to work. Have a good one.' Jonathan then disappeared into the crowd. Bernhard had finished his cookie before Monica or I had even started ours. A waitress came by and Bernhard held up three fingers and yelled over the music, 'Jagermeister!'

She put three shots down on the table and Bernhard gave one to me and one to Monica. I finished my cookie and downed my shot, watched a dirty ragged-looking guy with a canvas bag of long multi-colored candlesticks go from table to table trying to sell them. Bernhard began talking to the people across the table; a minute later he pulled Monica into the conversation. Soon he was introducing me to complete strangers as 'Tony from the States'. Once the hash kicked in the place began rocking as slender cool women in second-hand skirts danced in rhythm to my pulse. Monica looked at me and her eyes were wet and opaque and in them flashed the movie of our lives: a house far out in the countryside with everyday chores where I'd bring out the garbage and fix the fence and together we'd play with our young daughter on the swing set in the front grass yard; but it was nearly impossible to get the somber eyes of Victor Rudiyov's daughter out of that scenario.

Monica rested her head on my shoulder and I put my lips in her hair and breathed in a smoky desert. In candlelight she was the most beautiful creature I'd ever seen.

Walking to the car she put her arm through mine and gripped my biceps. The car groaned before kicking over, then Monica pointed me onto *Danzigerstrasse* as a gray BMW approached from the other direction. It was the same car Manny Simone drove.

I crouched down in the seat, sped up to hide behind a tram just in front of me. Monica looked in the rear-view mirror and I floored the pedal and the car jolted for a second, backfired, then shot forward. I screeched left onto *Greifswalderstrasse* and cut off a tram turning right onto *Danziger*; the angry bell rang like angry bells back in grammar school. Monica turned back from the rear window and said, 'No one comes.' But *Greifswalder* was a big street with four lanes and easy to be spotted from. I shifted into second and turned right onto *Kurischestrasse*, the cobblestone road bounced us in the shoddy car like beans; Monica mentioned that she used to live on this street. I turned right onto a small road with a domed church on the corner; at the second cross street where a billboard yelled in English to 'Smoke Marlboro cigarettes' I made a sharp left, stopped the car and rolled down the window, listened. A low rumble of traffic murmured in the distance. Monica told me to go to the corner and make a right. She pointed out the back streets to her flat. I parked four blocks away and knew that from now on this car marked me.

The hallway was pitch black and I appreciated the fact that she kept it that way. I put my hand on her back and followed her up the stairs. We reached her door and she opened it. I nearly knocked her over rushing inside and when she turned with a drunken grin, her front teeth looked like fangs. I leaned in and kissed her gently on the lips. She didn't stop me. I kissed her again and on the fourth kiss she kissed back. We held each other tightly; her strong bones pushed the air out of my lungs. I kissed her ear and she squeezed me even harder. I'd forgotten what it felt like to be held this way, clutched so desperately; the terrifying trauma of free-fall. When we parted, Monica's eyes were on fire. I took her hand and started toward the bedroom but she stopped and pulled back. 'No,' she said. 'I am tired,' she pronounced the 'r' in tired. 'I go *ins* bed now.'

She kissed me on the lips, then went into her room and closed the door. I made up my bed, lay on the floor and wondered what game Monica was playing. It didn't matter. Saturday morning, when she went to work, I would drive away.

'If they ask me, I'm gonna tell them the truth,' I announced.

She tried to dab her eyes, but they were still severely bruised; it seemed with every falling tear they darkened. Without saying a word she made me feel that it was my fault, that I was the one responsible; the things she never said were the things that hurt the most. But I was determined this time to end it. This was his third and final strike as far as the courts were concerned, and I was going to testify for the prosecution. I wanted him placed in an institution, where he could be looked after, taken care of; the fact that I even had to explain this to my mother was mind boggling to me. But in some ways she was as sick as he was, the periphery of his illness clung to all of us like mud. And so a few days later, after giving in to her wish, I moved out.

Rain pelted the windows like pebbles. The sky was dark gray and dense; thunder rumbled faintly in the distance. I lay on the floor feeling the raindrops inside me as if they were living cells. Monica slithered out of her room looking like the end of the world. I nearly chuckled at her hair standing straight up on the sides, but then, I didn't look like a sunny day at the beach either. After a quiet tea together Monica asked me what I was going to do. I told her I didn't know. She took out her atlas again and we planned my escape from Germany. Monica convinced me that anyplace in Czechoslovakia was better than my plan of driving to Transylvania. She again suggested Prague; she had friends there and had visited them once; she said the city was dark and had many back streets and tourists so that I could easily hide out until I had a more permanent plan. It certainly sounded more reasonable than my quest for Dracula. She plotted out a course over the *Autobahns*, then wrote it down step by step on a sheet of paper. She had no reaction to the news that I'd be leaving tomorrow at sunrise, not relief, not disappointment, nothing.

Monica pulled out some textbooks and told me she had to study. I went into her bedroom and watched TV with the sound off. Near eight o'clock I went out to the street to check on the car. I wore an old coat that Monica had in her closet and crept close to the buildings where the alleys and doorways were black and empty, until I reached a corner where I could see the car.

Monica looked up as I entered and told her everything

was cool. She went back to her book, a thick bound text-book of advanced biology; the fact that she could under-stand any of that stuff made me burn up inside. I stepped behind her and put my hands on her shoulders, she didn't protest. Her muscles were tight and solid but immediately loosened under my pressing fingers. Her back had hard knots that I worked out slowly, crunching out with my thumbs.

Carrie lay on her stomach and pulled her tee shirt up over her head. I sat over her and with my index finger began writing letters on her back. Carrie let out a breath and dug her face into the crook of her arm.

'Pony!' she said, popping her face up into the air.

'That's right. All right, good. Okay, get ready.' I traced my finger along the center of her spine, carefully doing each letter slowly, deliberately. She asked me to repeat it and I did.

'Money!' she exclaimed.

'No, that's wrong. It's honey. Now it's my turn.'

'Honey?! That didn't feel like honey. Do it again.'

I did and she again complained, 'That's money, not honey.'

'No, it's not. Feel, there's the h, then the o, then the n-e-y. Honey.'

'Wait a minute, you can't use capital letters for the first word then use all small letters for the second.'

'Why not?'

'Because that's cheating. You have to use the same kind of letters for all the words.'

'Who says?'

'It's the rule. You can't try and trick people.'

'Who made up this rule!?'

'It's always been the rule! Come on!'

She twisted around and looked into my eyes, her fierce

determination was blunted by the pleading underneath; I told her to lie down as I traced my finger along her back, using all capital letters.

'I want to kiss you,' I said, and kissed her on the lips. She kissed me back. When her arms wrapped around me and she pulled me close, her body felt like a warm plank of wood, stronger, more solid than my own, until she released her grip and stepped back.

'I want a glass wine,' she said, her face flush, slightly swollen, beautiful. She reached under the sink and I noticed how much wine she kept there, almost two cases. Monica opened a bottle with a wood-handled corkscrew and poured two tall glasses. We stood leaning against opposite sides of the counter, drinking and watching each other. Her eyes dimmed with indifference, she was fighting to keep whatever burned between us from getting out of control. Everything inside of me was pointing in the opposite direction.

'The first time I saw you, in the nightclub, when you saved your brother . . . I was there that night, in the crowd . . . I was struck by you. I know how crazy that sounds, but see, I felt like I'd been waiting my whole life to meet you. Never knowing if you really existed or not. But hoping. Wishing. Then when I saw you, when I looked into your eyes . . . I knew. I knew if I didn't meet you, get to know you, I'd miss my chance. And then I'd be lost forever.'

Monica took a sip of wine; a look of discomfort took her face. 'I like you very much, but I feel not the same.' She downed the rest of her glass and poured another.

'Is it a long drive to Prague? Maybe I should get some food.'

I lay on the floor staring up at the ceiling. Monica was sleeping in her room. The air outside was still, no wind, or traffic, nothing except for the sound of my own breathing. It had been a long time since I'd found myself so alone and lost, without anything, or anyone, like a leaf blowing in the fucking wind. I was both frightened and relieved.

Something in the room was dreadfully wrong. The air was dank, dirty. When I turned the corner red splotches screamed from the walls, the floor was a crimson sheet. I heard him behind me at the kitchen table, moaning in prayer. He clutched the knife in his palms, the blade pointing up to heaven and his body shaking in catatonia; whatever he'd done hadn't registered yet. My mother's body lay across the open oven door, the broiler was on and the right side of her dress had melted, polyester and human skin sizzled and roasted, gray-brown smoke hovered over the countertop. I crept up alongside him – he wasn't even aware that I was in the room – and bashed him on the head with a frying pan. He wailed and collapsed to the floor, landing with an unconscious thud. I slowly approached my mother's body and tried to keep my head together, tried to block out all feelings. Whatever took place here was over with; the only thing that mattered now, the only point of focus, was: What ... to ... do! There were deep stab wounds all over her torso, I stopped counting at twenty-one. I got her off the oven door, turned off the flame; the sweet-smelling wisps of burnt meat made me puke in the sink. I opened the two kitchen windows, turned around and saw my father twitching on the floor, his right side in a seizure of some sort. I wanted to bash him again with the pan. Instead I pulled several large trash bags out of a drawer, laid them on the floor and rolled my mother's body onto them, then dragged her into the back hallway leading to the laundry room. I doused the kitchen floor with two buckets of water then swept it all under the basement door to the left; using a mop I scrubbed down the walls. A stream of bloody water trickled under my father's head and he stirred awake, groggily sat up and looked around. After he asked me what happened I told him, matter of fact, 'You just murdered Mommy.'

Her kiss was warm and unexpected. She lay beside me on the floor. I thought at first I was still sleeping, until I wrapped my arms around her and felt the solid, tangible reality of her body. Her breath had that familiar, bitter scent of wine and smoked tobacco and I kissed her hard and pulled her underneath me and with my body weight held her down. Air came rushing out of her lungs and I kissed her again for a long time. Monica was wearing only panties and tee shirt, her legs were on fire, burning up against mine. I reached down and she was wet; I touched her with my fingertips and she moaned and licked my neck. We kissed while I touched her, slow, deliberate; she liked to be touched.

I made love to her and she told me she was sad. I taught her the word melancholy, then kissed away her tears. We laid wrapped in each other's arms with our legs entwined. We laid that way for an hour.

I awoke with a start, my body was covered in cold sweat and my legs wouldn't stop trembling. Monica slept on the floor beside me but as I started convulsing she stirred awake. My heart was beating ferociously, it burned with pain. Monica sat up and asked me what was wrong.

'I don't know. I'm so cold,' the words tripped over my lips.

She touched my forehead and her fingertips became wet.

'*Komm*,' she ordered, then took me by the hand and helped me into the bedroom. She pulled aside the blankets and put me to bed, tucked the blankets under my sides creating a tight cocoon.

She wiped my face with a towel from the kitchen, but I

was soaking wet underneath my clothes. I tried to will myself to stop shaking, over and over told myself to get a grip. It was only fear, the unknown, the buildup of everything having changed so suddenly. Once I looked at it rationally, faced my fear and marched through it, like I'd done throughout my life, then everything would stop. But something told me this wasn't just nerves and fear of the unknown. This was something more tangible, more powerful. I began to sob and Monica took me up in her arms, looked at me confused, maybe a little frightened. She kissed my head and I buried my face in her shoulder and cried like a girl.

Fortunately I had earlier dropped off ten cases of stolen liquor to the Rainbow Club, one of Marty Oppenheimer's new places, so there was enough room in the van to do what we were about to do. My father sat beside me, not saying a word, looking at the streets and the buildings with something akin to mystical wonder; he probably hadn't been out of the house in a year. I wiped my eyes but they were dry. I found it strange that I was able to do what I had done so far, without tears or sobs, no sign of remorse whatsoever; where did this inner strength come from? I blamed myself for what happened but not as much as I blamed her for it. Maybe that was the trick, blame the victim. But then, who wasn't a victim? I drove down along the service road that led to the Goethals Bridge, through south Elizabeth, through the traffic circle until I came to the local side streets that branched out to the Henry Hudson River. The streets at the end were always deserted as nobody wanted to live near the stench of the landfill. One street in particular, Manitoba Street, a dead end stopping at a narrow part of the river, was surrounded by tall weeds and brush. The brilliant crimson sun, shrouded in chemicals and pollutants, started its descent as I turned off the service road and drove down the narrow dirt path toward the water. Leaves and branches slapped the windshield and my father shielded his face as if they could reach in and pluck out his eyes. The road ended at the shore. Across the river, only a hundred yards away, a desolate field of abandoned oil tanks watched us. I sat with the van idling, not exactly sure what to do, but wanting to take my time as the next few minutes would determine the course my life would take for as long as I lived.

I checked out the shore, no one was lurking, hiking or making out in the woods. It was still daylight as I got out and ordered my father to follow. I carried the shovel through the brush, into a small clearing covered with sand and dead weeds; the river was green and putrid, lapping against oil-slicked mud just ten feet to our right. I started digging into the soft sand and my father watched silently, then sagged to his knees and shoveled out fistfuls with his hands. We didn't say a word to each other the whole time. Underneath the top layer of sand the cool smell of rain rose up into my nostrils.

My father dug out a little tunnel with his hand; with his other hand he pulled out sand from the other side of the small mountain we had made. Once his two hands connected he put several Matchbox cars inside, showed me the secret tunnel I now had. I took out my plastic miniature army men and began standing them up around the entrance. My father tied my sneaker, then helped me arrange the soldiers in orderly fashion, the way he said the military would like it. He told me that before I was born he was in the army and stationed in Korea, but that he didn't see any fighting. He said there was a famous baseball player in his company and they would play baseball games on the base. During night games this player would hit home runs over the fence that simply disappeared into the dark night sky; the next morning no one could find the baseballs. My father said it was unexplained phenomena, then chuckled. Carrie called him to watch her play with her new toy, a plastic ring that fit around her ankle connected to a string with a rubber ball on the end. Carrie spun the ball around with her leg and then hopped over the string. My father called back, 'That's wonderful, Carrie! You've gotten the hang of it. Beautiful! Princess.'

I stood up out of the hole, about three-feet deep, and told my father to get out. He looked around confused – I think he'd forgotten where he was – then he climbed out and followed me back to the van. We pulled my mother's body out of the back, wrapped and taped in plastic. A slimy film had leaked inside the wrapping and made her feet slip out of my hands. I gripped her firmly from underneath, then with my father taking the head, we carried her over to the hole and put her down. Before I rolled her in my father told me, 'No. Not like that.'

He hopped in the hole and reached back and lifted her gently from the middle, then eased her to the bottom. He crouched down over her and touched the blue plastic wrap, tracing the outline of her face. I thought I heard him sigh. Standing up he mumbled some kind of prayer, made the sign of the cross, and started to climb out.

'No Dad. You stay.'

He looked up puzzled, his eyes childlike. I recognized the same look in myself, from pictures taken when I was a young boy looking up with questions, innocence. With trust. My stomach twisted into barbed wire.

'Turn around,' I said and he tugged his trousers high up on his waist and turned away; his bare ankle bore the faint red scar from my knife six years before. I scoped out the surroundings, tall golden weeds and the river to my right, we were completely alone. My father stood over my mother's body waiting, very still. I raised the .22 rifle, the one he bought me for Boy Scouts when I was barely a teenager, and pointed it to the back of his head.

Whatever sane thoughts were left inside of me were drowned out by the prayers and the poison of the last ten years. I wanted it all to go away, to simply disappear and never come back, whatever would make that happen, but instead pictures of my mother's bruised face and my sister's ripped clothes flashed before me like a fugue, and as Carrie dropped from a chair and her neck snapped back, I squeezed the trigger. The rifle sparked in my hands and a patch of hair shot up from his head, a stream of red followed it, then he seemed to fall in slow motion, face first onto his wife. Wind blew silently through the weeds and made them sway; a seagull flew overhead as if in a vacuum. Down in the hole he was still breathing. I couldn't believe it. I checked the gun and tried to reload another round, but the firing pin was bent. Jammed into the chamber. Useless.

I fell to my knees and began to cry, from deep in my gut, until my eyeballs hurt. Cried for Carrie and my mother, my father, and most of all, I cried for myself. I didn't care who heard me, or who saw me. At that moment, I realized, with a shudder . . . I was as lost as a human being could possibly be. And there was no way to prepare for that kind of feeling, that kind of . . . thrill.

It was dark by the time my nose had stopped bleeding and I was finished heaving up my guts. I pulled myself up from the ground and filled in the hole. I didn't look to see if my father was still alive or not. When I finished I covered it with some brush and logs, then drove back to Newark. Delivered the rest of my liquor. Told Marty Oppenheimer I needed a favor done right away and he got Benny 'the Flame' Mataroni to torch my parent's house that very morning.

318

Monica told me I was going to wake the neighbors; it was the first time I realized how loud I'd been crying. The blankets were wet around us, I might have peed my pants. Monica gripped me close to her bosom; her arms were steel cables around my spine. I tried to catch my breath, to slow everything down. I was exhausted and aching from the retching in my stomach, yet I couldn't stop sobbing. I told her, haltingly, 'I've never told anybody that story. Ever! Not a soul.'

She put her lips in my hair and exhaled.

'Do you believe what I just told you?'

She nodded her head.

'Do you understand the words?'

She nodded her head again.

'Then how can you stand to touch me?'

She told me she didn't know.

24

'I*muss* work, *aber* when I come *nach Hause*, we go together. By night. I say them I make holiday.' My hands had finally stopped shaking. I was calming down to my old non-self again; the fact that she said she'd come with me took away some of the edge. She would visit her friends in Prague, help me settle myself in, then return to Berlin by train. Alone. It was more than I expected, and more than I deserved, and as she went into the bathroom to shower, I sat at the table staring at a red-and-white checkered towel hanging over the sink.

Monica came out dressed in pressed gray slacks and a black sweater. She felt my forehead for fever, then we had tea at the table; she tied her hair up neatly in a bun while her glasses hung crookedly on her nose. She told me she'd be back from work at three; that we'd leave then.

'I speak to my brother,' she said as an afterthought.

'Why?'

'He's my brother.'

'You won't have any furniture left when you return.'

She grinned and came around the table, kissed me hard on the lips, then stepped to the door with her jacket. I told her, 'If you change your mind, come home a half hour later. I'll wait till three-thirty. If you're not here by then, I'm gone. Okay?'

'Okay,' she said, then went out the door.

By one o'clock I was climbing the walls. I wanted her home now, not at three o'clock. I couldn't stay another hour in this place, it had become a cage. At two-thirty I decided to go out and get some food and water for the trip. It would give me a chance to check out the car and see if anyone was watching it. I crept out of the building into the gray cloudy day. The car was right where I left it and no one seemed to be paying any mind. I went three blocks south where I remembered seeing a small supermarket. Inside, the carts, all connected by chain, required a coin before you could take one. I took a small plastic basket near the cashier and went down the first aisle. Grimy looking canned fish and packages of ham and bologna sat on the shelves like prisoners on death row, some of them encased inside a clear gelatinous slime. I saved six cans of tuna fish from a dusty demise. The bread looked hard and dense; it was all brown and some of the loaves were solid, not sliced. I grabbed some sliced cheese and salami and a couple bottles of water, took a five-pack of Snickers and went to the cashier. She rang up my order, seventeen Marks, then sat back waiting for me to pay. The food just sat there naked on the conveyor belt.

I asked, 'How do I get my food home?'

The woman huffed something under her breath and a middle-aged man with a shaggy pooch in his arms leaned forward and said, 'You have to bring your own bag for groceries. They don't supply them.'

'Oh. I didn't know.'

'You can purchase a bag from the cashier, for fifty *pfennig*.'

'I'd like to do that. Can you help me, please?'

The guy with the pooch spoke to the cashier in German; then she pulled out a plastic bag and tossed it on the conveyor belt. I handed her a twenty-Mark bill and packed my bag, thanked the guy with the pooch and left.

I went to check one last time on the car. Monica would be home in ten minutes and we'd be leaving thirty seconds later. I felt good about that, positive. There was some hope to the situation; maybe I could convince her to stay with me; anything was possible. I stopped at the corner where the car was parked when someone walked out of an alley. I reached into an empty pocket and Jonathan laughed out loud, walking with his bike. 'What the fuck . . . You following me?' he said.

'I don't think so.'

'What are you doing here?' he asked.

'Meeting a friend. How about you?'

'I live here.'

'In this building?'

'Yeah.'

'It looks abandoned.'

I was suddenly surrounded by four huge Turkish guys in suits; two of them held .44s. One of them searched through my jacket for the weapon that was still in Monica's kitchen drawer, another took my bag of groceries, checked the contents, then said something to his friends and they laughed. I was led quickly and quietly to a sleek-looking grape-colored car with rear fins and hard angles, almost retro 1950's style. Guided into the back seat I caught a glimpse of Jonathan racing away on his bike in the other direction. The men drove off silently with me trapped among them. I regretted not killing Adam Gottlieb when I had the chance; my new change of heart was going to cost me dearly once Manny Simone, Riccardo Montefiore and the Countess finish questioning me. It was a somber ride back into *Kreuzberg*, over the *Oberbaumbrücke* where school had just let out and dark-skinned children ran wild in the street; the water of the Spree was rugged and choppy and a tugboat chugged lazily through the current. A dog peed in the gutter.

'What kind of car is this?' I asked the bearded guy to my right. He didn't understand and I made a driving motion with my hands and he grinned. He spoke in Turkish to his friends and they all cracked up.

'Citroën,' he growled. '*Französisch*.'

'Oh. This is the car that lifts itself when it drives.' They looked at me as if I was crazy. I thought of Monica coming home and finding me gone; her face pondering the empty apartment. Would she be relieved? I tried not to think about it.

The car sped past the dirt entrance of the squatters' camp; I glanced over my shoulder but there was no sign of Heike or Lars, or anyone for that matter. Continuing west along *Köpenickerstrasse* we turned left into the driveway of the factory complex where Heinrich was killed only two nights before. We were let through the guarded gate and proceeded to the rear factory where the Countess had dropped me off. No one came to greet me or to gloat; a minor inconvenience, that's all I was. The bearded guy to my right pulled me out of the back; the guy on my left gripped my arm and slid out behind me. Checking out the surroundings something was wrong; there were no Franchise workers in sight, only Turks. I saw my opening in the instant my bodyguards released my arms, both thinking the other had a firm hold. I creamed them simultaneously in the gut and took off, heading along the same route I took the last time. I figured I was at a distinct advantage having run the course before.

Cars came out of nowhere, screeching into my path and blocking the gates; tall wire fence closed in the rest of the complex. I was trapped in the yard with nowhere else to run. I picked up a pipe buried partially under some sacks of powdered cement and swung it low at his body, didn't want to crack his skull open, but he ran through it and tackled me. I was jumped by three or four others, then pounded by their fists and feet until I lost consciousness. With luck they'd beat me to death. The taste of blood filled my mouth, and for some reason I saw Monica's eyeglasses. Then I slept.

*

The room had been cleaned and repainted. There was no sign that anything had ever taken place here; even the hole had been filled in and covered over with fresh cement. It was very strange because I would think they'd want to play up the terror factor. My head throbbed with pressure, as if my brain were swelling up against my skull, breathing like lungs. The four Turkish guys who drove me here stood along the wall talking amongst themselves. One of them held a bloody handkerchief to his knuckles; I was sure some of my blood smeared that cloth. Broken blood vessels fought inside my brow; through bloated, tender eyes I saw a long stainless-steel table off to my right; around the edges was a drain to collect fluid. That was more like it, I thought. The cuffs holding my hands tightly to the back of the chair were cutting into my wrists. A warm line of blood leaked into my palm; I tried to slow my pulse.

The door opened behind me. The crisp, clear slap of polished leather on newly painted pavement and the strong musk cologne, expensive stuff, but too much of it, betrayed his entrance. But when he stepped into view I was startled by the sight. Gone was the youth and bewilderment, the confused naïvety, the puppy-dog pathos; instead his eyes were harsh, predatory. He looked taller, and older; his suit sat on him like a coat of fur. The air around him seemed to rush out of his way when he moved. The confidence, the swagger, it was almost . . . Montefiore-like.

'I was hoping I wouldn't have to see you again. I thought you would be smart enough to leave Berlin, and Germany.'

It was a little jarring to hear Vita speak such perfect English, with no hint at all of an accent. He answered my surprise with a cruel grin, 'I studied at Stanford for four years, lived in the United States for ten.'

Premig strolled into view. There was no pretense of a hand anymore. He had a prosthetic metal hook, one that picks up objects using radar; it looked more disturbing than anything he had worn up to then. When our eyes met he broke into a big, brown-toothed grin. I asked Vita, 'Where is everybody? What did you do with them?'

'Let's talk about you instead.'

I waited to hear what he had to say but he didn't say anything. I took the cue. 'I was leaving tonight,' I said. 'For good. I was going to my car when your guys picked me up.'

'You should have left sooner.'

'In hindsight, yes.'

Vita came up beside me, scowling; the temperature dropped twenty degrees. 'Do you think I'm playing a game with you?'

'No. I don't.'

'Then why do you want to die talking like an idiot?'

He waited for some gem of confession to fall from my mouth. It didn't fall. Finally he asked, 'Don't you have any remorse?'

'Is that what you want? Remorse? I don't know. It seems hypocritical to me, don't you think? I'm sorry for your father, that's the truth. He's a good guy and I always liked him; and I never disliked you.'

Someone stepped out of the back room, dressed in a custom-tailored pinstriped suit with shiny black shoes and a beaded skullcap on his crown, the image was totally incongruous with the person I'd been dealing with up to now. Jonathan gave Vita a kiss on both cheeks and said something in Turkish to him; all I caught was the word 'Allah'. When he grinned, his teeth were the only part of him still the same. He chuckled as he said, 'We worship at the same mosque.' Then he announced something in Turkish to the solidarity of himself and Vita, and the other four Turks slapped their chests and murmured.

'That's not going to keep the Russians and East Germans away from you now. They'll come in and take everything you got.'

Vita answered, 'That's what you were going to do.'

'They're gonna do it worse! You and your people won't be able to hold them off. You couldn't hold them off before and you can't hold them off now. I mean, what are you gonna do . . . outdress them?'

Vita threw me a cold, wicked glare. Not much shocked me anymore but what he then told me did. If it was, in fact, the truth. And I believed him. He knew certain details that very few people knew, the black fish, for instance, and the placement of the hooks over the bathtub. He could have gotten this from one of my former colleagues. But I didn't think so. I believed him because his version of events felt true, the way some things just do.

Vita told me the last thing he wanted was a deal between the Franchise and the Russians. He was smart enough to know that eventually he and his father would be cut out completely, and shortly after that, executed. He gave me a history lesson on the Turkish people as warriors, throughout the centuries of holy wars and massacres, the fierce independence and bloodshed. His voice boomed in the concrete room as he ranted about the strength and will of Allah! He began to stroll around me, stopped and pointed accusingly,

'You think we're all fanatics, terrorists, that we want to take over the world. Most Americans think that. Once you hear the name of Allah, you think immediately . . . fanatic! But we're not fanatics. We're only trying to protect our families, our beliefs. You have no idea what I'm talking about. Because you, and your kind, have no beliefs. Your world is

a godless, empty place! One where you murder and terror-
ize people, kill innocent children, then think you can go
and have a normal life with a student.'

I was struck by that last bit. Vita continued, 'As if the one
act doesn't poison the other.'

'Vita, she has nothing to do with any of this. She's a medical student. I fell in love with her; that's her only crime.'

Vita studied my eyes with mistrust. I told him, 'I met her
a few times in the East and fell in love with her. That's all.
She's not part of anything else.'

'She agreed to go with you to Czechoslovakia.'

'She's an unstable woman,' I insisted, dread bubbling up
inside me like a polluted lake. 'Completely nuts; she'll agree
to do anything from one minute to the next. I'm actually a
little relieved to be rid of her, if you know what I mean.'

Vita watched me for a long minute. 'We don't kill innocent people like you do,' he said, 'to torture the relatives.'

'Where is she now?'

'Forget the student; she's already forgotten you.'

Vita told me he knew where Hardy was, that he was
holed up in the outskirts of the city. 'What would you do to
redeem yourself,' he asked, 'if given the chance?'

Several cars pulled up outside and one of the larger Turks
called Vita over to the window in Turkish. Jonathan
watched me with discomfort. I said to him, 'Muslim, huh?
How does that jive with drug dealing?'

'I don't have to answer to a sick dog.'

Vita answered from across the room. 'We're fighting for
our lives! For our children's lives! We'll fight with any
means necessary. Up to and including mental, moral and
physical slaughter.'

'If that's the way you feel, why didn't you just do that
from the beginning?! Why did you ask us to come out here
in the first place?'

Vita stopped in front of me, took a weary breath. 'My father and I didn't agree on that,' he said. 'He wanted revenge for his brothers and friends, but he didn't want to subject his family to a war. Well, you can't have it both ways.'

'Is that why you sold him out?'

Vita slapped me hard across the face; fresh cuts opened up inside my mouth and I spit out a sliver of flesh.

'My father passed away yesterday morning,' he said, the words were crisp, cold. 'You should worry more about your own sins and less about my family.'

Vita ordered the cuffs to be unlocked from me and when Premig saw my wrists raw and bleeding he grinned. Jonathan walked toward the door, having to pass me in doing so; I clocked him square in the face and knocked him flat on the floor. I was beaten to the ground and kicked furiously in the ribs. I didn't see who or what hit me but when it ended Jonathan stood over me rubbing his chin. Vita appeared beside him, ordered his men to lift me up and I was carried by the arms outside to a white Mercedes sedan and shoved inside between two large thugs who reeked of horses. Vita sat in the front passenger seat and Premig got behind the wheel. It reminded me of my arrival, which now seemed like years ago. The car turned east on *Köpenickerstrasse* and I could only guess I was on my way to *Potsdamer Platz*.

25

The car drove out to the edge of *Pankow*, an eastern suburb overrun by weeds and wild grass. Small houses looked like bungalows at a seaside town, except that every structure was in need of serious repair and new paint. The gardens were dry dusty earth and the back yards had tool sheds leaning crookedly toward the west. Weather beaten old jalopies sat in driveways, all the same make and model – Trabant – but in different faded candy colors, like Matchbox cars for adults. At the end of tram line number 53, where the tracks stopped before a barren field, the taxi pulled over and the driver, a young Turk in jeans and a tee shirt, turned to me and said, '*Sechsunddreissig Mark.*' The meter read '36'. I wasn't sure if he was one of Vita's guys or not; it didn't matter. I gave him forty Marks and he opened a purse to give me change but I said, '*Nein*, it's okay,' and got out; he thanked me and drove away.

Wind howled through loose planks on the empty house to my left. In front of me was a tree-lined dirt road. I followed the tram tracks to the end and proceeded through the barren field. A dead, decayed bird lay crushed into the dirt; its beak hung partly off and its feathers were dried and desiccated; both feet were balled into brittle skeletal fists. Ten feet away a small rodent rustled in a bush; I tossed a rock and it scurried off. I continued along a dirt ravine, walking on what was once a stream, following a trail of smooth brown rocks. Ten minutes later I was lost in a weeded field; there was nothing but dead plants and fine dirt, plus the clouds frowning low overhead. I came to a pile of boulders and on the tallest one, spray-painted in red, was a swastika. I knew I was getting close.

I sat on the same couch in the same manner as I had done two weeks before when Manny Simone wanted to pop me for not killing Hans Kopp's son. Jonathan rubbed his chin and stared at me from across Heinrich's desk. In his eyes burned the same delirious flame of religion I used to see in my father's eyes; righteous indignation shining down from heaven, like radiation. Vita stood beside me, told me everyone had been rounded up. My friends, colleagues; co-assassins, he called them. He said there were a few loose ends still, but that soon the guilty would be punished, and the less guilty would be turned over to the authorities. I wasn't sure yet where I fit in. Vita pulled out a chair and sat down in front of me, handed me his beige silk handkerchief for my bleeding mouth, ordered someone to get a wet cloth for my cut-up wrists, asked if I wanted something to drink; Al Pacino couldn't have played it any better. I knew that whatever he wanted me to do, it involved Hardy; I had no doubt which category Hardy fit in, but I was certainly no messenger of God, either. I was about to make this point when a commotion broke out in the yard; skidding tires and men yelling. No one in the office seemed to notice. Premig stepped in from outside; the cuffs of his pants were soiled with mud, his hook dripped red.

The house appeared suddenly in the distance. Completely isolated, there wasn't anything around it except for a patch of dead trees in the rear. The first-floor windows were boarded up and a wooden gate surrounded the perimeter. With fear I started for the back yard, taking a long loop around the field; anyone peeking out an upstairs window could get a clean shot at me. I searched for movement in the shadows, a curtain moving in the breeze, anything, but it looked like there hadn't been anyone inside for years. It was possible Vita's information was wrong, though he had been right about everything else. I stood in the back yard looking up at the upper windows, thought of calling out, but then Hardy would be so freaked out he'd kill me on sight. I had to convince him first that I wasn't here to pop him, then convince him that the Franchise had been dismantled and he had till tonight to get out. The back door was locked, so I quietly pushed my elbow through a pane of glass and reached in to unlock it, but it still wouldn't budge; planks of wood nailed it shut from inside. I went around to the first-floor side window and it was covered by wood; rusted nail heads were hammered deep into the beams. The other first-floor windows were the same. I went to the front door and it was tall, solid; uninviting. When I turned the knob it broke off in my hand. I pushed on the door and the latch clicked softly. The front hall floors were dirty and splintered, wood the color of tar; there was a faded paisley-striped wallpaper peeling off the walls. A tall stone oven stood in the spacious room to the left; a pile of ashes sat at the foot of it. The kitchen was in back; it had a table and some broken wooden chairs; the counters were open with yellowed, cracked dishes inside them. The first floor was empty and I crept up the stairs to the second. The planks groaned and creaked under my weight; the seventh stair was missing. Behind the second door I heard a sound and crept up, listened for a moment, then turned the knob.

Hardy lay in bed snoring hoarsely; in his hand was a Glock .45 automatic; his mouth hung open and his teeth were flecked with brown; his hair was greasy and pointing in all directions; he looked filthy. Sunlight cut a sudden swath across the floor and Hardy moved in bed. I froze until he stopped, then I rushed up and punched his wrist and grabbed his gun and he jumped up screaming in shock; if I didn't have his gun right then he would have killed me before I could burp. He backed onto the bed; real horror screamed in his eyes. I had to somehow bring him down.

'I'm not here for what you think. I came to tell you a few things. Then you're completely on your own.'

'Fuckin' liar!' he screamed, eyeing his gun in my hand.

'This is only because of you, not me! I'm not here to pop you. If I were, believe me, you'd be popped already.'

'Bullshit!'

'Hardy, I'm unarmed.' I pulled aside my jacket to show him no gun in my waistband. 'The only gun here is yours. I'm here to talk.'

'If what you're sayin' is true, then put it down and we'll talk. I'm not talkin' to a friend like this.'

'Hardy, this ain't about friendship; it's about you being fucking paranoid. I know I'm not gonna pop you, as certain as I know anything. I'm not here to do that, but you're liable to do any-fucking-thing. I know you got knives and shit hidden all over the place, so I'm gonna hold the gun and tell you what I'm here to say. Then when I leave, you'll still be alive, and you can do whatever the fuck you want. Can we agree to that, please?'

'You expect me to believe you came all the way out here to tell me somethin'?!'

'As hard as that may seem, yes.'

'This is a fuckin' game, Tony! You're just gettin' back at me for that night at the social club. That ain't fair, chief; you said we were even. That's fucked. You're supposed to be a professional . . . If you're gonna do it, then do it professional!'

'You crazy fuck! I'm not gonna pop you! I only want to talk to you.'

He stopped. The possibility registered on his dim, 10-watt face. He was incredulous when he asked, 'You're not here to pop me?'

'Fuck, if you don't stop it, I really *am* gonna pop you.'

Hardy slumped down on the bed relieved. 'God man,

that was fuckin' close! You scared the Goddamn shit outta me.'

I warned him, 'Keep your hands in sight until I'm finished.'

'You're really not gonna pop me? Damn, what the fuck you doin' here?'

Vita grabbed me roughly by the collar; he didn't appreciate for one second the new me. But he wanted Hardy out of Berlin bad enough to agree to anything; he was really spooked over it. It seems Hardy had been right all along, the anti-Christ really *was* in Berlin; it just turned out to be Hardy himself.

Three bodyguards hopped up off their chairs and followed us out the door. In the yard there were several cars parked around the back of the office. The site was particularly empty today; then I remembered it was Saturday. Vita pulled me along the new foundation that houses Jesse Smith and Donnie Smokestack's crew.

'Did you do that?' I asked.

'No. But I didn't stop it either.'

'I lost a friend in that. A guy with a wife and two kids.'

'Shut up.'

Vita gave me a hard push toward the rear of the trailer. I was jolted by the sight of Hans Kopp and Victor Rudiyov standing there. In the Mercedes behind them sat Riccardo Montefiore with his left eye bandaged; a line of blood dripped from under the gauze; his hands were obviously bound behind his back. He didn't move at all, stoic, expressionless, his one eye staring off into space; I tried to ignore him. A dark gray BMW pulled around, crunching gravel under its tires. In the back seat sat the stubborn Lucretia Tigrit; at the sight of her husband she jumped up and slammed her palms against the glass, screamed hysterically, her voice a faint trombone in the closed metal

335

chamber. Premig drove with another Turk sitting in the passenger seat; neither of them reacted to her voice, which I knew up close could be shrill. As they headed out toward the exit she turned around and cried one last time for her husband who sat there watching, helpless to do anything. She disappeared onto *Stressemannstrasse* and into thin air and Riccardo Montefiore began to weep. While Vita talked to Victor Rudiyov, Hans Kopp eyed me suspiciously; the color in his glare spelled the opposite of life. Victor Rudiyov got in the front passenger seat of the Mercedes, two guys got in around Riccardo Montefiore in the back seat, then the car drove out toward the exit. A beige taxi pulled onto the site and slowly drove toward the office. Vita took my arm to lead me away when Hans Kopp stepped in our path and confronted him. They argued loud and hard and Vita refused to back down, standing chin to chin with him until finally Hans Kopp called over his shoulder to a coarse-looking guy with a square jaw who ran off to the next site. We stood there waiting, the three of us, silently, until the guy returned with Ulf Kopp in tow. Once I saw Ulf I knew it was over; Vita couldn't stop what would happen. Hans took his son roughly by the arm and pointed in my direction. Our eyes met and Ulf recognized me immediately; I didn't try and play it down. He glared at me, at my eyes, bruised and cut, then down at my wrists, also bruised and cut, turned to his dad and said, '*Nein.*' Ten seconds later I was in the taxi and driven off the construction site.

'They're all gone?!' Hardy gaped at me with bloodshot plums. I slid the clip out of the gun, cocked the chamber and dumped out the remaining round. After pulling the trigger twice to be certain there were no miracles pend-ing, I tossed it on the bed and dropped the clip in my pocket.

'Everyone except Manny Simone,' I answered, 'and

they're out hunting him like a dog. Why the hell are you still here? Why didn't you try and get away?'

'Where the fuck am I gonna go?! Europe?! It's the same as China to me! Without the Franchise I got nothin'. I was hopin' I could talk my way back in . . . until I heard about those four fuckin' detectives. Fuck, I didn't even do that!'

'What the hell smells in here?'

'Everything. I been here a long time. But not one minute more. Where's Heinrich? Who let you in?'

'Heinrich?'

I then told him the shameful story of Heinrich and when he told me Heinrich not only knew where he was but that Heinrich had been moving him to different houses and supplying him with food, I developed a newfound grudging respect for Heinrich, or at least his ability to withstand unimaginable pain. Hardy pulled an old suitcase from under the bed and opened it. I started for the door but he nearly screamed, 'Where you goin'?!'

'I'm leaving. I told you what you needed to know. Now you're on your own.'

'But ain't we goin' home?!'

'You can go wherever you want. I'm going somewhere else.'

'Wait, what are you talkin' about?! We can't split up! Let's stick together! We're friends, ain't we? I mean, you didn't pop me just then, when you had the chance.'

'Is that your idea of a friend?'

'Fuck yeah!'

With that Hardy grabbed a pair of shoes and some underwear and dirty tee shirts, stuffed them into the case, then looked around for anything else of value.

'Hardy, it's a little difficult for me to explain. I met someone. She's really special and I want to be with her.'

'So, that's great! I won't bother you! You won't even

know I'm there. Tony! I swear, you'll have your privacy. I know how that can be. But please, we're all we have of each other; I'm beggin' you; we can't split up. We're more powerful if we stay together than if we split up. Come on, it'll be just like old times, when we were startin' out, remember? We'll find a new crime family to join, one that's bigger and better! Maybe we'll start our own crime family!?'

Before I could tell him I wasn't interested in finding a new crime family or starting one of my own, I heard a buzzing sound coming from the window. On the floor a swarm of flies foraged on a piece of old cloth, a filthy, brown-stained rag; dyed into the material were faded cartoon figures.

'How did you get this number?' she was furious, her voice trembled with rage and grief. 'How did you get this number?!'

'Becky, please, just tell me what happened. Please!' My stomach squeezed into a suffocating knot as she would now confirm what I had been told a few minutes earlier by Manny Simone, who had given me the number; how the hell he got it I'll never know, or forgive him for not giving it to me sooner.

Becky choked back a sob – her voice was hoarse, cracked; she'd been crying all night and day – then she began. 'She was playing in the tub, taking a bath like she always does. I gave her some bubble soap to play with . . . I was drying my hair . . . with the dryer . . . the phone rang . . . before I left I told her not to touch anything. "Don't touch anything!" I said. I went to answer the phone . . . then the lights went out.'

I sagged against the wall of the booth, my head rung like I'd been hit with a sledgehammer. Every part of me screamed out her name until my insides hurt. The line was silent.

'When are the services?' I asked.

'What? Do you think you're coming to services?'

'When are the services?'

'You're not coming to any services.'

'Becky, I'm her father.'

'I know who you are, you bastard! You're not even supposed to know where I am. How did you get this number?'

'I have to see her. I have to, please, Becky. I love her too. I'm begging you!'

'The FBI will be there, so will the Justice Department. They'll be looking for you. They may be listening to us right now.'

'I don't care. I have to see her. God, Becky, please . . . I don't want to . . . We should be together now. We should be there for each other. This is . . . let's not hate each other. Please! I still love you!' On those words I lost it.

'Tony, please . . . don't do this . . .'

'Becky . . . Oh God . . . Becky! Fuck! This isn't supposed to happen. This isn't fair! I just want to . . . Ahhhh! Clarissa! I never dreamed anything could hurt so much.'

'Wake up, Tony. This is how my mother felt when you murdered her son.'

The toilet flushed and Hardy looked over as La Fontaine stepped out. Wearing a tank top shirt and nothing else, her legs were badly scratched, her bare genitals bruised. I was closer to the gun than Hardy; and he knew it.

'Tony, wait a minute! It's not what you think! It's completely legit! We're completely legitimate now! I made her an honest woman. Look! We got married last Saturday.'

Hardy held up his hand showing the gold wedding ring on his fourth finger. He called to La Fontaine and she lifted her hand to show the thin copper band on her finger.

'Heinrich got a friend of his, a real minister, to marry us, all perfectly legal! A real ordained minister. I got the paperwork to prove it! In the eyes of the Lord! Let no man undo what God has brought asunder!'

I went for the gun behind my back, the HK .44 Vita convinced me to take. Hardy's blade shimmered in the sunset but not fast enough as I blew his brains out the back of his skull; specks of bone and matter clung to the wall and smoke oozed from his hair, then his head kissed the floor with a wet pulpy smack. I stood there listening, waiting; rotted wood creaked and a dog barked in the distance, the last groan of stale air eased out of Hardy's noxious lungs. La Fontaine watched it all with nothing more than curiosity. I told her we were leaving and to pack her stuff but she just stood there looking at Hardy. I covered him with the filthy stained sheet off the bed and searched the closet for any clothes she might have brought. She didn't seem to have anything, only the panties on the floor and a pair of ripped socks. I grabbed what few of Hardy's clothes weren't spattered with blood and wrapped her in them, used Hardy's knife to cut the pants legs so they'd be short enough for her to wear, found a piece of wire to tie around her waist. She seemed to be in a trance as I led her out the door and through the field; her feet disappeared in the large spacious pants; she looked like a bundle of tragedy.

The tram stop was deserted. The sun slowly began its descent and I guessed it was around eight o'clock. We sat on the square metal-net seats and waited. La Fontaine hadn't said one word to me, ever, but she licked her lips constantly as if she were about to speak; I noticed her front teeth were chipped. She seemed content sitting there, swinging her legs underneath her as if she hadn't a care in the world, watching a baby rat nibble on a candy wrapper.

The tram approached; it would pass us and make a loop and the driver would switch tracks for the other direction. Except that this tram driver eyed me with suspicion, anger;

his fat officious face sat too large on his corpulent body; he was trouble. So I took La Fontaine by the hand and led her down the tree-lined street directly behind us. On my right was a small restaurant built out of logs like a mountain cabin. I asked La Fontaine if she was hungry, scooped imaginary food into my mouth but she looked straight ahead and tugged on my hand; she wanted to keep walking. We came to a stream on the other side of the street and she pulled me over to see it. The water rippled serenely underneath the road, leafy trees in full bloom flanked the sides. I slid the copper band from her finger, her wedding ring, and tossed it as far away as I could. La Fontaine watched it plop and disappear under the water's surface. A dirty plastic jug floated towards us, pulled aimlessly along by the current, stopping here and there, spinning off a boulder and passing under our feet before disappearing forever. She smiled faintly as that happened, then a gust of wind pushed back her hair and made her eyelids flutter.

'It's getting cold. We can't keep walking around, La Fontaine. If that's even your real name. You need help really bad. I'm gonna try and get somebody to call the police and get you to a hospital, okay?'

She didn't react, as if she hadn't heard, though I knew she heard every word. Quite possibly understood some of them.

'Come on, let's go.'

We walked further down the street and now I hunted for good Samaritans, somebody who wasn't going to risk their life trying to hold me for the police. We passed a newly opened ice-cream parlor with colorful flags and umbrellas, outdoor tables. I pointed to a giant plastic ice-cream cone and asked again if she was hungry but she tugged on my hand and we continued on. Everyone at the ice-cream parlor stared in shock, some gasped; it was only a matter of time before we were picked up. A middle-aged woman holding a small canvas bag approached from the opposite direction. Her eyes fell to La Fontaine and stopped. I whispered, 'I think we hit.' I crouched down and looked into her eyes; expressionless brown marbles stared back. I told her, 'This is it. This lady will help you, I know it. I wish you all the luck in the world, little girl. You got thrown some pretty hard breaks in your short life, but, somehow, you came through it, you survived. That makes you a very special person in my eyes. Very special.'

When the frightened middle-aged woman approached, I stood up. '*Sprechen Sie English*?' I remembered from my book.

'Yes, *ein bisschen*.'

'I found this little girl walking around by herself. I think she needs help. I don't know what to do. Can you call the police and an ambulance?'

'*Mein Gott*,' she sighed, and knelt to La Fontaine and took her hand. She spoke to her in German. I was sure she asked who I was and if I'd assaulted her. I began to walk away and the woman called after, '*Entschuldigung*! *Komm* back!'

I didn't answer or turn around, just put more distance between us. The woman yelled after me, calling for someone to stop the strange man from escaping. Fortunately nobody bothered and five minutes later I hopped on the tram. The driver had just finished his dinner break and pulled up to the platform and I took a seat and studied a map, found the line to get me back to my car.

The modern buildings all looked alike, but the older, non-renovated buildings had character and charm; a lion's head over a doorway, gables along the roof, bullet holes forming celestial patterns. I checked out the car from down the block and it looked safe, but that's how it looked the last time. I gripped the car keys in my fist; they were the last things Vita gave me before putting me in the cab; his way of conveying the importance of my departure. I took a step forward, then turned suddenly, desperately, and ran back in the other direction, ran with all my strength. I had to chance it, one last time. To see Monica.

I pushed the front door open and went up the stairs quietly until I reached the top floor. Stood outside her door, listening. I knocked. Then pushed on the door. It easily slid open. A radio played in the kitchen, it had never been on before. I called out her name. Survival ripped through my veins as I scoped the room . . . The kitchen was dark and I could see no sign of anything amiss. I saw legs on the bed and bolted into the bedroom. Monica lay there sleeping. I went to wake her up, touching her face and shaking her, when I noticed red lines around her throat – finger marks – she'd been choked unconscious; a professional terror tactic. I knew whose specialty this was and when I turned around Manny Simone grinned in the darkness. He took a step closer to where I could see him and the .38 he held on me. With his right hand he tossed three metal bolts at my feet.

'Looking for these?' he said.

'I don't know. What are they?'

'Spark plugs.'

'What are you talking about?'

'Didn't you go to your car yet?'

'No.'

Manny laughed. 'It's true, you've gone completely daffy.'

I moved toward Monica and Manny stopped me with his gun. 'You go near her and I'll plug her dead.'

'She needs a doctor.'

'She's fine.'

'What are you doing here? How did you find me?'

'Everybody thought he was an idiot; now he's running

the whole show. Did you know he went to Stanford? Seems like we underestimated him.'

I pictured Vita playing the same scene in the factory with Manny that he had played with me, except changing some of the words; turning us against each other; it was a risky ploy but one that had worked so far. Manny spoke as if on cue.

'Told me about you too, for instance. Emily Talbot? That was beautiful. And that scene with the four detectives?! I was gonna pop Hardy for that.'

'You still didn't answer my question. Why are you here?'

'You destroyed everything in my life, kid; my livelihood, my friendships, everything. And I wanted you to know how much I appreciate that.' Manny's hand squirmed on the gun. 'Give me the keys to the car, slowly.'

I reached into my pocket and tossed the keys to his feet. Manny took a step back. 'Pick them up,' he ordered. 'Now!'

Never taking my eyes from his gun I crouched down and retrieved them, dropped them in Manny's outstretched hand.

'Now wake up your girlfriend.'

'What are you going to do?'

'Just wake her up.'

'No.'

'Wake her up or she'll never wake up again!'

I leaned over and softly tapped her cheek, rubbed the marks on her neck. Monica rustled awake, choked several times, then sat up and puked on her dress. I clutched her trembling body close to mine and Manny chuckled. 'Yeah, hold her just like that. That's a nice picture.'

Manny aimed his gun and I pulled her behind me just as the front door opened and Monica's brother walked in. He took one look at Manny and reached into his jacket. The bullet smashed him against the door like an egg and I jumped on Manny and grabbed his .38, still hot and smoking, and we spun around the room like wrestlers. He got off two more shots before I cracked his wrist and the gun went flying. We tumbled into the kitchen and Manny got me from behind and tried to rip out my eyes with his fingernails. I butted his face with the back of my head, elbowed him in the gut and spun around kicking him in the balls. He fell back and I searched the floor for the .38; it was under the table. Manny jumped up and ripped open the first kitchen drawer. Before I could get to the gun he had plucked out a fistful of knives and came at me jabbing his arms like piston rods. I blocked most of his swings but my arms and hands got horribly cut. I clocked him in the face and that stopped him for an instant, then I karate kicked him across the room. He hit the wall and slipped in the blood pouring out of Monica's brother. Splayed on the floor he wasn't holding any knives. They were instead at my feet, except for one that was sticking out of my gut. I took a deep breath and the handle moved in and out with my respiration. There wasn't much blood, the knife was acting as a plug, and as long as I didn't pull it out . . . Manny lunged up for the handle and I bashed him in the head with a kettle from the stove and he hit the floor hard.

'Monica!'

She lay nearly folded in half on the rug. The bullet had entered the soft flesh just below her rib cage; it was still inside her. I couldn't tell how much damage there might be. Monica tried to lift herself up onto the bed.

'Don't move! I'll call an ambulance.'

'*Nein. Hilf mir.*'

Monica struggled to sit up and I gave her a painful lift onto the bed and she laid out flat, holding her side.

I went into the kitchen for the phone and Manny was reaching for his .38. I opened the second drawer, reached past the tin foil and pulled out my gun, calmly blasted a chunk of meat out of Manny's neck. He clutched at the wound and blood flushed through his fingers like a babbling stream, then he collapsed to a sitting position. I kicked his gun into the bedroom and lifted the phone from its cradle; the cord had been cut. Looking at Manny I wanted to bash his head in again; instead I noticed his cellphone on the floor by his ankle, the one he always carried in his inside pocket.

'What's the number for emergencies?'

Monica groaned out, '*Eins eins zwei.*'

A woman answered in German and I told her to send an ambulance and she said she doesn't speak English, in English.

Monica reached out for the phone, then spoke into the receiver, softly yet steadily, then let it drop to the floor. I clutched my stomach and sat beside her on the bed. She watched me calmly, with no expression; she could have been laying down for an afternoon nap. The clock next to her bed ticked faintly underneath the wind and the traffic outside.

'Monica, I can't be here when they come. I'm sorry. I'm sorry for everything. I want you to know . . . I . . . I tried to change my life. I really tried! I thought if I loved you, if I *truly* loved you, that our love would be strong enough to make up for some things. But some things can't be undone, and neither can some people. This is your lucky day, Monica. Now you can live your life. Help people! Do whatever the fuck you want to do. Just do one thing for me . . . forget we ever met. I was just a bad dream you had once.'

When I stood up the knife shifted in my gut and a tingle of heat burned like a line of pinpricks. I placed my fingers on her lips, felt her breath warm and steady. My heart ached as I started for the door, knowing I would never see her again.

In the kitchen Manny Simone had dragged himself over to the sink, reaching now for the gun I'd given Monica's brother ten days earlier; it was on the floor near his body. Manny stopped moving when the floor creaked under my feet, slowly turned around and slumped against the cabinet doors, the ones I'd repaired. Lifting his head from his shoulder, he grinned at my tears.

'Don't worry, kid. She won't be lonely. I'll rape her in Hell for you!'

'I don't think so, Manny. She's gonna live. She's gonna make it and survive. Which is more than I can say for you.'

'Looks like a lot of blood in there.'

'Lot of blood out here too.'

The floor was a pool of death and the walls were spattered with death, Monica's brother lay dead on his face while Manny sat against the cabinets clutching his neck still leaking with every pump of his dying heart. Death all around me. I was a chameleon with only one color, the color of death. It's the only thing I have to offer. It's all I've ever offered anyone. It was time to offer it to myself.

Manny grinned at the knife in my gut, defiant to the end.

'Why don't you let me help you with that?' he said. 'You help me, and I'll help you.'

'How will you help me?'

'I can take that knife out. I know a special way of pulling it out so it don't slice on the way.'

I chuckled. 'I think you have more immediate concerns.'

A red bubble grew out between his fingers and popped against his chin; plasma oozed like tomato paste down his arm. His face was pale and gaunt; I'd be surprised if he had more than a minute left. I felt bad for mocking him when he was helpless, but I didn't apologize either. I stepped over

Monica's brother's body and to the door and Manny rustled in the corner.

'So, you leaving me again?'

'Yeah.'

'One hell of a trip, huh kid?'

'Yeah. Memorable.'

'So, what are you gonna do now?'

'I don't know. What do you wanna do?'

He laughed weakly. 'Sick fuck. I'll rape you in Hell too.'

Manny sank low to the floor, his entire front was soaked to the skin, he couldn't lift his head, yet his teeth stayed clenched like a dead rat's.

I walked out the door and down the front stairs. On the street I held the ends of my jacket closed against the wind; the knife stuck out two inches past. The sky was still black. In the distance a siren cried and I hoped it cried out for Monica. The cobblestone seemed to shift unevenly under my feet, but the chilled night air kept me numb and feeling no pain. I walked deeper into the city, going east where entire blocks were nothing more than bricks and debris piled around demolition cranes. On *Blankenburgerstrasse* yellow-brick buildings were ancient and decrepit, but somehow standing solid. I noticed a stream of blood running down my pants, leaving a trail on the pavement. The sky breathed purple and blackbirds talked in the trees. An old woman waddled toward me carrying sacks of coal in each hand; she wore a scarf over her hair and the lines on her face spoke of Old World duty and hardship. On *Sleipnerplatz* a small construction trailer sat up on blocks and Heike and Lars came to mind; they were probably getting up now; the chickens would squawk and their hungry son would cry; the simple life of everyday survival and child rearing. If I somehow made it out of here I would go back and visit them one day, see if anything took root in the willing soil of Heike's womb. A young girl leaned against a lamppost at the corner, straight black hair covered the sides of her face and she stared down at her feet. Winged monkeys made of stone watched me from atop the facade across the way; their heads followed as I moved slowly in front of the girl, whose face was an oval void. She came up and walked beside me, step for step. I held out my hand and she at first wouldn't take it, but then she did; Victor Rudiyov's daughter was not that easily forgiving. She was a few years younger than I remember, maybe four or five years younger; I wondered if Clarissa was inside there with her.

'Do you know where we're going?' I asked and she didn't answer, just stared straight ahead and kept walking; a ragged fleshtone Bandaid swung from her scraped left knee. My head began to rock and I found it hard to keep my balance; I tumbled into some bicycles chained to a pole, bounced off a car not much bigger than a motorcycle. The whole time Victor Rudiyov's daughter kept a tight grip on my hand, helped me keep my footing. A truck rumbled by and the driver blared his horn and we moved out of the middle of the street.

We came to a main intersection where car lanes and tram tracks converged in a circle. No one converged at this hour. Somewhere a man sang at the top of his lungs; his voice was haunting, lonely; it made the hair on my neck stand up. When I turned to see what Victor Rudiyov's daughter thought about it, she was gone. Gripped in my hand instead was the knife. My shirt was emptying like a punctured oil can. I chucked the knife in the gutter and started off further east where the streets were dark gray and the pavement cracked and dirty and everywhere I looked neglected buildings looked back and I felt comforted by that.

I came to a highway with two lanes of cars driving at

incredible speeds. I crossed a wooden bridge as the sun began to peek up over a vista of tree tops. A great lake ran under the bridge and a man sat in a small canoe with a bright orange sail floating lazily in the current. My shoes were sopping wet and red but I continued on until I hit a cozy stone street where a small bakery opened for the day; the woman pulling up the blinds watched me with genuine fear in her eyes. I walked past houses that were boarded up or partially demolished, stores were closed and plate-glass windows caked with years of grime; a rusted tractor lay on its side and the further I walked the stranger the landscape became. I didn't feel like myself anymore, I was outside of my body, like a spirit floating beside it, until I pressed against my stomach and a mushy red tomato skin squeezed through my fingers. A group of people came towards me from up the road, rugged, simple faces in turn-of-the-century Sunday clothes; the men wore long coats with paisley vests underneath and pocket watches strung across the fronts; the women wore pastel-colored gowns and matching hats; they parted to let me through with a nervous murmur. I walked until there were no more homes or stores to pass, only the barren fields and deserted farmhouses, the mysterious woods and wilderness that complete the majesty of Berlin. A pack of wild dogs dug through a rabbit hole, the earth cracked into dust under my feet, church bells rang and I looked up just as the foreboding heavens poured down on me freezing sleet. I marveled at the absurdity of it all; the fact that I was still alive. The injustice of it. I screamed out her name as loud and as long as I could, spun in a circle until I fell flat on my back. I cried out for a sign, a symbol, proof that something mattered, that our actions here meant something, that it isn't all just random physics and a flushing toilet of probability.

But only loneliness snickered back at me, aloneness, the

laughter of the rain washing blood off my hands. I climbed to my feet and stumbled through the mud until I came to a deserted dirt road that ended at a silver point of light far off on the horizon. It reminded me of a movie I once saw when I was a child, before the world turned upside down, about a blind woman who turned into a bird one day when things went too far south. She endured as much hardship as she could possibly bear, kidnapped away from her family as a child and then having her own children taken away and then losing her eyesight and living as a slave in medieval Japan, until one evening she simply changed into a bird and soared off towards the horizon. Never to be seen again. The sun broke through the clouds and rays of light shone down in wide golden slats. I began to laugh, the maddened laugh of the wily survivor. Because I was alive and invincible and not even the poor gloomy soul of Victor Rudiyov's daughter could change that.

Nothing more poured out of me. I was as empty and as wretched as a dried-out slug. Just when I thought it couldn't get any worse, a sign up ahead welcomed me to Poland.